SECRETS

IN THE

MIRROR

SECRETS
IN THE
MIRROR

A NOVEL

LESLIE KAIN

atmosphere press

Published by Atmosphere Press

ISBN 978-1-63988-407-0

Cover design by Matthew Fielder

CAVEATS

This fictional family saga depicts how each member of an extended family deals differently with issues such as domestic abuse, substance use, mental illness and death. Readers who are sensitive to such subjects should be alert.

The fictional characters in this story use profanity, and one expresses racial bias and uses epithets that are abhorrent to reasonable, respectful people. That behavior is an aspect of the conflict in the fiction, and in no way represents the views or beliefs of the author.

1.

GAVIN WOULD ALWAYS REMEMBER THAT WEEKEND
as the turning point, when day turned to night and the earth
erupted, cleaving brothers apart. It all began innocuously
enough, but forces had been building unnoticed for years, like
the gradual movement of tectonic plates.

On that Friday, a ruthless July sun reflected serpentine
heat waves into motionless air above a parched field, with the
gothic buildings of Wellesley College punctuating the horizon.
Gavin's brow glistened sweat beads as he tossed baseballs into
the air and batted them into the distance. With each hit, he
cast a worried look toward his twin and wished the ball's
trajectory would go higher, farther, longer.

"That's not how you do it," Devon said. "Remember when
we were little, Dad said I was the champ?" He took the bat and
positioned himself opposite Gavin to demonstrate in mirrored
alignment how to swing. Devon was left-handed, his brother
was right-handed. Their signature red cowlicks peaked
Devon's left crown and Gavin's right. When one looked into a
mirror, he saw an exact replica of the other.

"You're hopeless, Baby Brother," Devon laughed and
messed Gavin's curly mop. "You're just a loser without me!"

Gavin cringed at the reminder of his brother's ten-minute

seniority over him, although he'd become numb to the jokes that were less than funny. "Coach says I have a great swing, and I had two base hits in our last game," he protested, and stabbed the toe of his sneaker into a clump of crabgrass.

"Coach is just humoring you, Gav. And you got lucky." Devon threw his arm around Gavin's neck in a controlling headlock.

Gavin pulled away. "Hey, we have to get home and clean up before everyone comes," he said, as he gathered balls from the field. "And Mom and I have to set up all the food."

"Oh, yeah, our own little Julia Child," Devon snickered.

That day was the boys' sixteenth birthday. They would have a party with their friends the next day, but the first celebration was with their extended family.

"Race you!" Gavin called out and bounded forward, for once getting a few steps ahead of his brother. Even carrying the bat and balls, his long legs conditioned by running cross-country easily outmatched Devon, who had channeled his energy into wrestling. Whenever Gavin ran, he felt distinct and unique, not just the other half of a set of twins. He became larger, better, stronger with each stride, each breath. He wanted to run forever. Some day he would.

"Hey, wait! You cheated," Devon yelled. "We had to start at the same time!"

Gavin arrived home first, followed by his panting brother nearly fifty yards behind. While he enjoyed a brief sense of victory, Devon disregarded the evidence of that gap and objected, "I'd have kicked your ass if you hadn't cheated."

Gavin had already taken the stairs two at a time to the second floor of the house and jumped into the shower. He was in the middle of shampooing when he was startled by muscled arms circling him from behind.

"You're a real wuss, Gav," Devon hissed into his twin's ear, simultaneously grabbing Gavin's genitals.

Gavin yelled and jumped away, swung his arm around but

missed his target, with shampoo stinging his eyes. But Devon was gone, leaving him enraged and frozen in disbelief.

After Gavin finished his shower, still seething, he stomped down the hall to their bedroom and confronted his brother. "Why'd you do that, Dev?"

"Do what?"

"Your sick little joke in the shower."

"What're you talking about?"

"You know, asshole. You grabbed my balls, pulled on my dick—"

"Wow, you're imagining things, baby brother," Devon laughed.

"No I'm not, cocksucker, and it isn't funny!"

"I think you're having some wishful fantasies, Gav."

"Don't ever do anything like that again," Gavin spat, while some invisible force restrained his twitching arms from flailing at his tormentor. He stormed out of the room and slammed the door behind him. Devon's mocking guffaw echoed down the hall in his wake.

The twins' DiMasi grandparents pulled up in their new black 1994 Cadillac DeVille Concours, as the first guests to arrive at Tony and Colleen's early-1900s home. Grand by most measures, the house was modest compared to many of the vintage mansions in Wellesley Hills. Tony, barrel-chested and imposing, ushered his parents into the family room and handed them drinks he'd already prepared. Martini for his mother, bourbon on the rocks for his father, who greeted his middle son in a raspy dialect that reflected his old-world upbringing in Italy and Boston's Italian North End.

Shortly afterward, the O'Malleys—Colleen's parents—arrived and walked into the bustling kitchen with gifts for the twins and flowers for their only daughter. Her father, a tall patrician professor of constitutional law at Harvard, surveyed all the preparations for the expected crowd and grumbled, "Tony should've let us throw a party like this for you last month when you got your PhD."

Under faded red hair, her tired eyes darting over her shoulder, Colleen shrugged with a wan smile that annulled the pain of the seminal day of her hooding and its aftermath. "Oh, Dad," she sighed. "You know Tony was too busy with his new stores. And it doesn't matter."

Her father scowled and opened his mouth to object, but his wife—a well-known authority in Middle East history at Wellesley College—put her hand on his arm and interjected, "Colleen, what can I do to help? You have a lot of mouths to feed today."

"Not a thing, Mom, but thanks," Colleen squeezed her mother's shoulder in a sideways embrace. "Gavin has everything under control. He made some sangria," she pointed to a pitcher on the kitchen island. "Can I pour some for you, so you can join Tony's parents in the family room?"

At that moment Gavin entered the kitchen after setting up two long tables on the patio. "Grandma and Grandpa! It's good to see you," he said with a hug for each of them. "Are you taking the summer off? Let me get you some drinks." Although Gavin was in the middle of preparing for the 'show' his father had planned, and for the day's cookout, making everyone happy was his first priority.

Uncles, aunts, grand-aunts and -uncles, along with a gaggle of female cousins, arrived next. Many of the guests gravitated into the sunny kitchen. As the hub of food prep activity, it was awash in delicious aromas.

Tony called out to the crowd in an accent less noticeable than his father's and directed them further through the open arch into the spacious family room, which exuded the static perfection of a seldom lived-in designer showroom. Colleen's muted watercolors graced the walls below a wood-beamed vaulted ceiling, and a large Heriz rug joined overstuffed sofas atop gleaming hardwood floors. Tony began taking drink orders. His liquor cabinet was well-stocked; he owned a string of liquor stores, having inherited the first in the North End from his father, then expanded over the years to more locations west of Boston.

While relatives chatted and drank, aligned in DiMasi or O'Malley clusters, Gavin and his mother worked with coordinated synchrony in the kitchen. As Colleen pulled out Gavin's culinary creations from the fridge, he set out trays, serving utensils, tools for the outdoor grill, and began transferring everything to the patio. Colleen busied herself by passing around the hors d'oeuvres she and Gavin had made that morning.

In a short-sleeved madras plaid shirt like his twin's, Devon wandered among relatives oozing charisma, boasting of his achievements and spreading his singular charm, smooth as whipped cream topped with a devilish grin. After weaving his way through the crowd, he progressed to the brick patio to talk with Marco, his father's younger brother.

But Devon's attention focused on Gavin, who at that moment carried two large pitchers of sangria as he walked through the family room, greeting each relative with his self-effacing smile. There were tags hanging around each pitcher; one indicating non-alcoholic, the other alcoholic.

When Gavin exited the patio with the sangria, Devon lunged for the spiked pitcher and said, "I'll have some of that, Gav."

"And get Mom all upset," Gavin grumbled. He gave his brother a sideways look and set the pitchers down on a patio table.

"Oh, Goodie Gavin, I'm sure it'll be harmless for me to have a sample," Devon insisted, and snatched a tumbler from the table.

"I don't think that's a good idea," Gavin snapped. Still

angry with his brother for his prank in the shower, he added, "Devious Devon."

"Ah, don't be a candy-ass, Gav," Devon laughed. "Uncle Marco doesn't mind, do you?" he winked. As the DiMasi 'caboose,' Marco was a twenty-years-younger version of Tony. The bluster of his youth, firmly rooted in the working-class macho culture of the North End, made him seem more reckless than his brother. He nodded to Devon with a conspiratorial grin.

Tony's older brother Joey, whose slightly hunched back evidenced an old injury, poured himself a second scotch from the bar in the corner of the family room just as Tony arrived to mix another drink for their father. "Hey, Antony," Joey drew out his words haltingly between gulps, "how's business?"

"Couldn't be better, Man," Tony crowed. "I'm rakin' it in with all my new stores, and I'm gonna be opening more pretty soon. Can't wait for Devon to get old enough to take over some of it."

"Devon?" Joey stammered and downed his drink. "And what about Gavin?"

"Devon's the one with balls. His brother's a nerd, like Colleen."

"Yeah, but he can usually keep Devon from doing crazy stuff," Joey nodded, then lowered his voice. "You better watch your wonder boy; he'll be wantin' to flirt with Salemme or 'Cue Ball.'"

Tony whipped an angry face around to his brother. "Shut your trap on the mob shit, Joey. You know how that turned out."

Joey smirked ruefully and changed the subject. "You comin' tomorrow night for cards? We got some new girls lined up. Real hot."

"Nah, I gotta chaperone the boys' birthday party at the arcade," Tony rolled his eyes. "But you keep 'em warmed up and I'll check 'em out next week," he muttered with a wink.

"I told you before, you never should'a married that snooty little bitch." He paused. "Just because you knocked her up didn't mean—"

"Hey, can it," Tony broke in. "That's my wife you're talking about. Look, she was sixteen—that's old enough." Tony flicked his hand dismissively.

"May be legal age, but she don't know nothing about what's real. Then she went and got that stupid-ass degree. Ivory tower twit."

"She's the boys' mother, good enough," Tony growled, visibly annoyed at being cornered by his brother. He walked away and called out to the crowd in the family room. "Before we go out to the patio for dinner, I'd like to propose a toast to our birthday boys."

After taking something from Marco and stuffing it into his pocket, Devon came to the open slider of the family room. He leaned against the doorway with a self-satisfied smirk and crossed arms like a celebrity. Tony raised his glass toward him and began, "Devon Umberto DiMasi, named after my dad. You make me proud. And Gavin O'Malley DiMasi, you're like your mother. To my twins!" Tony tipped his glass then downed his drink.

Colleen cringed upon hearing her husband's singular possession of their boys.

Gavin stood at the edge of the crowd, looked down at his feet and shifted as if he couldn't find a comfortable position.

Tony rambled on about how the boys would soon begin driving, have girlfriends, go off to college, get married, and make him a grandfather.

Everyone laughed, nodding agreement on the inevitable path to maturity. Then Tony cleared his throat with a flourish and said, "Some of you might know my friend Vic. He's a film engineer at 'GBH. He did me a big favor and copied a bunch of photos and home movies of the boys and put all of it on this VHS cassette," he said as he turned on the latest 35-inch Sony

Trinitron TV and loaded the VCR. "In honor of the boys' sixteenth birthday, this'll show how they've grown over the years. Some of you may have already seen a few of these pictures. I don't want to bore you—I'll just let the tape run, and I may comment on a few of the shots."

Several family members, who'd likely had their fill of twin propaganda over the years, responded with restless smirks and dug into the trays of hors d'oeuvres.

Tony clicked the remote. The first image was a video of the twins' pre-birth ultrasound. "We'd always only had a photo of the boys' ultrasound; they don't send people home with a video of the results," he began. "Well, being on the board at the hospital has its perks. So I asked Dr. Ricci, the president, how far back they keep the originals in archives. He checked, and bingo! Here's the first live movie of the boys!"

And there they were in black and white, locked in fraternal embrace, as if no one else in the world would ever matter, floating gracefully in maternal plasma, turning pirouettes with each other and seemingly miming via sign language.

That was followed by a montage of photos chronicling the typical phases of toddlerhood. Then a home movie showed the two-year-olds 'talking' with each other in their unique private language. One of the twins—apparently Devon, Tony noted as he pointed to the vigorous use of that boy's left hand—did most of the talking, adamantly gesturing to his brother while emphatically shouting unintelligible 'words' and stomping his feet in a frenzied dance, to which Gavin responded with similar utterances that were quickly overcome by Devon's vociferous shouting and gesticulation. While Devon put on this display that seemed to oscillate from pontificating to berating, Gavin took a cracker from a table. Devon then screeched and lunged, spewing apparent invectives, and yanked the cracker from Gavin's hand.

Tony chuckled, "So Devon got the upper hand really early, eh?"

Everyone snickered. Except Gavin, who ducked into the kitchen.

Some family members began losing attention, talking among themselves. Tony frowned as his audience fidgeted. But the next home movie of Tony playing with the boys as older toddlers reined them back. In it, Tony commanded, "Okay Devon, let's fight like I showed you." He positioned little Devon and swung his fists near his son's head while Devon flailed his fists. Next Tony pulled Gavin in and stood him in front of his twin. "Okay, Champ, show your brother how it's done," Tony instructed and guided Devon's hands toward his brother's face. "C'mon, Gavin, get in there and take a swing, fight back!" Gavin's little face contorted in something between confusion and fear. He turned to his mother with outstretched arms and a beseeching look. Colleen picked him up, clutched tightly, and turned away.

"Did you see that left hook on Devon?" Tony crowed. "He showed his chops even before he was out of training pants!"

Everyone laughed. Except Gavin, who turned on the garbage disposal.

Tony's show continued with a string of more photos and home movies of the twins in various activities and contexts, and finally ended with, "So here's to my identical twins." He lifted his glass in an air toast. "They've always been close, insisting on doing everything together...well, until recently. I guess they're growing up, each becoming his own man. May they always be best friends to each other. Devon's going to rule the world, and Gavin's gonna feed it—so time to eat all that grub he made!"

Scattered cheers rose from the group as they quickly exited to the patio, as if they couldn't get away from Tony's PR pitch fast enough. Tony's brother Joey grumbled to his father, the patriarch, "But it's not Italian, Pops. You see what's happening here?"

Although it was a hot July day, a gentle breeze had risen

from the north to provide relief while Gavin manned the large Weber grill. He arranged Beef Bourguignon Kabobs and Poulet Moutarde on the grill and had a big pan of vegetables waiting to blister. After days of planning and preparation, he was in his element, wielding the grill tools with the practiced ease of a seasoned conductor. Colleen directed everyone to the food table holding the sangrias, two large bowls of different salads, bread and setups. On the brick floor beside the table, Tony had placed a metal tub filled with ice and beer.

Colleen's teenage niece joined Gavin at the grill. "Look what Devon just gave me," she beamed, and held out a furry white rabbit's foot on a little chain. Then she giggled, "He'd make a good politician, wouldn't he?"

Gavin shrugged, "Yeah, I guess so."

"You two may be identical, but I can always tell you apart."

"We're mirror twins, so we're opposite from each other. Reversed. In more ways than one," Gavin smirked.

"Oh, that's so true!" she laughed, with a glance over at Devon. "Well, all this food smells so good, Gavin. How did you make the different sauces?"

Gavin was pleased to find someone interested in his cooking, and eagerly began explaining his techniques.

"How did you get started cooking?"

"I was kind of experimenting with it, and then Grandma O'Malley gave me a copy of Julia Child's *Mastering The Art of French Cooking*—I was hooked," Gavin said with an embarrassed shrug. "I watched all her *Master Chef* TV series that aired last year, got another of her cookbooks, and I even met her one day when she was at her favorite butcher in Cambridge. She's amazing."

"So you're really good at this, huh?"

"Oh, I've got a lot to learn, but I'm having fun with it," Gavin said, then lowered his voice. "Don't mention it around Devon or Dad, though. They think it's gay."

"I don't think that at all. I follow all the celebrity chefs in

Boston and New York. They're so creative. And I love how some of them have cool tattoos!" she gushed. "Do you want to be a chef?"

"I don't think my dad would approve of that. Maybe it'll just be my hobby."

"Have you started thinking about college?"

"A little. How about you?"

"I'm not sure. Definitely Harvard, with the free ride thanks to Grandpa O'Malley's tenure."

"I know Dad wants us to go to Harvard," Gavin said, turning the chicken on the grill. "He never went to college, so he thinks Harvard is the epitome of success," Gavin smirked as he spooned sauce over the kabobs. "But I'd like to go away for college, maybe on the West Coast, like Stanford. Or maybe even a culinary school," he said with a nervous laugh, then quickly amended, "Just kidding."

———

Residual smells of hours-ago barbeque and alcohol hung in the air like soured memories, enticing when separate and fresh, but conflicted and foul in desiccated blend. Echoes of words said, words unsaid, assaulted Gavin as he worked in the kitchen, completing the final stages of cleanup.

Tony and Colleen had already disappeared upstairs for the night. Devon sat on a stool at the kitchen island drinking the last of the sangria, which at that point was watered down from melted ice cubes. Gavin worked around him to clean the island counter and the floor beneath him.

"Jeez, Gav," Devon said. "Are you going to take all night to finish this shit?"

"You could help, you know," Gavin grumbled. "Why are you even here?" He lugged a big plastic bag full of trash out to the garage.

"I wanted to tell you about Marco. He's going to take me

to see his new apartment in Boston!"

"Have a ball."

"You went all-out on the food tonight, Gav," Devon emptied his glass. "Some of it was actually okay. You know I'm just joking when I razz you about your cooking, right?"

Gavin looked sideways at his twin. He waited for the usual put-down. "Sure. Thanks."

"But you really should consult with me on the menu next time. I know more about food combinations and preparation than anyone—even your precious Julia Child."

"*Right,*" Gavin drawled with an eye roll, declining to point out the groundless absurdity of Devon's claim. "So you can do all the cooking next time."

"No way. I'll just have Dad cater it all."

"Good luck with that." Gavin turned to go upstairs.

"You're in a bitchy mood, aren't you?"

Gavin turned on his heel, spun around and glared at his brother. He turned off the kitchen chandelier, leaving the room in semi-darkness, illuminated only by undercounter lights casting gloomy shadows. The sound of water spray rhythmically turned in the dishwasher. Swish, swish. "Why did you say I'm a loser when Dad told everyone you're the winner at everything?"

"Oh, that," Devon laughed. "I was just joking."

"Wasn't funny. Why did you say I'm a loser?" Gavin stood stiff and unyielding.

"You know I always have to agree with Dad. Keep him happy, or he gets pissed." Devon waved his hands like batting away a mosquito.

"But why did you volunteer that I'm a loser?" Swish. Swish.

"It didn't mean anything, Gav. Trust me." Devon's hands thrust out helplessly. "And you know I love my brother."

"But you don't stand up for me like I do for you. Why'd you say I'm a loser?"

"You're just overly sensitive, Julia." Devon began pacing.

"Is that why you say I'm a loser?" Gavin didn't move.

"Well, if you wouldn't be so uptight, and sucked up to Dad a little like I do, maybe he wouldn't think you're a loser."

"But why did *you* say I'm a loser? What happened to all those years we've had each other's back?"

"Oh, grow up, Twinkie." Devon fidgeted, then turned to face Gavin with a pitying look. "But I understand. You can't help the way you are. Poor little wimp just doesn't see who really loves him—Me. Sorry if you felt offended." He walked past Gavin, slightly bumping shoulders, pulled a package of popcorn from the cabinet and popped it into the microwave. "Let's you and me pig out on popcorn and watch TV in the family room like we used to when we were kids."

Gavin felt like he'd just been sparring with a cloud of smoke. His anger felt fruitless and gradually subsided as he and Devon shared a big bowl of popcorn on the family room sofa. But when angry sounds from their parents' bedroom overcame the volume of the TV, Gavin cringed. "Arguing again," he mumbled and shook his head.

"It's called fighting," Devon said with a flippant shrug, and turned up the volume on the television.

It must have been Italian night on Jay Leno's show; his guests were Tony Danza and Tony Bennett. Danza's TV show, "Who's the Boss" had been off for two years, but his new movie was being released that weekend, so he was there to hype it. The boys knew their father listened to Tony Bennett's recordings, but as teenagers they weren't too impressed.

"You missed some crap when you cleaned up this room," Devon said, pulling an olive from between the sofa cushions and throwing it at his brother.

Gavin caught it in mid-air, then in the same movement with smooth wrist action, tossed it in a perfect arc over the kitchen island straight into the sink holding the garbage disposal. Swish.

Devon either didn't recognize or didn't acknowledge that singular feat.

Nor did Gavin. "So…You pumped for our party tomorrow night?" he asked.

Tony had rented out the local arcade for their birthday party with all their friends. Catered pizzas, soft drinks, a DJ, and unlimited game plays for all.

"I gave the DJ a list of my favorite songs, but other than that, I'm not sure how much fun it'll be," Devon grunted and grabbed another handful of popcorn.

"I hope Katie comes."

"Katie Goodwin? That nerd?"

"I think she's amazing," Gavin said. He had been intrigued by her from the first day she transferred into his Trig class. "Cute, fun, and wicked smart. She gets top grades even while holding down a part-time job. Her dad died when she was little, and her mom has some sort of sickness."

"Well, I guess another nerd is a good match for you, but most girls are like stupid Barbie Dolls."

"What do you mean?"

"You know—silly, boring. Most of them are a real turn off."

"Really?" Gavin's eyebrows shot up. "How do you get that?"

"Oh, I'm just so tired of girls throwing themselves at me," Devon shook his head and made a face, as if he'd just tasted something disgusting. "They are *so* not exciting."

"Oh, sure," Gavin scoffed. "You're so magnetic that hordes of girls are clamoring for your attention, rolling over for you."

"Well, yeah, for obvious reasons," Devon chuckled with an innocent grin.

"So, aside from yourself, what else do you consider exciting?" Gavin challenged.

"You, little Twinkie. You're a carbon copy of me—I see you whenever I look in the mirror!" Devon laughed and grabbed Gavin in a chokehold.

"Fuck you," Gavin gurgled through his constricted throat, then broke his brother's hold. "Didn't that Narcissus guy fall in love with his own reflection?"

Devon rolled his eyes. "I'm bored. Where's the chess set?"

"Oh, come on, you just want to wipe my ass." Gavin thought back to the last time they played. It had been a few years. He suspected Devon had switched the position of two pieces when he'd gone to the bathroom. But he pulled out the board and pieces from a cabinet below the bookshelves, and Devon dived in to set up the white pieces as always—so he could go first.

Devon moved his pawn. "This should be a quick game. You always lose, Gav," he snickered. "You can't beat me in anything."

"Yeah, you usually win in chess," Gavin conceded, then countered with his own pawn. "But you don't always win in everything. I can think of a lot of things where I'm better than you."

"Like what?" Devon laughed as he moved his bishop.

"Well," Gavin stammered, and moved his knight. "I can run faster than you, I get better grades in English and French, I'm better at basketball—"

"I think my dear brother is imagining things," Devon interrupted, and captured Gavin's pawn with his bishop.

The match progressed rapidly. Gavin studied the board after Devon's last move. He saw that he now had an advantageous position over his brother. Maybe he could win this time. But he had to test his theory. He stood and took a mental picture of the board, then headed for the kitchen. "I'm getting a Coke. Want anything?"

"You're stalling, Twinkie," Devon said, then joined Gavin at the fridge. He gave his twin a condescending pat. "But that's okay. You'll always need me, and I'll always be there for you."

"Oh sure, you'll always be there, telling me what to do and how you're god's gift," Gavin mumbled, and opened his Coke.

Devon pulled one of Tony's beers out of the fridge.

"You know you're not supposed to drink Dad's beer," Gavin said.

Devon popped the cap and took a long gulp. "Oh, Goodie Gavin. Don't you worry about me," he laughed.

Gavin grumbled and returned to the chess board. He checked the position of each piece against his mental picture. Devon had moved his rook in his last turn. Okay.

"You having a problem figuring out your next move, Gav?" Devon goaded.

But one of Devon's knights was in a different position than where it was, which set up a clear attack pattern. Shit, he finally confirmed it. His brother cheats.

"Since when can you move two pieces in the same turn, Dev?"

"What are you talking about?"

Gavin jabbed his finger at the board. "So how'd that knight get from here to there, at the same time you moved your rook?"

"Jeez, Gav, will you pay attention? I advanced my knight to that square three moves ago."

"No you didn't. You moved it while my back was turned, dipshit."

"Your delusions are starting to get the best of you, little brother. Maybe you should see your pediatrician."

"Yeah, that's right, Dev. You always win, one way or another."

To argue with his brother was futile. It always opened more opportunities for Devon to escalate his insults and counterarguments, which ended up making Gavin feel hopelessly cornered. Devon never backed down from anything, and certainly wouldn't from this cheat.

"Just sit down, dear twin, and make your move," Devon said, his voice soft as if he were soothing an upset child. "Maybe I'll let you win." He drained his beer with a swagger and went back for another.

"TWO beers?" Gavin challenged.

"Oh, grow up, baby brother."

There was zero chance of recovering the match at this point. Gavin stiffened, his fists clenched and jaw set. He wanted to send the board and pieces airborne, off the table with one swing of his arm. He could see it all in his mind—kings, queens and their courts flying in slow motion like a swarm of attacking locusts. His arm twitched with the urge. But that would give Devon what he wanted—evidence he was getting under his twin's skin. Instead, Gavin walked out, leaving the board and his brother behind.

2.

TEENAGERS OFTEN BECOME WRAPPED UP IN THEIR own world, blithely oblivious of impending danger. That Saturday night was no exception, as the Fun and Games Arcade vibrated with more than thirty hormone-fueled kids whose energy competed with blaring music and raucous game machines. Several adult chaperones, including Tony, patrolled the group, but the looming crisis went undetected.

If anyone were to listen to the playlist Devon compiled for the twins' party, they would have discerned a roadmap to his future. The songs included a variety of genres, primarily by male artists and mostly devoid of slow dance tunes, with lyrics that would ultimately prove prescient. The single blasting at that moment was Snoop Dog's *Gin & Juice*, its subtle rap throbbing lyrics of weed and alcohol. The long-haired DJ was in his own world, showing off his skills during the instrumentals by licking his finger, slowing the record down, intently listening on his headphones, then speeding it up.

Not that the teenagers were paying much attention. The room writhed in complex interplay like a disturbed ant colony. The kids engaged in groups, clusters and pairs, in nearly constant movement. They competed for turns at the games, which were not the pinball consoles of their chaperones' day.

Instead of the harmonic bells and pings of those mechanical devices, these games featured digitized videos with 3D graphics, full music tracks and sound effects that reflected the actions of the player—or players. Several of the games, such as *Galaxian,* were multi-player.

Inner Circle's *Bad Boys* played as kids stepped into the blue interior of *Turbo Kourier*'s rendering module to get their image superimposed into the computer-generated graphics of *Kourier*'s 3D virtual reality game. With all the music blasting, neon flashing and action sounds from game machines, mixed with boisterous chatter from amped-up teenagers, the arcade pulsated with overwhelming cacophony.

As Devon commandeered *Mortal Kombat II,* the newest and most difficult game, one of his favorite songs from Cypress Hill—*Insane in the Brain*—pounded like a herd of wild horses, its knock-down lyrics slamming reckless crazy.

Devon was surrounded by several giggling girls along with a few boys hoping to claim one of his cute discards. He performed like a showy virtuoso with exaggerated bravado, calling attention to every score, advertising his superiority and finally ending the game with arms raised high in victory, surrounded by cheering fans.

In a less noisy corner of the arcade, Gavin engaged in conversation over pizza with Katie, the pert blonde of his fascination. She had a dimpled smile and large glasses that overwhelmed her delicate face. Gavin had sneaked out a shirt different from the one Devon had planned for them and changed into it in the arcade's restroom. While he talked with Katie, he kept a wary eye on Devon, hoping his brother would keep his distance so he could talk with Katie without his twin taking over.

But Devon seemed to know Gavin's whereabouts in the crowd even while fully engaged in his game with his back turned. After defeating Shao Kahn, the underworld emperor and MK2's final boss, he attempted an aimless air while sauntering directly to Gavin and Katie. He was accompanied by a thin pimpled boy whose gaze on Devon verged on hero worship.

Gavin cringed when he saw Devon walk toward him. Just as his and Katie's discussion was warming up.

"Hey Gav," Devon cracked a scheming grin. "I almost didn't recognize you in that shirt. You know I'm the twin with better taste, and I don't remember saying you could wear it." He let loose a roar of laughter, then turned to Katie. "Katie, you're looking especially beautiful tonight!"

Katie looked mildly surprised but managed to squeak an embarrassed "Thank you."

Devon threw his arm around Gavin's shoulder. "So, little brother, why don't you show Katie how you can beat me in that *Virtua Racing* game over there?"

"Oh, I wouldn't try to challenge you—you're the expert on these things," Gavin struggled to keep annoyance out of his tone. "And I don't really want to play right now. Katie and I were talking."

"I'm sure Katie won't mind," Devon flashed a charming smile in her direction. "Right, Katie? Cecil here will keep you company."

Before a befuddled Katie could respond, Gavin interjected in a controlled flat tone, "Well, I mind, Devon."

A chuckle slithered out of Devon, but his face wasn't laughing. In the tense moment while he tried to assert control, Michael Jackson's *Will You Be There* thrummed its anthem, its plaintive lyrics yearning for brotherhood, love and salvation.

"You look thirsty, Gav. Want some of my soda?" Devon shoved his drink under his brother's nose.

Vapors of strong alcohol rippled the air above the cup. Gavin could smell the rum in the Coke. He glowered at his brother. He knew Devon wanted him to know that he was drinking, to rub it in and upset him. "No thanks," Gavin growled, losing his battle to keep annoyance out of his tone.

Any other teenage boy might exhibit more than that, showing anger or even rage. But Gavin felt constrained from acting, as if he didn't have the right to oppose his brother. He turned and strode away, pulling Katie's hand behind him and leaving Devon with his skinny admirer.

The kids had dug into the pizza like the growing teens they were. More than half of it was gone when Devon approached Tony. "Dad, some of our friends here are allergic and can't eat regular pizza," he began. "So I have to go get some no-cheese pizza."

"Damn picky kids—that's a bunch of bullshit," Tony said.

"They're lactose intolerant, Dad," Devon drawled in his flat 'you're so ignorant' tone.

Tony shook his head with disgust. "So where you gonna get it and how are you getting there? Can't they deliver?"

"Bill's in Natick is the only place that'll make it that way, but they don't deliver," Devon said. "I called them. Trayvon Harris is here with his brother's car; he'll drive me. Can I have some money?"

Tony pulled out his wallet. "Hurry right back. Are you taking Gavin with you?"

"I offered, but he's occupied. With *Katie*," he sniggered.

Almost an hour passed before Tony realized Devon hadn't returned. But Gavin noticed his absence right away and had become increasingly anxious as time went on, knowing that Devon had been drinking. He worried what kind of trouble his brother might have gotten into.

"Dad, where's Devon?"

"He went with someone—Trayvon something-or-other—to get some no-cheese pizza—can you believe it?" Tony checked his watch. "They should be back by now, though."

Gavin had just seen Tray, and Devon wasn't with him. He

barreled through crowds of kids and rushed back to where he'd last seen his friend and blurted out, "Where's Devon?"

Tray looked surprised and confused. "I don't know, man. He's your twin. Can't you keep track of him?"

"He said he was going with you to get some no-cheese pizza."

"Some what?" Tray laughed. "That's news to me!"

"He said you have a car here and would drive him."

Tray moved closer to Gavin and whispered, "Look, man, your brother lied. You know he's been drinking heavy duty tonight."

Gavin knew his brother all too well. And now his panic multiplied. "Do you have your keys with you?"

Tray patted each of his pockets. Multiple times. "Shit!" he spat.

The boys ran out to the parking lot. Tray stared at the empty space where his car had been. "What kind of car is it," Gavin's words rushed with urgency, "and do you know your license plate number?"

Armed with that information, Gavin ran back inside to tell his father—not that Devon had been drinking, only that he had taken Tray's car.

"Well crap!" Tony barked. "He's only practiced driving a couple times in an empty parking lot, so now he thinks he can drive—without his license?"

"He's been gone more than an hour, Dad," Gavin said. "Do you think you should call the police to look for Tray's car?"

"Or call hospitals," Tony mumbled, pulling out his Nokia 1011 mobile phone.

Tony DiMasi knew most of the local police force. He didn't tell them his son had taken the car without permission, only that he'd borrowed it. The officer took his contact information and said they'd let him know if his son or the car showed up.

Tony turned to Gavin and snarled, "What the fuck, boy, why weren't you watching him?" then ran to the arcade exit, with Gavin close behind. As they left, Nine Inch Nails' *Hurt* moaned its pathetic dirge of self-destruction.

3.

GAVIN

THIS ROOM. THE SO-CALLED FAMILY ROOM. WE
have a living room, but that's for show, for people we don't
know very well. So we don't really live in that room. We spend
most of our time in our bedrooms, the kitchen and this family
room. This is where some of us watch TV, where we put up
the tree at Christmas, where Devon and I played games when
we were little, where Mom taught us our ABCs, where Dad
shows off for relatives, but is that 'family'? What makes a
family any different than a few strangers randomly together?

So we're all just suspended here, in darkness and shadows.
Waiting for a phone call, waiting for Devon, the most important person in our family...our group of resident strangers. It's
after midnight and we still don't know where he is. Nothing
from the police.

It's all my fault. I should've been watching out for him.
Should've told Dad he was drinking. Broke the stupid twin
code of silence.

Dad just poured himself another scotch. What's that, three or
four? Doesn't matter. They're all double anyway. Mom and Dad
got into an argument about Devon, but now she's just curled
into a knot over in the corner in the dark, rocking back and
forth, staring out the window at nothing. My legs are cramp-

ing up, from hours of pacing around this room. The family room, where no one really talks with each other, or whatever it is that families do.

We all jump when the phone rings. Dad grabs it. "What happened? Is he hurt? How bad? Where is he?" He keeps bellowing questions, then finally shuts up so whoever it is can answer. Mom is up, back to life, and now Dad slams down the phone, grabs the car keys and we all follow him in a stampede to the door. "That's the police. He was in an accident and he's in the hospital now."

The phone rings again. Dad almost trips over his own feet to get it. "He has an identical twin, so they must have the same blood type. We'll be there in five minutes." He throws the phone on the floor, clamps the back of my neck and shoves me to the door. "C'mon, boy, you're gonna save your brother's life."

Oh god...How bad is it? What if I can't save him?

Dad peels out of our driveway. "That was someone from Newton-Wellesley. Devon's in emergency surgery. They need blood. Why don't they have any on hand?" He's driving too fast. I tighten my seat belt. He just went through a red light without even slowing down. Hope he isn't drunk now...

I think Mom is freaked about Dad's driving, too. She's mumbling. "AB negative. It's rare. They probably have O-negative—universal type—but want Gavin's, just in case." Sometimes Mom's like that when she's upset. She goes all intellectual. Or else she disappears somewhere into her head if she's really weirded out. Wonder which way she'll go when we get to the hospital? But Dad only has one way to react— ballistic. I usually crawl into my hole, but Devon just tells us all how dumb we are and what an expert he is.

Dad screeches up to the emergency door of this plain old brick hospital and jumps out of the car. Doesn't park it, just leaves it. Mom and I run in after him. There's a woman behind a desk talking to a guy who's bent over moaning. Looks like he just puked on the floor. Dad barks at her, "My son's in emergency surgery and they told us to go to the lab so his twin can give blood. Where's the lab? And where's my son?"

She looks at him with half closed eyelids, like she's bored, hears stuff like this all the time. "Are you Mr. and Mrs. DiMasi?"

Mom stands there fidgeting. Jeez, she's actually shaking. Like I feel inside. And Dad's coming unglued and yells, "So where's the lab? Just so you know, I'm on the board of this hospital!" As if that'll make any difference.

"They're expecting you," the woman says, flat and calm. I don't think she gives a shit about Dad's board position. She points down the hall. "Ms. Mahoney the lab technician will be waiting for you. And your son is in the second-floor surgery unit."

Mom gives the lady one of her tight half-smiles and whispers "Thank you," like she's apologizing for Dad's asshole behavior.

We run down the hall. Dad slams the elevator button. Repeatedly, like that will make it come any faster. The lighted number says it's up on the sixth floor now. So Dad starts giving orders. "Colleen, you take Gavin to the lab down that hall. I'll go up to surgery to find out what's happening."

Mom and I wander around looking for the lab technician. The place is deserted at this time of night, so our footsteps sound hollow, echoing off bare walls. When we find Ms. Mahoney she says, "Yes, we have the doctor's order here to take your son's blood. How old is he?"

Mom tells her, and she says Mom has to sign a form so I can give blood under age seventeen, then looks me up and down and says "He looks to be over 110 pounds, I assume. Is he on any medication?"

Mom says 'no.' They're talking to each other like I'm not even there, like I can't answer for myself. Which is probably about half right. I don't know whether to run or shit myself.

What's it like to give up some of your blood?

Mom takes in a long slow breath like she's counting to a hundred, trying to be calm, then says "Ma'am, I'll be in the second-floor surgery area with my husband, checking on the status of Gavin's twin brother. Please let us know if there are problems of any sort." She turns to me and says, "Have Ms. Mahoney or someone bring you up to the surgical unit when you're all done here." She hugs me and whispers, "Thank you for doing this, Sweetie. And don't blame yourself for Devon's accident. I love you."

Well, Dad blames me and told me I had to do this. Whatever it takes to save Devon.

Ms. Mahoney hands me a bottle of water and takes me to the lab. I've never done this before. No one told me how this works, so I'm nervous. But I'm more worried that Devon could die, so I'm willing to do anything. Even though I've been mad at him, resenting him, none of that is as bad as if I lost my brother. I can't catch my breath now, thinking about it, like I might lose part of myself or even die if that happened.

I know how identical twins are made; we learned it in biology class. We start out as one cell that's supposed to become one baby, then divide into two duplicate babies. But Mom explained to me how Devon and I shared the same of everything else even before we were born. Not just that original cell, but also the same amniotic sac we developed in, and even the same umbilical cord that delivered nourishment to us. In fact, Devon hogged more from that cord than I did, so he was born bigger than me. And also first, as he likes to remind me. So if we came from all that sameness, how could one half survive if the other half dies?

My blood-letting wasn't so bad, if you don't mind a needle stuck in your arm. The worst part was having to sit there and wait afterward. They made me drink water and gave me a candy bar. I guess they want to make sure you're not having any kind of reaction or faintness. But I just want to know how

Devon's surgery is going.

By the time they take me upstairs, Dad is already in top form. I hear his voice booming from behind a door marked Family Waiting Room. I go in and see him and Mom with another woman. Her name tag says Irma Garfield, House Supervisor, Nursing Department. She's trying to show some sort of sympathy, but she's pretty stiff like she's reading from a script. "I'm sorry I wasn't called the moment you came to the ER. I was supposed to have escorted you. I'm here to help you. I'll facilitate getting information from the Operating Room to keep you informed. Either I or another member of our team will stay here with you."

Dad sure isn't comforted, stomping around like a prehistoric T-Rex. "Look, I've been waiting too long already, and I want to see a real doctor who can tell me about my son." He's loud enough for everyone in the county to hear. "I'm on the board of this hospital, and I expect better service than you just being a useless messenger."

Ms. Garfield offers excuses and a lame attempt at apology, and slinks out of the room.

Our family doesn't talk much in this 'family' room. We just wait: sitting, pacing, watching the clock as time crawls and our worry grows. Hospital night noises—beeps and pings of patient monitors, occasional voices over loudspeakers—are the only sounds, which we eventually tune out. Mom just sits with her arms crossed tight, like she's trying to hold herself together. She's always hated the color yellow, so maybe that's why she has her head down, not looking at the bright daffodil walls. She just stares with blank eyes at the patterned carpet that seems way too cheerful for what must usually happen in this kind of room. Even though we occasionally go to mass, we aren't very religious, so I don't think there's much praying happening now.

Around two o'clock, a guy comes in and introduces himself as an Emergency Room Resident to give us an update. He recites mechanically like he's going down a checklist: "Your son was brought in at eleven-thirty, was assessed and prepped with bloodwork, x-rays and MRI—with close monitoring during all processes. Specialists were consulted, priorities defined and a treatment plan was developed, with surgery commencing shortly before one a.m. Surgery is proceeding without major incident so far."

Dad looks really irritated, like he expected more specific information. "So you're saying they've been operating on my son for more than an hour and they're still not done?" he snaps.

The guy fidgets and nods.

Mom cuts in before Dad can rant, "What are his injuries?"

"There are broken bones," the Resident says, sort of hesitating like he's holding something back. "But I will defer to the Chief to provide details."

This was about as helpful as a sharp stick in the eye, as Grandpa DiMasi likes to say.

It feels like days crawl by with no news, when finally, around four-thirty in the morning, a short thin sixty-something man comes in. He has those weird half-glasses that some people slide down their nose and look over. We all turn to him. He's obviously a doctor. A real doctor. He sort of stops short when he sees me, and then he goes to Dad and Mom. Mom gives him a smile that's both tired and relieved, then turns to Dad and says "Tony, this is Dr. Khatri. He was part of the review team when I defended my dissertation."

Dad scowls. He doesn't like to be reminded about Mom's PhD.

"And an outstanding piece of research it was, Dr. DiMasi," he says. "There's been scarce work on the psychological and epigenetic impact to patients suffering physical trauma."

I wonder what that is? I've got to ask Mom about 'epigenetic impact,' since Devon has just had physical trauma. Lots of it.

The doctor turns to Dad. "Mr. DiMasi, I'm Chief of General Surgery here. I'm sorry your son has been in an accident. I'm sure you've been quite worried."

"General Surgery?" Dad says, surprised. Or insulted. "Shouldn't my son be treated by specialists?"

"In cases of trauma, the Chief of General Surgery coordinates the entire team of specialists," the doctor explains.

That seems to satisfy Dad. For now. But he launches into his usual barrage of questions without waiting for answers. "What took so long in surgery? What's his condition now? When can we see him? Have the police got the guy that hit him? You know who I am, right? And I expect the best care for my son, even if that means calling in experts from Tufts, or even Harvard!"

Dr. Khatri looks really tired, but everything about him almost glows with genuine care. He looks at Dad, then to Mom and me, and back to Dad. He clears his throat and begins speaking in a slightly accented voice. "I understand your concerns. Rest assured that we always exert the utmost effort, expertise and professionalism to provide the best care for all our patients," he begins. "As you know, we're a Teaching Hospital of Tufts Medical School, and also associated with Harvard Medical School, so we've had a large multi-discipline team, including three surgeons, working in stages on your son for more than four hours," he explains patiently. "This was particularly challenging because at the same time we were also coordinating a surgical team for another critically injured patient." He sort of emphasizes that last bit with a fixed gaze on Dad.

Mom's eyes widen and Dad sucks in his breath at that, but then he pushes on, "So what exactly are Devon's injuries, and what's his condition?"

"Would you mind if I sit?" the doctor asks.

"Please do," Mom says, then pulls one of the ugly green upholstered chairs to him.

Khatri starts, laying his hands out like he has to organize what's going to be a very complicated story. "Overall, his condition is serious, but he has a reasonable chance of complete recovery, given time and care."

That's a relief, but it sounds like there's going to be more. A catch somewhere.

He goes on. "The impact of collision was to the driver side door of his vehicle, inflicting damage to the left side of his body and causing internal bleeding, which we've controlled. His left arm, pelvis, leg and several ribs suffered fractures, ranging from minor to compound. We've set his arm and leg during our surgery. We've immobilized him, so the rib and pelvic fractures should heal on their own without surgical intervention, given his youth. We will provide supportive wraps and devices to help keep your son comfortable while he's on restricted activity levels. He was not wearing a seatbelt, and we're told that his car flipped over. He's fortunate not to have injured his spine, but he does have a concussion, which will require time and attention to address possible intracranial swelling, on which we will act to relieve in that case. We'll be coordinating care with the Neurology Chief to manage that injury. Your son's kidney and liver were damaged by the impact and his liver is also compromised by the toxicity of substances he ingested..."

Dad pops up straight with his mouth open. "What're you talking about—substances? What substances?" His voice just doubled in decibels.

Mom's head spins to Dad and she gives him one of her 'told-you-so' looks.

"Your son came in with toxic levels of both alcohol and THC," Dr. Khatri says. He sees Dad's confused expression, then adds, "That's the psychoactive component in marijuana."

I know what Devon has been doing, but no way am I going to say anything now. Dad shakes his head hard, like he can make it all untrue, then opens his mouth to argue.

Khatri rushes to go on, like if he keeps talking he can stop Dad from flipping out, maybe manage to get the truth through to him. "We've brought in Nephrology and Gastroenterology for intraoperative consults."

Dad was speechless. A rare thing. Mom breaks in and asks, "How bad is the concussion, Dr. Khatri?"

Khatri looks sideways at Dad like he's expecting an explosion and says, "It appears to be Grade Three at this point, but we can't be sure until he wakes from surgery. Your son lost consciousness at the scene of the accident; we will continue to monitor his neurological status closely."

I'm totally buried under all that information, trying to understand and sort it all out. Devon has a lot of different injuries. And damage. The booze and pot probably contributed to him having the accident. I just hope those won't make the damage worse. I should have stopped him. The doctor looks at me now like there's something wrong, or weird.

"The damage to your son's liver," he starts, "was affected by the point of impact on his left side, which is reverse from the liver's normal location. He didn't have identification on him, so we couldn't check his medical records, and he wasn't wearing a medical alert bracelet indicating *dextrocardia* with *situs inversus*. Discovering that during prep complicated matters a bit."

What the hell is *that?*

Dad almost spits, "What's that dextro...whatever it is you said?"

Mom turns to him and says low, almost whispers, "Remember that's what they told us before the boys were born, from the ultrasound. Devon's organs are reversed—on the opposite side of his body from normal." Then she looks at Khatri like she's in pain, "But no one ever told us he should wear a medical alert bracelet."

Khatri pats Mom's arm, "I'm sorry, Dr. DiMasi. Some physicians don't always consider it a medical risk."

Dad's head spins around to Mom. He's pissed. "You think you're so damn smart, why the hell didn't you know that?"

But Devon probably wouldn't agree to wearing that kind of thing anyway. It would advertise his flaw. Unless he thought it would show how special and unique he is.

Dr. Khatri smiles at Mom like he's apologizing for something, then says, "I'm assuming his mirror twin," he looks at me, "doesn't have the same condition?"

"No, he doesn't—or at least they didn't tell us he does," Mom shrinks into her chair.

It's sort of bizarre—well, coincidental I guess, that Devon and I are mirror twins and we're not only reversed in our outward appearance, but internally too. But who's the reverse of the other? My organs are what's considered normal, but Devon came out first, so am I the reverse of Devon or the other way around? Maybe nature caught its mistake in the first twin and corrected it in me? Now that would be ironic.

I know Dad hates surprises, so of course he's furious now. And he really hates to be upstaged by Mom and her PhD, so hearing Khatri call her 'Doctor' just makes it even worse. His scowl is so deep it could split his skull. "My boys were born here, at this hospital," Dad roars. "I'm going to make sure the hospital pays for this incompetence. You shouldn't have had a problem with my son's condition if you did x-rays and an MRI."

The doctor starts to explain, "Yes, that's when we recognized his condition, which required altering the surgical approach, and—"

But I'm not interested in that, so I interrupt, "What are you doing about Devon's organs—his liver and kidney? Did you operate on them?"

The doctor smiles at me, like he appreciates the diversion from Dad's tirade. "There was no detachment, so at this point, the best thing we can do is watch closely, monitor his vitals and respond if and when required," he says. "That's why we're consulting with Nephrology and Gastroenterology experts. In most cases where there's no disease, those organs can heal by themselves. We'll be tracking their function with lab tests, imaging and fluid administration, and of course detoxification of substances will help."

Mom looks like she's trying to figure something out, then asks, "Will Devon's organ reversal complicate his prognosis and recovery, Doctor?"

"There have been some anomalous disorders reported in a few cases of the condition," he says, shaking his head like it's not a serious issue, "but it's so rare that no statistical probability has been established. But from your research, Dr. DiMasi, you understand that we'll be watching for epigenetic alterations as well."

There's that word again. I have to ask Mom later.

Dad looks confused but dismissive, like it's just mumbo-jumbo. "So what does all this mean, Doc? Give it to me in English. What are the next steps, and when will we know he's out of the woods? What happens now? How long will he have to stay in the hospital?"

Jeez Dad, just take a breath.

Dr. Khatri waits for Dad to finally wind down, then says, "It all depends. The next forty-eight hours will be key." He nods, letting that sink in, then goes on to explain. "The absence of injury to the spine is encouraging. Of some concern is his concussion. We don't know at this point what might be the extent or duration of any cognitive impairment. This is something that will be closely monitored by our Neurology department. Your son is unconscious now, but it's too early to tell whether that will continue for any length of time."

That sounds serious. Now I'm even more worried. "Is he in a coma?" I ask.

Khatri turns to me with a kind face. I like this guy. "As I'm sure your mother knows, a coma is just a prolonged state of unconsciousness," he says. "In some cases, the patient's recovery can proceed more effectively if he is in a comatose state for a while, allowing him to rest without conscious stress that could slow the healing process. In the meantime, we must watch and wait, monitor your brother closely and adjust as needed. We have him in the Recovery Room now, prior to transfer to ICU, connected to monitoring devices for that purpose, overseen by our Critical Care Team."

My head hurts. I'm overwhelmed with fear, guilt, panic. I can't sort it all out. And something else that doesn't feel right. Relief...that my brother is alive? Or that Devon is out of my face for a little while? I push that contradiction out of my mind. For now. "Can we see him?" I ask.

"Not yet," Khatri says. "The Recovery Room team must assess his condition and make sure he's stable." The doctor looks at me like he really cares. "You can look through the window of the Room as you leave to go home and get a little sleep, then return in the afternoon. You can be sure that if there's any change in status, we'll notify you immediately."

I look at Mom and see tears have gone down her cheeks in wiggly tracks like they navigated an obstacle course around her freckles. She seems to have aged ten years in the past few hours, like she's seen a ghost. I've never seen my father cry, but now he's turning away, and I think his eyes are a little watery. Like mine.

In the car back home, I'm in the back seat and ask Mom about the 'epigenetic' term I heard.

She turns around and talks soft to me, probably to avoid disturbing Dad. Or pissing him off even more. "Epigenetic alteration is a change to DNA as a result of physical, chemical or emotional trauma—or a combination thereof. What changes is the chemical structure of the DNA, not its coding sequence, but the result is how the DNA is expressed. It gets a lot more technical and complicated after that, like what happens molecularly—"

"Thanks, Mom. I think I get the idea." I don't need the intellectual stuff right now.

But I'm really worried.

This epigenetic thing has made me think about the similarities and differences in our brains. How Devon's concussion might affect his brain, which I've learned is supposed to be like mine. At least physically, because we're identical. I wonder whether his injuries might change his brain in some way. He's already begun to change in the past year. More domineering and obnoxious toward me and other people. How much of that is based in someone's brain? And then he's been experimenting with alcohol and drugs, and Mom said 'chemical' trauma can be one cause of epigenetic alteration. Would Devon's accident and concussion change him even more, or differently? For better, or worse?

Despite our recent differences, I've always thought of him as my closest companion and friend. I have to make sure my brother doesn't die.

When we get back home from the hospital, there's a police car in front of our house. Dad pulls into our garage. "That's Gus. You two go on inside. I'll deal with this."

Mom frowns and looks at Dad like she wants to know what's happening, but she doesn't say anything. Dad just scowls at her and shakes his head. Mom tilts her head up with an unspoken 'ah-ha'—she gets it, whatever it is, and turns to go in the house. I've always been amazed at how everything in our house is so pre-programmed that interactions—when they happen—are conducted by facial expressions and body language, with no one talking or discussing what really matters.

Once in the house, I go to the library window but don't turn the lights on. I look out at Dad and the policeman. Apparently someone named Gus, and Dad knows him. The sky has started to get lighter, although sun won't crest the horizon for several minutes. So I can see that Gus has a pencil and tablet of paper, lays it on the hood of his cruiser and writes some stuff. He and Dad talk some more, but I can't hear them. Dad gestures with his shoulders up, arms out, palms up, like when someone says, 'Jeez, how the fuck should I know?' or something like that. Gus nods, puts his paper in his back pocket, pats Dad on the back and shakes his hand. Then he gets back in his car and leaves Dad standing in the driveway with his shoulders slumped, like he's either exhausted or relieved.

I guess I had assumed there would have to be a police report of some sort on Devon's accident, but I thought it would be a bigger deal, or take longer, be more complicated. That seemed too easy.

4.

DEVON

LOOK AT THEM CLUSTERED DOWN THE HALL.
Nurses, doctors, interns, technicians, therapists, dieticians, in
their cute little uniforms, all together yapping like it's a gossip
session, probably talking about me. How special I am, how
unique my case is. Instead of standing around talking, they
should be taking care of me, getting me out of here!

I've been here half my lifetime. Well, not quite two
months, but it feels like forever. So long I lose track of what
day it is, or even what month. And now I see it's the week after
Labor Day, school is back in session and I'm still stuck in this
place. I feel like a prisoner, for crissake. Someone has to get
me out of here. It's like they're all out to get me, everyone from
the nurses to the doctors, even the floor sweepers. I'm
trapped, out of my element. I can feel myself coming apart,
dying bit by bit...and it's all their fault.

It's like they're punishing me. So I assed out at my own
damn birthday party. Big deal. Sixteen's a cause for celebration, right? I ran out of dope, no one else had anything, so I
had to get more. I was just going the speed limit, but those
idiot police told Dad I was going thirty over! How the fuck
could they know? They weren't there. So I figured I could
beat the light. Not my fault they have shorter time cycles on

those signals late at night. Then the incompetent shits at this dump of a hospital made things worse. No way should I have gone into a *coma* from a little fender-bender. And then sepsis? What the hell?

I am so fucking tired of these idiots. You'd think I could get some real professionals who actually know what they're doing, since Dad is on the board of this hell hole and donates a ton of money to the place. I told him he should sue them, but he doesn't want to screw with his board status and connections, so he's playing it cool. Guess he's not as stupid as I thought. At least we won't have to pay anything for their lousy 'care.' Whatever insurance doesn't cover, the hospital will eat.

I can't wait to get out of here. I'm convinced this place is slowing my recovery on purpose. Making up issues that don't exist, so they can keep me here longer, with more specialists. I'm fine. Minor stuff like a little car accident can't hold me down. I got out of the body cast last month and I'm already walking. Sort of, with this boot cast on my left leg.

Here comes the Chief Idiot, Dr. Khatri. Just because all those doctors that operated on me kiss his ass, he thinks I should too. Just the opposite. Arrogant asshole. But he has to sign off on letting me out of here, so I have to butter him up.

"Good morning, Mister DiMasi."

I hate that Indian accent—or is it Pakistani, like that slimy creep in history class? It sounds like they have a mouth full of marbles. But at least he calls me 'Mister.' He knows who's in charge.

"Good morning, Doctor. It's always a pleasure to see you. I've told my family and friends all about your excellent care, the miraculous work you performed after my accident. I can't thank you enough!"

"I'm sorry to hear that you missed your physical therapy session yesterday."

Missed? I refused to go, especially not with that mousey dimwit Rachel something-or-other who says she's a licensed whatever. But I have to be nice to this guy now. "Yes, I'm so sorry. I was getting exercise by using my walker down the halls and became so engrossed in that, I forgot. I really appreciate how physical therapy has been key to my remarkable recovery." I've told him before that those routines are a waste of my time. I can do it all with no effort. There's nothing that's challenging me. He should just discharge me and stop wasting my time.

"Mister DiMasi," he begins. Maybe he isn't buying my line; I can see him gearing up into lecture mode. "But you've told us that the physical therapy routines are unnecessary. Although you may be able to do each exercise with little effort, the value to your recovering bones, tendons and muscles is repetition. Like the pushups I know you did before your accident. One, five, or ten can be done with ease, but real sustainable strength and balance come from more than that, in number and in frequency."

I've tuned him out. Uncle Marco is supposed to be coming to see me in a few minutes, bringing me some stuff to make all this bearable.

I make my voice soft now, cajoling. "I know that's true, Doctor, and I will make a sincere effort to do those routines at home, too. My father is renting the necessary equipment and my brother will be there to help me." I hope that'll shut him up. But then I see him open his mouth to say something else. I'm really tired of him and everyone else trying to tell me how to run my life, instead of just fixing things and be done with it, like real medical professionals. "I'm sorry if you feel offended by my independence, Doctor. I know it's just part of your job, how you validate yourself." I turn away from him, pick up my magazine and begin reading. He sighs and slinks away; his geeky hospital shoes make a squeaky sound going down the hall.

Gavin, Dad, and Mom have been visiting me almost every day. Gavin has to come see me because he can't live without me; I'm his better half. And of course Dad makes sure Twinkie comes. But I can do without Mom coming, and I can tolerate Dad. I guess it makes them feel good to visit me, like they're trying to be good parents.

Dad bought a car for Gavin's black friend Trayvon—replacing that beat-up old junker I totaled with a *new* one? Those Roxbury coons will strip it or steal it in a week. I think Dad had to pay off someone in the police, too, so they wouldn't charge me with reckless driving, or worse. And he's paying off the family of the woman who crashed into me. Too bad she died; sorry about that. Everyone's feeling so bad for her, but what about *me*? It's not like being here is a vacation! Even though I'm out of traction, I'm in pain! Good thing they're giving me good drugs. I've managed to swipe a lot more of it, enough to take home with me if I can ever get out of here. But their damn physical therapy is torture, and even worse, they force me into group therapy and sessions with that stupid shrink.

I'm stuck here and hardly anyone from school visits me—I'm just all alone, like in prison. It could drive me crazy. Some friends! They're just jealous. They know I'm the smartest and all-around best in the school. Or maybe they're all so worried about me they're afraid, uncomfortable in hospitals. That's it! They all care too much about me. Well, they'll be relieved when I come back to school. It'll be like old times again.

So I gotta get home. And Gavin really needs me. For his own completion, to be whole. It's fitting karma that he gave his blood. That makes us *really* together for life, blended into one. I'm the most important part of his life. I can't wait to go home, to be with him again. And now that school has started up again, if I'm still here he won't be able to visit me as often, so I absolutely have to go home. He'll miss me if he can't see me every day.

I see Uncle Marco walking in now, carrying what looks like a restaurant doggy bag. I love how he walks, like all tough and 'fuck you.' Is that how guys in the North End walk?

"Here are some brownies for you, Nephew." He grins and winks.

He's playing it straight. "Oh, thanks, Uncle. The food here is so bad it makes me sick."

Marco comes closer and talks low. "There's a packet with a couple capsules in there too, but don't take any more than one per trip, definitely not at the same time you have the brownies."

"Why not?" I say, and grin. I can feel my sense of adventure tingling.

"You don't want to be a vegetable, or die, Dummy," he says.

"Oh, is that all?" I joke. It feels like a challenge, a dare, one I find hard to resist.

"Don't be stupid, man," he says. He claps me on the back and gives me two issues of Rolling Stone. The June 2 issue with an article about Kurt Cobain's suicide and the latest September one, with Trent Reznor of Nine Inch Nails on the cover. I think Marco's trying to give me a message.

I put the doggy bag away for uninterrupted enjoyment later and kick back with the Rolling Stone mags. Someone will be coming to take me to the shrink in a few minutes. The dumb-ass Dr. Epstein. I suppose Jews think they're the 'chosen people,' that they're somehow superior. And they think that because Freud invented modern psychiatry, the only good shrink is a Jewish one. But this poor sap has met his match with me. I have him totally fooled. Just because I got a concussion doesn't mean I've lost my sanity or my superior edge. They're trying to tell me the concussion may have affected my cognitive capacity, at least temporarily. Bullshit. I haven't lost anything. And even if I lost half of my 'cognitive capacity,' I'd still be miles ahead of all these morons.

I told Dad this jerk *has* to agree to discharge me. So when I get to his office, I start the bullshit right away. "Doctor Epstein, how nice to see you." I gotta stroke this guy's ego so he'll think he's the hero who 'cured' me and approve my discharge. "I can't tell you how much I appreciate your wise counsel. My brother has been bringing me summer reading and assignments from school so I can keep up with my class, and I can see that my functioning is totally back to normal, even better than before my accident." I watch his face. He's buying it. "Thanks so much for your insight and guidance. You're a genius."

"Well, Devon, I never doubted your capacity—"

"Yes," I break in. I've got him. "Thank you for your recognition of my intelligence, Doctor. It's true that not too many people can measure up to my abilities."

"Well," he smiles now. "You're very quick-witted and you've charmed many people here during your stay."

He loves me! I give him one of my award-winning smiles. "I'm going to miss you and many others here when I'm discharged."

But now he starts up again. "What I'd like you to focus on is your concept of relationships with other people, your capacity to appreciate the value and rights of others, and your willingness to play by the same rules you expect from others. You're not always entitled to special treatment."

What a pompous ass he is. I'm different, special, and he knows it. Why shouldn't I have the advantage over inferior people? Shrinks want their patients to be screwed up, so they can justify their existence. Like this guy is trying to tell me I have symptoms of Narcissistic Personality Disorder. Even has an acronym—NPD—trying to legitimize the idea. Some asshole looked up stuff in this huge pretentious 'Diagnostic Statistical Manual of Mental Disorders'—DSM, the Bible for shrinks. Then they twisted what it says and came to the asinine conclusion that I'm a Narcissist, like there's something clinically wrong about recognizing my own superiority. What a crock.

But I have to give this guy a point now to keep him on my side. "That's a good idea, Doctor. I'll keep that in mind when I get back to my normal life. I've enjoyed my time here with you and all the staff, but it's so important that I go home as soon as possible. My dear twin brother needs me to be with him. He's incomplete without me. I'm his better half. I can't let him down." See? I care about Twinkie. Epstein tries to tell me I abuse inferior people, even my little brother who can't live without me, with "gaslighting", whatever that is. Horseshit.

"But just yesterday you said your brother is a weak dependent sycophant."

"I never said that. I love my brother!" Oops, I have to tone it down. "I'm sorry; you must not have heard me correctly... Which of course is not to question your competence, Doctor."

"See there?" Epstein says. "You just tried to do it to me. Tried to tell me I'm imagining something, that I don't know what reality is, trying to make me doubt myself. That's gaslighting, one thing you're an expert at. You seem to think you can convince people they must depend on you for their reality."

"I'm so sorry, Doctor," I make my voice whiny so he'll feel sorry for me. "That's my weakness, my failing. I see and understand so much, I feel compelled to share that insight with everyone. I must learn to control myself."

Epstein starts chuckling. Actually bends forward like he's trying to squelch a big guffaw. Finally swallows it and tries to regain his composure. I have him over a barrel and he knows it.

"Devon, I know you are eager to be discharged. But we do have concerns about your cognitive abilities."

"What do you mean? Everyone knows I'm the smartest person in school, definitely smarter than everyone in this department, including the staff."

Epstein puts his hand over his mouth, but I can see his eyes laughing. "We've conducted numerous tests, Devon. Of course we don't have a baseline on your abilities prior to your accident, but current results show sporadic deficits in reasoning and memory."

I can't deal with this jerk any longer. I start to walk away.

"And we've chronicled your tendency to repeat yourself. Frequently, as if you don't remember you've said the same thing to the same audience numerous times previously. That's another indication of cognitive deficiency."

"That's bullshit. My Grandpa DiMasi repeats himself, and—"

"Exactly. How old is he?"

"Not much older than you, Doctor." This idiot is grasping at straws. "But even if there's been some minor impact from my accident, when I get out of here, back home, I'll get back to my totally superior abilities."

He's just pulling this bullshit to make me lose my temper so he can say I'm crazy or something. I turn and grab my walker to get away from him. Still a little painful, but that's what the meds are for. It'll work itself out once I get out of here.

This place is messing with my head. Like, last week I had the craziest dream. A nightmare, really. I was somewhere in the middle of a big crowd and I was telling them all about something, talking. I'm an expert on so many subjects, it could have been anything. But all of a sudden, some people in the crowd started turning away from me, walking away, and I yelled at them, like, "Where do you think you're going? I'm talking to you!" But then more people left and I was all alone. I yelled again, so everyone turned back and started yelling at me, throwing stuff at me, shouting, "You're a fraud! A god damned fraud! You're nothing!" I woke up sweating and screaming, I couldn't catch my breath, I was shaking and my heart was pounding out of my chest.

I've had that dream, and ones like it, a few times since I've been here. This place really is making me crazy. There've even been a couple times when I've had weird sensations when I'm awake, like things around me are distant, unconnected. Unreal. Maybe it's the medicine they're giving me? It can feel like some kind of psycho trip, even without Marco's goodies. I kind of relish the experience when it happens. Sort of out-of-body. Shit like that has been happening for a couple weeks now. It's bizarre and a little scary. In a way, I sort of enjoy it...

But I'm not going to fall for Epstein's shrink-speak. Lots of people do; they believe that crap about having psychological issues and become dependent on their shrink. Ka-ching. How to get rich on peoples' gullibility. I think Dad will probably want me to take over his liquor business, but I really should be a shrink. I understand people better than anyone else. I'd be world-renowned. I would attract such a following, I'd have to turn patients away.

I could start on my parents. I've been doing the research. I swiped the latest DSM—the 4th edition that just came out this year—out of Epstein's office. Epstein got it wrong on NPD for me, but the DSM has my family down to a 'T.' Talk about screwed up. Dad's an alcoholic with Bipolar tendencies. Even though in some ways he's a role model for me—he's so tough—but in other ways he's so lame I can easily manipulate him. Mom's a shrink herself, so she must know she's neurotic, along with clinical anxiety and depression, definitely Cluster C Personality Disorder—either Avoidant or Dependent—maybe both. It's a miracle I'm sane. The only one in the family. Gavin needs me to save him.

5.

COLLEEN AND TONY HAD ARGUED ABOUT BRING-
ing Devon home from the hospital, against the recom-
mendation of his care team, but Tony prevailed.

When they arrived for the final meeting to discuss Devon's
discharge, they were instructed to go to a larger room than in
prior weeks. There was an unusual collection of senior physicians in the room, which—from Colleen's experience, suggested
the day would include a high concentration of weighty, possibly
contentious, issues. Tedious at best and distressing at worst.
Whether Tony could handle all that was yet another issue.

Dr. Stevenson, the Medical Director of Rehabilitation,
offered refreshments when they arrived, then began the
meeting. "At your request, today we will discuss and consult
with you on the issues associated with discharging your son
Devon from the hospital."

Tony flashed a satisfied smile and muttered, "It's about
time." He had consistently dismissed the diplomatically word-
ed weekly staff reports suggesting that Devon had become
uncooperative and unmanageable.

A small nondescript man with wireframe glasses, Dr.
Stevenson began introducing each participant, which included Dr.
Khatri, Chief of General Surgery and Dr. Epstein, Chief of

Psychiatry, along with doctors from Physical Therapy, Neurology, Orthopedics, Nephrology and Substance Use.

Tony drew back in puzzled surprise when the last doctor was introduced. But Dr. Stevenson broke in just as Tony's mouth opened to object. "Mr. and Mrs. DiMasi, considering his condition when he came to us, your son Devon has made significant progress over the last two months and he has been very eager to return home."

"Well, yeah," Tony said. "He's been bugging me about that ever since he came out of his coma."

A few of the assembled doctors cracked knowing smiles.

"Of course we're eager to understand your assessment of Devon's readiness to return home," Colleen said, "and what will be required to ensure his success."

Dr. Stevenson spoke, "Yes, that's our intent, Dr. DiMasi. We will discuss Devon's progress to date, along with our recommendations for his wellbeing after discharge, and to answer any questions you may have."

"Well, the first thing I want to know is why this woman from Substance Use is here," Tony barked. "What's that have to do with my son?"

"We can discuss that aspect of Devon's wellbeing after Dr. Khatri and others have had the opportunity to address the state of his physical health," Dr. Epstein said.

The entire team seemed to stiffen in tense apprehension, having become aware of Tony's mercurial temperament. Dr. Khatri rushed in to divert the discussion from what could be combative. "Yes, Mr. and Dr. DiMasi," he began, "Regarding Devon's physical health...As you know, Devon incurred several fractures in his accident. Thanks to his youth, they are healing nicely. However, he has been a reluctant participant in physical therapy," nodding to the rehab doctor, "so his progress has stalled. Dr. White, could you speak to that?"

"Certainly," Dr. White began. "We all like your son. He can be very charismatic. But his lack of full commitment to doing his physical therapy has slowed his functional progress. We prefer the patient to have taken accountability, to be motivated and committed to what is required to ensure his well-being, before discharge. We've tried a number of strategies to address his resistance, including counseling to explore reasons for his unwillingness. Sometimes, shame or fear of failure can be the problem. But few of our efforts have made much difference."

Tony waved his hand as if all that were trivial. "What my son needs is to be back home, back in his environment. We'll make sure he's committed. You can count on that. If Devon's back home, with his brother, back with his friends, that's what'll make sure he's motivated. And his twin will help him."

Colleen glanced at Tony with pursed lips as if she were constraining a mouthful of bile.

With a single grim nod, Dr. White continued. "In the short term, he will need to use either a cane or a walker when going more than twenty or thirty feet, and on inclines or slopes. And he currently has difficulty with stairs." He paused, his face betraying his concern.

Colleen's eyes pivoted to Tony, who simply shrugged and said, "He'll get there, no problem."

Dr. White went on, "Normally we don't like to require that parents be responsible for ensuring a sixteen-year-old participates in his rehab program. But if you are committed to taking that on, we can have someone from our team instruct you and Devon's twin on the exercise routines, on basic equipment you can rent and place in your home. We'd nevertheless like Devon to come here weekly for progress checkups and assignment of next-level routines."

Dr. Khatri broke in, "If we work together, your son's full recovery is more likely to be realized. Devon could be back to normal soon if he adheres to the program."

Tony waved all this away with a flick of his hand and "Yeah, yeah. Devon's a winner, he'll be fine."

Dr. White concluded, "In the beginning he'll need to have a bedroom on the first floor of your home, and a ramp if there are stairs to the first floor. Fortunately, his school has handicap entry, but he'll need an aide to help him get around to classes."

"Well, his brother Gavin can help with that, since they're in the same classes," Tony insisted.

Several of the team exchanged nervous glances. Dr. Zhang from Neurology spoke up now. "We think it will be good, for a while at least, if Devon can ease back into classes a little slowly." He coughed. "Devon is a bright young man, as you know. However, our tests are showing some degree of deficiency in his understanding and retention, which frustrates him a great deal, so he denies having any problems at all, instead finding excuses elsewhere."

"You'll see he's smarter than all you guys," Tony said, impatiently shifting in his chair.

"Those deficiencies," Zhang persisted, "are likely the result of his concussion and may disappear in time. But in the interim, we think it wise to avoid pushing him faster than he can go, which could only cause more frustration and defensiveness."

"So he might be in some different classes when he first returns to school," Dr. Stevenson clarified. "We will work with the school to devise an accommodation plan that's best for Devon."

Dr. Zhang added, "We'd also like to conduct neurological testing on Devon monthly and give him brain-training exercises to do at home. If he's willing to cooperate in doing that, it should facilitate his progress."

Tony's facial muscles began to twitch. Whether all this was overload or he had doubts about his son's capabilities, whatever it was seemed to be under control for the moment.

Dr. Stevenson assured the parents, "We will provide you with all the information and assistance you'll need to fully support Devon upon release. Referrals, schedules, appointments, medication, equipment...and we're always here for you when Devon and your family need anything."

Colleen's eyes focused out the window, unblinking, as a large flock of geese passed overhead, honking so loudly they could be heard in the room. Everything the doctors said aligned with what she already suspected. Although it wasn't good, she knew it could be worse because of Tony's and Devon's denial. And because of the burden it placed on Gavin. She shuddered.

Tony broke in, "So what's the story with substance use? You said you'd come back to that, Epstein."

Dr. Epstein hesitated as he eyed Colleen's detachment. "Are you all right, Dr. DiMasi?"

Colleen blinked, turned back from the window and sat up straight. "Yes. Please go on."

Tony glowered at her with a disapproving look.

Dr. Epstein began. "We don't know anything about your son's condition before the accident, aside from his having used substances that night. During the time he's been with us, we've seen evidence of his being under the influence of certain substances, the source of which is unclear—"

Colleen broke in, "Who has come to visit Devon?"

Dr. Epstein sputtered, "He hasn't had many visitors other than family, but we can check the visitor logs."

"Are all medications kept under tight security and inventory control?" Colleen challenged.

"Yes of course. And we have concerns about the possibility of uncontrolled substances conflicting with the medications prescribed for your son's injuries—pain, inflammation."

Tony waved a dismissive hand. "My son doesn't use any illegal 'substances.' You guys are probably just over-medicating him."

Colleen aimed a disapproving scowl at Tony.

With a hesitant glance at Tony and then at Colleen, Dr.

Epstein took a deep breath and continued. "Well, in long sessions and discussions with him while he's been here, and in observing his behavior and interactions with staff and other patients, we've seen that he is driven by certain needs, a craving for stimulus and excitement, which can sometimes manifest in drug use. And in analysis and testing, he has exhibited nascent symptoms of a condition known as Narcissistic Personality Disorder."

Tony began turning red, sputtering, "Narcissist? So he's self-centered! So what? A lot of teenagers are. That doesn't mean he's a nut case or has a *disorder*," he objected, his voice increasing volume.

While several team members looked down uncomfortably, Colleen whispered, "Let them explain, Tony."

Dr. Epstein smiled and attempted to lighten the tension. "Well of course 'nut case' isn't covered in the DSM, which is the professional manual that serves as the standard for diagnoses." He didn't cite the DSM's full name, which could have sent Tony barreling out of the room at hearing the word 'Mental' in the title.

But Tony was teed off anyway, rising from his chair and barking, "The only *diagnosis* of my son is that he's smarter than everyone else."

Colleen whispered, "Tony, please sit and listen to the doctor." Tony glowered at her but finally sat, flushed and still fuming.

Dr. Epstein cleared his throat. "The symptoms of this condition—let's call it NPD for short—can severely affect the patient's life course, his ability to be happy and integrated into society."

Colleen placed her hand on her husband's arm as he was about to launch another outburst and asked, "Please describe the symptoms, Doctor." Although with her PhD in psychology she was quite familiar with NPD—which she'd already suspected in Devon, she needed Tony to hear it from someone other than her. He had responded angrily on the few occasions in the past when she had tried to discuss their son's behavior and the ways in which Tony's indulgence toward him encouraged it.

"Well, first of all I should clarify what a 'personality disorder' is," Dr. Epstein began, with a smile and fingers in air quotes to frame the words. "It's a term used to describe a pattern of behavior driven by someone's inner experience that's different than most people's, how they view, interpret and accommodate reality, to one degree or another."

"We already know he's different—he's exceptional!" Tony objected.

Epstein looked to Colleen with one eyebrow raised, seemingly questioning whether he should continue. She nodded her encouragement, lips drawn tight in determination.

The doctor went on, "This particular difference is typically seen in the patient's cognition and their affect—how they exhibit feelings—and in their interpersonal functioning and impulse control." He handed Tony and Colleen each a printed document. "You can take this with you. It describes the symptoms and behavioral traits of NPD, with references to scientific research if you're interested in the evidence. I'll just cover some of the highlights now, if that's okay?"

Tony looked at the paper with a dismissive eyeroll. Colleen said, "Yes, Dr. Epstein. Please go on."

Epstein took a deep breath and continued, quoting rapidly from the paper like a kid just wanting his turn to be over quickly. "The symptoms of NPD include a grandiose sense of importance, either in fantasy or in behavior; preoccupation with unlimited success; persistent need for admiration; lack of empathy toward others; and belief they are special and unique."

"But everyone knows he's special," Tony said. His voice had shifted from anger to almost pleading.

With a quick glance to Colleen, Dr. Epstein then softened

his tone, modulating from technical recitation to a casual conversational voice to avoid any hint of negativity or blaming. He inserted pauses between phrases and sentences to be sure the meanings were getting through. Colleen relaxed her tense grip around herself a bit, in response to Epstein's efforts to throttle down the tension in the room. At least for the moment.

"As you see in that document," Dr. Epstein resumed at a slow pace, "people with this disorder have a number of behavioral characteristics that can make life difficult for them and people around them." He peered at Tony and Colleen as they scanned the document. "Patients with this disorder can have disdainful or patronizing attitudes...be exploitative, arrogant or manipulative of others...or become enraged when people don't cater to their superiority." He paused, waiting for a reaction from Tony or Colleen. "Have you witnessed any of these symptoms or behaviors in Devon?"

Colleen had seen many of those indicators emerging in Devon for some time and nodded slowly. But Tony was silent. Although his scowl and clenched mouth suggested disbelief, his eyes were hooded in fear and worry. He had just heard an irrefutable description of his son.

Colleen interjected with a question. Although she knew the answer from her training and experience, she wanted Tony to hear. "What else can you tell us? Are there complications associated with the disorder?"

Tony's chest heaved with labored breathing. He didn't look at her.

"There are some...side effects that may accompany the disorder," Dr. Epstein stammered. "One that I mentioned previously is an intense desire for excitement and attention, which can result in risky behavior or substance abuse, sometimes both. The patient may also turn to substances to alleviate the pain he experiences when his desires for adulation aren't met. Dr. Malone has been addressing these issues with Devon during his stay."

Colleen looked expectantly at Tony. But he just stared straight ahead, his jaw set and fists clenched.

Dr. Epstein looked at them and went on. "Another condition that sometimes accompanies NPD is paranoia, as a reaction to unsatisfied or stymied visions of superiority. Devon has occasionally shown these symptoms during his stay here, and we've seen at least two instances in which he seems to have had a break from reality."

Tony's tense muscles began to give way to aggressive restlessness; his arms and legs vibrated, as if he were about to become physically violent.

Dr. Epstein looked warily from Tony to Colleen, then with a nervous cough concluded. "Finally, I should mention that another consequence of the disorder can impact people close to the patient—parents, siblings, or acquaintances who may be affected by the patient's behavior. This Narcissistic Abuse—bullying, manipulation, humiliation—can drive away those who would be friends or caregivers, exactly the opposite of what the patient needs or wants. Such abuse often includes gaslighting, in which the patient negates other people's reality. This can be psychologically damaging for the victim, robbing them of their own self-esteem and identity—their *agency*, the ability to feel in control of their own life. We will want to coordinate with your sons' school to be sure Devon's twin is not being affected in that way."

Tony broke in, "Well, don't try to blame Devon for Gavin being a candy-ass little wimp—that's just what he's always—"

Colleen cut to Tony with quiet admonishment, "Tony—," ending in stern upspeak.

Tony's head shook slowly, almost imperceptibly, as he stared down at the floor. It was unclear whether he was dismissing what he'd heard from the doctors, or was stricken with its undeniable reality.

Colleen nodded, her mouth grim. "You've made clear the

treatment plan for Devon's physical and cognitive issues," Colleen said. "What do you recommend to address his psychological issues?"

"Now wait a minute," Tony snapped. He stood up and began pacing and huffing. "I'm not sure I buy this. I think you shrinks are making a mountain out of a molehill, making normal teenage boys' behavior into something weird. I mean, if this *disorder* even exists, tell me how someone gets it? Will his identical twin get it, too?"

"That's a good question, Mr. DiMasi," Dr. Epstein nodded. "There have been one or two cases that suggest a possibility of predisposition for the disorder, but most research has shown that the patient's environment plays a much larger determining role."

"Yeah?" Tony challenged. "Like what?"

"Well, for example, where caregivers are over-indulgent, promoting the notion that the child is unique, special, or entitled; or who use authoritarian methods that insist on perfection, winning and toughness from the child. Those factors can establish in the child both behavioral habits as well as a deeply engrained belief system that diverges from the realities the rest of the world lives by."

"That's complete bullshit!" Tony flailed his fist in the air. "How could just one of my twins have this *disorder,* when I treat both my twins exactly the same?"

"No, Tony, you don't," Colleen whispered to him, with a firm look.

Tony paused, as if air had been let out of his balloon. "Well, I want a second opinion," he mumbled like a petulant child.

"You're certainly welcome to do that, sir, and we encourage it," Dr. Epstein nodded. "But do keep in mind that this diagnosis isn't just my opinion. We've had an entire team and staff treating and caring for your son, including renowned specialists from Harvard's McLean, with everyone scrupulously recording his behaviors and statements."

"We understand, Doctor. What would you recommend?" Colleen murmured.

Epstein nodded. "We recommend weekly one-on-one therapy sessions—you and Devon are encouraged to select your preferred therapist—and group therapy every other week, which is important to help him understand how he affects others. And we'd like to meet with the entire family once a month."

"Christ, we'll be camping out at the shrink's office," Tony grumbled.

"And as time goes on, if there's little progress, low doses of approved medication may be necessary," Dr. Epstein concluded.

"Oh, so he'll go from one *substance*," Tony drawled, "to another?"

Colleen frowned at Tony, her mouth puckered in a grimace of disapproval. But Tony was eyeing the doorway, like he'd had enough and couldn't wait to run out of there.

Dr. Stevenson handed them a packet of information. "Because we believe Devon's full recovery is incomplete and dependent upon adherence to a full multimodal program, we'll need you to sign a waiver before taking him home. There's a copy in this packet for you to review in advance." He eyed Tony cautiously, who sat rigidly frozen like a fierce gargoyle. Stevenson continued in a tone eager to appease, "Social Services can help your family with all the supplies and equipment for Devon's return home. If you want, we can also provide home health aides, nursing assistants, or a visiting nurse to support his transition to home. Let us know how we can help you."

Colleen glanced at Tony. "Thanks, Dr. Stevenson. We'll let you know." She reached over to shake Dr. Epstein's hand. "I'm sure we'll have more questions as time goes on. You've all been very helpful."

A tense silence emerged like a dense cloud of smoke between

Tony and Colleen when they left the meeting, all the way down the elevator, to their car, becoming impenetrable during their drive home. As they pulled into their driveway, Colleen turned to Tony and said, "Bet you any money your little brother was responsible for Devon's drug use in the hospital. Tell him to stop it."

Tony acknowledged nothing, but mumbled in a resigned voice, "I'll call someone to have a ramp built and get the equipment delivered to put in the family room. You need to make space in the library for him and order a bed."

Colleen's muscles tightened. She would try to discuss all this calmly with Tony the next day. But his quiet often served as the lull before a fierce storm.

Later that night Colleen lay awake, unable to sleep, while Tony snored beside her. Tortured by memories of what had been, what might have been, and thoughts of what may lie ahead.

She recalled a night long ago when she was sixteen. A party, her first taste of beer, a charming older man. Handsome, boastful and confident. Making the biggest mistake of her life. Followed two months later by her worst mistake: giving in to his sorrowful begging and pleading to marry.

Then the most joyful blessing of her life. Their twins.

She had managed to overcome the mistakes of a sixteen-year-old by working years to earn academic and professional degrees despite Tony's resentment. Which perpetuated a sort of ongoing class warfare.

But the root causes beneath that conflict were threatening to destroy two innocent victims. Their twins.

Colleen loved her husband, despite—or because of—his insecurities and fears. She understood him, even though he didn't understand himself. She knew that his love for her was distorted by his own self-doubts.

But the twisted dysfunction of their family had become toxic. The arguments, the fights, Tony's rages, had to stop. Colleen knew she must find a way to reverse the destructive trajectory their family was on. To save Tony, their marriage, their sons. And herself.

6.

SHADOWS BOBBED ACROSS THE CEILING, AS gentle night breezes ruffled trees illuminated by the streetlight below. Gavin construed images of creatures in the shadow shapes as he lay awake in the dark, two a.m. on a school night. He'd been tossing around in bed like a deranged gymnast for almost two hours, after studying for his precalculus exam. He could tell the class would be a tough one. Since when are exams given before October? Quizzes, sure, but exams?

He kicked himself for beginning to study for the test so late, but there were other demands on his time each day after school. Cross-country or basketball practice on alternating days, going to see Devon in the hospital, coming home to fix dinner, cleaning up the kitchen after, other homework, never-ending shit. He felt exhausted, defeated, as he recalled last night's dinner, when his father repeatedly yelled at him and his mother. With too much to drink, making it impossible for anyone to eat.

A waning moon streamed its light through the window, illuminating his brother's empty bed across the room with a hallowed glow. From all appearances, a visitor might assume the room was tranquil, everything in neat order, tastefully furnished and decorated for teenage boys. But the ghost of

Devon's pernicious toxicity still lingered, more than two months after he was hospitalized. No amount of Gavin's obsessive neatness could vanquish his brother's shadow.

He hated that room. Having to share it with Devon felt like imprisonment, being trapped with an unpredictable animal, one minute fun and brotherly, pulling him under his captivating spell. The next minute he might attack Gavin and remind him he was a loser. The threat was always there, constraining belief, thought, joy, or even breathing. Gavin often wondered if this was how all siblings treated each other, or whether there was something different about him, or Devon, or their relationship.

But Devon was supposed to come home sometime next week and the room would revert to chaos. There was no such thing as Devon's side and Gavin's side. Devon's detritus invaded every cubic inch. Even though there was plenty of space in the house where Gavin could have his own bedroom, Devon and Tony had always insisted that the twins stay together. There was always Tony's clear expectation that Gavin would take care of his brother. Clean up after him, keep him from doing stupid stuff. Gavin never understood why their father seemed to have crowned Devon as the winner, The Chosen One. Or why Dad disliked him so much.

He sank back into the depths of self-loathing. He must be a loser. But then as he thought of his twin in the hospital, guilt flooded him and he berated himself all over again. Maybe it was his fault. Maybe he should've been watching Devon at the arcade, like their father said, to keep him from driving off. Gavin figured he owed something to his brother now, to help him recover.

But he hoped this wasn't a life sentence.

The high school hallway before first period was crowded and noisy with locker doors slamming and teenage chattering. That day seemed even noisier because it was Friday, the day before the big football game. But the metallic clangs echoing off hard floors and walls hammered in Gavin's head, ringing with urgency, warning of impending doom.

As he opened his locker, he heard Tray call out to him. "Hey, Gav, you okay?" he said in his laid-back way, the same tone he might use to casually comment 'cool shirt, man.' Gavin admired Tray's attitude, like nothing could bother him. They had become tight friends over the summer. Which was surprising, since Devon had totaled Tray's family car.

"Oh sure," Gavin said, hoping his sleep-deprived eyes weren't showing. He didn't want anyone to know he was having a hard time concentrating and sleeping. But then he counted to three and blurted out, "Devon will probably be coming home from the hospital soon."

"Is he all better now?"

Gavin was glad Tray didn't spout the Pollyanna bit that it was good Devon was coming home. His friend got it—that it might not be so great. "He still has a little trouble walking, even though they started him on physical therapy soon after he came out of the coma."

When Devon first landed in the hospital, his classmates had bombarded Gavin with questions—What happened? Was he drunk? How bad was it? Was he in a coma? Gavin had managed to create a script that evaded most of the details, like "Devon was in a coma at first, he (Gavin) donated blood, Devon was going to live, he hadn't lost a testicle (as one rumor claimed) or any other body parts, he broke some bones." Eventually, the questions stopped, except from Tray who was more interested in how Gavin was dealing with it all.

"You gave blood, so Devon owes his life to you."

"Only because he had a lot of internal bleeding then got

that sepsis infection. I don't think he sees it like I saved his life."

"Well, that's Devon," Tray laughed, then changed the subject, to Gavin's relief. "I saw you running cross-country yesterday when we were working out on the field. You got good form, man." Tray was quarterback on the football team. Which was a testament to how good he was—a METCO kid bussed from Roxbury being quarterback in a snooty suburb like Wellesley was rare.

"Keeps me in shape for basketball, too," Gavin nodded. "Hope I can fit them both into my schedule this year." He didn't want to think about how Devon's demands might overwhelm his life.

"You still going to the Grateful Dead concert with me and Kyrone Tuesday?" Tray asked. "Garcia's a legendary old white fart; this could be his last tour."

"Too bad Kyrone wasn't assigned duty to their weekend shows."

"Oh shit, there's the bell. By the way, we have to get together on our history project Sunday. We can end with a run," he elbowed Gavin's ribs then rushed to his class.

In the middle of Gavin's first period English Lit, a kid walked in and handed the teacher a piece of paper. She looked at it and gave it to Gavin. The school counselor, Dr. Pedersen, wanted to see him during third period, which was when he had French. He wondered what Pedersen wanted and couldn't think of anything he'd done wrong recently.

On the way to Precalc after English, Gavin spotted Katie in the hall. He thought she seemed a little distant since Devon's accident. Maybe it was because he had been preoccupied with Devon. Or because she had second thoughts about hanging out with someone whose brother got drunk, stole his friend's car and totaled it. Maybe that kind of crazy shit runs in the family, especially between identical twins. He nodded to her and smiled. She returned a tight smile, put her head down and increased her pace.

His exam was easy. He realized he hadn't needed to study. He could've gone to bed earlier. Maybe even slept.

Gavin thought about Dr. Pedersen on his way to meet him. He'd always liked him; he seemed to genuinely care. Gavin knew kids from schools in other towns, where teachers and faculty didn't get involved in students' lives like they did at Wellesley High. But that's how it had always been in his experience, so he guessed maybe having the college in town was what made the school more attentive to kids' success. He remembered his mother taking him and Devon to Wellesley College's Child Study Center when they were younger. Colleen told him Harvard was somehow associated with work the Center does with public schools in town. But sometimes he wished certain teachers would butt out a little.

Gavin always felt comfortable, at ease, in Dr. Pedersen's little office, which seemed to reflect his personality. It was sort of homey, with incandescent lamps instead of fluorescent ceiling lights, plants in the window, framed artwork on the walls, shelves crammed with books, interspersed with pictures and things he'd collected from around the world. As Gavin came to the doorway, the warmth of the room relaxed him a little, but he was still nervous about what the counselor wanted.

Dr. Pedersen stood when Gavin entered the room. His salt and pepper hair was rumpled like an absent-minded professor. Or a shrink. Although there was an official school psychologist, Pedersen had his doctorate in psychology and used to have a private practice. The rumor was that he had a breakdown of some sort after his wife died, and no longer had that practice. But Gavin thought he 'practiced' on the kids he counseled anyway.

"Hi Dr. Pedersen. You wanted to see me?"

Pedersen extended his hand to shake. "Welcome, Gavin! Sit down, young man." He was very proper, old school, as if he should have a British accent.

Gavin detected the sweet smell of incense, which he knew wasn't allowed in the school. He sat in a straight chair in front of Pedersen's desk and watched his counselor settle into his own chair with measured ease. He liked how Pedersen was a little quirky but didn't seem to have a hidden agenda. "What did you want to talk to me about, Sir?"

"I just wanted to hear how you're doing. I understand you've had a challenging summer."

"Yeah, but it's okay now. My brother will be coming home soon."

"Yes, we've been told. How do you feel about that?"

Gavin put on his happy face. "Well, it'll be good when everything gets back to normal," he said, fingers virtually crossed.

"By normal, do you mean how things were before your brother's accident?"

"Yeah, I guess."

"Do you like that 'normal?'" His fingers went up in air quotes.

"Well, define normal," Gavin punted, forcing a sideways half-smile.

"The reports we're getting from your teachers are that you've been a lot more outgoing and engaged since returning from summer vacation. More so than you were last year."

Gavin didn't know what to say. He didn't think anyone could see anything different in him. He just shrugged.

"Of course we all know that identical twins don't necessarily have identical personalities, right?"

"Well, sure," he mumbled. *No shit, Sherlock.'*

"So what has triggered your sudden blossoming into a confident individual? It seems like you've felt a little more free to be yourself. Your unique self. What's different this term?"

Gavin tensed, like Pedersen had just seen him naked. "I don't know. I haven't really thought about it, Sir." He looked down and toyed with a hangnail. Of course he knew. The only thing different about this term was that Devon wasn't around. But he wasn't sure what his 'unique self' was supposed to be or feel like.

Pedersen didn't say anything, just sat casually and looked at Gavin, who didn't feel like he was being challenged. More like Pedersen was inviting him to...he wasn't sure...Spill his guts? Fess up? Be honest? With Pedersen, or with himself?

"It's okay if you do feel a little less..." he chose his words carefully, "constrained when your brother's somewhere else, Gavin. It would be perfectly *normal*." No air quotes this time, but he emphasized the word. Gavin looked down at his feet.

"Your father called yesterday to tell us that Devon is coming back to school next week and that there would need to be some accommodations." Pedersen paused. Gavin felt like the man's gaze on him was seeing inside him, knowing something he'd hidden. "When did you learn of your brother's imminent return?"

"Last weekend," Gavin mumbled, scrunching his shoulders in.

"Mm-hmm," Pedersen nodded. "Your coach told us that all of a sudden this week you seemed to revert to your old self, not as confident and outgoing as you were when you first returned to school."

Gavin looked out the window and shrugged. Again. He was afraid the gesture was becoming his habit; a dumb cop-out.

"Are you worried that when your brother comes back he'll resume overshadowing you?"

Gavin's head jerked up. He was startled that someone could say exactly what he was thinking, stuff he didn't even want to say to himself. It was intimidating, almost scary. He wondered if that's what shrinks do, even seeing things that aren't good. Like Pedersen might start talking about how trapped he felt, as if the guy could get inside his head.

Gavin realized he must look like an idiotic puppet with all

his shrugging, so then he just hunched his shoulders and tried to disappear.

"That would be most unfortunate if your brother were to overshadow you. You seem to have become a more fully realized individual this term and attracted a wider circle of friends. Everyone has really been enjoying this version of Gavin. It seems more alive and real." He paused and locked his eyes on Gavin's. "Do you like it?"

"I don't know. I didn't realize I was any different." He couldn't acknowledge it, like that would jinx it or something.

"Well, we've all seen the difference and would like to keep that Gavin around," Pedersen smiled. "I told you that the school will be required to make some accommodations for Devon when he returns. These measures have been recommended by his care team at the hospital, to address his not-yet-fully-regained capabilities, both physical and cognitive. That will necessitate the two of you being in different classes for some of your subjects, at least for a while. And he'll have aides to get him to and from classes."

Gavin was speechless. He didn't know whether those arrangements would be a negative for Devon or a get-out-of-jail-free card for himself.

"Would that be okay with you, Gavin?"

"Yeah, I guess." Shrugging again.

"And if it's okay with you, we'd love to keep the conversation going with you, to ensure you can retain and nurture the advances you've made this fall."

"How?" Gavin asked, wary.

Devon's care team had asked the school to monitor Gavin for signs of Narcissistic Abuse, but Pedersen didn't mention it yet on that day. "Oh, just by stopping in to chat with either Dr. Jankowski or myself now and then. Maybe once a week or so for a while, then less frequently after that," Pedersen looked at him. "Whatever helps."

Gavin groaned internally. How was he going to squeeze

that into his schedule? "What time of what day? Like I'm missing French now. I don't want my academics to suffer."

"Why don't you look at your schedule and decide what would be the best timing? It could even be before first period, or during lunch if you prefer. Twenty minutes a week should be enough. This isn't a big deal, son."

Gavin stared at his feet again.

"Of course you can discuss it with your parents," Pedersen said.

Gavin swallowed hard. "Uh, I don't think that'll be necessary. Like you said, it isn't a big deal." He didn't want his father to know anything about this. He knew his dad would go totally ballistic and remind him he's a wimp.

"Well, just let us know what day and time works for you and whether you'd like to chat with me or Dr. Jankowski."

Gavin sat and stared past Dr. Pedersen, out the window, at nothing in particular.

"Do you have any questions, Gavin, or have anything else you'd like to talk about now?"

He definitely didn't want to keep talking about this. The 'overshadowing' Pedersen mentioned. Gavin thought that was the least of his problems. Or maybe that was code for the job Devon does on him. Gavin ducked his head and stood. "No, that's okay. I'll get back to you later."

He couldn't get out of there fast enough.

Gavin stopped at the boys' room on his way to catch the last half hour of French class. He felt unbalanced, not knowing whether to puke or take a dump. He went into a stall and then heard two guys talking at the urinals.

"You hear Devon DiMasi's coming back next week?"

He suddenly felt sick, realizing how fast news travels. Maybe that's why Katie was acting strange.

"Yeah. So Gavin will be his bitch all over again. Poor bastard. He *was* having fun."

"That didn't last long, did it?"

7.

GAVIN HUMMED A TUNE FROM THE PREVIOUS
night's Grateful Dead concert as he rearranged furniture in the
library and set up Devon's temporary bed. It was just delivered
that morning, so he couldn't go with his father to get Devon,
and had to skip school to set it up. The exercise equipment was
delivered then as well, so the family room was next—move
stuff around and set up that contraption. He hummed more
intensely. Snippets of lyrics thrummed his brain. *"I will get by,
I will survive..."*

He hadn't expected to like the Dead so much, but their
music had gotten into his head, imprinted on him. He realized
that words and thoughts from old white guys don't become
obsolete or irrelevant with age.

The phone rang, interrupting Gavin's rhythm. Tony was
calling from his cell phone to say they were finally through the
discharge process and on their way home. Gavin had to hurry.
If his father arrived and saw that everything wasn't all set up,
he'd be pissed. He rushed through the kitchen, where Colleen
was completing all the 'Welcome Home' decorations, into the
family room. Yes, the Chosen One would soon return. The
music in his head died.

Thirty minutes later, he and Colleen went outside, where

colorful ribbons and balloons spread across the front of the house to celebrate Devon's return. They stood side by side in the driveway to greet him as the car pulled in. It reminded Gavin of a movie he once saw, where all the servants lined up to greet the master returning to the estate. When the car came to a stop, he unwittingly conformed to character and strode forward to open the car door for his brother.

"Twinkie!" Devon squealed and turned to Gavin with open arms, awaiting assistance to rise from the back seat.

"Do you need your walker or cane to get into the house?" he asked.

"Nah, I can walk without any of that. If you walk with me."

Devon reached out to Gavin and linked his arm with his twin's. Gavin turned to lead him up the ramp Tony had ordered, but Devon said, "I don't need that pussy thing," and instead shuffled toward the garage for the entry door to the kitchen, wincing pain whenever he stepped forward with his left leg. He pulled Gavin's arm tight against him and stroked it with his other hand as Gavin struggled to help him up the three low steps. "Good to be back with you again, Gav. Just like old times, right?"

"Sure," Gavin grunted.

On that Wednesday in early October, thunder rumbled in the distance as black clouds rushed to obscure the sun. Residual autumn leaves surrendered their brilliant glow, beginning to flail violently in the advancing wind. Birds went silent, taking cover. Gavin hummed another Dead song. *"If the thunder don't get you then the lightning will..."*

"Always said I'd be there for you, Gav. And you'll always be here for me, baby brother."

Gavin swallowed Devon's assertion and helped his brother up the few stairs into the kitchen. It was a struggle. He had learned that his brother's recovery was proceeding more slowly than expected because he had frequently avoided his physical therapy routines in the hospital. So now it was his responsibility to help Devon with his exercises, as well as with his brain-training program. Gavin felt like he'd been trapped into indentured servitude to his brother, just like those servants in the movie.

Colleen rushed into the kitchen ahead of them, carrying Devon's bag. When the boys entered the kitchen, she turned to Devon with a broad smile and reached out to embrace him, "Welcome home, Devon!" She had affixed posters heralding his return all around the first floor of the house, along with streamers and balloons.

"Cool posters, Mom—thanks!" Devon crowed, then shirked away from her arms. "Hey, Gav, let's go up to our room. Can't wait to sleep in a comfortable bed again."

Colleen spoke up with strained cheerfulness. "Oh, Sweetie, do you remember that your care team said you shouldn't be climbing stairs until you've regained your strength and balance? We've set up the library especially for you—it'll be perfect! Near all the action in the kitchen and family room—Gavin can show you!"

Devon's face mirrored the thunder and dark clouds fulminating outside. Just as he was winding up to object, Tony came in from the garage. "Yeah, so being stuck downstairs should be incentive for you to work on your exercises, m'boy," he said, clapping Devon on the back. "And Gavin's gonna help you."

Gavin's new daily routine would play out like a tragicomedy and dominate his life, relentlessly torturing him over the ensuing months.

Gavin had gotten his driver's license over the summer, after his father told him he'd have to drive Devon until he could drive himself. Now with both parents going off to work each day, Gavin had to drive his brother to school, rather than bike the short distance as he always did. Then after classes he had to drive Devon home, then rush back for his after-school activities. After which he'd return home to work with his brother. Cognitive drills in workbooks the hospital provided and physical routines on the equipment they'd rented, which Gavin had assembled in the family room. All before preparing dinner for the family.

There wasn't much time to meet with Dr. Pedersen, although Gavin did manage to stop in to see him sporadically during lunch breaks. Each visit was like coming into sunlight.

"Come in, Gavin," Dr Petersen said. "I've just made a pot of tea. Would you like honey in yours?"

Gavin juggled the lunch he'd grabbed from the cafeteria and sat in the straight-backed chair in front of Pedersen's desk, eyeing the colorful little porcelain pot resting on a trivet in front of him. He recognized it was a teapot; his mother had one she'd inherited from her grandmother, but it sat on display in the dining room, never actually used. Drinking tea wasn't a habit in their family, but on the rare occasions they did, he'd only seen paper tea bags put into a cup with hot water. He hesitated. "Uh, sure, a little honey sounds good."

As Pedersen poured from the pot, a pleasant fragrance wafted from it. Gavin didn't recognize it. "What kind of tea is that?"

"Chamomile. I think you'll like it." Pedersen handed him the steaming cup and a small pot of honey with a wooden dipper protruding from it. In response to Gavin's quizzical expression, he said, "That's a dipper made just for honey. Turn it a little, lift it out and drizzle a bit into your tea. And go ahead eating your lunch! It's quite all right to talk with your mouth full. I'll be eating, too." He extracted a small tin box from his desk, opened it and selected from an assortment of delicate little multi-layered crust-less tea sandwiches and took a bite. "So what has it been like having your brother back home?" he asked, with his mouth full.

"That tea is awesome," Gavin said after a few sips. He paused and took a bite of pizza. "Well, uh, Devon needs a lot of attention."

"Mm-hmm..."

"He didn't always do the physical therapy exercises he was supposed to do in the hospital. Now I have to get him to do them."

"I wonder why he didn't do them in hospital?"

"I dunno. I guess he thinks he's perfect without all that. Or doing them would admit he isn't perfect."

Pedersen smiled. "You're pretty insightful, Gavin."

"Yeah, well, Dad always tells me I'm really dumb."

"If that were true, I wonder why he thinks you're capable of helping Devon with his physical therapy?"

Gavin hesitated. "He uh...seems to have this idea that because we're twins, I have the most influence on Devon. Some kind of magical ju-ju."

"And do you?"

Gavin scoffed in sardonic dismissal. "Are you kidding me? Devon pulls out every trick in the book to avoid doing the exercises the hospital prescribed. He eventually does most of them, but he makes me pay. Then he refuses to do any of his brain-training stuff."

"How do you deal with that?"

"It's hard..." Gavin took a deep breath. "I cajole, bribe, coerce, pamper him, make a joke of it, even try to feed his ego with stuff like 'You're so strong, this'll make you like Superman.'"

"Does that work?"

"Eventually. But he whines, goes into self-pity, insults me and tells me he's already ten times stronger and smarter than I am, that I'm a loser..." Gavin stuffed the rest of his lunch back into its bag and put it away. He hung his head low.

"Do you think that's true?"

"I guess it is. That's what Dad always says, too."

"C'mon, where did that smart kid go, the one I was talking with a few minutes ago? The one who's making straight As in all the advanced classes, the one who's star of our cross-country team?"

Gavin fell silent.

"There's a trick that some people use to try controlling other people. They keep repeating the same lies, the same distorted versions of reality, figuring if they say it often enough, people will believe them and conform to their version of truth. Which puts them in control of you."

"Like Devon and Dad are always saying I'm a loser."

"But you know the truth, the reality, of you. Only you can define who and what you are. Not your brother. Not even your father."

Just then the bell rang. This time Gavin didn't want to run out or escape. He wished he could stay. He wondered why he felt so much more relaxed, calmer, than when he came in. Maybe it was the tea. He smiled at Pedersen and turned to go. "Thanks. What kind of tea did you say that was?"

———

Gavin struggled to fulfill his new job of getting Devon to do his physical and cognitive exercises. His brother was a reluctant complaining participant. It wasn't as if Gavin could get his brother set up and started, then go take a shower or begin dinner prep. He had to be there with him at every step. Every minute, or Devon wouldn't do the required routines. But the process typically devolved into mind games. With Gavin as victim.

"Ah, there's my dear brother again. I really appreciate you spending time with me, helping me. But why do you think I need to do this brain-training stuff? You know I'm already smarter than you are—why don't *you* do them instead?" And then there were other forms of abuse. "Hey Twinkie, I need help with this exercise. The pain is really bad today. Can you just hold my leg...around on my inner thigh...a little higher... higher..."

By dinner time, Gavin's resentment often left him tied in such a knot that he could barely stomach the food he'd prepared. His mother fretted, "Gavin dear, please eat. You can't run cross-country if you're under-nourished."

On the evenings Tony came home, he typically joked in ways that demeaned Gavin. "Don't bother, he's going to be a cook, not a jock. So he doesn't need to eat a lot."

To which Devon always chimed in with a similar remark, "Yeah, our little Julia Child."

Colleen became stuck in the middle and tried to intervene, "You guys have to stop your snide remarks. Be civil and polite. We're family." Which invariably elicited eye-rolls from Devon and dismissive grunts from Tony.

But Gavin made a show of shrugging it all off. "It's okay, Mom. I know they're just trying to toughen me up." And then he laughed. To show he wasn't upset, that they hadn't gotten to him, they hadn't won. That he wasn't a wimp.

In addition to his responsibility for his brother's rehab routines, Gavin withstood Devon's frequent demands at other times. Devon even found a silver bell from the glass cabinet in the dining room, where family heirlooms were displayed. He kept it by his bedside and carried it everywhere, ringing it whenever he wanted his brother. "Hey, Gav, I'm in a lot of pain. Get me some more of my pain meds." Even though he'd had his daily maximum half an hour before. Or, "I'm thirsty. Get me some water." Sometimes he'd ask for a beer, but Gavin wouldn't comply. Devon's demands could be outrageous, contrived, and designed to control his twin. "I'm bored. How about a game of chess?" Or, "Where's my notebook? Go find it for me." Or, "Hey, you gotta drive me into town!" His expectations were constant, persistently interrupting Gavin's concentration on his homework, or preventing him from pursuing his social life, even interrupting his dreams and stifling sleep. It seemed deliberate, the timing calculated to hijack Gavin's independence, keeping him tethered to his twin. Even in the middle of the night, like a dependent child. Or a manipulative one.

A week after Devon's return home, Tony decided to throw a 'welcome home' party for him. "You're such a great cook, Gavin, you can show off your Julia skills for all those kids," he said, then directed Colleen to manage all the other preparations. He invited the entire junior class and several of the twins' other friends, along with Tony's two brothers.

"This'll be great, m'boy," he crowed, clapping Devon on his shoulder. "I bet the whole school is glad you're finally back and healthy, so this is cause for celebration!"

Gavin spent most of Saturday preparing food for the party. Devon conducted a running commentary over his brother's shoulder, telling him how he did things wrong or not good enough. Gavin ground his teeth and internally grumbled, *as if Devon has ever cooked anything.*

Everything was all set at five o'clock. Time for the party. Tony's brothers arrived earlier, bringing cases of beer. Colleen spoke up right away. "I'm sorry, but you can't bring that into the house with a bunch of teenagers."

Tony and Devon spoke almost simultaneously. "Aw, don't worry. It'll be fine."

Colleen had become more outspoken and assertive since Devon's accident, having to step into the breach with the medical professionals. Now she insisted—in front of Tony's brothers, despite knowing Tony's resentment would manifest later. The beer went back into Marco's truck.

No one arrived during the next half hour. Gavin became anxious as he watched his father and brother becoming agitated. He anticipated trouble. Tony grabbed a beer from the fridge, took a swig and grumbled, "Maybe they're all trying to be fashionably late." Finally, shortly after five-thirty, the doorbell rang. Cecil, Devon's skinny admirer, stood on the doorstep looking hesitant. Over the next half hour, three other boys from the junior class arrived. Then another guy walked in. Gavin knew him as 'Jimbo,' a former student who'd been kicked out for drug dealing. Only two years older than the twins, his eyes had the sallow look of someone who lived a hard life. He sidled up to Devon with a sleazy grin dripping from his face.

That was all. No one else came. Gavin wondered if parents had prevented their kids from coming, because of what Devon had done. He hoped that wouldn't bias their assessment of him too. After an awkward hour, everyone left. Tony was outraged. "What the fuck?" he fumed. "These dumb-ass kids have no class, no manners, no appreciation for the leader of their class! What the hell happened to the rest of them?" He began dumping all the food into the trash in a frenzied manner, much of it scattering onto the floor.

Colleen gasped and scowled at Tony, but to intervene during his tantrum would be counterproductive. Devon blew it all off. "Well, nice try Gav, but the food you made wasn't that good anyway," he said.

"It was delicious, Gavin," Colleen insisted.

Tony stomped out to his car, followed by his brothers. He tried to drag Devon with him, but Colleen stopped them at the door.

After so few people came to the party, Devon's behavior became aggressive, perhaps to redeem himself from the humiliation of being ignored. Gavin was the most accessible victim of his brother's revenge.

The following Monday at school, most students' demeanor seemed to indicate they knew what had happened. Except for the aide assigned to help Devon, not many students interacted with him, as if the rest thought he had a contagious disease. He was no longer the center of attention. He wasn't trailed by a legion of admirers. Only a few students greeted him and hung on his every word, or even made eye contact with him.

That lack of attention from his usual coterie of admirers seemed to challenge Devon's ego. He struck out, targeting his brother as proxy for the kids who ignored him. Whenever Gavin passed his brother in the hall between classes, Devon called out to get his attention—loud enough for everyone to hear—with a belittling tease, "Hey, Twinkie! How's my favorite twin?"

Gavin looked down like he wanted to hide, ignored him and kept walking.

Devon yelled, "Hey, wimp, I'm talking to you!"

Gavin had gone to all the latest movies that summer with Tray and other friends, so could quote most of the iconic lines. At that moment, he wasn't sure what prompted him to dredge up his inner *Ace Ventura* with a perfect Jim Carrey imitation, "Well all righty then," he aped with a goofy Carrey smile. Which elicited hilarious laughter from everyone. Except Devon, who looked around at his classmates and recoiled, like it was a replay of his bad dreams in the hospital.

But back home that evening, Devon announced at the dinner table, "My baby brother thinks he's a comedian now. Give us one of your funny routines, Twinkie."

Tony looked at Gavin, "What's this all about? I thought you wanted to be a cook or something like that."

"Nothing, Dad," Gavin said. "I just quoted a line from a movie I saw this summer. Devon hasn't seen it—maybe he can rent it from Blockbuster."

"That would be nice, Gavin," Colleen said. "Maybe you can watch it together."

The next day, Devon resumed his taunts. Lacking positive attention from his classmates, he was forced to up his game. "There's little Julia Child! What's for din-din tonight?"

Gavin stopped in his tracks and stiffened. He had enjoyed an entire summer and the first month of school as a free person. He didn't want to revert to captivity. Turning to his classmates while pointing to his brother, he called on *Buffy The Vampire Slayer* to channel a condescending Lothos from the movie. "He tends to drool before supper," he deadpanned.

It cut through his classmates' discomfort to elicit laughter and palpable relief.

Devon's game escalated daily, becoming increasingly loud and more belittling. Classmates turned away, loath to get caught between the brothers. "Hey, Gav," Devon called out, "this guy isn't a very good aide. Why don't you come help me take a dump?" Unsure whether to laugh or run for cover, embarrassed kids ducked their heads and scurried past. "Hey, you morons," Devon yelled after them. "Shit happens."

Gavin deflected, "But yours is better than anyone else's. I wouldn't want to deprive your aide of this special opportunity." He joined the crowd in laughing.

At lunch that day, Tray joined Gavin at his table in the cafeteria. "Way to go, Gav!" He said, landing a playful punch to his friend's bicep. "You really put Devon in his place. Like, finally!"

"That effect will last about two minutes," Gavin grumbled. "Or back home at the latest. He'll find a way to get back at me."

"You can't let him get to you, man. You're better than that."

Tray wasn't alone in this opinion. The cathartic effect on their classmates was obvious. It unleashed laughter and freed them from their embarrassment and fear of getting involved. Which encouraged Gavin. It felt better than being Devon's whipping boy.

Despite turning on his abundant charms, Devon seemed powerless to regain the same level of influence he'd once had over his classmates. Many of his former fans seemed to have cooled toward him, in some cases shifting their allegiance to align with his twin. But Devon made Gavin pay at home, with escalating humiliation. His father, smelling blood in the water, often joined the attacks. Colleen heroically tried to intervene, bearing the brunt of Tony's disdain.

But Dr. Pedersen had heard about Devon's public torturing of his brother. After it had been going on for a few weeks, during which Gavin hadn't had time to visit him, Pedersen called him into his office.

Gavin dragged himself into Pedersen's office with the look of a defeated victim.

Pedersen poured a cup of chamomile tea and passed the honey pot.

Gavin eagerly sipped the tea, clutching its warmth. But it took a great deal of prodding to coax him into talking about the stress he was under, both from Devon and their father. As if admitting it would reveal weakness.

"That must be hard, Gavin," Pedersen said. "Having to play nursemaid to an unwilling patient has to be frustrating. And being insulted by your twin—your closest friend all your life—must be especially hurtful."

"Yeah," Gavin grunted, leaning forward, elbows on his knees, clenched fists supporting his bowed forehead. "But he's my brother. And if I don't help him, he won't fully recover."

"He has to want to recover, Gavin. He has to want it for himself, more than he wants to dominate you."

"Maybe he dominates me because I'm weak," Gavin mused. "He's always saying that I'm nothing without him, that I can't live without him."

"But it looks to me like he can't live without *you*. Can't let you go, let you be your own person." Pedersen anchored his elbows on his desk and leaned forward with an intensity Gavin hadn't seen from the counselor. "What Devon is doing is called Narcissistic Abuse. He's attempting to undermine your personhood, your agency, your ability to pursue your own reality, in order to elevate himself, make you dependent on him and his distorted version of reality. Keep you tied to him." Pedersen had just violated a cardinal rule of counseling by displaying an outrage, a ferocity, that revealed his determination to protect his client. Blurring the line between professional and personal interest.

Gavin went silent, stricken by the depth of his counselor's concern and the gravity of his entrapment by his twin. He stared into the distance as if deciphering some inscrutable truth written there.

"You're so focused on saving your twin, but he has to want to be saved, for himself." Pedersen paused, letting Gavin digest this. "In the end, you have to save yourself."

A few weeks later, a day of reckoning arrived.

As Gavin attempted to cajole Devon into his exercises, his twin became especially perverse, insulting and badgering his brother, then switching to a pitying tone to camouflage the hopeless demeaning 'reality' he imposed on Gavin. "I understand, Twinkie. You can't help the way you are—a wimpy pussy. But I love you anyway."

At first Gavin felt deflated and beaten, but then remembered what Dr. Pedersen said about Devon trying to steal his own reality from him. Anger rose in him, as if he were fighting for his life. He'd had enough. He didn't want to be intimidated or lessened—by anyone, certainly not by his brother. "Look, asshole, I'm done with babysitting you," he snapped, as he pounded on the table beside Devon with each word. "You want to walk, to run, get your driver's license, regain function in your brain? You're on your own. I'm done."

Gavin turned to leave, but then turned back to Devon, who was momentarily speechless with his mouth agape. "You have no conscience, do you? It doesn't matter to you at all that someone died because of your illegal asshole move. And Dad's just as bad, buying everyone off—he's equally guilty. I can't wait to get away from this sick-ass family!"

As Gavin stomped away, Devon recovered before his twin could even get out of the room.

"You're a total loser, Twinkie."

Gavin slammed the door.

"Just you wait—I'm going to tell Dad!" Devon yelled.

8.

THREE MONTHS AFTER DEVON LEFT THE HOS-
pital, he'd regained enough strength to climb stairs and return
to the shared bedroom with his twin. Three months after that,
Gavin finally convinced his father to let him move into the
small bedroom at the end of the hall. He had help from his
mother in that appeal, and Devon had actually supported the
idea, too. At first Gavin was surprised by that, but gradually
began to suspect his twin had something going on, for which
he needed privacy. Jimbo and Cecil often visited him—
separately, sequestered with Devon in his newly private room,
behind a closed door. With music blaring to mask any
indication of what transpired behind it.

Gavin wondered if one or both of those teens were Devon's
new victims. But he figured it wasn't his problem. At least
Devon hadn't hassled him as often recently.

Devon remained vague about what he and his 'friends'
were doing. Well-ingrained twin allegiance prevented Gavin
from sharing his suspicions. When their mother asked him if
he knew anything about Devon's closed-door meetings with
Jimbo and Cecil, Gavin just shrugged in code-of-silence ignor-
ance. Something he'd sworn he wouldn't do again.

Now as a colorful spring sunset painted the sky outside his

window, Gavin relished the view as he lay on the bed in his own room, which he'd painted a deep Prussian blue. Bookshelves, bureau, desk and closets all neat and organized. At least he could control that little corner of his world. As he sipped from a can of Coke and buried himself in the SAT prep manual, he didn't notice his brother had walked in—finally without a limp—and stood staring at him.

"Why are you doing that, Gav?"

"What?"

"Bothering with the SAT. You won't need that for Harvard because Grandpa will get us in."

"I'm not so sure that by itself will get us in. Tray and I are studying up to take the test in May, then re-take it in the fall if we have to. Anyway, maybe I might want to go to a different school."

"Jeez, idiot. You know we both have a full ride to Harvard because of Grandpa."

"Maybe I don't want to go there."

"What do you mean, you don't *want* to go to Harvard? Are you nuts?"

"Maybe they don't have the courses I'm interested in."

"You're not still on that cooking kick, are you?"

Gavin didn't respond. After he resigned as Devon's physical therapy assistant, he was able to carve out more time to talk with Dr. Pedersen. He was beginning to understand more about the twindom that ensnared him and the mind tricks his brother played on him. He now recognized what Devon had been doing and what drove him to be so controlling. Although that didn't make it any easier to deal with his brother. He was often sucked in by his twin, back into captivity, pulled into a bottomless hole.

"Culinary, not just 'cooking,'" he stated in a flat tone. "And I'm looking at the best—the Culinary Institute of America, in New York. CIA."

"Well, you could major in business at Harvard and go to

CIA after that, then open your own restaurant," Devon insisted. "That way, if you changed your mind, you'd have a solid Harvard degree in business—you could make a ton of money, not just cooking and baking."

"As opposed to your conniving and cheating," Gavin tried to deflect Devon's attempts to shame and control him.

"Ha. I'm going to be a *professional*, not just a struggling poor-ass cook."

"So I assume you're going to Harvard," Gavin mumbled with a full stop, suggesting the subject was closed. He didn't take his gaze from the book.

"Of course. I'm going to be a shrink and get rich. I know more about the human mind than anyone," Devon boasted. "I'm not sure yet if I want to go the pre-med route. That takes so damned long before you can even start getting any money out of it."

"Yeah, it's all about the money, right," Gavin muttered. "But dude, your grades have fallen this year. Do you think you can turn it around enough to get into Harvard?"

"I've been recovering from my accident. It's only junior year. I'll be back to my usual top performance next year. It doesn't matter, though. Grandpa will get me in. And my brain still works."

"Twisted though it be," Gavin said under his breath.

"I heard that," Devon said. "Might be twisted, but that's why I'm going to be a shrink. Goes with the territory."

"Physician, heal thyself."

"Seriously, Gav," Devon said, as he plopped down on the bed next to his twin. "You really *have* to go to Harvard with me. I need you," he whined pathetically. "You can't just abandon me, your better half. And what would you do without *me?*"

"Devon," Gavin sighed. He spotted his brother's attempt to manipulate him. He stood and looked at his twin, almost with pity. "We've never been apart for more than a few hours all our life. It's time to grow up and be individuals, not just the other half of a pair of twins."

Devon crossed his arms and leaned back. "Don't be ridiculous, Gav. You'll always be just a half. You don't know what 'individual' is. You're nothing without me."

"Now who's being ridiculous," Gavin snapped and turned to the window. "While you were in the hospital, I made more friends, had more fun, did better in school and was happier than I'd ever been. I could finally live my own life." Gavin was worked up now. He paced and gestured as if he were shaking off restraints. "You may think I need you, but I can do just fine without you."

Devon crossed his legs and sneered. "Right, dear twin," he drawled. "But you came to visit me almost every day when I was in the hospital. You couldn't stand to be away from me. If you go off to some other school—"

Gavin broke in. "I went to see you in the hospital because Mom and Dad wanted me to. It had nothing to do with you." In that moment he realized that he still wasn't able to fully live his own life. Some day he would.

"And they also want you to go to Harvard, dipshit."

Gavin tried to maintain his resolve, although it felt like he was barely hanging onto the edge of that bottomless hole. "I can't always live my life exactly like my parents think I should—or anyone else, especially you," Gavin asserted in a tentative voice that suggested an effort to convince himself. "So there's CIA of course, but also both Johnson & Wales and Drexel have high academic standards for admission. And they all offer dual degrees in culinary arts and business."

"And if you decide you don't want to be a *chef*," Devon dramatized the word, "what kind of career could you have with a degree from any of those half-ass schools?"

"Let me worry about that, Dev. You just worry about yourself," Gavin snapped. He grabbed his Coke and stomped out of his room.

"Do Dad and Mom know about your stupid little plan?" Devon yelled as he trailed behind his brother down the hall.

Gavin slowed. "Not yet."

"Little Momma's Boy Gavin may have her approval, but you know damn well Dad won't go along with it." Devon caught up and took the Coke from Gavin's hand. "You can't just abandon me, Gav. You're not allowed to! Just wait till I tell Dad. You *are* going to Harvard with me."

"How's the SAT studying?" Tray asked, taking a big bite of pizza as the two sat at their favorite table in the school cafeteria. Then he stopped chewing and stared at his friend. "Are you okay, Gav?"

"Yeah, yeah. I'm good."

"You don't look like it."

Gavin shrugged. "Not sleeping much, I guess."

"It's not the SAT thing, is it? You could probably ace it without studying."

Gavin dropped his head, shrinking into himself. "Devon's trying to force me into going to Harvard with him," he mumbled.

Tray put his pizza down with a groan. "Shit, Gav. You really have to get away from him."

At that moment, Gavin was overcome with a desire to run. Anywhere, far away. To breathe, escape the suffocating weight upon him and keep on running. When he spotted his twin coming his way he abruptly stood, left his lunch behind and ran out of the cafeteria. With no destination in mind, he was driven by a desperate need to escape, to survive. As he rounded the corner, he collided with Dr. Pedersen, knocking him against the wall outside his office door.

"Oh, I'm so sorry, Dr. Pedersen!" Gavin reached out to pull the counselor upright.

"Is there a fire somewhere, Gavin?"

"No sir," Gavin said. "I'm sorry," he apologized again.

"My pot of tea is steeping," Pedersen said, stepping into his office. "Would you like to join me?"

"Chamomile?"

Pedersen smiled and nodded. He poured the steaming tea into the blue and white Bavarian cup he always reserved for Gavin, drizzled a little honey in, and handed it to Gavin.

Gavin slumped down into his usual chair, his eyes downcast, clutching the warmth of the cup. Pedersen leaned back in his desk chair.

"So what's going on?"

"The usual."

Pedersen remained still. Waiting.

"I was hoping I could go to college somewhere else. Far away. Out of state, West Coast, or even the other side of the world."

"Mmm-hmm..."

"That's not going to happen. Devon and Dad aren't going to *allow* it." He did an air quote with his free left hand and took a slow sip of his tea. "They won't let me go anywhere but Harvard. With Devon."

"How does that make you feel?" Pedersen leaned forward, put his elbows up on his desk and steepled his raised fingers in a gesture of thoughtful attention.

A low vibration, like the warmup to a growl, rumbled in Gavin's throat. "Like my life doesn't belong to me. Like Devon and Dad decide what I can and can't do, who I am, even what I'm supposed to think and feel." Gavin sat upright, as if he'd just experienced a revelation. "What's scary though, is...I can see that's actually what I often do. I accept it and...live their version of what I am. Who I am."

Pedersen nodded, a grave expression clouding his eyes. "You're still a minor. So you're still under parental control when it comes to what college you can attend. I don't know enough about your father to understand what drives him, but I have a good understanding of what drives your brother. If he can make you believe you're weak and he's your only hope of survival, that you're nothing without him, even when he belittles and mistreats you, he thinks you'll never abandon him."

Although Dr. Pedersen had explained variations of that concept over the past few months, on that day it seemed to have made a dent in Gavin's understanding. His eyes widened, realizing the implications of that truth. For himself as well as for Devon.

"For someone like Devon, abandonment is the worst thing he could ever experience. If you, the object of his desperate manipulation—his victim—were to leave him, that would invalidate his entire persona he projects to the world, make it all a lie, making him a fraud. That would be the death of who he thinks he is, exposing nothing real underneath."

"So I can't abandon him."

"It seems that you'll have to go to the same college for the time being, but 'abandonment' can be cognitively and emotionally based. In Devon's mind, you must not leave him. You may be forced, for now, to accept physical proximity, but if you reject the distorted vision he has imposed on you and craft your own version of who you are, he will become desperate to reel you back under his control."

"So it's hopeless."

"Not completely. And there's hope over time. You must detach your thoughts and feelings from him. From his contrived domain. Build your own self, one who is far superior to what he and your father inflict upon you. But don't challenge openly; that only escalates the manipulation and assault. Appear to concede, but then proceed to live your own reality to the extent you can—if only internally, until you can emancipate from family control."

"Sort of like Walter Mitty's secret life, right? Easy to say though."

"Yes, easier said than done. Where's your mother in all this?"

Gavin abruptly shifted, becoming tense, as if a stranger had entered the room. "She tries to intervene as much as she can," he stated, his voice flat. "But she's a victim too," he mumbled, almost under his breath, then stood and turned to the door. "Thanks for the tea, Dr. Pedersen. I gotta go."

As Gavin rushed to his next class, his mind reeled from all that Pedersen had said. It felt like he would have to exist as a paradox, live a dual personality, just to survive long enough to become free. In that moment, he wondered how his mother managed it all, whether she had attained any kind of freedom.

9.

ONE WEDNESDAY NIGHT A YEAR LATER, TONY came home late, in an unusually bad mood. If black clouds could follow someone, the one above him would fill the entire room. He went straight to the liquor cabinet, pulled out a bottle of scotch and drained the last two fingers into his glass. He pulled out another bottle and set it on the side table next to his easy chair in the family room, ready for his next round. He sat down and flipped on the television. He scowled. It was halfway through the third period in the first game of the NHL Stanley Cup's Eastern Conference Quarterfinals, Bruins against the Panthers in Miami. Boston was behind 2–5 and a fight was in progress on the ice. Tony yelled, "Yeah, sure, you dummies! If you can't beat 'em in the net, maybe you can just beat their heads in!" He emptied his glass.

Dinner was already over and the boys were in their rooms presumably doing their homework. "We just finished dinner, Tony," Colleen said, wiping her hands on her stained blue apron. "But we saved some of Gavin's Bouillabaisse for you. Would you like me to heat it up for you?"

"No, I don't want any of his Julia Child crap," he snapped.

"Can I get you anything else?"

"No." He opened the second bottle and poured.

"Did something happen today? Is something bothering you?"

"You're bothering me." He put his feet up on the ottoman and loosened his tie.

"Well, let me know if there's anything I can do," Colleen said and turned to leave the room.

"One of my trucks got highjacked today," Tony mumbled. "Took the whole shipment."

Colleen turned back. "Oh no, did anyone get hurt?"

"No," Tony snapped, as if Colleen had asked an offensive question.

"Where was this?" She sat down on the sofa next to his chair.

"Medford. I thought that location was safe."

"Beyond the reach of the mob?"

Tony's head spun around, his face fierce. "Don't ever say that word."

"Not saying it won't make it disappear."

"Yeah, well. I don't want the boys to ever hear it."

"But Devon seems to know anyway. I heard him talking to that boy Jimbo Halloran about your liquor business and then they started making jokes about the mob."

"Jokes? It's no joking matter."

"Well Tony, I'm concerned about Devon." She reached over and took a sip of his drink. "I got a call from the school today."

"What's he done now?" Tony grabbed his drink from Colleen's hand and took a long gulp.

"He's been bullying and harassing one particular boy, whose parents complained to the principal, and—"

"Yeah, well the kid's probably a sorry-ass wimp that deserved it."

"He's been skipping classes."

"So, if the teachers can't keep Devon interested and challenged, do you blame him?"

"But Tony," Colleen began, taking a deep breath to prepare for what could be a battle. "That's the problem. You excuse Devon's self-important and entitled behavior. That feeds his narcissism. You encourage him to bully and harass his own brother, too, which is seriously damaging Gavin's self-esteem and confidence. That's the narcissistic abuse the doctors have warned us about."

"See, that's it, Colleen! I've always said you pamper Gavin and make him a wimp. Life is tough, and my boys have to be tough, too."

"They're not just *your* boys, Tony. They're *our* boys."

"Yeah, and if you were around here more, like a real mother, instead of going off every day trying to fix other people's heads, maybe Devon wouldn't be skipping school!"

"I *am* a real mother, Tony. That's why I want our boys to be psychologically well-adjusted. They can't succeed in life without that. So both of us need to work together on that as parents."

"There you go again, with that psychology bullshit!" Tony turned off the television, got up from his chair and began pacing. The hockey game was over and the Bruins had lost 3–6. "You think you're so god damned superior, so fucking smart you think you know what a guy has to do to survive in this world. But you don't know shit!"

"Tony, did anyone ever bully you when you were a boy?"

Tony stopped pacing and whirled around to her, glaring. "What do you mean? Why would you ask that?" He was shouting at this point, loudly, his neck muscles bulging with the look of a cornered animal on his reddened face.

"I just wondered if you know how it feels." Colleen spoke softly, motioning her hands palm-down in a signal to lower the volume.

But her question must have struck a nerve in Tony. He swung around and grabbed a floral embroidered pillow from the sofa and flung it across the room.

Colleen stood to leave. In deliberate tiptoe steps as if to avoid landmines, she walked into the kitchen toward the back stairs. More pillows hit her back. Next, Tony's half-empty glass smacked against her head then shattered onto the floor. She stumbled but managed to catch herself with her hand on the kitchen island. She continued on, moving quickly, up the stairs to her and Tony's bedroom, his rageful bellows resounding behind her.

10.

TWO MONTHS LATER, AT 5:10 ON THE MORNING of commencement, Gavin woke to the smell of bacon. The sky outside his window had begun to lighten, although the sun hadn't yet broken through the trees surrounding the house. Who was making bacon at this hour? His mother never got up this early, his father wouldn't be caught dead over the stove, and Devon would starve if he had to cook anything. Gavin rubbed his eyes and remembered that it was graduation day. A conflicted blur of excitement and dread wrestled within him. The day could be either very good or very bad.

But Gavin held onto the hope that it could be the beginning of a new stage in his life. Although he lost the battle to go to a different college, at least he and Devon would certainly be assigned to different dorms at Harvard. It was a sprawling campus, so he could easily evade his twin. He climbed into his sweatpants and went down the back stairs to the kitchen.

Colleen was bent over the stove in her oversized pink terrycloth robe, poking at the pan in front of her.

"Mom, what are you doing up so early?" Gavin said as he walked toward her and grabbed a banana from the basket on the kitchen island.

"Oh, Gavin, I'm sorry if I woke you," she mumbled and

hunched her shoulders over the pan.

Gavin approached to get a piece of bacon and put his hand on his mother's back. But Colleen turned away. He thought that was strange; his mother usually greeted him in the morning with a smile and a pat.

"Mom, is something wrong?" he asked.

"No, of course not," she said and walked away from him. "You should go back to bed and get some sleep. Or shower and get dressed. Your breakfast will be here when you're ready." She busied herself with something in the sink.

Gavin jumped forward and stuck his face in front of hers. Tear tracks creased her cheeks. There was a welt on her upper lip and a purple bulge below one eye. "Oh no," he groaned, recalling the arguing he'd heard the night before from his parents' room. He rushed to the freezer to get ice. His dread turned to anger.

"Oh, honey," Colleen whispered. Her head shook and her voice cracked.

Gavin brought over the ice in a plastic bag wrapped in a cloth napkin, and steered his mother to a stool next to the island counter. "Here, Mom," he said as he put the ice on her face and placed her hand to hold it. Words failed him. He set his jaw and clenched his fists. Then he turned off the burner under the bacon pan and ran to open the door into the garage. His father's car was gone.

He came back and pulled another stool next to his mother and sat. "I'm so sorry, Mom. You want to talk about it?"

"No. Your father just lost his temper." She kept looking down, her eyes averted.

"Do you still want to go to graduation today? It's okay if you don't feel like it."

"I don't know. Maybe the ice will help. Then with makeup and sunglasses..." She trailed off and shrugged hopelessly.

"Do you think Dad will come?" he asked. "I hope not."

"Oh, he wouldn't miss it," she said. "I can't guarantee his

condition though..."

"Mom, is there anything we can do?" Gavin pleaded. "Like maybe ask Father Decker to talk to him?"

"Oh, that won't help," Colleen almost laughed. "Father Decker is a *Jesuit*," she drew out the word with drama. "Your father prefers Franciscans. You know he grew up in the North End, right? The Franciscans *own* St. Leonard's there."

"So what's the difference? A priest is a priest."

"Well, no. Jesuits are more intellectual. And Tony thinks Father Decker, and most of Wellesley, look down on him."

Gavin suspected the reasons. But he wanted his mother to talk about it. "Why?" he asked. "Dad has a really successful business."

"A liquor business. Without a college degree. And he's from a working-class neighborhood in the North End."

"So why did Dad decide to move here, to Wellesley?"

Colleen coughed a sarcastic chortle again. "I don't know for sure. Part of it was wanting what was best for you and Devon, but I suspect he also hoped his money might warrant respect, that he could become part of the 'upper class.'"

"Oh," Gavin grunted. He thought about how his father sometimes acted like a bully, sort of tough-guy gangster style. Which would probably give the lie to any respect he might hope for from Wellesley-ites.

"But of course that hasn't really happened, despite his big donations to Wellesley institutions," Colleen smirked. "The hospital, the church, Rotary..."

It occurred to Gavin that his father's thwarted desire to be "upper class" could be why he often seemed resentful toward his mother's PhD and professional career.

As always, Colleen read Gavin's mind. "He's never forgiven me for getting my degree and a job."

"But he doesn't have to beat you up about it," Gavin growled, pounding his fist on the counter.

His mother dropped her head and fidgeted with the tie on

her robe. "Gavin, despite what your father thinks, it isn't your job to save everyone. Not your brother, not me. You just need to be responsible for yourself and allow others to do the same for themselves."

"But Mom, I can't stand by and watch Dad hurt you!"

"Your father isn't a bad man, Gavin. I know he'll be remorseful about this later. It's just...well, the model for manhood in the Italian North End where your father grew up was different than what you see here in Wellesley," she muttered, then smiled. "I remember the first time I met your dad's family and friends at a party in the North End. It was so obvious...all the men were tough, macho, swaggering and boasting, the undisputed boss of their women, who all just got in line with what was expected of them. It's like all their roles were predetermined, pre-programmed."

"That's crazy!" Gavin snapped. "And what's that pre-programmed bullshit?" Gavin said. "So Dad can't help himself?"

"Sort of," Colleen nodded. "But he eventually came to understand that I wasn't going to accept those models in our family. And to his credit, I know he wanted to distance himself—and you two boys—from what was going on in the North End."

"What was going on? You mean the forced role model thing?"

"Well, I guess that could be at the heart of it all. Have you ever heard names like Frank Salemme or Raymond Patriarca?"

"No. Who are they, and what do they have to do with Dad?"

"Some guys from your dad's old neighborhood. Like I said, it's complicated. Did you ever wonder why your grandfather DiMasi gave his business to your father instead of your Uncle Joey, the oldest son?"

"I never really thought about it. Maybe Uncle Joey didn't want it?"

"You should ask your father, Sweetie. It's not my story to

tell."

"But I think it's a story you have to live with, not in a good way, right, Mom?"

Colleen was silent.

Gavin felt like he'd been granted only one lick from the lollipop, not enough to even determine what flavor it was. Or what was the truth. He stood up and began banging cabinet doors, pots, bowls and utensils. Gathering oatmeal and other ingredients, he announced, "I'm going to make us a *healthy* breakfast, so we can both feel better."

Colleen sighed out a small laugh, a final tear escaping her eye.

A few minutes later, as they sat eating steaming oatmeal with chopped nuts, raisins and cinnamon, Gavin asked, "What are you going to do, Mom?"

"I've always wanted to be here for you and Devon," Colleen mumbled, her mouth full. Then as she swallowed hard, "And I took my marriage vows seriously...I really do love your father. I understand him and tried to get him to go to counseling with me, but..." she shrugged.

"Well, Devon and I are going off to college this fall, Mom." Gavin put his spoon down and bent his head over, trying to connect with his mother's eyes. "You don't need to worry about us. But I do worry about you, whether you'll be okay when I'm not here. After Devon's accident, you started to assert yourself more, stand up to Dad. What happened with that, where'd you go? What do you *want*, Mom? It's your life. I can't imagine you want it to go on like this."

Colleen smiled. "That's a good question. Your father and I really do love each other, even though sometimes it might not look like it to you. Let me ask you the same thing—what do *you* want, Gavin?"

"Nice dodge, Mom," Gavin grinned. He paused, looked down and poked at his oatmeal. His mother's question threw him off guard, spinning his thoughts into forbidden realms, the fantasy life he'd only dreamed of. He'd never undertaken the risk of seriously considering what he wanted, beyond his enjoyable escape into cooking. It was orderly, something he could usually control and create. Even though his father and Devon thought it was sissy. He hoped that once he's finally away at college, he could figure it out. All he really knew for sure at this point is that he wanted to be his own person, whatever that was. And he knew what he *didn't* want to be. Not just a twin. And certainly not the weak inferior twin his father and brother said he was. More than anything, he had to escape the daily tension that lay thick as quicksand in their family, choking the very life out of him.

But there would be no escape that day from the quicksand. They heard feet padding down the back stairs. Colleen stood, cast a weary glance toward Gavin, turned away from the back stairs and scurried through the dining room and up the front stairs.

"What're you doing up so early?" Devon asked. "The ceremony isn't until five tonight. Is there any of that for me?" he said, grabbing Gavin's bowl.

"We're supposed to be at the school at eight this morning for rehearsal," Gavin said. "We should leave here at quarter of, so you could go back to bed for another hour and a half."

"Maybe you need to rehearse, baby brother, but I sure don't," Devon mumbled, spooning more oatmeal into his mouth.

"They won't let you graduate unless you come to rehearsal, smart ass," Gavin said. "You haven't told Dad yet, have you? It'll be a lot worse if he's surprised at the ceremony. He's expecting you to—"

"Oh, shut up, wuss. I've got this handled."

As the first rays of sun pierced through the family room sliders, Gavin heard the garage door go up. He scooped up dishes and listened for it: Car door slamming, trunk opening then slamming, garage door coming down. He braced himself as his father barreled in from the garage and deposited a large box full of liquor bottles on the kitchen counter. Rancid odors of consumed alcohol and old cigars wafted from him like a noxious cloud of gas.

"Whatcha got there, Dad?" Devon asked, opening the box and pulling out bottles.

"Just keep your hands off, buster," Tony said. "Wait till after graduation. Your uncles and grandpa are coming over to celebrate."

"Y'know, Dad, you guys shouldn't even come to the stupid ceremony," Devon said. "It's going to be so hot out there in the middle of the field in the sun. I don't even want to go, but I'll be doing the rounds of my friends' parties afterward. That's the only good part about graduation."

"Your friends will be around all summer. Family comes first. I told your uncles and Pop that you're valedictorian and they can't wait to toast you!"

Gavin suppressed a derisive snort. *They just want to get toasted.*

Devon frowned, looking down at his feet. "Uh, Dad, I've been meaning to tell you…"

"It's a great day, my boy!" Tony said, grabbing a beer from the fridge.

Gavin wondered how his father might react during the ceremony. Gavin knew the truth would have to come out then. He hoped Devon would swallow his pride and tell him before then.

"Dad, they won't let me be valedictorian."

Gavin exhaled relief.

"What do you mean, they won't *let* you?" Tony snapped.

Gavin rolled his eyes and turned away. He knew that no one prevented Devon from being valedictorian. Flunking three classes is what did it.

"After my accident, I had a hard time getting to my classes and getting my schoolwork done," Devon said in a plaintive tone. "And Gavin didn't help me," he whined.

Gavin whipped around. "Oh, poor baby," he sneered. "You always have to blame someone else instead of taking responsibility for your own shit. You know damn well I bent over backward trying to help you, but you kept blowing me off. But if that's the only way you can salvage your superiority myth, just keep on lying. To yourself."

Gavin spun around to avoid losing control of his temper and stomped off, silently fuming as he vaulted the stairs two at a time. He knew that Devon wouldn't actually graduate that day, although the school was letting him go through the ceremony and accept a blank 'diploma' until he re-took those classes in the summer. But Devon would never admit that to their father and would probably make more excuses and blame Gavin. He couldn't wait to get away from what he termed his 'so-called family.'

Tony shook his head and glowered at Devon.

The day was unusually hot. Late afternoon sun beat mercilessly upon the crowd assembled in the open field on uncomfortable chairs. Rows of seniors squeezed together in their black robes, radiating heat and shared odors of sweat. There was no air. Devon fidgeted like a caged animal, desperate to escape. He pounded his shoulder into Gavin's. His brother wouldn't acknowledge him, staring straight ahead. Gavin finally leaned toward him and whispered, "I can't believe you haven't told Dad and Mom you aren't really graduating yet."

Devon turned around to look for his father and uncles among the guests. He hoped they'd decided not to come. Many among the rows of guests were fanning themselves with commencement programs. Tony wedged between Uncle Marco and Grandpa DiMasi, beside Uncle Joey. Colleen hunched a couple chairs away, between her parents. The broad rim of her hat extended over her sunglasses, shading her bruised face.

Superintendent Russell wisely kept his remarks brief, saying nothing meaningful at all before handing the podium over to Principal Jefferson, who wasn't as considerate. He droned on about responsibility and the road ahead, oblivious to the restlessness and discomfort of the crowd, while repeatedly wiping his handkerchief across his glistening brow.

Finally done, he began his introduction of the class salutatorian. "Our Salutatorian this year didn't just have the second highest GPA in the class. Her scores were within a half a point of our valedictorian. On top of that, she's active in the jazz band, head of our winning debate team, tutors disadvantaged kids, captain of our champion girls' soccer team, *and* holds down a part-time job! We know she's destined for great things! Everyone give a cheer for Katie Goodwin!"

Katie quickly made her way out of the row and almost skipped up to the podium with a shy grin. The humidity of the day had kinked her curls and a few wisps were plastered to her sweaty brow. She began with a soft voice, "Thank you, Principal Jefferson. And thanks to all the families and guests who've come here today to enjoy our sauna."

Chuckles rippled throughout the crowd and a choreographed group of her classmates swished their robes in unison to circulate some air beneath.

"I wanted to take this opportunity to thank our wonderful faculty and staff for all the wisdom and knowledge they've managed to stuff into our heads these past few years," she began, turning around and nodding to the department heads seated behind the podium. "But more than that," Katie's voice became stronger and more assured, "I wanted to thank them for their support of us students as individuals, recognizing our strengths as well as our weaknesses, helping us to grow in confidence and self-discipline. They've always seemed to understand that the path to maturity isn't necessarily easy, having one foot in childhood and the other in adulthood.

Knowing what to do and how to do it in these transition years isn't always perfect."

She looked up to the back row and smiled. Her mother was beaming. "We make mistakes, but our teachers and counselors know that sometimes we're still finding our way and they don't give up on us. Armed with that support, their unshaking belief in us, we've become victorious as individuals and as a class. State football championship—Trayvon Harris, give a wave—" she paused while the crowd cheered, then resumed. "Our marching band was second in the state," gesturing to the bandleader, "our track team competed in statewide contests, winning big in cross-country," pointing to Gavin. "Our debate team won awards," nodding to her co-captain, "and the list goes on. We also have a record percentage of our class going on to college and winning scholarships. So faculty, families and students should all be proud. But more than the accomplishments of individual students or teams, we as a class are very connected to each other and to our community, which makes it all so much more worthwhile. Success is sweeter and failure is more tolerable when we can share it with family— both our birth families as well as the school family we've developed during our years at Wellesley High. I hope we continue to be connected with each other, support each other and grow together. Thank you all for your goodness—past, present and future."

A standing ovation greeted Katie as she accepted her award and made her way off the stage. Her cheeks blushed pink. Gavin was happy for her and couldn't help but worry over how she would cope if her mother's illness became worse. He made a vow to himself that he would be there to support her.

Principal Jefferson returned to the podium. "Thank you, Katie. We're proud of you and all our wonderful graduating class. Now to honor this year's valedictorian, the student who topped Katie's GPA by a hair, who is very much at the top of his class in more ways than one..."

Devon sank lower in his seat. Ashamed that he wasn't valedictorian like his father expected. And at that point he didn't know or care who was.

"The student with the highest grade point average each year is recognized as class valedictorian. But that's not the only measure of excellence in a student. This year's valedictorian should also be recognized for his outstanding citizenship, leadership in his class, helping others in the school and in the community, and his respect for the rights of all. He should also be recognized as being supremely well-liked by students and faculty, for his good humor, excellence in sports, hard work and participation in student government."

Devon mumbled under his breath, "Oh sure, some goody-two-shoes pinhead."

"Well, awards for all those attributes haven't been formal-ized—yet!" Principal Jefferson smiled. "So today we're giving him *official* recognition for merely having the highest grades in the class, but we all know what an incredible all-around person he is. Let's have a round of applause for this year's valedictorian, Gavin O'Malley DiMasi!"

Devon's head spun around, aiming an angry glower at his brother. When Gavin stood to walk out of the row, Devon stuck out his foot to trip him.

But Gavin stepped over it and made his way to the stage while the entire senior class applauded and hooted wildly. He hurried up the steps, aware of the audible gasps and mutters rising above the buzz of the crowd, coming from where his father was sitting. He hadn't told his family. He wanted to avoid the inevitable taunts and put-downs from his father and brother, the presumptive Best In Class. Now he was sort of enjoying the effect of his surprise on his family.

The crowd quieted down as Gavin placed his speech notes on the podium. He looked to where parents and families were seated, as one last DiMasi voice pierced the hushed silence.

"Thought you said Devon was supposed to be the best," Grandpa DiMasi's deep bass rumbled, followed by Tony and the uncles animatedly whispering among themselves.

Gavin took a sip of water and began. "Thank you, Principal Jefferson and Superintendent Russell. It's very hot today, so I promise to be brief." Many among the graduating class cheered. Gavin picked up his notes, crumpled them into a ball and tossed it into the middle of his gathered classmates. There must have been a bit of a breeze after all; he didn't intend for it to sail like a curve ball onto his brother. Devon picked it up, stood and threw it back. His aim veered off course and the ball fell into Tray's lap, who wisely held onto it. That avoided what could have become a free-for-all of teenagers tossing it around like a game.

Gavin nodded to his friend and watched as Devon plowed through the row and rushed out. Gavin looked to the rear and saw his father leading his uncles and grandfather out of their row, rudely bumping people along the way. That was a painful confirmation of his father's opinion of him. He looked down, grim, then took a deep breath and went on. "Well, we've had a great ride here at Wellesley High, haven't we? Made a lot of friends, learned a lot, forgotten some of it..."

A chuckle came from the parents and guests section, laughter and applause from the students.

Gavin smiled and nodded. "One thing I hope we've learned, and won't forget, is who each of us is. Although who we are is determined in part by family and the gifts given us at birth, our identity is also shaped by friends, environment and a whole variety of factors that are external to us. Things like fads, customs, norms...And also expectations. What other people *expect* of us. Our friends may assume a tall guy will be great at basketball, or that an intelligent girl may be nerdy." He looked to where Katie sat in the class rows. "Katie sure demolishes that myth, right?"

The class turned to her with a few huzzahs and clapped.

Gavin continued, "And a parent may have always wanted to be a football star, so encourages his kid to do that. Or a mother was an actress, so urges her kid into drama. And a grandfather may assume his grandkid will take over the family business. You get the idea. We've seen a few examples of this in our class, among our friends."

Some of Gavin's classmates snickered as they whispered and pointed. Gavin saw his mother's face smiling, while Grandpa O'Malley squeezed her shoulder.

"But is that really you? Are the expectations of others the same as how we see ourselves, what we want to be, our vision for *our* future? Well, I'm going to share some good news and some scary news. The good news is that we can decide for ourselves. Who we are, who we will become, is also a product of our interests, our efforts, our work, our passions. Each of us can chart our own path, chase our dreams, be the person we want to be. On the other hand, the scary news is that we can decide for ourselves—which is exciting, but can be sort of daunting and intimidating! We may not be what everyone thinks we should be, yet defining who we really are can lead into unfamiliar territory. But the reward of being true to our real self—and to the world around us, our community, regardless of how modest or grand—is far more rewarding than the predetermined path other people may have assumed *for* us."

Gavin paused, looking out to his classmates. He was surprised to see that most of them were actually paying attention, their eyes locked on him. He nodded to them and continued, "So we can use the critical thinking skills we've gained here at Wellesley High to determine who we really are, what we want, and devote ourselves to achieving that. So ten years from now, at our class reunion, it'll be exciting to see what each of us has become, for himself or herself." He exhaled the breath he'd been holding and thrust his fist high, his private salute to emancipation. "Let's enjoy the journey!"

As Gavin left the stage amid a standing ovation, he saw his mother dabbing a tissue to her eyes and cheeks.

———————

Devon had run off the field, past the school, with hurt and anger churning his stomach and shame burning his brain. He had disappointed his father—the most unforgivable crime, the last thing he wanted to do. His father expected him to be tops in his class, best at everything. How many times had Tony said that? But now he wasn't. In fact, he wasn't even close to tops, even if he completed those last three classes this summer with top grades. And he knew it was all glaringly apparent to his classmates and their families. The memory of the dream he had in the hospital—which had recurred in various forms many times since—continued to haunt and taunt him. He was *not* a fraud, he argued to no one in particular. He wanted to find a hole and crawl into it. He wanted to get so high he never came back down.

He caught up with his father and uncles in the parking lot. "That god damn Principal Jefferson!" he yelled and punched his fist wildly, like he'd done as a toddler. "Just because I missed some classes after my accident, he thinks he can keep me from being valedictorian! Everyone knows I'm the smartest one in the class!"

"Well, I'll have a talk with Jefferson," Tony said, his voice deflated and resigned.

Tony's disappointment hurt Devon more than his father's usual anger.

"But boy, you knew this," Tony added. "You should've told me earlier. Maybe we could've done something about it."

Grandpa DiMasi shrugged, "At least one of you DiMasi boys got your shit together."

11.

WITH THEIR USUAL TACTICS OF BADGERING AND humiliation, Devon and Tony prevailed over Gavin's desire to attend a different college. Even worse, Tony had bullied—and bribed—Harvard's administrators to change Devon and Gavin's room assignment in different dorms so that the two would now be sharing a double in the same dorm. That served as the ultimate evidence to Gavin of his lack of agency in his own life. He was headed to Harvard, not to culinary school, captive in the same room with his brother. He had been defeated.

"You think you guys are going off to Timbuktu for four years?" Tony grumbled as he struggled to fit all the boys' suitcases, boxes and gear into and on top of his new black Lexus LX 450.

"Dad, we checked out our dorm room this weekend," Devon said. "It's really bleak. Harvard only gives each of us the basics—a little twin bed, bureau, bookcase, desk and chair. All shitty quality stuff. It's like a prison cell."

"How would you know?" Gavin interjected. "You've never been in prison—well, not yet, anyway."

"Shut up, baby brother," Devon snapped and went on. "So then we had to go buy all this crap to take with us. It's like furnishing a whole house! Bedding—it's not like anyone has twin bedding sitting around their house, right? Pillows, rugs, bathroom stuff, reading lights, window curtains, a whole ton of stuff. Just the essentials. And then we'll have to add bling to make it comfortable and homey—posters and shit, y'know."

"Well, you can just come back here any time to get whatever else you might need."

"I don't know about Twinkie, but I want to make sure I have everything where I want it, when I want it," Devon said.

"You're too lazy to do your own laundry," Gavin said, lifting one of his brother's boxes to the roof of the SUV. "So you'll be coming home anyway to have Mom do it for you."

"Maybe I'll have you do my laundry, Julia."

"Nice try, asshole."

"All right, you guys," Tony said. "Cut the crap and finish loading this shit."

Gavin was still bitterly disappointed that he would have to share a dorm suite with Devon. Gavin had overheard his parents arguing about it. Tony insisted that Gavin would watch out for his brother and keep him focused, while Colleen argued that it was time for each of them to achieve success independently. Tony always won such debates, and due to his "generous donation" to the school, Harvard conceded. Gavin feared the worst, with oppressive dread.

Just then Colleen came out of the house carrying an electric fry pan. "Gavin, did you want to take this with you?"

"Thanks, Mom," Gavin smiled abashedly. "I'll wait to see what kind of food they have over in Annenberg, and whether appliances like that are allowed in the dorm. I think there's a microwave in the kitchenette in the basement common room."

All first-year Harvard students lived in one of several freshman dormitory buildings, in singles to quads, in Harvard Yard or very close to it. Gavin and Devon had been reassigned to a double in Thayer Hall, in the Oak Yard corner of Harvard Yard. Thayer was one of the biggest dorms at Harvard, a sprawling 1870 brick building with limestone trim, having multiple wings of four- and five-floors. Many famous people like James Agee and E.E. Cummings once lived there. A bronze sculpture of John Harvard sat in the Yard nearby, the toe of his left boot shiny from frequent student and visitor rubs for luck.

There was scant room for the family in the fully packed SUV as they drove into Cambridge on that hot September Move-In Day. Once in the Square, they took their place in the long line of cars directed by campus police through Johnston Gate into the Yard. The line moved very slowly. The twins' room was at the far end of Thayer, near the exit from the Yard into the Science Center Plaza.

"You can pull up to that door, Dad," Gavin said, pointing. "Lucky for us, Thayer's one of the few dorms with elevators. We have to get all this stuff up to the fourth floor."

Once the family had unloaded everything from the SUV onto the lawn, Tony drove through Meyer Gate out of the Yard to find a parking lot, while the boys and Colleen began hauling it all into the building. "Now Mom, don't you go trying to carry the heavy stuff," Gavin said. "We can do that."

"*You* can do that, Julia," Devon said. "My old injury's acting up today."

"Sure it is, jerk," Gavin muttered.

After multiple elevator trips, the three of them surveyed the boys' two-room suite, hollow-sounding with its gleaming hardwood floors and bare walls. The entry to the suite from the hallway opened to the first room into which the school had delivered the requisite basic furnishings in scattered disarray. Everything the family brought from home lay cluttered there in random disorganized piles. A doorway led from the first room into the second room.

"This should be great, Twinkie," Devon said. "We can use this room for entertaining and the other one for our bedroom. We'll be bunking together again!"

"There is No. Fucking. Way," Gavin ground out word by word as if each were a complete sentence. "Don't even think about it." He picked up his box and headed for the next room.

"Hey, wait a minute!" Devon objected. "I get that room. It has more privacy."

"You're going to be the Big Man On Campus. You'll be entertaining your fan club in the first room, so I'll need privacy for studying. I *am* taking this room," Gavin declared with a tone of finality. Then he tilted his head, aimed a pointed look to his brother and lowered his voice. "If you want privacy for other stuff, do it somewhere else. Nowhere near me."

Colleen's right eyebrow shot up. She'd caught what Gavin was implying, made a mental note to talk with Tony about it later and diverted the conversation from potential confrontation. "I'm sure Devon knows how important it will be to practice good citizenship and study habits here at Harvard. And you two have different sleep patterns, so it's probably best to have separate bedrooms." She picked up a bag of bedding and busied herself with putting a mattress pad and sheets on the bed in what would be Devon's room. "We can get you some bolster pillows to match the spread, so you can use this as a sofa when you have visitors, Devon."

Gavin dragged the other twin bed into what would be his room and began unpacking. Devon wandered out into the hallway, turned on his charm and introduced himself in glowing terms to other arriving freshmen, just as Tony returned from parking the car. "You already settled in so fast, kid?" he boomed.

Devon cringed, embarrassed to be called a kid. And by his father's provincial accent echoing down the Halls of Ivy. "Well, not really," he said, pointing his father into their suite. "Just taking a break. Maybe you can help."

———

During the twins' first week in Harvard, they learned they had to meet with pre-concentration advisors to discuss their interests and readiness for certain courses. Devon was offended by this. "Who do they think they are?" he complained. "I know exactly what I want and need. Why would I want people who don't even know me telling me what to do!"

Gavin hesitated. He didn't want to get involved in his brother's rant. But he couldn't resist. "I think they might have information on the nature of the courses—how they're structured, their expectations, the curricula and so forth," he said. "They'll share all that with you so you can decide whether a course is right for you."

"Yeah, well, I bet I could teach any one of those courses better than they could."

"Right." Gavin retreated to his room and closed the door.

Devon barged in without knocking. "And get this! I had to take a writing test and now they tell me I have to take two semesters of Expository Writing this year! That's so much bullshit! I'm not in Harvard to take dumb-ass writing classes!"

Gavin suppressed a smile. He had already taken the test and was exempted from having to take even one semester of Expository Writing. "Oh, I'm sure it'll be fun, an easy 'A,' Devon." He turned his back and bent over his book.

Gavin would forever resent his father for insisting that he and Devon share a suite. His time—in fact, his life—was not his own whenever he was in their suite when Devon was there. Not even when he was in his room with the door closed. Devon's harassment, bullying and gaslighting were constant, particularly when he was "entertaining" the visiting acolytes he'd collected. Gavin had to admit that his brother had a dynamic personality that attracted followers like a powerful magnet. Devon seemed to have a need to boast about fictitious accomplishments while demeaning Gavin, to demonstrate his superiority and control over his twin when other people were around.

As a consequence, Gavin spent most of his time outside classes in other places where he could study or talk with people without his brother taking over. Harvard was replete with libraries in every corner. Lamont was one of Gavin's favorites; it was usually open twenty-four hours. It was also situated in the far diagonal corner of the Yard from Thayer, making it least likely that Devon would show up there. Widener Library and the Science Center were his other preferred hangouts. He managed to meet other students in those locations with whom he felt comfortable. Some were lost souls like he was, struggling to adapt to Harvard for a variety of reasons, although none of them had to room with an abusive identical twin.

As Gavin studied in Lamont one evening with three students from his Economics class, a guy named Wei excused himself by saying he was going to Room 13.

"Is that on this floor?" Gavin asked, looking around for room numbers.

"Not here. In Thayer. In the basement."

"Oh. Well, I live in Thayer," Gavin said, gathering his books and papers into his backpack. "I'm just about studied out, so I can walk with you."

It was almost midnight when the two walked through the Yard. The DiMasi twins had grown to six foot three at this point, so Gavin towered over Wei, who looked like he spent long hours working out in the gym. He chattered in rapid staccato as they walked. Autumn leaves crunched under their feet and Gavin breathed deep, relishing the musty fragrance of fall.

"I hate this time of year," Wei said, sniffling followed by three sneezes.

"Oh, I love it!" Gavin said. "It always smells so great, the air is crisp and cool—"

"That's just it. The smells. From mold spores released from decaying leaves," Wei muttered through his handkerchief. "Kills my allergies."

"Wow. That's too bad."

"Yeah, I can only hope for a heavy icy snowstorm. Soon. Meantime I get migraines and depression. I miss home."

"Where's that?"

"Phoenix. No autumn leaves there."

"So I guess you didn't know about these spores before you came here?"

"No. But it helps to go to Room 13."

"What, do they have something for your allergies?"

"No, but I can talk about my depression."

"But wait—it's almost midnight! Who's there to talk to?"

"Dude, you live in Thayer and you don't know about Room 13?" Wei looked up at Gavin, shaking his head. "It's a peer counseling place in the basement, vetted and sanctioned by Harvard. Where students can come for a little support when things hurt the most. Like in the middle of the night."

"Wow. That...that's great," Gavin said. "I always like to cook when I feel down. Except I can't really do that here."

Back in his room later, as Gavin fell asleep in the early morning hours, his last thoughts were of Room 13.

12.

AFTER A MONTH AT HARVARD, GAVIN STILL HADN'T fully settled in. Or felt happy. But he hoped a couple days back home would let him catch his breath, so he pulled the old family Subaru out of the Harvard Square parking garage to drive home on Columbus Day weekend.

Devon piled in at the last minute, jamming two fully stuffed pillowcases into the back of the car.

"What's all that?" Gavin asked.

"My dirty clothes. Sheets and towels too."

"There's a laundry just down the hall from our dorm room, Dev. Why are you taking your stuff home?"

"I don't *do* laundry, little brother. Mom can do it."

"Oh yeah, she doesn't have anything to do except wipe your ass."

"She loves being needed. Just like Dad loves when I need his money. Makes him feel important," Devon laughed.

"So that's your real game, huh?" Gavin snorted. "I can guess what you want to do with that money."

"Well, I'm the leader of the class—eventually the entire school! Being in that role takes money."

Gavin stared ahead and continued driving. Responding to Devon's fantasy would be useless.

The moment Gavin got home and greeted his parents, he bounded up the stairs to his old room and called Katie. He hadn't realized how much he missed her.

Katie's mother answered. "Hi, Mrs. Goodwin," he said. "This is Gavin."

"I know it's you, dear boy," she said. "How are you doing over there at Harvard?"

"Okay I guess. But more importantly, how are you feeling?"

"Not too bad today, for a change. But I never know from one day to the next."

"I'm sorry to hear that. I hope tomorrow's good for you, too," Gavin said. "And please let me know if there's anything I can do to help; I'm home today. Is Katie home with you this weekend?"

"No, she's got some kind of group project she's doing on campus. She and a few other girls are working on it in her dorm." Mrs. Goodwin giggled, "You should hurry on over there and give her a break!"

Gavin ran to the garage. He'd taken his good bike to Harvard for getting around the Square and along the river, but was relieved his old bike was still around. He checked the tires; they were low. Just as he reached for the pump, Devon came out from the kitchen. "Hey, Twinkie, what're you doing?"

"Nothing special. Just thought I'd ride around a little. It's a nice day." He finished pumping the tires.

"You're going to see that nerd Katie, right?"

"What do you care?" Gavin snarled and sped off.

The day was so beautiful it swelled Gavin's heart to overflowing and expunged the tension that gripped him. The fall air crisp and clean, the skies a spotless cerulean canvas against which golden and ruby leaves danced a gypsy rhythm. Gavin couldn't help but smile as he pedaled along the winding paths of Wellesley College's sprawling campus, past water lily-covered ponds, giant spreading mature trees, vast expanses of rolling lawns and towering clusters of Gothic Revival-style buildings. He gulped in deep breaths. He felt worlds apart from the tension and anxiety that engulfed him daily. He finally stopped the bike as he came to the footpath along Lake Waban and looked across its glassy surface, an undisturbed mirror reflecting the surrounding landscape. At that time of day, crew practice was already over, the skulls returned to the boat house, but a few students remained on the dock studying, chatting, or simply relishing the sun.

He turned to Katie's dorm, Claflin Hall, which, along with Tower Court and Severance Hall, overlooked the lake in a U-shaped cluster. Claflin and Severance were long five-story buildings flanking Tower Court, a narrower stately six-story structure. The three were built in the early 1900s with brick, cast stone trim and slate roofs. A sundial sat prominently in the center of the courtyard. Gavin found it hard to believe that young women actually lived in these castle-like buildings that seemed plucked out of royal English countryside estates.

He parked his bike and called Katie. He knew her quad suite was on the third floor, but not exactly where along the length of the building. He couldn't wait to see her. He scanned the third floor windows and waited for her to appear. Then there she was, opening a window with her phone in hand, leaning out and squealing in delight. Even Christmas was never this good.

When Katie emerged from Claflin, she ran to Gavin and took a flying leap into his arms, wrapped her legs around him and held on like a front-loaded knapsack, giggling. They swayed, glued together until Katie's friends who'd been working with her on their project stuck their heads out the window and began teasing them, something about nuclear fusion.

Gavin and Katie walked along Waban's footpath, hand in hand, talking. About her courses, teachers and roommates. And Katie's mother.

"How's she doing?" he asked. "You said it's lupus, right?"

"Yes. systemic lupus," Katie said. "But it's been getting worse. I just hope she won't be part of the forty percent whose lupus attacks their kidneys, graduating to nephritis. That would force her into dialysis."

"I'm so sorry." He squeezed her hand. A gentle breeze harmonized with the silence that enveloped them.

Katie squeezed Gavin's hand and broke the silence. "So tell me about Harvard."

Gavin rattled on about his courses, professors and friends he'd made. Then ground to an excruciating halt when he began telling about his roommate.

Katie cast a worried look in his direction. "From what you're telling me, Gav, being stuck in the same dorm room with Devon...the way he is...has to be so stressful," she said. "Nonstop."

"I should be used to it by now, but just when I think things couldn't get any worse, they do. Meaner, nastier, unrelenting. There's something about his behavior, like he's headed over a cliff and trying to take me with him."

"Well, don't let him. I hope it doesn't run in the family," Katie said. "Have you talked to Tray since we've all gone off to our different colleges? He's always been so good with perspective."

"Yeah, he really has his shit together. Like he understands stuff about you that you don't even get. Too bad he won't be home for Thanksgiving. Football."

"You should call him."

"I did, about a week after we started classes, but I need to hear his sane voice again. You know he's majoring in criminal justice? Wants to go into law enforcement like his dad and brothers. A family of cops."

Gavin and Katie finally stopped to perch on a large boulder that jutted over the lake. As they sat fused together on this rock, gazing out at the mirrored surface of the lake, shimmering in the dying light of the day, silence felt precious and warm. Their kisses were deep and long. Gavin didn't want to leave. He especially didn't want to return to what he'd just escaped.

———

When Gavin returned to his parents' house, his mother, having just returned from shopping at Whole Foods, rushed out to greet him. "Gavin! Don't you look happy and full of energy!" she said with a hug. "Harvard must be treating you well."

"I just came from visiting Katie," he blushed. He was relieved it was his mother who intercepted him, rather than Devon or his father. She was the only one in the family who really got him, the only one with whom he felt totally safe. "How've you been, Mom?" He was happy to see no bruises on her.

"Busy," Colleen said. "I've gotten several new patients, some tough cases. It can really weigh on me, and stays with me long after office hours. And now with all the new reporting and insurance requirements..."

Gavin put his arm on her shoulder and squeezed. "Mom, you need to take care of yourself. You're no good for your patients if you aren't good for yourself. Take a break now and then."

"Oh, so the Harvard boy is now giving his mother lectures on mental health?" Colleen teased.

Gavin ducked his head, embarrassed. "Sorry." He paused. "Did you know there's a peer counseling center in the basement of Thayer? They're open from seven at night till seven in the morning, to support any student who needs to talk about anything bothering them. They take calls and students can drop in to talk, too."

Colleen eyed her son. "Have you used their services?"

"No. Not yet anyway," Gavin shrugged. "One of my study friends told me about it. He gets allergy-related migraines and depression."

"Hmm...I can always tell when you're feeling down," Colleen said. "You cook. You pull out every pan, pot, knife and cutting board in the place and away you go, making a real mess—and absolutely divine concoctions."

"There's a kitchenette in Thayer basement," Gavin said with a sheepish grin. "I found out they don't mind if you bring in appliances as long as it doesn't blow a breaker or have an open flame. And clean up your mess."

After dinner that evening, as the boys prepared to leave, Colleen gave Gavin a large box to take with him. Once back in his dorm room, he opened the box to find a new set of professional chef's knives in their special carrying case. He almost cried as he opened and inspected that most awesome gift from his mother. Below it was the old electric fry pan, a crockpot, cooking utensils, cutting board, spices and his old chef's apron. He buried his nose into the apron. It still held delirious fragrances.

———

Later that night Gavin was in Lamont, deep into the online readings for his Economics course when Wei—accompanied by two other guys he didn't know—interrupted him. "Hey, Gavin," Wei began. "We were thinking about having a little party. Y'know, to celebrate still surviving...or something like that."

Gavin didn't know if that meant Wei was inviting him, or if he wanted to ask something. "Well, great," he said. "Glad to hear you're surviving!"

"This is Murray, my roommate," Wei said. "And Scott. He's down the hall from us in Gray's."

Both of Wei's friends stuffed their hands into their pockets, nodded and shuffled their feet almost in unison.

"We were thinking that some night when we go over to Room 13 you might want to meet us there, since you live in Thayer."

Gavin hesitated again. "Uh, well, sure. I guess."

"Oh, I don't mean in Room 13 unless you want to," Wei added. "You said you like to cook. So maybe we could meet in your kitchen and you could make something and we could... y'know—celebrate."

"Celebrate surviving, right?" Gavin laughed, finally understanding Wei's intention. "Yeah, I guess so. As long as it isn't the night before an exam."

"How about tomorrow night?" Wei wiggled like an excited puppy.

Devon found Gavin the next afternoon, whistling in the kitchenette while chopping garlic, onions and peppers for crockpot chili. "What the hell are you doing, Twinkie?"

"What do you care?"

"Oh, I don't *care*," Devon drawled. "I just hope none of my friends find out my twin wears an apron and thinks he's Julia Child."

"Oh, I wouldn't want to sully your reputation," Gavin said, without pausing his chopping. "I promise I'll never tell."

Devon mumbled something dismissive and walked away, sneering and shaking his head.

Gavin was notorious in his family for cooking way too much of everything. That was fortunate, because Wei—or his friends—had apparently told other students, who told others, about the "celebration." By ten o'clock that night the little kitchenette was crowded with more than a dozen students, with more milling around in the hallway and in the common room. Many had brought soft drinks. Wei brought paper plates and plastic utensils. Someone else brought napkins.

Combined aromas of chili, fried chicken and vegetarian pad thai rose throughout Thayer and captured the attention of more students, who joined the crowd. Surrounded by appreciative comments, belches and grunts, Gavin hummed inside. He'd clicked into his resonance, like a runner's high in a 10K cross-country.

"Hey, Gavin, didn't you tell me you share a double with your twin?" Wei said. "Where's he? I was looking forward to seeing your other half!"

Gavin plummeted back to earth with the worried realization that Devon wasn't part of the crowd. It wasn't like his brother to miss an opportunity to advance himself as the superior leader.

"Oh, I don't know. He really likes to eat, so he must have something else going on," Gavin shrugged. Only a few students remained as he looked around. "You guys gonna help me clean up this mess?"

Wei, his friends and a girl from Greenough—one of four freshman dorms outside the Yard—all plunged in, and the kitchenette was soon fairly presentable with an overflowing trash barrel.

Wei took Gavin aside and spoke low. "Would you mind walking Aniyah back to Greenough? It's the opposite direction from us. She'll act all tough and say it isn't necessary, but I don't think she should be walking alone so late at night."

Aniyah declined as predicted. Gavin insisted. After delivering her to her dorm, as he walked back to Thayer, he couldn't wipe the smile from his face. Stars shone brighter and he was free. For the moment.

Gavin's stride opened up with an energy he hadn't felt in some time as he walked up Prescott Street and cut between the Carpenter Center and the Fogg Museum. He was almost to Quincy Street when he noticed legs protruding from bushes at the end of Fogg. He stopped. Was it a homeless person, or someone drunk? Or maybe someone hurt? He approached cautiously and peered into the darkness.

It was Devon. His other half.

Panic gripped Gavin like a giant fist. His head spun as if all oxygen had deserted him.

In a wild frenzy he tore the bush aside to look for injuries in the streetlight. None visible. His brother's eyes were closed. He desperately felt Devon's neck for a pulse. His hands trembled. He found a thready beat, then realized he'd been holding his breath in his tightened chest. He gasped a deep lungful of air and paused to consider whether his brother's condition warranted calling 911. But that could result in the incident going into Devon's record.

Torn between his fear of losing his brother or getting him into trouble, he tried to rouse him. He shook him, slapped his cheeks, pried open his eyelids, lifted his torso, wished he had water, shook him again, blew in his face...Finally Devon began mumbling incoherently. Gavin pulled him up to a standing position, although he certainly couldn't stand on his own. As he did, he saw a syringe on the ground.

It took a slow halting effort to finally drag his twin back to their room in Thayer. After splashing water on Devon's face, he placed cold wet washcloths on his forehead and neck.

Eyes still dilated. Checked his pulse again. Stronger finally, regular rhythm.

Gavin sat beside Devon's bed and watched him breathe the rest of the night. He didn't want to contemplate what may lay ahead.

———

The young woman reading a book turned to Gavin when he walked into Room 13 the following night. "Hi, can I help you?" she smiled.

13.

IT WAS ALMOST AS IF DEVON'S NEAR-BRUSH WITH
death had emboldened him, encouraging even riskier behavior. More frequent drug use and concomitant manipulation of his brother. When Gavin tried to talk with him
about consequences, Devon blew it off as if it were trivial. "Oh,
Twinkie, grow up. You know that nothing bad can ever
happen to me. I'm smarter than that."

"But what about your grades? You hardly ever go to
classes or do the work. Dad will blow a gasket if you get kicked
out of Harvard."

"I can handle Dad, little brother. Don't worry. He donated
a ton of money to this shithole place, so they won't dare kick
me out."

It seemed to Gavin that he was trying to reason with a
holographic mirage.

As time went on, Gavin spiraled down, like he was drowning, struggling to reach the surface, to breathe. In fact, he was
often short of breath, as if he couldn't get enough air. Each day
seemed worse than the day before. He wasn't sure how much
longer he could hold himself together. Or even go on living
this way.

He sank lower every day as Devon's abuse became more

depraved whenever he was high.

"Aww, Twinkie. You need to lighten up, relax," Devon mumbled when Gavin attempted to divert him from his drugs *du jour*. "Don't be such a goody-two-shoes, little Momma's Boy. Chill! You're a real loser, y'know. Here, try this, maybe it'll help." He opened his hand, revealing a white capsule, then laughed.

Gavin hoped to gain a little breathing room during Thanksgiving weekend at home. After classes on Wednesday, Gavin planned to drive himself and his brother home to Wellesley. When he walked into their suite, he found Devon in the middle of a giggling fit. "What's funny, Dev?"

"Hoo, I just farted so big, don't light a match!"

"What's not funny is that you're high. I'm going home without you."

Devon rolled onto his bed, doubling into uncontrolled giggles.

Gavin was worn down from worrying about his brother. He tried to keep reminding himself of Pedersen's two-part mantra: *You can't save anyone unless they want to be saved. And you can't save anyone until you save yourself.* "If you decide to come home for Thanksgiving, you'll have to get a ride from one of your ass-fuck friends."

"Ooo, gobble-gobble!" More giggles.

Gavin turned and left, slamming the door behind him.

He decided to take the backroads to Wellesley. He relished the quiet aloneness of the car's protective bubble, where all sounds were either blocked out or muffled from a faraway distance. He floated, suspended in space and time, free, escaping the bonds of earth. He wanted to drive above and beyond the horizon.

That sunny afternoon was the picture-book image of late November in New England, cold and crisp. Gavin floated through the perfect world passing outside his windows, far from strife, a blur of ancient trees having shed their leaves, crystalline ponds, two-hundred-year-old homes, iconic town squares and children playing along narrow winding roads. He drove slowly, a circuitous route through Belmont, Waltham, Lexington, Lincoln, Weston and Newton to Wellesley, finally easing into his driveway. He was unsure whether he'd find relief there or an alternate version of stress.

Colleen was outside hanging a ribboned cluster of colorful Indian corn on the front door. She turned to the Subaru's hum and brightened when she saw Gavin. She ran to him as he emerged from the car. "Gavin, dear! I'm so glad you could come home this weekend. Where's Devon?"

Gavin enveloped his mother with a prolonged hug. "He... was taking a nap, Mom, but he'll get a ride with a friend and come later."

"Harvard must be working you boys awfully hard," she cast a worried look at Gavin. "You look tired, too. And you've lost weight!"

"That's why I'm here, Mom. So you can fatten me up. Is Dad home?"

"Not right now. He's dealing with a problem at the North End store."

"Is there anything I can help with, either for tonight's dinner or the big feast tomorrow? How many people are coming?"

"Just your dad's side of the family. Mom and Dad are going to your uncle's house for Thanksgiving this year."

Gavin ushered Colleen into the house, to the kitchen. "What can I do, Mom? Make pies?"

"Oh, that would be great, Gavin! You know I've never been able to master pie crusts." Colleen began opening every kitchen cabinet to check through her supplies. "Could you do your famous pumpkin-ginger mousse pie and your French apple pie?"

"Do you have all the ingredients we need?"

"I don't have the candied ginger, or the...Oh, we should

make a list." She opened the fridge and looked into the drawers. "I don't have fresh rosemary and sage. I was going to brine the bird this year...if you could help."

"I can go to Whole Foods and pick up the rosemary and sage. Let me do a quick inventory to be sure you have everything else I'll need for the pies and the brine. How big is the turkey?"

A few minutes later Gavin had grabbed his backpack, mounted his old bike and was sailing down Cliff Road. He recalled how he and Devon used to race each other down the steep hill, their trajectories often briefly airborne. It was a small miracle neither of them had incurred anything more than a skinned knee or elbow in their reckless pursuit of flight.

Whole Foods was predictably crowded the day before Thanksgiving. Just as Gavin had lugged his full handbasket to join the end of a long checkout line, he heard a familiar voice calling his name.

He looked around and saw Dr. Pedersen, in an even longer line next to him.

"So did Harvard let you out for the weekend?" Gavin's confidante from high school cracked his boyish grin and chuckled.

"Dr. Pedersen! Good to see you," Gavin said. A warm calm, a sense of relief, came over him upon seeing Pedersen.

"Did you bring a picnic? We may not get out of here for a long time, considering the length of this line."

"Well at least we're in a grocery store."

"Sure, we can mainline sweets from the bakery while we're stuck here." His line edged one step forward. "How's Harvard treating you?"

Gavin looked down at his feet. "Uh...well...It's a good school," he shrugged.

Dr. Pedersen paused and eyed Gavin. "Hey, I saw a pot of Portuguese Kale Soup over at the self-serve bar. Want to get a seat and have a little warmup snack or cup of coffee? Maybe the lines won't be so long after we're done."

Gavin got a baguette and cocoa and joined Dr. Pedersen at the table. He broke the baguette in half and handed it across the table, "For your soup."

"So talk to me," Pedersen nodded to Gavin and slurped his soup. "Needs more pepper."

Gavin pulled up short, astonished that Pedersen had obviously recognized something was bothering him, despite his best efforts to hide it. Just like he always did.

As if in reply, Pedersen dipped the baguette into his soup and without looking at Gavin mumbled, "It's written all over you."

Gavin sighed. "I have to share a dorm room with Devon."

"Well, that explains everything."

"It's gotten worse."

"Mm-hm..."

Gavin swirled the cocoa in his cup and clutched both hands around its warmth. "He's doing drugs. Like almost every day."

"How is that impacting you?"

"I try to stay out of our suite as much as I can. But it's like I can't avoid him. He and his fellow druggies manage to find me everywhere. His badgering has become more nasty, relentless. And his cult members do the same." He took a slow sip of cocoa. "I think some of them are off-campus suppliers, along with some fellow students who use, same as Devon does. So whenever I'm out on campus or even somewhere in the Square, I can usually count on encountering at least one of those assholes." He caught himself. "Sorry."

"It's okay, son," Pedersen smiled.

"I remember what you tried to grill into me. That what Devon—and his surrogates in this case—say or do has little to do with me, it's a reflection of who they are."

"Yes." Pedersen rested his gaze on Gavin. Accepting, waiting.

"It's hard though. I know all that in my head, but I keep

getting pulled back into the mind games he plays on me, so I feel like the loser he says I am. And then I think back to when we were kids. We were always so close. He was my best friend."

"And now it must be especially cruel that your best friend—the guy you see in your mirror every morning—is your tormentor."

"Yeah." Gavin's head hung low. "It's weird. Even though he makes my life miserable, when I think about his reckless drug use, I get really panicked. If anything were to happen to him, I don't know what I'd do. Like some part of me would be threatened, or could die right along with him." He bit off a chunk of baguette and chewed slowly.

Pedersen put down his spoon. "There's been some research that says identical twins often form an almost unnatural bond, as if they never really separated in the womb. Some even become codependent on each other."

"I've heard that term, but what exactly is that?"

"When two people can't really function on their own as individuals. Their thinking and behaviors are constantly focused on the other person, to the detriment of their own needs. When that's the case with one and the other one recognizes it, they can use it to manipulate the first. It can almost be like an addiction, pulling each party back into it, like moths to flame."

"Like I keep being suckered into it with Devon, even though in my head I know what you've told me so many times is right."

Pedersen nodded. "If your life were fiction, you'd hear it once and change how you react. Instead, you're sort of stuck, static, because challenging the status quo seems too risky. So you need to hear it many times before you can believe in yourself enough to overcome Devon's manipulation and act on the truth of who he is and who you are."

*The truth of who I am...*Gavin looked into the bottom of his empty cocoa cup, as if the answers could be divined in the patterns of brown flecks. "Maybe it's even harder for us to be separate individuals because we shared everything in the womb—egg, amniotic sac and placenta."

"You two hit the trifecta of twindom. Doesn't happen very often. I don't think that research I mentioned included trifecta twins," Pedersen mused.

"Well, I can save them the trouble. I can tell them all about it," Gavin mumbled.

"I'm sure you could," Pedersen laughed. "Anyway, remember what we talked about a few times, about root causes?"

Gavin paused, as if rewinding his memory tapes. "Uh, yeah...something about what's behind someone's behavior, behind their visible actions—what started it all, and continues to drive it."

"Uh-huh. And buried deep in their emotions, hidden even from themselves. So what emotions do you think are compelling Devon's behaviors? And the root causes of those feelings?" Pedersen asked.

Gavin was silent as he thought about this. His shoulders raised a shrug of bafflement.

"Remember, everything Devon does, says and thinks is about him and his image."

"Yeah, Dad always said Devon's the best, the smartest, all that shit. So that's what Devon tells everyone. But that was what Dad wanted him to be. I don't think that's what he actually is."

"What if some part of him finally realizes it's not the case? That it's all an act, he isn't superior at all, in fact he's inferior? He's not so naïve that he doesn't know his behavior is self-destructive. So why would he willingly destroy himself?"

Gavin looked down, toying with his napkin, oblivious to the flow of shoppers passing by. Suddenly he sat up straight, staring beyond Pedersen in shock, as if someone had just died. "He isn't trying to, uh, *eliminate* that 'inferior person,' is he?"

Gavin air-quoted, panic choking his breath.

"I don't think so. Like most narcissists, Devon thinks he's invincible. But he may be afraid that he can't live up to his own—and his father's—hype, which would reveal that he's a fraud."

"So, if he didn't ever have to actually *do* anything great, he can't be sure that he *is* great."

"Yes. It would be hard to define himself if his cover is blown. In playing a charade all these years, he has failed to invest in his true self."

Gavin paused to ponder that notion. It occurred to him that the same might be said for himself. All these years he had been conforming his thoughts, his life, to what his father and brother asserted, failing to believe and invest in defining his own self.

"So the only way you *might* be able to help Devon is to tell him you know there's a good vulnerable person underneath his façade, and you hope *he* can find and rescue that part of himself."

Silence settled over the table between them like a cloud of incense.

"But remember. You can care, but you can't *do* the work. He has to want that for himself."

"I know that in my head, but it's hard to watch my other half self-destruct."

"Other half? That implies you aren't complete without him, which is the myth he uses to control you. Keep your identity separate from Devon's, separate from the twinship." Pedersen's eyes bore into Gavin's. "Devon's personality disorder drives who he is, his behavior and everything he thinks. Changing that is almost impossible, but it's wholly in *his* hands, not yours. So the only thing in your control is saving yourself."

Gavin knew he'd heard that before. From Pedersen and Tray. And from Katie. But for some reason he didn't understand, he couldn't hold fast to that maxim, maintain his resolve. He was invariably sucked back into Devon's clutches—like that moth to the flame, and couldn't turn his back on his twin. As if the mitosis of their twin development were incomplete, keeping him tethered to his brother. How could he save himself if he wasn't sure who his own 'self' was? He wondered whether Devon's narcissistic abuse of him had destroyed his personhood, his agency, like Pedersen warned?

When Gavin got home, he unloaded his groceries as Colleen walked into the kitchen. "Thank you, Gavin." She looked distracted and a little flushed. "Your father just called. He's picking up Devon from campus and on his way home now. Can you help me throw together some soup for dinner? We have lentils and some Italian sausage...sweet potatoes, onions, green peppers..." she began furiously pulling out ingredients.

"Of course, Mom," Gavin took his mother's hands away from her task and sat her down at the kitchen island. "I've got this." He snatched kale from the crisper drawer and poured his mother a glass of pinot. Soon the savory Portuguese kale and sausage stew was simmering in a big pot and the giant turkey was in its brine.

Gavin inhaled the stew's fragrance and poured a second portion of wine into Colleen's glass, along with a cup into the stew. Cooking always freed his mind, helped him see things that had been eluding him, discover new ways to approach difficult things. Over the stove on that day, he finally decided to lift the twin code of silence. "Mom, I think you and Dad should know about Devon."

"Is he giving you a hard time again?" Colleen put down her glass.

"More than that," Gavin gathered strength to tell it. Then with another deep breath, he blurted, "He's doing drugs most days and rarely going to classes."

Colleen drooped like a felled bird over the island counter. "I should have expected that," she whispered with a weak cough. "The signs were all there, but I kept hoping it was just a phase, like your father said." She straightened, gathered herself and stood. "I'll tell him. You shouldn't have to be the messenger who gets decimated by his defensive anger."

Gavin put his hand over his mother's and thrust his sincere face into hers, speaking in an urgent tone. "Let me be with you when you tell him, Mom. I don't want him to take it out on you."

"No. He'll find some way to blame you if you're there, and it won't make any difference in what might come after."

Gavin sighed. "When are you going to tell him? I suspect Devon will still be a little high when Dad gets here with him."

"Now I realize why your father was being so curt when he called me," Colleen said. "He obviously saw Devon's state and was upset. I'll wait till you and Devon aren't here, to have the talk with him."

"You don't think you should do it in Devon's presence?"

"Oh, Gavin. Think about it. That would be like lighting a bonfire. No, Tony will need space to digest it. He may blow it off at first, but I know he'll think on what to do about it."

"Please promise you'll call me if there's any problem."

———

Thanksgiving morning was relatively calm on the surface. Devon slept the entire morning, while Gavin and Colleen cooked and baked. Tony left the house without saying where he was going, then finally reappeared just in time to greet his parents and brothers when they arrived in the afternoon. Devon slumped red-eyed at the table, playing with his food. Dinner proceeded with no one acknowledging the elephant in the room, although Tony kept eyeing Devon and was altogether too cheery and chatty in his attempt to cover up his favorite son's condition.

Gavin escaped to Katie's house for the rest of the weekend. It was late Friday evening after he and Katie had finished cleaning up from dinner and her mother was in bed, when a moan came from Mrs. Goodwin's bedroom. Katie popped up to listen, then ran to check on her mother. She soon came out, with a phone to her ear. "Yes, Doctor. She has a fever and pain in the area of her left kidney. She really doesn't want me to call an ambulance." She paused. "Yes, my boyfriend is here so he can help me get her to the car and bring her in. You'll be waiting for her in the ER, right?"

Katie's mother was even smaller than she was, so it wasn't difficult for Gavin to get her to the car. Katie held her in the back seat, reassuring her, while he drove carefully, avoiding any sudden stops or turns. When they got to the hospital, the doctor met them and began examining Mrs. Goodwin immediately while Katie sat rigidly, shivering with anxiety. Gavin held her hand, feeling her pulse throb. "I can't lose her, Gav," she whispered into his chest. "Not yet."

During the two days Katie's mother was in the hospital undergoing tests and observation, Gavin spent hours at her bedside and intermittently pestered the staff for results. Katie was almost paralyzed with worry. Whenever they weren't at the hospital, Gavin cleaned and cooked and tried to get Katie to eat. At night he held her in his arms. He longed to make love with her, but now was not the right time. Instead, he was a rock, the unwavering support system for Katie. Despite his worry about Mrs. Goodwin and Katie, he felt appreciated and validated, something he rarely experienced.

14.

THE WEEKS BACK ON CAMPUS BETWEEN THANKS-
giving and Christmas break were tense. Devon's behavior
changed after his brother broke the twin code of silence; he
now alternated between cajoling and retribution. Gavin
assumed their father had threatened him in some way,
because he wasn't getting high as often.

"Sweet Gavin," he purred. "I know I've been a bad boy. I
appreciate that you're trying to save me."

"I'm trying to keep you from destroying yourself," Gavin
said. He pulled Devon's desk chair over beside where his twin
was lying on his bed and sat down facing him. He attempted
to project empathy in his voice. "You're my brother. I know
there's a good, capable human inside you, vulnerable underneath your tough façade, victim of Dad's expectations." He
paused, seeing some inscrutable conflict in Devon's face.
Gratitude and relief, sparring with fear and anger. Gavin
called on his inner Pedersen and went on, "So you try numb-
ing yourself to that dichotomy with drugs, which only bury
that decent human even deeper. But those drugs can destroy
you. I don't want to see you hurting yourself, or worse." With
a final Pedersen axiom, he added, "But you have to want to
save yourself. You're too good to lose."

Devon quickly snapped himself back behind his protective shield. "Ah, Twinkie," Devon scoffed. "You've been spending too much time listening to that garbage in Room 13. Don't you worry about me. I understand you need me. You're nothing without me, so I'll always be around to take care of my poor little brother."

Gavin sighed. It seemed hopeless.

December was torture, but finally Christmas break arrived. It felt like getting out of a prison cell. Away from having to share a room with his brother or being harassed by Devon's clones, he could breathe, at least was allowed outside in the prison yard. He spent most of his time either locked in his old bedroom or at Katie's house.

"I can see how hopeless it makes you feel, Gav," Katie said one evening as they sat cuddled on her sofa enjoying the Christmas tree they'd just decorated. "I do hope whatever it is that makes your brother and father so abusive doesn't run in the family. Or is genetic."

Gavin nodded. "Me too."

"What are you going to do? You can't go on with things as they are. I can see and feel the tension all through your body."

"Oh, I guess I could run away and join the circus," he deadpanned. "Or slit my wrists."

Katie drew back and slapped his hand. "Don't even joke about such a thing, Gavin!"

"Yeah, that was a sick joke, wasn't it?" Gavin sighed. "Of course I'd never do anything like that, Kat."

"But you have to do something, Gav. Devon isn't going to change."

"Well, there's always the circus. Better than the zoo I've been living in," he grinned. "By the way, I'm meeting Tray tomorrow. We're doing a run—just two laps around Fresh

Pond. Then probably grab some pizza. You want to join us?"

"No way I would intrude on your guy time, Tiger. Anyway, I need to spend time with my mother. Tell Tray I said 'hi.'"

————————

Balducci's was crowded and warm. Their brick ovens radiated heat throughout the entire restaurant. Gavin and Tray were famished after their five-and-a-half-mile run. Gavin felt almost euphoric to be free of his brother and hanging out with his friend, but kept looking around guardedly, expecting Devon to appear any minute.

"So," Gavin said between guzzles of water. "How've you been doing out there in the boonies at Amherst?"

"Y'know," Tray said, "out there they don't pronounce the 'H'—they say it like 'Amerst.'"

"Like I said, the boonies," Gavin laughed.

"Yeah, and you go to Hah-vad."

"Right," Gavin said with a slight grimace and grabbed a menu. "You look like you've beefed up since I last saw you. They must have worked you hard on the football team."

"Oh yeah. Gotta be competitive."

"I see UMass' record has improved, but I haven't been keeping up."

"Well, after I became quarterback—"

"No shit! QB as a freshman! They finally wised up, huh?"

"They didn't have much choice. Blake got injured in early November and the second-string guy was sidelined with the flu. Coach didn't really have anyone else who could do the job, so..."

"Do you think they'll keep you in as QB after those guys return?"

"With my stats, coach says it's a possibility. He said he'll make a decision during spring training." Tray paused. "But Blake's dad is a big donor to the school, so I'm not holding my breath. And as long as they pay my scholarship, it doesn't matter. It's not like I want to go pro."

The two of them dug into the two large pizzas they ordered—one vegetarian, one meat.

"How's Katie?" Tray asked.

"Her mother's not doing very well, so she's really stressed. But I gotta give Mrs. Goodwin credit; she's tough and refuses to be a martyr. She keeps telling Katie to just go ahead and live her life, follow her dreams."

"That must be hard for Katie to do."

"I'm trying to do as much as I can to help out, take care of some of her errands and routines, but..." Gavin shrugged and toyed with a slice of pizza. "Hey, have you been dating anyone at UMass? Hotshot football star and all that."

Tray laughed. "I was dating one girl for a while, up until Thanksgiving. Becky."

"Was?"

"Yeah, until her parents came up to visit over Thanksgiving and I joined them for dinner."

"What, you chewed with your mouth open, used the wrong fork or something?"

"Her parents didn't think our dating was a good idea."

"Becky, huh? Let me guess.... like 'Becky-Sue'?" He feigned a deep-South accent.

"Pretty obvious, huh?" Tray chuckled with a shrug. "But that's okay. It's not like we were going to get married or anything. And I don't think she'd ever want to have Thanksgiving dinner at my parents' house."

"Not your 'type,' right?" Gavin laughed and gave Tray the anchovies that were inexplicably added to his veggie pizza.

"It's almost 1997, for shit's sake. Things never change," Tray shook his head.

"It's gotta change eventually...our generation has to make sure of it."

Tray eyed his friend with skepticism. "Not gonna be easy," he mumbled, his mouth full. "Did you see that Chris Rock special on HBO? I missed it when it first aired—that was around graduation—but they replayed it this fall."

"Yeah, I loved it—he's hilarious. Irreverent and in your face."

"His bit on *Black People vs Niggaz* cracked me up. But underneath the humor, it isn't really very funny."

"Yeah. Sorry, man," Gavin said. "Sucks." He finished his pizza slice and reached for another. "Oh,—how's your family?"

"Okay," Tray hesitated and took a gulp of his soda. "As the youngest kid, I get to learn stuff from my brothers. What to do, what not to. Takes on a different vibe in a family of cops. Abe just got shot in his arm when he was going after some guy robbing a store."

"Oh no!" Gavin said. "He's the oldest, right? Is he okay?"

"Yeah, Abraham Junior. He's good, all healed now. Kyrone I worry about."

"Narcotics detail is high risk, huh?"

"In more ways than you know."

Gavin raised a questioning eyebrow.

"Some undercover cops have gotten pulled down into the life they're pretending to be part of. Get too close. They can get hooked, or they can get made. Both risky, in different ways."

"I hear Roxbury is dangerous. Where your family lives."

"That's a myth. The narcotics business is mostly dominated by the mob. Little guys in the hoods just peddle it, small-time." Tray had devoured all his meat pizza and pointed to Gavin's. "You gonna finish all that?"

"Nah, help yourself."

"Anyway," Tray continued with his mouth full, "Roxbury actually has less crime than some other neighborhoods around Boston. My family lives in this big old Victorian that my dad grew up in. Parts of Roxbury might be considered sort of a black ghetto, I guess. But other places outside Roxbury are more dangerous for black guys. From jerks on the 'T' to over-zealous or racist cops on the street."

"Jeez, Tray. So I guess I shouldn't complain about having just two pains on my ass."

Tray slapped the table, laughing. Then becoming serious, "Yeah, but those two are in your own backyard, relentless. Sorry, Man."

Gavin thought about what Tray said. "So what do you do about that kind of danger? The harassment?"

"Dad taught us to not take anyone's bait, just not-react and move on," Tray said. "That doesn't always work, though. So that's why he made this 'Boston Police Family Member' card for me a couple years ago," He pulled it out and flashed it to Gavin. "It's something Dad ginned up to look official, complete with BPD insignia and artwork, all laminated and shit. There's a very small disclaimer in the scrollwork around the edges saying that it doesn't represent BPD official endorsement, but it's saved my ass a few times."

"I had no idea things might get so bad you'd need something like that."

"You lead a sheltered life, white boy," Tray teased. "My mom keeps bugging my dad to move out of Boston, but there's no guarantee it'd be any different elsewhere. Besides, if you're on the Boston police force you have to live somewhere in Boston. And there's no part of Boston outside Roxbury where Dad would feel more at home."

"Well, I'd like to move out of our house in Wellesley. Permanently."

"I get it. Someday you will. But sharing a dorm room with Devon isn't headed in the right direction."

"And he's getting worse all the time. He's into drugs now, too. Like all the time."

"I bet his bullshit gets worse when he's high."

"You got that right. Maybe we could have Kyrone scare the shit out of him,"

"Somehow I doubt that would have much impact on Devon."

"Well, I can't tell you how hard it is to just sit and watch my twin destroy himself."

Tray sighed, shaking his head almost imperceptibly. "Gav, don't beat yourself up for not saving Devon. He's famous for thinking he's smarter than everyone else and can out-maneuver all the rules. No matter how many times you talk to him, or what you say, you're not going to change him."

"Yeah, I know you're right," Gavin slumped, resigned. Then suddenly his head popped up, looking around urgently as if spies were lurking nearby.

As if on cue, he saw his brother coming into the restaurant with Jimbo Halloran, the dropout druggie from high school. Devon frequently managed to intrude into Gavin's escape spaces, and that day his twin had tracked him down again, heading directly to their table. Gavin stiffened, expecting the usual...

When Gavin went to bed that night, he couldn't get Katie's and Tray's words out of his head. They were right. As he drifted off to sleep, he vowed to put permanent distance between himself and his brother...someday...

In blackness, he is surrounded by bars spaced a few inches apart. Walls of bars enclose him. Bars above. Bars underfoot, resting on rough cement, cold and clammy to his touch. How did he get here? How can he get out? He shouts. No sound comes out. He grabs the bars and shakes. Nary a rattle. Deadbolts clang shut all around him. No way out. He shouts again. Still no sound. The cage vibrates. It moves. Then plummets. Icy water engulfs him. He and the cage plunge deeper. He cannot breathe. His chest tightens. He struggles, pulls on the bars. Can't breathe...

Gavin popped up from bed, gasping for air, coughing, heart pounding.

15.

AFTER THE HOLIDAY BREAK WAS OVER, GAVIN had to return to campus with Devon, back to the daily regimen of torture. No matter where he went or how long he hid himself away, Devon or his acolytes found him. If one of Gavin's campus friends were with him during his brother's ambush, they'd either steer him away or try to defend him. But that would make them one of Devon's targets, too, so they began to steer away from Gavin to avoid being collateral damage.

"Twinkie, you must miss me when you're off in the library all the time. You still love me, don't you?" Devon whined. "You know you're nothing without me."

Every night Gavin spent almost an hour in Room 13. But Devon even found him there. "Is my little Twinkie sad?" he taunted, in front of the peer counselor. "I know what can cheer you up, baby brother," with a sly wink, patting something in his pocket.

One week into the term, Gavin realized he hadn't seen Wei. He spotted Wei's friend Murray the next day and ran to catch up with him. "Hi Murray! How was your Christmas break?"

Murray seemed uncomfortable, looking down. "Okay, I

guess."

"Have you seen Wei?"

"Uh...," Murray stammered. He wouldn't look at Gavin. "You haven't heard." He dragged the words out slowly, with a flat tone.

"Heard what? Is he all right? He didn't drop out or anything, did he?"

"He isn't coming back. He didn't have the money to get home to Phoenix for break, so he stayed in his dorm."

Gavin was surprised. If he had known that about Wei, he'd have invited him to come home with him. That is, if he wanted to share some DiMasi family dysfunction.

Murray cleared his throat. "He hanged himself." He glared at Gavin, resentment contorting his face, as though he were angry he had to say the words, give voice to grief. He slumped and walked away.

Guilt flooded Gavin. He'd assumed...but he hadn't asked. He berated himself for being so wrapped up in his own problems that he hadn't thought to inquire about Wei's plans for break. Instead Wei was left all alone in his cold dorm room for more than two weeks.

Gavin skipped class, wandering aimlessly around campus. And beyond. On that gray January day, he found himself standing on the John W. Weeks footbridge staring down into the murky depths of the Charles River. A cold wind rippled the surface of the water. Thin patches of ice hugged the shores. A typhoon of emotions swirled within him. Grief for his friend, guilt that he'd failed to recognize and act on Wei's vulnerable state. And bitter outrage, that the genuine problems of good people are superseded by the self-centered entitled expectations of people like his brother. Something inside almost vaulted him over the side of the bridge in despair. He could feel it in his muscles and pictured himself catapulting through the air, splashing into the frigid water, disappearing into oblivion.

"Is that you, Gavin, or your evil twin?" Aniyah giggled as she walked past him on the footbridge. He could barely discern her face, she was so bundled up, as if she was ready to climb Everest. "Damn, it's cold today, so don't jump! On days like this I hate walking across the bridge to my job."

He hadn't seen Aniyah except in passing since the night he walked her to her dorm in Greenough. The night he'd rescued his brother from a drug stupor in the bushes. The night of his and Wei's 'survival celebration.' But Wei hadn't survived.

"Hi, Aniyah. I know this isn't like your home in Niger, but try to stay warm. I'd better head back inside myself." He turned decisively on his heels. He knew what he must do, where he must go.

———————

Gavin slowly opened the dorm room door. The hinge needed WD40. True to form, Devon wasn't there. He knew his brother's schedule. Well, usually, but this was Friday and Devon could be unpredictable. He did know where his brother hid his stash. Or at least he thought he did. He stood back for a minute and surveyed the mess before him. It was if a marauding band of gorillas had torn through the place looking for bananas and, failing that, decided to deface, break, or destroy everything in revenge. Gavin knew his brother had always been a lazy slob, but resented Devon's expectation that he would always clean up his mess.

Gavin reached up to the top of Devon's bookcase. High above shelves crammed with magazines, dirty empty food containers, socks and an occasional book, was his brother's prized wooden chess box. He pulled it down and shook it gently. It seemed mostly full. He debated whether to take the box or just the stuff inside.

He checked his watch. Only five or six minutes until Devon might walk in the door. Gavin knew how to open the flimsy lock on the box. It was like the kind on young girls' diaries. A sneeze could easily pop it open; he just needed a paper clip now. He rushed into his bedroom, where he knew how to find everything, unlike in Devon's trash heap. Every paper clip he had in a round jar on his desk was the jumbo kind, but the lock had a small slot. He had seen one somewhere...on a paper he'd written, on which his professor had attached a note...he began to breathe heavily, racing for time.

Gavin found the little paper clip and waded back through Devon's debris. He heard Devon down the hall outside, pontificating to a group of students. He rushed to get the box and opened it. Devon had already made a dent in his usual collection, but at least Gavin could empty the rest, save his brother from himself for a few weeks. He dumped the collection of pills and small plastic bags of white powder into his pockets, re-locked the box and returned it to the top shelf just as the door opened.

"Hey, what're you doing?" Devon barked, his voice sharp.

"You never returned my Ethics textbook, dipshit," Gavin snapped, taking the offense and rifling through the book-shelves. "I'm sure you didn't read it and now I need it back."

"Of course I read it. It's all bullshit. If you clean up the room like I told you to, I'm sure you'll find it."

"Forget it. Clean you own damn room. I'll go borrow Murray's copy." Gavin stormed out of their dorm, hoping his brother wouldn't notice the bulges in his pockets.

Dark sets in early on January evenings in the Northeast. It was 4:35 p.m. as Gavin sat near a cluster of evergreens in Cambridge Common. The sun had already sunk below the trees, leaving a vibrant glow above the western horizon thrusting its fluorescent fingers through branches and tendrils of vines. Two men sat under the eponymous Washington Oak near

Garden Street, trading swigs from a bottle swaddled in brown paper bag. They watched a disheveled woman dancing to absent music in the playground adjacent to Waterhouse Street.

Gavin felt as untethered and homeless as those men, and less free than the woman dancing to her own music. He reached into his left pocket and felt the pills from Devon's box. They trickled through his fingers like miniature pennies falling into a wishing well. He withdrew his hand and studied the four in his palm. What was the hold they had on his brother? Did they fill some emptiness in him? Anesthetize some pain? What remained after? A paved-over hole, an aching bruise where injury had struck?

Gavin flicked his tongue into his palm, raking the four white discs down his throat in a single motion. He breathed in, awaiting some sort of epiphany, surcease of despair, music to dance. He waited. Impatiently. There must be something... more. He reached into his right pocket, stroking the smooth plastic bulges, several miniature bags bound and tied, captive white pillows inside. He pulled one out and examined it in the waning light. He untied it, slowly. Passing his nose over its opening, he wondered what hold this fungal cirrhus had on his brother...

Tray had called Gavin three times with no answer. His criminal justice class was on a field trip visiting the FBI's Boston Division in Chelsea. It was Friday, so he could spend time with his friend over the weekend. He decided to go over to the Square, hoping to find Gavin in one of his favorite spots or on campus. When he came out of the Harvard Square 'T' station, he saw that traffic was blocked off around Cambridge Common, so he walked up Garden Street to see what was going on. Police were questioning two homeless men. An ambulance sat at the curb. Paramedics emerged from the bushes carrying someone on a stretcher. The first thing Tray noticed was the inside-out pockets protruding from the man's pants like arms of surrender. Then he saw, above a clear plastic orinasal mask and oxygen feed, the curly red hair.

He broke through the crowd of onlookers and rushed to see if it was Gavin. Or Devon. A policeman caught him and turned him away. "You're not allowed in here, unless you want to get arrested."

Tray pulled out his mobile phone and called Gavin's number, his head cocked to hear it ringing somewhere close. There was too much ambient noise to hear anything. But then a shout came from a policewoman searching the park, who soon appeared waving a phone she'd heard ringing in one of the trash barrels.

"That's Gavin's phone, I just called!" He turned to the sergeant, pointing to the stretcher, "That's my friend," Tray said and pulled out his Boston Police Family Member I.D.

A police sergeant looked at him and his I.D. "Well, your friend doesn't have identification on him. Who is he, and do you know his next of kin?"

Tray's breath caught upon hearing that last term, as if his best friend was at death's door. "Gavin DiMasi. He's going to be okay, isn't he?"

"Depends on what he took, kid," the officer brushed him away.

"Took? But he doesn't do drugs," Tray said, then mumbled, "unless you got his twin."

"Yeah, so you say. We gave him naloxone but it didn't totally work, so we're taking him to the ER."

"What hospital? I'll call his parents."

"Mount Auburn. But we'll make the call."

———

Tray was already pacing in the waiting area of Mount Auburn's ER before Tony and Colleen could get there from Wellesley. He tried using his police family ID to get some—any—bits of information, but it didn't work. He wasn't DiMasi family. He tried contacting Devon, but got no response.

A resident soon came out to talk with him. "I understand you know the patient that was brought in. He's awake now; we're waiting for his parents to pick him up. Do you know what substances he took?"

"No, like I told the officer at the park, Gavin doesn't do drugs."

"There was some residue in his pockets. We'll be getting it tested. Do you know where he could've gotten anything like that?"

Tray hesitated. Although he suspected Gavin had gotten it from his brother, and he'd love to blow the whistle on Devon, it might blow back onto Gavin. "I have no idea. What did Gavin say?"

The resident shook his head. "We can't disclose details except to his parents."

Tray nodded, "I understand."

No sooner had the resident left the room than Tony and Colleen rushed in. Tray cringed when Tony spotted him and snarled, "So now you've fucked up my other son?" Tray wondered whether Tony was implying Devon's years-ago accident in his car was *his* fault, or had just tacitly acknowledged that Gavin's twin was 'fucked up.'

Colleen cast an apologetic smile in Tray's direction and pulled her husband away. "Tony, don't jump to conclusions. Trayvon's a good boy."

When Tony and Colleen went in to see Gavin, he tried to protect his twin. "Dad, I don't know what it was. I found a bag of candy in the dorm break room and stuffed some into my pockets to snack on later. Next thing I knew, I was passing out in the park."

Tony didn't know whether to believe his first instinct—that Trayvon had supplied his son with drugs—or to believe Gavin's story. Neither one made much difference to the bottom line, as far as Tony was concerned. "You stupid shit. I don't know how you're Devon's twin and yet so damn dumb."

Gavin's explanation didn't feel right to Colleen. She walked down the hall and found the ER doctor, showing her Clinical Psychologist business card.

"Ma'am," the doctor hesitated. "You may want to have your son evaluated. Kids are under a lot of pressure their first year away from home in college, you know?"

Colleen's faraway gaze pondered the unthinkable. "Do you think he was feeling suicidal?"

"Hard to say. Could have been just experimental, but his story doesn't make sense, as I'm sure you realize."

Colleen nodded, thanked the doctor and went to the waiting room to talk with Tray. "Could you please take Gavin with you, Trayvon?"

"Uh, sure, Dr. DiMasi. Do you want me to take him back to campus?"

"Anywhere but his dorm room." Colleen's lips pursed. "You understand, don't you? Katie's house, or yours, or the room of one of his classmates. At least for the weekend."

"I understand you're worried about him. I'll spend time with him, talk to him. And I'll let you know where he is." Tray had always liked Gavin's mother, and puzzled over how different she was from Gavin's father.

Colleen gave him her business card. "Let me know by text, to this number."

Gavin's mouth watered as Tray's mother pulled a pan of meatloaf from the oven and placed it on a trivet in front of him, along with mushroom gravy, baked potatoes and baby limas with diced tomatoes. Mrs. Harris had set six places at the large oval kitchen table, but so far only Tray and Gavin sat in the warm fragrant room. The Harris policemen hadn't yet come home from their shifts. "You two go ahead and eat, before it gets cold," she said, wiping her hands on her apron. "I'll warm it up for the men when they get here."

Tray cut a large slice of meatloaf for himself and passed it to Gavin, who eyed the pan with concern. "You gonna leave enough for your dad and brothers?"

"Mom has two more of these in the oven. She has this down to a science."

Gavin served himself a smaller slice and took a bite. "Mmm...this is really good!"

"It's one of Mom's specialties. She mixes oatmeal in with the meat, instead of breadcrumbs like most people do. Always trying to stuff the best nutrients into us."

"Smart woman." Gavin ladled gravy over his meatloaf and potato, and took a big serving of lima beans. "This is a really great house, Tray. Thanks for bringing me here."

"You can thank your mom. She didn't buy your story for a minute."

"Yeah, she knows me. My dad just believes what he wants to believe."

"What the hell were you thinking?"

"I don't know. I wanted to get Devon's drugs away from him, empty his stash." Gavin looked down, playing with his food. "Then for some reason I was curious about what that stuff does for him, wanted to experience what he does."

"Well, that wasn't too smart at all, man. You could've croaked."

"He'll shit a brick when he sees his stash is gone. He'll know I did it."

"Just tell him you were doing him a favor."

"That won't help."

"You gotta stay away from Devon, at least for the weekend.

Then can you get transferred to a different dorm room? A different building would be even better."

"I already tried that. Devon had a fit, said he'd find me no matter where I went."

"You can't go on this way. It's like he's obsessed with owning you or something."

"Yeah, it sucks." Gavin grimaced and buried his head into his hand. "Being 'owned' feels like slavery."

"I get it, man. More than you know."

16.

NEWS OF THE SPRING BREAK PARTY SPREAD BY
word of mouth. Gavin had finally moved into Wei's old double
with Murray, so on that night the two of them took the subway
together to Kendall Square. Almost immediately upon
entering the host apartment, Gavin spotted Devon, who was
pontificating to a cluster of students on some topic that
glorified himself. Gavin noticed that a couple of them—
obviously new to his brother's hollow grandiosity—were duly
enthralled, while three others were fidgeting, trying to escape.
Gavin slipped past them into another room.

The place was jammed with Harvard and MIT students—
mostly freshmen, along with some from neighboring schools,
who hadn't opted, or couldn't afford, to escape to Florida for
spring break. There were kegs in each room of whoever's
barely furnished apartment it was. 2Pac's *How Do U Want It*
pounded from the stereo. It appeared that most of the students
holding large red dixie cups were drinking the beer, even
though Gavin was certain that some of them weren't twenty-
one. It was nevertheless a tame party at that point, but the
night was still young.

Gavin felt a nudge to his rib from behind and turned to see
Katie. "You decided to come!" he greeted her with a big hug.

He hadn't seen her since he took her to dinner on Valentine's Day. On this night she looked especially beautiful, energetic and confident in that dingy apartment. "How's your mother?"

"She's been having new complications," she said with a worried shake of her head. "Thanks for asking though."

"I'm so sorry. Is there anything I can do?"

"I'm afraid not, Gav. I wish there were."

Gavin put an arm around her shoulder and squeezed.

Katie changed the topic, "I finally finished with that big project," she said with a puckered smile, one shoulder shrugging, like it was no big deal.

"So has it got you any closer to settling on your major?"

"Well, it's been eye-opening, for sure. I went into it thinking I'd go dual—French and Art. But now I'm having second thoughts. What about you? Sticking with your business major?"

Gavin let out an ironic laugh. "Okay, I guess. But I think I might be ambivalent about my major, like you are. I'm having second thoughts, too."

Katie motioned to a sparsely populated corner of the flat, somewhat away from the blaring music. Gavin followed. She looked up at him. "I knew that was going to happen, Gav. And so did you."

Gavin dropped his head and stuffed his fists into his jean pockets. "Was it that obvious?"

"Well, you've had a passion for the culinary arts for as long as I've known you. You're so creative."

"Uhm...thanks," Gavin nodded, looking down. "But I don't want to leave Harvard to do something just because I like it. I mean, being a chef or even owning a restaurant is sort of weak and...*sissy.*" He hunched his shoulders, digging the toe of his boot into the dingy olive-green shag carpet.

"Wait a minute," Katie interjected, her voice sharp with annoyance. "Where'd you get that? Is that what Devon and your dad are telling you?"

"Well, yeah," Gavin shrugged. "They may be right. It's a hard life, with high risk, no sure path to sustainable success."

"Nothing ever is," Katie declared, throwing a hand up, palm out, miming the obvious. She eyed him and took a sip of her Coke.

Gavin stammered, looking out a window that only revealed the brick of an adjoining apartment building. "I guess being a chef and owning a restaurant isn't the only reason I'm thinking about changing schools."

"Yes, Gav. I know," Katie said softly, peering deeply into his face. "You need to get away from your twin, have a life of your own. Right?"

"Yeah, for sure," Gavin exhaled. "It's sort of weird. We're mirror twins, but I don't want to be just the reflection of my twin. Or anything like him, actually."

Katie nodded sympathy, withholding comment, waiting for Gavin to say what was apparent.

But Gavin was eager to change the subject. "So what are your 'second thoughts' on your major?"

Katie chuckled. "Nice dodge, Gav. Well, I'm thinking Art and Business. Maybe I'll open an art gallery, or a women's version of *Burning Man.*"

"Burning Woman," Gavin grinned.

"Right. But Wellesley doesn't offer much in business management, so I may have to transfer. Maybe to B.U." She put her hand on Gavin's forearm. "I'm not letting you run away from this subject, Gavin. What are you going to do? I can see you're nothing short of miserable."

A smile escaped Gavin's mouth, gradually spreading ear-to-ear as he looked at Katie. "Are you sure you aren't majoring in psychology?" he teased. "I've looked into it. Once I finish this first year at Harvard, I can transfer all my liberal arts and business credits to CIA and get my Bachelor's in Culinary Arts there in three years. Along with internships with top chefs in award-winning restaurants, maybe even trips to France or

Italy!" He was so excited, he was virtually hopping.

"And you wouldn't even be in the same state as Devon."

"*YES-sss*," he hissed. "I've already filled out the application form. Maybe I'll send it in."

Just then Devon barged in, wedging between Gavin and Katie. "Baby brother! Here you are. Where's your beer?"

Gavin grimaced. "Katie and I were just going into the next room to get some of those chips," he said, hooking his arm into Katie's and pulling her away from his brother.

Devon began to object, but Gavin and Katie were already well ahead of him. He sputtered after them, "There goes a cute couple—of nerds!"

Gavin and Katie both rolled their eyes in perfect synchrony, then began giggling when they realized their unintended choreography.

"Hey, guys!" Tray had just walked into the apartment.

"Well, look what the cat dragged in," Gavin laughed, greeting his friend with a fist bump and back clap.

"Hi, Katie," Tray said after Gavin released him. "Great to see you're still putting up with this guy."

"Oh, he can't get rid of me," Katie laughed. "Is UMass on break now, too?"

"Amherst is," Tray said. "I guess Boston is too."

"Did your coach expect the team to train this week?" Gavin asked.

"Yeah, but he let us take a long weekend off. My friends on the baseball team didn't catch a break, though."

"Has your coach promoted you to quarterback yet?" Katie asked.

"Well, coach put me in for the last three games of the season after the regular QB was injured and the second-string got the flu. But nothing's official yet. The current QB won't be graduating until next year, so once he recovers, I may have another year as running back."

"UMass' record immediately improved when Tray was QB,"

Gavin noted to Katie.

"You were the main reason Wellesley won state champion-ship two years running," Katie chimed in, "and why UMass recruited you with a scholarship. Now Gavin tells me you're majoring in criminal justice?"

"Definitely. UMass has a really great program."

"And you're planning to be a police officer?" Katie asked.

"Uh-huh. At least long enough to get someone to pay for me to go to law school," Tray grinned. "And are you two still in those wimpy Ivy League schools?"

Gavin and Katie laughed at the same time. "Actually," Katie said, "we were just talking about switching."

"Oh, so Gavin'll transfer to Wellesley and Katie'll go to Harvard?"

"Sure, and I'll start wearing skirts," said Gavin, giving a playful punch to Tray's shoulder.

"No, seriously," Katie said. "I'm considering transferring to B.U.'s Questrom School of Business, and—"

"—I'm going to transfer to the Culinary Institute of America in Hyde Park," Gavin finished. "CIA." Then added, "Dad'll shit a brick..."

"But it's your life!" Tray put both hands up and simulta-neously landed high fives to both Gavin and Katie. "It's about time you guys got real." He then began sniffing, turning his head from side to side. "I smell weed."

"Yeah, I smelled it earlier, too," Gavin said.

Just then Devon emerged from another room, bringing with him a cloud of marijuana fragrance. "Hey, Twin. I see you're slumming with that *colored boy* from Roxbury."

Gavin lunged toward his brother, his fist pulled back, about to swing. "You ignorant asshole," he spat as Tray restrained him. Devon walked away laughing, leaving the three of them stunned.

As Tray kept a grip on his friend, Gavin grabbed Katie and pulled them all toward the door. "Let's get out of here." As he passed his suite mate, he nodded and muttered, "Hey Murray, we're leaving. See you back at the ranch."

The trio of pals walked to the nearby Area Four restaurant in grim silence. Finally Gavin opened his mouth to speak, huffing. Tray put a hand on his shoulder and stuck his face eyeball-to-eyeball with his friend. "Gav, you do not have to apologize for your brother. What he does and says has nothing to do with you. You're not responsible for him and you can't let him get to you. Got it?"

Gavin stood still. His eyes stared through his friend, somewhere beyond space. It was as if he were witnessing a life-altering event, like the end of slavery. His own. He nodded slowly and returned his focus to the present. "Yeah. Thanks. I guess it's about fucking time I got that, right?"

Katie and Tray laughed and sandwiched Gavin in their embrace. "Let's top that off with a pizza!" Katie said, opening the door to the warm aromas of late-night food. Once their order arrived, Katie marveled, "I've never seen you chow down like this, Gav," as he tore into his fourth slice of pizza.

Gavin felt almost giddy as if an enormous weight had lifted from him. The three of them talked nonstop until the restaurant closed at midnight. "Great seeing you guys tonight," Tray said as he headed to the subway station. "Keep me posted on your new directions!"

After he'd gone, Katie turned to Gavin. "I have Mom's car here, Gav. I can drop you back at your house." She hesitated. "Or you can come with me to my dorm. My roommate went to Florida for spring break."

They made love for the first time that night, flooding Gavin with emotions. Glory and strength in his manhood, freedom and wonder that this beautiful woman loved him, a connection so deep and profound. As he lay back, exhausted, relishing the feel of Katie curled into him, another Grateful Dead tune hummed in his mind. *In the attics of my life...when there was no ear to hear, you sang to me...*

Gavin woke the next morning in Katie's arms, feeling like a new man. "Good morning, Katie-Kat," he whispered in her ear.

17.

AFTER THE END OF DEVON'S SECOND YEAR AT Harvard, Tony called him to come meet at one of his liquor stores. He wanted to discuss something with him. Devon was a little concerned. Had his father learned of one of his recent escapades? If so, Devon thought he could probably talk himself out of trouble.

That location of DiMasi Liquors was in a working-class section of Framingham. It was one of Tony's more recent additions to his current twelve-store chain throughout Eastern Massachusetts, west of Boston. It was close to three highways— Mass Pike, Routes 9 and 30—and also near Framingham State University, tapping both the trucker and college student markets. The exterior was modest—a renovated one-story wood-frame stand-alone building.

An electronic doorbell chimed when Devon walked in. There was a subtle smell that reminded him of every liquor store he'd been in. His first thought was that lots of kids from Framingham State were probably using fake I.D.s all the time here. He noticed several convex security mirrors placed strategically throughout the store, to give the clerk working at the register full view of shoplifters or troublemakers. The aisles were narrow, crammed with alcohol of all sorts. Not much that was exotic or expensive, mostly the standard mainstream categories and brands. Every bottle and can were lined up perfectly on the shelves, labels facing outward, no empty out-of-stock spaces. Lighting verged on industrial, but the floor and shelves were spotless.

Tony came out of the back room, undoubtedly alerted by the chime. "Well, son, congratulations!" he laughed. "For a change, you're less than half an hour late." He clapped Devon on the back.

"Sorry, Dad. Traffic sucked."

"Sure it did. Ten o'clock on a Tuesday morning can be brutal."

Devon rolled his eyes. The sarcasm wasn't lost on him. "So what did you want to talk about?"

Tony called out to his store manager, "Hey Joe, I'm going out for a couple hours. You're in charge. I probably won't get back here till later in the week."

Joe grunted, "Sure thing, Boss."

Tony steered Devon to the door, toward his Buick in the parking lot. "We're going for a ride, son. I want to show you where all this started," he said, gesturing back to the store.

Devon silently grumbled. *Oh, shit. A field trip.*

Tony drove aggressively, over the speed limit, cutting off cars, talking all the while about how his father had opened the first store in the North End in 1950, then how he took it over in 1976—"I was only twenty-five, only a few years older than you!"—and began opening new stores. "I've been successful by only stocking high-demand stuff with the highest profit margins and I pay distributors under the table to make sure we get preferential delivery and never run low on inventory," he boasted. "But we're getting pressure from the Rizzo family. Frankie—we grew up together in the North End—him and his boy Tommy over in Charlestown—typical Townie—think they can muscle their way around and force me out. And now his little brother Mickie over in Chelsea, is trying to play tough."

Devon perked up. He was intrigued. "How are they trying to muscle you out?"

"Well, I don't want to scare you, son. But the Rizzos are trying to play like old 'mob' games with me," using both hands for air quotes at seventy-five miles an hour down the Pike. "They intercept my distributors and hijack my deliveries. I hear Tommy's goons even have guns. Tommy's your age!"

Devon's eyes lit up, seemingly energized by this, as if it was a new arcade game. "Jesus, Dad! What are you going to do?"

"Fight fire with fire, m'boy," Tony said with a determined wink. "Meantime, I'm opening two high-end stores. One in Wayland. Weston next door to it is dry, you know. And one in Concord. Next year I'm opening one on the North Shore, in Gloucester. All the top-shelf stuff. And I want you to get involved with managing the high-end locations."

"Dad, that sounds great, but what about college?"

"I've seen your grades, boy. You've been a real fuck-off, haven't you?"

Devon cringed and ducked his head like a turtle retreating into its shell.

"That's because you're wasting your talents on those *psychology* courses, like your *mother*. You'd be better off if you focused on business!"

"You want me to switch my major?"

"Damn straight, boy," Tony barked, like he was surprised his favorite son hadn't figured it out before now. "So while you're getting your business degree at *Hahvad,*" Tony mocked the patrician Boston accent, "you can spend half your time learning real-world business, store by store, like a management trainee—while you're finishing your last two years of college. A Harvard grad will impress the snobs in those towns. See if you can keep your act together long enough to graduate," Tony shot a warning look at Devon. "Besides, I've got to hand the business down to one of my sons, and it sure ain't gonna be

Little Julia. He's already deep into that cooking bullshit, even off now to some highbrow restaurant in Chicago for four months on an 'externship' or something like that."

Devon's mind buzzed with ideas on how he could grow the business, make a lot of money, become well-known as a powerful business mogul...When they finally pulled into the space marked off by rickety chairs on Prince Street outside the North End store.

This was the first time Tony had taken either of his twins to his old neighborhood. Prince Street was a narrow one-way street lined with brick buildings from the nineteenth and early-twentieth centuries, most of them abutting each other with no space in between. A fire in one would wipe out an entire block. Most of the four- and five-story buildings had a store of one sort or another on the ground floor and what appeared to be residences in the floors above. Delivery trucks and vans crowded the congested street.

Tony got out of the Buick and went into his store, but Devon stood, looking around, taking in the surroundings. He was curious to see old men sitting on the sidewalk in flimsy chairs they had apparently brought from their own apartment, holding court with passing neighbors. It was a sweltering August day and the narrow street bounded by walls of multi-story buildings concentrated the heat. Devon could see windows open with no air conditioners and figured the men had escaped to the shady side of the street to catch any available breeze outside.

Young men walking by stopped to talk with the old men, showing exaggerated deference. Although Devon couldn't hear what they were saying, it appeared that some transactions or agreements were being exchanged. Women—young and old—passed by, their arms full of grocery bags or children, nodding, smiling, and kissing the old men's cheeks. It seemed as if the men were tribal elders who must be honored.

Devon took all this in like a tourist in another country,

carefully scrutinizing every detail. He noticed a burly young man standing across the street with his hands stuffed into a black leather jacket that seemed out of place on this hot day. Although the man moved about as if he were waiting for someone, his eyes never veered from Tony's store, specifically locked on Devon.

Devon thought the guy looked like someone he would never want to encounter in a dark alley. Yet there was something about that idea that excited him. He smiled as he anticipated this new chapter in his life. This is what he was made for. He was only twenty, but running liquor stores sounded a lot more like his style than sitting in classes at Harvard. And of course there would be fringe benefits...

Tony opened the door of DiMasi Liquors and called out to his son. "Hey, you gonna stand there forever? Get in here!"

Devon reluctantly turned to join his father. "Dad, who are those old guys sitting out there on the sidewalk?"

"Ah, just a bunch of goons," he said. Pointing to one, "That one down there's 'Sonny Boy' Rizzo." He drew out the full name as if he were mocking the title of royalty. "Alexander Santoro Rizzo's his real name. He just got out of prison a couple years ago and decided to move here instead of going back to his home turf in Revere. But everyone knows him anyway."

"Rizzo? Any relation to the family you said is giving you a hard time?"

"Yeah, the same. The old man is Frankie's grandfather." Tony looked around. "And I think the kid across the street trying to look tough is one of Tommy's goons."

Devon's gaze shifted from the old man to the guy across the street, who had begun walking away. *Doesn't look too tough to me.*

18.

ALTHOUGH MAY AND JUNE ARE TYPICAL MONTHS for graduations, Gavin's graduation from the Culinary Institute wouldn't happen until August because of CIA's rolling calendar. But that didn't keep Gavin from driving three and a half hours from Hyde Park to Katie's graduation on May 21st and Devon's on June 8th.

Katie wasn't expecting Gavin to break away during his final term at CIA for her graduation from Boston University's Questrom School of Business. But when her name was called to receive her diploma, Gavin stood and wildly cheered, making a complete fool of himself, causing everyone around him to laugh. That caught Katie's attention and when she spotted him, she gasped, breaking down in giggles.

"Wow, I'm really intimidated," Gavin chuckled as he hugged her after the ceremony and handed her a bouquet. "Magna *and* Phi Beta Kappa? Are you sure you want to associate with me?"

"Oh, Gavin," Katie beamed and wiped her watery eyes. "I'm so happy you could come! Are you on break from CIA?"

"No, unfortunately," he said. "I have to drive back tonight; I have a demonstration first thing in the morning."

"That's too bad! Well, let's make the most of the little time we have. When do you have to leave?"

"I figure nine or ten o'clock might be okay. Traffic should be thinned out by then. At least I got to see you graduate, and hear the great Tom Wolfe speak. Do you think he had his iconic white suit on under that red-trimmed white robe?"

"I heard that President Silber had it made just for him, for this occasion," Katie said. "Oh, there's my mother."

Gavin saw the woman struggling with her walker and rushed forward to help. "Mrs. Goodwin, how wonderful to see you again!"

"Gavin dear, you're a sight for sore eyes," she hugged him. "Did you drive here all the way from Hyde Park?"

"Yes, Ma'am. Do you have your car here?"

"No, I took a taxi. I sure didn't want to deal with Boston traffic."

"Well then, let me be your chariot."

Although Mrs. Goodwin had planned to take her daughter out to dinner to celebrate her graduation, Gavin and Katie could see that her mother was too tired to endure that. She asked Gavin to drive them back to their home in Wellesley, where he cooked dinner for them. As they were finishing their meal, he noticed that Mrs. Goodwin seemed to be having difficulty breathing and swallowing her food. He frowned, recalling that Katie told him about pleurisy developing in some cases of advanced lupus.

While Katie helped her mother into bed after dinner, Gavin smiled at the warmth of their chatter from the bedroom as he cleaned up the kitchen. He regretted having to drive back to Hyde Park that night, but relished his time with Katie later as they relaxed and snuggled on the sofa, surrounded by several needlepointed pillows Mrs. Goodwin had created over the years. Katie buried herself in Gavin's arms, then finally stood and said, "I need a beer. You want one?"

"Sure, thanks. Just one, though. I'll be driving."

They sipped their beers in silence. Gavin couldn't imagine

life without Katie. He took a deep breath and asked, "What are you going to do now that you've graduated?"

"As a matter of fact," Katie sneaked a grin. "I do have an offer from a small gallery in Manhattan to come manage the business."

"That's wonderful!" Gavin lunged to embrace her, almost knocking the bottle from her hands. "I'll be graduating in August, and I have offers from three restaurants in the city. So we'll be in the same town!" He was ebullient, almost vibrating.

Katie just smiled, looking at him expectantly with her arms crossed.

"Then after I graduate, would you consider sharing an apartment with me?" He was almost afraid to ask.

Katie laughed and said, "Of course, silly. Can you join me to look for an apartment there? I'll be moving in before you, and I want to make sure it suits you, too." Then she paused. "But I do worry about my mother if I'm not nearby to help her."

"Do you think we should move her in with us?"

"I could talk with her about that. But she likes her doctors here...and just last week she surprised me by saying she's ready to have a home health care aid. She wants me to go on and pursue a career, chase my dreams." Katie looked down, fidgeting with her hands. "It sort of sounded like Mom feels it's the beginning of the end for her."

Next came Devon's graduation from Harvard.

"Dad, I don't want to go to commencement," Devon griped. He pushed aside his meal and gulped the last of his drink. He tolerated Sunday afternoon dinners with his parents because he could typically get some money from his father, even though he had only picked at the filet mignon and vegetables his mother had prepared that day.

"Devon honey, your dinner's getting cold," Colleen said, and appealed directly to her son's tired eyes. "I roasted the potatoes the way you always like them."

Devon got up from the table for the third time during the meal, opened the liquor cabinet and poured himself another scotch.

"What do you mean, you don't want to go to graduation?" Tony asked. "You *are* going to graduate, aren't you?"

"Yeah, yeah, Dad," Devon snapped with an eye roll. "But I'm not going to be valedictorian or any of that shit, so get that out of your head." He sat back down to the dining room table, pushing his potatoes into the blood pooled around his steak, then lined up his peas one at a time across the top of the potatoes like a row of green bugs. He looked up from his plate and smirked, "Not that I couldn't if I wanted, though."

Colleen studied Devon's eyes. His pupils seemed to be occupying too much of his hazel iris. She'd seen that a lot in her practice. She wondered whether he was just overly tired, or that he'd taken some sort of drugs. He seemed unable to sit still that day. "Now that your exams are over, Devon, I hope you can catch up on your sleep. And...have you been using drugs again?"

"Jeez, no, Mom. Don't be ridiculous! You know I stopped that after my first freshman semester. I'm just really tired. I'm gonna crash for a week after this is all over," Devon nodded, sniffling behind his napkin.

"If you don't go to the ceremony, how will you get your diploma?" Tony asked. "Y'know, the official sheepskin you can frame and hang in one of the stores you're managing?"

"Dad, they'll just send it to me. No big deal."

"Who's the commencement speaker this year?" Colleen asked. "And are you coming down with a cold?"

"Some Indian economist I never heard of," Devon mumbled, taking a gulp of his drink. "They had Alan Greenspan last year, but this year we got a nobody. And no, I don't have a cold. Probably just allergies. The pollen's heavy this year."

"Well, son, I want to go watch you get your degree," Tony declared, more of a command than a statement. "And I know Pops does too. You're the first DiMasi to graduate from any college—and Harvard at that!"

"I'd like to be there as well, Sweetie," Colleen said softly. "Your O'Malley grandparents are really happy for you, and I know your brother will want to come down from Hyde Park to celebrate with you."

"All right, all right, you guys!" Devon huffed and stood up. "I gotta get back to campus. Thanks for the dinner, Mom. Sorry I wasn't very hungry. Dad, I need some money."

"Again? How much?"

"If I have to do this commencement gig, they charge for stuff. Do you have a couple hundred on you?"

"Jeez, boy, Harvard's expensive!"

"You just now figuring that out, man?"

———

All Devon's final exams and papers were complete and graded before the first week in June. He did manage to pass, but it was unclear whether his grades reflected his actual work, or the result of some outside influence. The week before commencement was filled with parties and winding-up activities. After a brief cameo appearance at the Dean's Reception the day before commencement, he found some big boxes and began tossing in almost everything he had from his dorm room on the top floor of Dunster House.

Although Devon had originally wanted to live in an off-campus apartment after freshman year, for the privacy it afforded, he was actually glad his father had resisted. Dunster House was an historic 1930s brick building that needed some updating, but its 197-foot-tall clock tower, gleaming white topped in red, was an iconic symbol of Harvard's grandeur.

The imposing structure sat directly across from the Charles River and the Weeks Footbridge into Boston. Dunster was the most social of Harvard's twelve undergrad Houses, and the fourth floor was populated by mostly chill guys who knew how to party. Devon was a member in two of Dunster's Stein Clubs, and a prominent participant in the annual Keg Race and Goat Roast.

He was sort of sorry it was all over. He gloated that he'd become a genuine BMOC—Big Man On Campus. He felt certain that everyone knew him as the best in his class. Although he hadn't achieved the highest grades or athletic glory, those weren't the only, or most significant measures of being best. It was influence. He'd learned the value of influence by managing his father's stores, and it worked like magic at Harvard, and especially in Dunster House. He was the expert at getting people to do things for him. He was recognized as the guy who could game the system, get away with flouting rules and authority, score the best stuff, manipulate people's opinions, and use fear to his advantage. He knew he could continue to use certain guys from Harvard to do things for him even after graduation.

Once graduation was over, he could devote all his time to managing DiMasi Liquor stores and expand his influence beyond just the few upscale suburban stores his father had assigned him. But he'd come to see that there were things beyond peddling liquor that could make a lot more money, by leveraging the DiMasi base. He could become the most powerful man in New England, easily outsmarting those slick rubes in the North End...

"This all you got?" Tony asked, interrupting Devon's reverie when he saw the few boxes. He looked inside one. "What'd you do, just throw your things in without folding or organizing anything? This looks like a pile of trash!"

"It isn't everything, Dad. I have to come back tonight to get ready for the whole fucking day of commencement hoopla. I don't know why they have to do all that, instead of just handing out degrees. I'm only packing what I won't need tomorrow. Mom'll take care of all this crap when we dump it back at the house."

"Yeah, leave it all to your mother. Lazy slob."

As they dragged the boxes down the hall, Tony heard someone behind them grumble, "Sure won't miss that asshole..." Tony nodded internally. He knew his son all too well. Devon hadn't completely fooled him.

While Tony drove his new Infiniti QX from Harvard Square to Wellesley, he peppered his son with talk. "It'll be great to have you back home. You can start working fulltime managing the stores you've been working on, and then we need to talk about other stores, and what your pay will be, and—"

"Yeah, Dad, I have some ideas..."

"Gavin doesn't graduate till August, so you'll have the house all to yourself till then."

"Except for you and Mom," Devon grunted. "Dad, I have my eye on a place in the North End." He talked fast, not looking at his father, hoping Tony wouldn't break in and nix his deal. "It's on Hull Street, between that old cemetery and the Old North Church. It's a nice little condo and I'd be just a couple blocks from the main store!"

"Son, I don't want you living in that neighborhood. And your Nonno doesn't, either. Why do you think I raised you boys in Wellesley?"

"Aw, Dad, it's perfectly safe!"

"It may be safe, but the life there is dangerous for someone in our business."

"Don't be ridiculous, Dad. I'm gonna be twenty-two next month. I'm a grown man. I can take care of myself."

"You don't realize what you're up against, kid."

"I'm not a kid, Dad. The people and connections to help the business aren't in Wellesley."

The discussion ended, unresolved, when Tony pulled the SUV into their driveway. Devon saw Gavin's Jeep ragtop there and bolted out to greet his brother just as Gavin emerged from the side door of the house.

"Twinkie!" Devon hooted, rushing to greet his brother. "You drove here to see me graduate!"

"No way I'd miss it, Bro," Gavin grimaced in the suffocating crush of Devon's embrace.

"You gonna make us an amazing dinner tonight, Gav? I have to go back to the dorm after that. All the crazy shit starts at eight tomorrow morning, for crissake."

"What time do we need to be there?"

"It's complicated. Let's talk about it with Dad and Mom over dinner."

"Okay, I'll help take your boxes in and you can help me with the meal."

"Don't try to make me into Julia Child, baby brother."

Gavin laughed and gave his brother a playful punch to his shoulder. He considered how much more pleasant things seemed with Devon than they were just a few years earlier. Going to different schools in different states may have been the best decision he ever made.

Or maybe Devon was just showing the charming, manipulative side of his narcissism now, Gavin reminded himself.

Sitting around the dining room table digging into arugula salad, glazed salmon and truffle pasta with grilled asparagus, Gavin thought it almost felt like they were a normal family. He emptied the last of the dry Riesling into everyone's glasses and served the chocolate ganache soufflé cake he'd prepared for dessert. But he couldn't help being privately wary, expecting the old humiliation and abuse to show up any minute.

"Well, Twinkie, at least I know you won't be upstaging me tomorrow, delivering the valedictorian speech."

Gavin rolled his eyes. There it was. For a moment he'd hoped things could actually be different. Colleen's eyes took a subtle roll, too.

"But Devon doesn't need to be a valedictorian in order to take over the DiMasi Liquor business," Tony said. "Right, Dev?"

"Yes, Dad," Devon smiled. "And some of the connections I've made at Harvard are going to be a big help, too."

"Gavin, could you take Devon back to his dorm tonight?" Colleen asked. "I'm sure you two have a lot to catch up on."

"And we can have a drink in the Square before you drive back home," Devon chimed in.

"But first, let's talk about the logistics for tomorrow," Tony began. "Parking will be impossible, so I'll park at Fresh Pond and we'll take the 'T' in."

"What time should we plan on being there, Devon?" Colleen asked.

"The first ceremony—when the president awards the degrees like a mass blessing—doesn't start till quarter of ten. But your tickets don't come with a seat assignment—just a section, so unless you want to take binoculars, you might want to get there early."

"Where exactly do we go in?" Gavin asked.

"Probably the same as when Mom got her PhD," Devon assumed. Colleen's parents were the only family members who had attended that ceremony six years ago. "You enter at Gate D on Mass Ave., between the two long Wigglesworth buildings. There'll be signs. You can't miss it. The big ceremony is set up in the Yard, between the Widener Library and Memorial Church. I gave Dad a map. The section where Dunster House seniors sit is directly in front of the stage, on the left side of the center aisle, so if you get there really early, you'll be seated in the section right behind us. The gates open at quarter of seven, and all guests have to be in their seats by eight-thirty because the big procession thing starts then. So you can watch all that before the ceremony. Seniors don't come in till around nine."

"Wow," Gavin whistled. "Maybe we should just pitch our tents there tonight!"

"Don't laugh, little brother. All the hotels in a twenty-mile radius were fully booked as much as a year ago. And the thing with the president throwing holy water at everyone is only the start. To get your actual diploma, you then have to go to your residence house—Dunster in my case—for lunch and *that* ceremony. And finally, if you have an ounce of tolerance left—which I will NOT—there's the afternoon thing where they give out medals and listen to the commencement speaker—some economist this year that no one has ever heard of. I just want to bolt after I get my diploma."

On the drive into Cambridge and later over drinks at Russell House Tavern, the brothers—mostly Devon—talked.

"Hey, Gav, I can't wait for you to get out of that cooking school up in New York."

"Culinary Institute."

"Whatever. Good thing I'm taking over Dad's business."

"The whole thing, right away?"

"Well, not right away. But soon. And I want you to join me."

"Doing what?"

"I know they're teaching you all about wine in your school. You can recommend what wines I should be stocking in my premier stores, and the lower-price wines in my other locations. I bet with your CIA connection you can get big discounts for me."

"I wouldn't bet on that."

"And you can open a restaurant here in the North End, or maybe some other town near Boston, and my business can supply the liquor. And there are other things we can do to make a ton of money."

"Like what?"

"There are ways to move goods around."

"That sounds vague."

"Well, come join me and I can explain all the details."

"That doesn't fit with my plans, Dev. I already have offers from three chefs who own restaurants in Manhattan, to come work for them."

"As chef?"

"Sous Chef to start—I'm flattered they aren't expecting me to start as line cook. But no one can expect to be Executive Chef right out of the gate."

"But see, if you opened a restaurant here—I can get Dad to back you—you can be your own Executive Chef right away!"

"That isn't really how it works in this business, Dev."

"Well, I like my business better. I bet I'll make a whole lot more money than you do, with your cooking and baking thing."

"While you're wheeling and dealing your way into trouble."

Devon paused, staring at his brother.

"I wasn't born yesterday, Dev. Y'know, that crazy shit operates in New York, too, but I'm not playing. Ever."

At five-thirty the next morning, Tony stormed around the house, determined to be the first parent at the ceremony. He rushed Colleen and Gavin out to the car and drove too fast down Mass Pike while calling on his new Nokia 3110 to coordinate meeting his father and brothers at the gate at six-thirty. He parked at the Fresh Pond garage, they all caught the Red line into the Square and arrived exactly on time. One of the first twenty people in line at the gate.

Gavin was still rubbing sleep out of his eyes when they sat down in the uncomfortable folding chairs. Colleen had taken an oversized purse with her and pulled out breakfast bars and water for the group. As a faculty member, her father was given a reserved seat in the F section, so could afford to arrive not so early. Her mother joined Colleen and the rest of the family in the front of the section for seniors' guests, right behind the Dunster House section.

Tony, his father, and two brothers sat out the wait, restlessly fidgeting in their seats. They all took turns using the toilet facilities. Around eight-thirty, after alumni came in, masters level graduates began arriving in stately procession, with the University Band playing in the background. All the grads had colorful—predominately red—adornments in hoods, scarves, shawls, trim, or tassels. Colleen whispered to Gavin, "The various colors and add-ons to the robes signify certain grad schools or honors. You need a decoding ring to figure it all out."

And then the procession continued, where everyone was wearing only black robes with no adornments. "Now the seniors are coming in. Devon should be in this group," Colleen whispered. They watched as one after another senior traipsed in, settling into the sections in front of them. Then they saw Devon, his curly red hair sticking out from under his mortarboard cap, which perched rakishly back on his head. He was weaving a bit out of line from the rest and leaving a gap behind the person in front of him. "I think Devon may have partied a little too much last night," Colleen murmured, hoping that was all he'd done. Gavin grimaced and nodded.

Once the processions were complete and everyone was seated, after a few student orator speeches, the Provost and Deans introduced each college's masters or doctorate programs and then the senior class, by House. After each group was announced, President Rudenstine officially conferred relevant degrees *en masse* to the graduates of each group. There could be no jubilant throwing of caps in the air at this point. The graduates next had to proceed to their various Halls and Houses to endure yet more speeches, after which they would each be called to receive his or her diploma and finally all have lunch with families and guests.

The day was overcast and humid. The DiMasi and O'Malley group made their way out of the Yard and proceeded slowly along with clusters of other families to Dunster House, ordinarily just a few minutes' walk. Tents were set up in the Dunster courtyard for the occasion. The graduating seniors who lived in this House all gathered in chatting groups, the excitement and relief apparent in their energetic laughter. Gavin spotted Devon standing alone, with no one around him, glowering into the clusters of his fellow graduates and jutting his chin up as if he were above all the pageantry. The Dean called out to everyone to find their seats—seniors in their alphabetically ordered front rows and guests behind, at tables assigned by graduates' names, where they would later enjoy lunch.

After a blessedly short speech, the Dean of Dunster House announced the awarding of diplomas. The graduating seniors filed out of their rows and lined up adjacent to the stage. Gavin noticed that Devon seemed distracted, fidgeting, shifting from one foot to the other. As the graduates' names were called one by one, they stepped up onto the stage to receive their diploma and shake the Dean's hand, frequently to applause and cheers from their family. Reactions and demeanor varied among the graduating seniors. Some fairly danced across the stage to accept their diploma, beaming wide, arms raised in victory, a few literally jumped for joy, and one young man cartwheeled off the stage, diploma in hand. When Devon's name was called, at first he didn't respond. The classmate behind him gave a nudge and he moved forward, finally mounting the three steps. He caught his toe on the last one and nearly took a tumble, but righted himself before reaching the Dean's podium. Gavin stiffened, fearing the worst. Devon accepted his diploma but didn't shake the Dean's hand. It was unclear whether that was intentional or simply negligent distraction. As he began to exit the stage, he collapsed. He didn't trip, miss a step or fall. He just dropped like a felled tree, and the momentum of his fall sent him over onto the ground in front of the stage, snagging bunting along the way.

Everyone froze in motionless concern, like a stopped movie frame. Although his fellow classmates and many in the audience understood the cause of his fall and looked away in embarrassment, no one moved to help him. Except Gavin, who had jumped up, running, while Devon was still airborne.

As Gavin pulled Devon up and dragged him to their family's table, Tony waved off the concerned gazes of the crowd with a resigned shrug. He didn't want anyone calling 911 for an ambulance. Colleen assessed Devon's condition. He was semi-conscious and mumbling. Clearly under the influence of something, but she wasn't certain exactly what at the time. She smelled alcohol but thought there must have been something else, too. Tony knew there could be legal problems if drugs were involved. "Do you think he'll be all right if we just take him home and let him sleep it off?" he whispered.

"I think so," Colleen said, below a deeply furrowed worry.

Tony and Gavin lift-walked Devon out to Memorial Drive and waved down a taxi. Colleen monitored his condition in the back seat, all the way to Wellesley.

It was probably the longest twelve-mile cab ride ever. By the time the family arrived in Wellesley, Devon had become totally dead weight. Tony and Gavin together had difficulty dragging him into the house.

"Don't take him up to his room," Colleen said. "I have to keep checking on him. Take off his robe and shoes and put him on the family room sofa, where I can keep an eye on him in case he aspirates vomit."

———————

It was a sleepless night for Colleen, while Tony snored upstairs. Devon gurgled on the sofa and became incontinent in his stupor. Gavin found a small plastic bag with white powdery residue in his brother's pocket and gave it to his mother, for her office to analyze. After that, he stayed to keep her company, snoozing sporadically in the recliner chair.

Devon didn't awaken until after noon the next day.

"Well, well," Tony greeted him. "I guess the Big Man On Campus must have been the life of the party, eh son?"

"Oh, yeah," Devon cracked a grin below drooping eyes and puffed out his chest. "All my friends kept giving me drinks, toasting me. That's what happens when you're the leader of the class, the smartest of the bunch."

"So tomorrow let's talk about how you're going to use your Harvard education to make my business even more successful."

"It's my business now, Dad." Devon turned to go to his bedroom.

"Not so fast, smart ass," Tony said. "You haven't proven yourself yet."

"And we need to talk about your drug use, Devon," Colleen said. "You're flirting with danger."

But Devon wasn't listening. He collided with his brother as he rounded the corner.

"Twinkie!" he said, with a haughty tip of his chin. "Now that I'm a Harvard alum, when are you going to join me in my business?"

"What kinds of shit did you take, you ignorant druggie?" Gavin growled in Devon's ear. "You embarrassed yourself and your family yesterday, and almost OD'd."

19.

GAVIN'S GRADUATION FROM THE CULINARY INSTI-
tute was scheduled for August 3, at the culmination of his
fifteen-week stint at CIA's farm-to-table American Bounty
Restaurant on the edge of campus. He was full of competing
emotions as he anticipated the event. Relief, satisfaction, and
a sense of pride to have completed this phase of his journey
toward attaining his goal. Excitement to begin working as
Sous Chef at Del Posto in Manhattan and that he'd be living
with Katie in the New York apartment they'd chosen in June.
But he was also feeling anxious about seeing his father and
Devon, wondering whether there would be conflict or tension
as was so often the case.

That time of year in Hyde Park was typically miserable at
CIA, situated on the banks of the Hudson. Temperatures
ranged in the high 80s, raising the surface temperature of the
river and resulting in oppressive humidity. The air was still,
with no hint of breeze. Flies buzzed languorously as if they
were sedated. The usual clean fresh scents from densely
wooded surrounding areas curdled like overcooked sauce.

Katie called Gavin from Manhattan the night before his
graduation. "I can't wait to see you, Gav! I'm driving up in a
rental car first thing in the morning."

"I can't wait to see you too, Kat!" he gushed. "It's about a two-and-a-half-hour drive, so you'll probably be early. I can show you around the campus. Did you know there's an old Jesuit cemetery here? They had the property before CIA bought it."

"So it's holy ground, is it?" Katie teased. "Where should I park?"

"They're supposed to have signs for where to park for graduation. Call me when you get here and I'll come walk you to Pick-Herndon. I have all my stuff packed in boxes..."

"So we'll finally be together in our apartment!"

"Ah, but we have a stop on the way back—I've arranged a special diversion for us!"

"Ooo...can you give me a hint? Should I wear anything special?"

"No hints! And you don't need to wear anything special. You're beautiful no matter what you wear."

"Aww...You sure know how to flatter a girl. What time do you expect your family?"

"My dad's driving the whole gang in an eight-passenger Toyota Previa he borrowed, so it'll probably be a challenge to get them all rounded up, especially Devon. If they make it here by doors opening at two-thirty, I'll be surprised." Gavin paused. The more he thought about that undertaking, the more anxious he became. "CIA isn't a big deal to my father, like Harvard."

"Well, I think it's a huge deal, Gav. And my mother does too—she sends her love. She really wishes she could come..."

"How is she doing with her home health aide?"

"Hanging in there...for now."

"I want to go see her as soon as I get settled at Del Posto. Oh, by the way, Tray said to tell you hi. He's in police academy training so he can't come today."

"How was his graduation?"

"Huge. Long. And pouring rain. But Tray earned cum

laude!"

"That's awesome. That's hard for a guy on football scholarship. The practices and games can be so exhausting and time-consuming, it's a wonder any of them have time to study."

"Tray's always been so smart," Gavin said. "And driven. Remember he was named MVP in his junior year when UMass won Division championship? That was amazing!"

"And he still isn't resting for a minute, training to get on the police force."

"Yeah, he'll probably be Chief in a year or two, knowing him," Gavin said. "Or head of the FBI! I'm really lucky to have a friend like Tray."

"Yeah, considering..."

The memory of that birthday night six years ago brought Gavin's mood thudding to a stop. "Oh wow, you have to get to bed if you're getting up early in the morning. Make sure you get a good night's sleep, and drive carefully tomorrow! No big rush. I love you, Kat."

"I love you too, Gav. Good night. See you tomorrow!"

———

Katie arrived a little before ten the next morning, looking fresh in a long gauzy white sleeveless dress that was perfect for the weather. Gavin nearly dissolved upon seeing her.

On this morning of graduation, the air was liquid. Dark clouds were visible on the distant horizon, but the sun was still beating down ferociously. Whereas most graduating college students don long gowns and mortarboard caps, CIA was distinctively different. Here, white-jacketed seniors walked across campus from their residence houses to Roth Hall, where they would receive their diplomas in air-conditioned comfort. Drenched in perspiration, they carried their pleated white chef's hats.

As each member of the graduating class donned their hats and filed into the cavernous dining hall of Roth, many turned their heads to the guest section to look for family and friends. Which created a humorous choreography resembling cat-in-the-hat caricatures, white foot-tall stovepipes bobbing atop varying heights of graduates. Gavin was one of the tallest in his class. When his head spun around to look for his family, his hat waved like a semaphore above the class.

He saw his mother seated next to Katie, with Grandma and Grandpa O'Malley, who had funded his tuition at CIA after Tony blew up when Gavin left Harvard. Gavin scanned the crowd. He didn't see his father or Devon. Katie caught his eye and touched two fingers to her puckered lips. A kiss, above which her blue eyes telegraphed comforting regret.

The commencement ceremony wasn't as formal or lengthy as Devon's had been at Harvard, but Gavin suffered through each minute nevertheless. Nothing else seemed to matter to him without knowing where his father and brother were. He couldn't bask in the honor of graduating summa cum laude, nor of being the first CIA student to earn the hat trick of awards: Julius Wile Academic Achievement, Jacob Rosenthal Leadership, and President's Humanities. He kept looking into the rows of guests, desperately seeking recognition and approval from the two people who'd denied him that all his life.

When the program ended, Gavin waded through the crowd to his mother and Katie. "What happened to Dad?" he blurted before Colleen could open her mouth to speak.

"Your father would be so proud of you, Gavin," she said. "But he and Devon had an emergency at the main store. He really wanted to be here."

Gavin didn't know whether to buy that story, at least not its critical urgency that would prevent his father from coming today. He shrugged, trying to show dismissal of his father's and brother's absence, as if it weren't important. But he retreated into an internal dialogue, reminding himself of what Dr. Pedersen had always told him. *Adjust your expectations. You are the only one hurt when other people don't live up to your expectations. It's their issue and it doesn't have anything to do with your worth, your value.* He tried to embrace that mantra, with limited success.

Katie seemed to read his mind. "Whether they're here or not doesn't take away from your achievement, Gav," she whispered into his ear as she embraced him. "You're awesome, and I love you."

Gavin swallowed the lump in his throat and tried to look on the bright side: at least the day wasn't marred by a scene from his dad or Devon. "I'm just glad you could be here," he said. "Mom, I've made reservations for all of us at American Bounty, so we can spend time together over a great meal before you have to drive back."

"Gavin has worked with the chef and staff there," Katie added. "So he'll make sure the meal is extra special."

Gavin took his guests on a tour through the pristine, white-tiled kitchen, bustling with student interns, staff and chefs, all white-coated with tall white pleated chef's hats. Several of those working paused to greet and congratulate him before he led his family to show off the vast wine storage area behind glass. They then settled into plush chairs surrounded by tall arched windows under elaborate chandeliers hanging from the ultra-high ceiling. After enjoying an exquisite gourmet meal, Gavin and Katie escorted Colleen and her parents to their car. His mother pulled him aside. "Gavin dear, I'm so sorry your father and brother didn't come today," she spoke low. "Things are a little rocky at home."

Gavin stiffened, alert with immediate concern. "Are you okay, Mom?" he asked. "Should I come home to help you? What's going on?"

"It's Devon," she murmured. "I think he has a serious drug problem."

"Oh, shit." Gavin paused, taking a deep breath and shaking his head. Devon's issues always managed to encroach on every DiMasi family scene, even remotely. "But we could see that happening."

"And I think he's getting mixed up with the wrong crowd in Boston."

"Crap!" Gavin almost punched the air. "I warned him about that!"

"Which would make it all the more appealing to him, of course."

"Yeah, I should know that by now." He crossed his arms tightly across his chest and turned, poised to stomp and pace, then turned back to his mother with anguish distorting his grim mouth.

"Well, don't you worry," Colleen made an effort to assure him. "We're trying to handle it, and if anything disastrous happens, we'll let you know." She rubbed her son's back. "You just move forward with your life, which is great, and will be wonderful."

———

Katie had dropped off her car at the Hyde Park rental location before the commencement ceremony, and now all Gavin's boxes were loaded into his Jeep. Gavin watched the campus recede in the rearview mirror as he turned south onto Route Nine toward Poughkeepsie. A diverse tangle of emotions vied for prominence in his head. But at least he and Katie were on their way to a future together.

Again, Katie read his mind. "I'm so glad we're together, Gav. And it's all going to be good, regardless of what's in the past."

He reached his hand over and squeezed her thigh. "I love you too, Kat. I don't know what I'd do without you."

"So where are you taking me—this 'special diversion' you

teased me with?"

"You'll see. We'll be there in less than half an hour." The Hudson River sparkled below them as they crossed over the Mid-Hudson Bridge. Twenty minutes later, Gavin turned into a side road on the outskirts of Marlboro, New York, then left at a sign reading 'Benmarl Winery.'

Katie squealed with delight. "Oh, so after you dined me, you're now going to wine me, then have your way with me!"

"I can only hope."

"You won't have to twist my arm, big guy."

Benmarl was one of the oldest wineries in the country, its rustic thirty-seven acres overlooking the Hudson River Valley. It was one of many wineries that supplied wines to CIA, so when Gavin requested they stay open a little later that evening, they were happy to oblige. He and Katie had the place to themselves. The owners gave them a private tour of the vineyards and barrel rooms, and finally provided cheeses and bread as they sat at an outside table with a bottle of cabernet franc, enjoying the waning light of the day.

"This is so nice, Gav," Katie said, clasping his hand. She then became pensive. "Y'know, I never developed many really close friendships like you have with Tray. Probably because I was so busy, so focused on taking care of my mother. She's actually my best friend. I don't know what I'd do without her."

"I know it's hard to think about, Kat."

"You're right. I guess I'm just trying to pretend she'll go on forever, but of course pretending won't stop the inevitable."

"I'll always be here for you," Gavin said. "We'll build a life together, and new phases of your life—relationships and friendships—will evolve for you. And for us."

"Yes." Katie looked into Gavin's eyes, clinking her glass to his. "We're in this together."

As they were taking the last sip of wine from their glasses and corking the bottle to begin their drive into Manhattan, Katie's cell phone rang.

"Yes, this is she....Margaret Angela Goodwin, yes..." Katie's face went pale and her shoulders dropped.

"Katie?" Gavin rushed to hold her up.

"That was the hospital. My mother has to go on dialysis..."

20.

THE TELEPHONE ON TONY'S SIDE OF THE BED rang several times before he roused sufficiently to answer it. His voice was the groggy mumble of someone who'd had too much bourbon the night before. It was almost four in the morning. Mass General was calling.

Devon had been in an accident.

"*Déjà vu* all over again," Tony muttered the iconic Yogi Berra malapropism as he drove with Colleen to Boston. When they arrived at the hospital, they were relieved to learn that Devon was not in the ICU, and that his injuries were not severe. Beeps and hums of vital signs monitors emanated from patients' rooms as their heels clicked through the halls to Devon's room. There was a police officer standing outside his room, who stopped them and asked for identification.

"What's the big deal, buddy? I just want to see my son," Tony challenged.

At this point a young doctor appeared. He looked as if he were only sixteen years old, just beginning to shave. "Are you the patient's family?" he asked in a scratchy tenor.

"Yes," Colleen said. "Can you tell us something about our son's condition?"

"And why this guy is here," Tony growled, flipping his

thumb toward the policeman.

"I was part of the team that triaged your son when he came into the ER. I'm Dr. Carlson," he said, extending his hand. "Your son is not awake yet, but his injuries are only minor, not the cause of his unconsciousness."

Tony was silent, anticipating more information. Waiting for the other shoe to drop.

"What more can you tell us?" Colleen prodded.

"I can tell you he will recover physically," the doctor said. "But you'll need to speak with law enforcement for other details."

Tony turned away and walked a short distance down the hall, away from the doctor and police officer. He pulled out his cell phone and called one of his friends on the Boston police force. "Hey, Ralph, Tony DiMasi. Sorry to wake you." Pause. "Yeah, I'm at Mass General. Devon's been in some kind of accident, and there's a Boston Cop outside his room. Can you find out what's going on?"

Tony and Colleen sat and paced in the drab windowless waiting room. Then Colleen spotted the ER Chief leading an entourage of interns and residents through on morning rounds. She pulled Tony up and the two of them trailed the parade at a respectful distance, hovering outside Devon's room. They heard diagnostic snippets, perking up at "cocaine".

"I knew it," Tony growled. "He's using again." He turned away.

"But that alone wouldn't explain the police detail," Colleen noted.

Tony's cell phone rang. He walked down the hall to take the call.

"Hey, Tony. Ralph here."

"What did you find out?"

"Your son was found unconscious behind the wheel of his car, crashed into a utility pole."

"But why the fuzz?"

"They found a couple kilos of coke in his trunk. And an unregistered .45 under the seat."

"Fuck."

"So they're going to charge him with trafficking, minimally dealing. And illegal possession of a weapon."

"Jesus." Tony rubbed his head, eyes closed tight. After a moment he exhaled and whispered, "What are our options?"

"One sure way to stay out of jail on this, is to give up his supplier."

"You know he can't do that. He'd be dead in a week."

"But you could get your kid to tell you and then you tell me," Ralph said, his voice smooth as silk. "We'd take the guy down, out of the way, and it wouldn't have any connection to you or your kid. Trust me."

Tony knew from experience that whenever anyone urged "trust me" they were not to be trusted. He wasn't sure what Ralph's game was, but he knew not to trust him now. Or ever again.

"Well, I'm not sure Devon even knows the real name of whoever he got the stuff from," Tony said. "I'll ask him when he wakes up and let you know."

"It could be his only way to avoid time," Ralph said,

Tony thanked Ralph and walked back to Colleen. "It's bad. Not only was he under the influence, but he had a ton of the shit in his trunk and a gun with him. Unregistered." Tony's mouth tightened as he shook his head. "So that's why the cop is here. They'll arrest him when he wakes up. And now that fucker Ralph Patrone's trying to play some kind of angle."

"What do you mean?"

"He was trying to get me to spill the name of our wonder boy's supplier, which would make Devon a target. So he's either trying to get a medal for bringing in a big fish, or he'll try to gain favor with the mob by ratting on Devon."

"So what're we going to do?" Colleen asked. She spoke low so the policeman wouldn't hear. "I don't think jail would be good for him at all. But this is his first actual arrest, so given his prior hospitalization, maybe we could convince a judge to put him in rehab."

"Well you're the fucking shrink. Go find the best place that'll take him," Tony mumbled, resigned. "And fix the damn kid."

"I'll make some calls. But Tony, we've known this for a few years," Colleen said. She shook her head, "You've always blown it off, like it's just a rite of passage for kids to play around with drugs."

"Well, you're just a woman," Tony said. "Most boys and young men go through those phases on the way to growing up."

"But ignoring the fact that Devon has a problem has only reinforced his belief that it's okay, that he's unique and entitled. Meantime it's become a bigger, more entrenched problem."

"Just shut the fuck up and do it," Tony snapped. He abruptly stood and walked away.

———————

A short time later, Devon emerged from his drug-induced twilight screaming and flailing. "NO!" he shouted, his eyes wide with fear, as if the Grim Reaper were wielding the scythe of death at his neck. "That's not true—don't you call me a phony, and don't walk away from me! You'll be sorry—I'm in charge here, the expert—the real deal. I can make you or break you—I know everything!"

Like a poorly coordinated swat team, medical personnel, Devon's parents, and police rushed into Devon's hospital room, interrupting his diatribe. "What're you doing here?" Devon's head whipped from side to side, confused and frightened by so many people closing in on him. He popped up in his bed, poised to defend against his detractors.

———

Tony didn't even have to pay someone off to get his favorite son sentenced to rehab for six months followed by probation. Devon's bizarre behavior in the hospital, history of mental health disorders and drug use were sufficiently overwhelming evidence for the judge to make that ruling.

Tony and Colleen drove in complete silence to the facility in Quincy, with Devon huddled in the back seat of the car. Arms crossed tightly across his chest, a deep scowl creasing his forehead, he thrust his lower lip out like a pouting child. The car drove through a leafy suburban neighborhood and turned down a neat residential road, slowing as it approached a stately white clapboard colonial perched on a grassy knoll adorned with well-manicured landscaping. Its five long windows on the second floor and four windows and door on the first floor were all flanked by black shutters like expressive eyebrows. The four small windows of the attic scrunched together like a random afterthought in a dormer that jutted from its slate gambrel roof. One window was missing a shutter. The structure looked refined, yet comfortably lived in. Tranquil. Peaceful.

Devon sat up, looking around. He smiled. "...piece of cake," he muttered under his breath.

———

Anger, worry, resentment, fear, and an inexplicable guilt churned in Gavin as he paced in the pristine waiting room. Each chair arranged in perfect geometric alignment. Plastic floral arrangement on a dust-free table. A faint scent of Lysol toggled memories of hospital and another pacing, in the surgical unit the night of Devon's accident on their sixteenth birthday. A stark poster on a white wall exhorted, "Appreciate

Those Who Don't Give Up On You."

And that was why Gavin was there, instead of creating Michelin-grade gourmet delights in his Manhattan restaurant. Tony had called last week, demanding that he come help his brother.

Then his mother had come on the line and pleaded. "He'll listen to you, Gavin."

"I'm not so sure about that, Mom."

"I think this is a turning point, sweetie," Colleen whispered. "We talked to his doctors, and they believe that Devon's multiple accidents, along with his substance abuse, may have resulted in irreversible epigenetic alterations."

Gavin searched his memory. He knew his mother had mentioned that before...something about how environment and lifestyle choices can trigger changes in someone's chemical infrastructure—an epigenome—that switches genes on and off. Changes that would make his twin's identical DNA function differently. "What would that do, Mom? I mean, how would that affect him?"

"It's unpredictable, and unique to each person. I just hope it doesn't escalate his Narcissism to Antisocial Personality Disorder, where the behavioral symptoms are much more dangerous."

Gavin didn't want to imagine how bad that could be, but he agreed to go see his brother. He doubted whether Devon would appreciate his mission. An absolute belief in his own perfection resisted any need for help.

But Gavin was there to try. A mechanical whir and click sounded from behind the interior door to the room before it opened. Devon walked in, followed by a young woman in baggy pants and a black long-sleeved t-shirt bearing the facility's logo. Devon sauntered toward Gavin with the confident air of being in charge.

"Hey, Twinkie," Devon's face opened to a conspiratorial grin. "I bet you thought I'd be in leg irons and handcuffs," he drawled, and threw a chokehold around his brother's neck. Gavin pulled away.

"I'll leave you two here," the woman said. "I'm sure you have a lot to catch up on. Visiting hours are over at five. Feel free to help yourselves to water from the case over there in the corner." Then with a grim smile, "And let's be sure the right twin leaves at five."

After she'd gone, Gavin noticed there was an obvious two-way mirror on the wall.

Devon plopped onto one of the sofas and put his feet on the coffee table in front of it. Gavin sat stiffly in an adjoining chair. "How are you doing here, Dev?" he began, thinking that was a pretty lame way to begin a conversation with his brother in a drug rehab facility.

"Just super, Little Brother! I've got a cool gig going on here." He stretched and leaned back, clasping his hands behind his head. As if he were posing for a celebrity photo-op.

"Gig?" Gavin was confused. "You mean therapy?"

"Oh, get real, Twinkie. I don't need *therapy*."

"Yeah, so why are you here?"

"Twinkie, Twinkie. You're so naïve. This is my 'get-out-of-jail free' card."

"Jail?" Gavin's breath deflated, along with any hope that his brother might finally turn his life around. "What'd you do this time?"

"Nothing serious," Devon scoffed. "Some people just don't have a sense of humor." He slapped his thigh and emitted a roaring guffaw.

Gavin realized nothing had changed. He studied the mirror, wondering whether anyone was observing on the other side.

Devon sat up, leaned toward Gavin and whispered, "The idiots in this place—and I don't mean just the patients—are so desperate for their dope that I'm making a ton of money real easy here, scratching their itch."

"And *your* itch, too, Dev?" Gavin mumbled, shaking his head. He didn't want to hear any more. He suspected Uncle Marco was somehow involved in his brother's supply chain, just as he had been when Devon was hospitalized after his car accident. He slammed his hands onto the arms of his chair and stood, in a single propelled motion. He turned to the mirror, as if to engage with whomever was on the other side. "You asshole," he growled. "Dad and Mom are so worried about you, they begged me to leave my restaurant and drive here from New York to support you. Give you some encouragement..."

"Aww, Twinkie," Devon purred. "And I'm so glad you came."

"But you don't need any 'support,' do you?" Gavin turned on his heel to glower at his twin. "This is like a Las Vegas vacation for you, playing craps, winning some, risking everything."

Devon smirked, shaking his head. "But I *am* a winner, Gav. That's what I was born to be."

"Don't kid yourself, Devon." Gavin returned to his chair, poised over it, as if undecided whether to sit or flee. "If you keep doing these things—playing with fire—sooner or later you're going to get burned. Or worse."

Devon remained in his preening pose, indifferent.

Gavin sat in a crouch, his gaze bent on his brother. "Devon, you're a pain in my ass, but you're my brother. I don't want to see you all fucked up. Or dead. Please don't assume you're invincible."

For a brief nanosecond, a small cloud of vulnerability passed over Devon's face. And then it was gone. "Well, I've made a lot of friends here. Even got a girlfriend, sort of. So don't worry about me, Little Brother."

21.

GAVIN SAT DOWN ON THE PEW BESIDE HIS MOTHER. He could see she was worried. That twitch in her right cheek above her jaw was a sure sign her TMJ was flaring up. The next day, July 15. was a big day: Devon's wedding. On his and Gavin's twenty-third birthday. But on that day it was all about Devon.

"People will be coming for the rehearsal in a few minutes, Mom. Is there something wrong, or are you just nervous?" Gavin peered into Colleen's face, his hand on her shoulder, seeking eye contact.

"Your father is all worked up about this," she said, biting her lip and looking down. "I don't know whether to expect a mild tremor or a total earthquake."

Gavin stared up at the stained-glass windows of St. John The Evangelist Church, where the late afternoon sun had set the bright colors of the Virgin Mary aglow. Her eyes bored into him.

"Why? Are you afraid he might make a scene?" Gavin asked.

Colleen nodded. "Depends, I suppose."

"On how much he's had to drink?"

"Well, yes," she sighed. "That's tonight. And tomorrow

could be even worse." Colleen turned to her son. "I really appreciate that you're here, Gavin. I know things haven't been good between you and Devon. Or your father, for that matter. Since you've been away in New York, you haven't had to deal with all the drama that's been going on."

Gavin stiffened. "What drama, Mom? Are you okay?"

"Oh, not that drama, Dear." Colleen smiled and patted Gavin's hand. She took a long inhale and exhale, as if gathering strength to explain. "This sounds so old-world, but it's almost as if Devon's marriage has been 'arranged,'" she said, air-quoting. "Devon met Maria in rehab, and then Tony found out she's Frank Rizzo's daughter—Tommy's kid sister."

Gavin looked completely baffled. "Who are they?"

"The Rizzo family. Frank grew up with your dad in the North End, and his son Tommy over in Charlestown is around Devon's age. Their liquor business competes with your dad's business. And it isn't polite competition, if you know what I mean," Colleen raised one eyebrow with a meaningful glance. "Now that Devon's taking over your dad's business, the competition has gotten pretty rancorous. Sort of like the Hatfields and McCoys."

"Macho against macho."

"Right. So your dad started pressuring Devon to court Maria so he could...well, I guess, hold all the aces. A month later, they're engaged and two months after that, here's the wedding. In *Wellesley* instead of the North End in St. Leonard's. And the reception at the *Wellesley Country Club*, for god's sake. How much more elitist could it get?"

Gavin recalled what his mother had told him about St. Leonard's, where his father had grown up. This didn't make sense. "Doesn't the bride's family decide where the wedding should be, because they pay for it?" Gavin mused. "So did *they* want to have it here? If Dad muscled them into it, that would be a real poke in their family's eye," he grimaced, shaking his head. "Like 'look at me, here in *Wellesley*, you low-life rubes.'"

"I'm not sure. You know your father doesn't consult me on these things. I suspect he has something on Frank, but I don't know what exactly. But I am sure of one thing. It won't be the last volley between them."

Gavin's head snapped to attention. "You mean Rizzo may try to get back at Dad in the future?" He stood and began pacing across the chancel. "Maybe the two families could merge their liquor businesses?" Gavin wondered. "Like, keep your friends close and your enemies even closer?"

Colleen let out a snort. "Not a chance. From what I've picked up here and there, I think Frank Rizzo might have bullied your father when they were kids in the North End. Of course Tony would never admit it. And certainly never forgive."

"Y'know, if the wedding had been in St. Leonard's—where Dad and the Rizzos grew up, that would put everyone on the same level, the same playing field."

Colleen almost laughed. "You know your dad and Devon will never settle for being on the same level with anyone."

"But this way, the rivalry and resentment are magnified. It sounds like a recipe for disaster."

"I just hope no one lights a match."

They were silent, just picturing how bad things could get. Gavin was incredulous. All this...what—tribalism? It was beyond his understanding.

"Well, we just need to brace ourselves for whatever happens," Colleen sighed and stood. She walked into the aisle and began aimlessly pacing, fidgeting with her rosary.

"Dad's coming, isn't he?"

"I'm guessing he'll be late on purpose," Colleen smiled. "Wait till after the Rizzo clan gets here, so he can make a grand entrance."

Gavin rolled his eyes at how transparent his father's showmanship was. Then as he gazed at the large golden crucifix hanging from the majestic lancet arches framing the apse, he wondered if there would ever be peace in his family. Although he wasn't very religious, he grew up here and had always felt small in this place. Humbled. But today he only felt disquiet as he noticed the first installations of white ribbons in the grand hundred-year-old church.

"Looks like they hired an expensive wedding planner," Gavin mused.

"Oh, that's Eric's handiwork. Devon's friend," Colleen said. "He's quite creative. By tomorrow at eleven, I'm sure there won't be a square inch of this place that isn't an over-flowing jungle of flowers, bows and all that."

Gavin looked puzzled. He'd never met Eric. For that matter, he hadn't met Maria either. "So tell me about Maria? And who's this Eric guy?"

"Maria is quiet, sort of mousy. A couple years younger than you and Devon. Had a drug problem—that's how she ended up in rehab, but seems to be okay now, I guess." Colleen shrugged. "Eric was in rehab, too. Both he and Maria worship Devon, in a fawning sort of way. I find the dynamic a bit unsettling, to be honest."

"But that's just what he needs. Or wants," Gavin grunted. "By the way, what's a 'best man' supposed to do? Devon asked me to be his best man. Well, commanded, more than asked. But I don't really know what I'm supposed to do."

"That's what the rehearsal is for." Colleen said. "The Best Man usually holds the bride's wedding ring in his pocket and hands it to the groom at a specific prompt in the ceremony. I'm sure Devon will make everything clear."

"I hope I don't have any holes in my pockets."

"By the way, did Katie drive here with you from Man-hattan?"

"Yes, I dropped her off at her mother's for a visit. She'll join us at the dinner, providing her mother isn't doing any worse than expected."

"When are you two going to tie the knot?"

"Well, now that Devon has managed to do it first, Katie and I are free to get married without him resenting us," Gavin smiled. "Of course he'll still manage to make it all about him. So maybe we'll elope. But we're still young. No reason to rush it."

Just then the double doors behind them banged open, sending an echo down the nave and ushering in three men with slicked-back hair in leather jackets. Gavin noticed they all seemed to have the same swaggering strut as his father. *Maybe that's a thing in the North End.* The oldest of the trio had a lined face as leathery as his tailored jacket, and about the same tawny shade. Obviously a Grecian Formula devotee, Gavin assumed he was Frank Rizzo, father of the bride. He was flanked by the two younger men in black motorcycle jackets. Gavin guessed they were the bride's brothers, one of whom was presumably Tommy. He walked up the aisle to greet them, his hand out. All three men glared at him, their hands unmoving at their sides.

"Where's my daughter?" the older man demanded.

Colleen stepped in. "Mr. Rizzo, this is Gavin, Devon's twin brother. Gavin, this is Frank Rizzo, Maria's father, and these are her brothers, Tommy and Mickie."

All three men appeared to loosen their stances slightly, but didn't proffer a handshake. "Oh," the elder Rizzo said. "When Devon said he had a twin, he didn't say it was a clone."

The man Colleen identified as Tommy mumbled, "Yeah. Freaky."

From what his mother had told him, Gavin knew this evening might be difficult, or even incendiary. He tried to lighten the mood. "I can assure you Devon and I are very different. We're mirror twins, which makes me the exact opposite of my brother," he forced a nervous laugh. He summoned the hospitality skills he'd developed in the restaurant industry and gestured down the aisle toward the chancel. "I'm sure everyone else will be here soon, won't you please join us and make yourselves comfortable? How was the traffic coming here?"

The men didn't answer, but began following Gavin and Colleen. The elder Rizzo spoke loudly, to no one in particular, "This place is nothing compared to Saint Leonard's. A real dump is what it is."

Gavin looked again at the golden crucifix ahead. Something in him felt he owed an apology to someone—God?—for Rizzo's insult. But he also knew he had to maintain peace, despite every nerve in his body so tensed that he felt like he was vibrating. "I would love to come visit Saint Leonard's, sir," he said. "I hope you can appreciate our humble little church as much as I do. My brother and I have been coming here since we were kids."

"Yeah, well, Maria and her brothers grew up in Saint Leonard's. And their mother was buried there."

"I'm sorry, sir. I hope that with your blessing, Maria and Devon's wedding here will help create some wonderful memories for them." Gavin searched the men's faces and could see he wasn't making much headway with the Rizzo family.

Luckily, the bridesmaids and groomsmen arrived soon— delivered by stretch limousine—to relieve some of the tension with their animated chatter, likely facilitated by champagne in their hotel rooms and the limo. Tony had arranged an entire floor of the stately Wellesley Inn for the party, although he and most of the guests were probably oblivious to its seminal 1860 origins. Then the doors opened again and in Devon slinked, followed by a giggling duo whom Gavin assumed were Maria and Eric. Maria was very thin, almost gaunt, with untamed straw-like brown hair. Her eyes flitted nervously. Eric was short and round, with frizzy hair that was a lighter shade of red than Devon and Gavin's. He seemed nervous and a bit fussy, as if conflicting music was swirling in his head, a pounding rap battling a waltz.

Devon had a grim look on his face, as if he were about to

undertake an unpleasant task. When he spotted Gavin, he broke away from his companions and rushed forward, sweeping his brother into a crushing hug. "Twinkie, I am *SO* glad you're here!"

The Rizzo men exchanged glances. "Twinkie?" Tommy sneered.

Gavin smiled. "Yeah, well, when we were little, Devon came up with that—a form of 'twin'-key—get it? And he's never let it go." With that, Gavin gave a playful punch to his brother's upper bicep.

"Where's Dad?" Devon asked, his eyes darting in panic.

Just then Tony made his grand entrance, trailed by his two brothers and their father. It seemed to Gavin that his father's strut was more pronounced than ever.

Colleen's face clouded over. She crossed her arms protectively across her stiffened body, shivering as if an arctic blast had entered the church.

Receding daylight through the stained-glass windows seemed to extinguish the earlier glow of the Virgin Mary, as if the sun had been eclipsed by an other-worldly object. Mary's eyes took on a frightened dullness. Gavin noticed for the first time what looked like a single tear on her cheek.

Gavin doubted that the marital cross-pollination between the Hatfields and McCoys had been as awkward and tense as this wedding between the DiMasi and Rizzo families. The rehearsal was bad enough, with Frank Rizzo glowering threateningly at the point where he practiced giving his daughter to marriage. As if he were warning Tony and Devon to never cross his daughter or his family. Then after rehearsal they were all supposed to go to dinner together, arranged by the DiMasi family. But Frank Rizzo said he and his sons couldn't stay. "We have to get back to our *business*," he said, looking pointedly at Tony. "That bullshit is for kids."

Colleen intervened. "Mr. Rizzo, I wish you would please stay for dinner," she pleaded in a low voice, up close to him and apart from everyone else, so he could save face. "It would mean so much to Maria and Devon. They need your blessing. I know we would all like them to have a happy marriage, and your presence would get it off on the right foot."

Frank Rizzo looked at Colleen. Her sincerity and lack of ulterior motives were apparent in her kind voice and face. He paused, looked at his daughter, and muttered, "I guess we could stay for a little while." He allowed Colleen to link her arm in his and lead him to the waiting limousines. "But only if I can sit next to you."

As soon as the fleet of limos arrived at Il Capriccio, a high-end Italian restaurant in Waltham, Colleen rushed into the banquet room and quickly rearranged the placement of name cards at place settings on the table.

As the crowd of young people streamed into the dining area, most went directly to the bar. Minutes later, Katie arrived to join Gavin for the dinner. The tension headache he'd developed during the rehearsal suddenly lifted at the sight of her; she was the bright spot in the evening for him. "How's your mother?" he asked.

"Not so good," she whispered. "The hospice worker was there. We'll talk about it later."

Gavin squeezed her hand in his. "I'm sorry, sweetheart. Are you up to meeting the bride and her family?"

"I think I can handle that," she said with a weak smile.

Gavin saw Maria and Eric talking together like conspirators. He held back, hesitating, then with apologies interrupted them to introduce Katie. Their responses were not what he expected. They reacted as if Katie were some sort of interloper to their closed society.

"Oh, so this is the one Devon told me about," Eric said with pursed lips, peering at Katie above his uplifted nose.

"Yeah, I guess she's the one that stole his brother from him," Maria giggled.

Gavin tried to hide his shocked discomfort by making a

joke of the situation. "Well, I guess Siamese twins have to be separated sooner or later, you think?" He forced a laugh and pulled Katie away.

"Holy shit, what the hell was that about?" he whispered.

"Whatever it was, I hope it doesn't run in her family. Otherwise don't even bother to introduce me to her father."

Frank Rizzo seemed to have been transformed by Colleen's intervention. As Gavin approached with Katie in hand, Rizzo smiled benevolently. "Young man, I can see you've chosen a mate who's just as lovely as your mother is."

"Thank you, sir," Gavin managed a smile that he hoped would mask his surprise. "Katie Goodwin, this is Mr. Frank Rizzo, Maria's father. Katie and I have known each other since high school." He purposely avoided mentioning the obvious corollary to Frank's childhood association with Tony. That would certainly have derailed the positive mood.

Frank took Katie's hand and graciously kissed it in old-world fashion. "You two take good care of each other. I hope to dance at your wedding someday."

Katie and Gavin looked at each other and laughed. "We'll look forward to that, sir," Gavin said. "I hope you and your family will enjoy the evening and the big day tomorrow."

As Gavin and Katie walked away speechless, all they managed to say—in unison—was "Wow."

It wasn't until the entire party was seated at their assigned places that Tony realized Frank Rizzo was sitting beside his wife, to her right, while he sat on her left. He gave a squint-eyed look at Colleen. She defensively hitched her tensed left shoulder, an instinctive fear coursing through her. But she was determined to keep the peace, regardless of the consequences, and immediately commandeered the proceedings by clinking her glass for attention and stood to speak, refusing to look at Tony.

"Tony and I are so glad all of Maria and Devon's family and friends could come together to honor them at this very special time in their lives," she began. "Maria, you're making not only Devon very happy but his family as well. And I hope that your family and ours will blend our lives and interests for mutual support in the many years to come. The whole will become greater than the sum of its parts. Frank Rizzo, your wonderful father, is entrusting your wellbeing to Devon, and I can promise you that Devon's family shares that honor and responsibility." She paused, looking around to everyone, including Rizzo's sons Tommy and Mickie. "I think there are many people here tonight who'd like to say a few words and toast your union. Let's start with your father. I know he's very proud of you." She turned to Frank.

As Colleen sat, she could feel the hostility emanating from Tony like heat from a furnace.

Frank took his time to stand, while everyone waited in silence. "Y'know, the measure of a man can usually be seen in his family. Devon and Maria had a sort of whirlwind courtship, so we're only now getting to know Devon's family. And if his mother," he gestured to Colleen, "and his brother," nodding to Gavin, "are any indication, then my daughter is in good hands."

Colleen noticed that Frank didn't mention Tony.

Frank continued. "Sometimes the heads of families have to set aside competition or rivalry in the interest of making sure the next generation can live in peace and prosper. We're doing that here tonight, because the genuine good heart of the DiMasi's has shown us that my daughter Maria will be cared for and loved."

Gavin saw that Maria's face was softening. She looked to Devon with an entreating smile. Eric frowned, curling his lower lip.

Tony would not be outdone and was about to rise from his chair, but Colleen beat him to it. "Thank you so much, Frank. Maria, we love you. I hope you know that. Now I see that Devon's brother Gavin would like to say a word."

Gavin was caught off guard. He wasn't prepared to make a speech, or even a simple toast. But he realized his mother was trying to orchestrate—engineer would probably be more accurate—a harmonious détente between the Hatfields and McCoys. He took a deep breath and stood. "Some of you may know that Devon and I are identical mirror twins. Which means we're the same, but in reverse. So whereas Devon likes to eat, I like to cook. And while he sells wine, I like to select and drink it. But I do need to warn you, Maria. Don't ever play chess with my brother. He plays to *win*. Every. Damned. Time. And he brings that determination to everything he does. Which means he'll do anything to make you happy and to have a good marriage." Gavin could feel his skin crawling and his stomach retching at this lie. He could only hope that by verbalizing this publicly in his brother's presence, Devon might convince himself it's true, and live up to it. Maybe. "So here's to my brother and his life partner Maria. Thank god he finally has someone else to annoy instead of me."

To which everyone laughed. Except Devon.

By this time, Tony's alcohol consumption meter had tipped to 'FULL.' But he stood anyway, lifting his glass and swaying a little. "I always thought that of my twins, Devon would be the first, the best, the winner in everything."

Colleen scowled and kicked him under the table.

"And here he is, the first of my twins to get married. To a great little girl from a great family." He turned to Frank with a nod. And a grimace he failed to suppress.

At that moment Colleen realized that Tony had no intention of joining her campaign to get along with the Rizzos. He had to win at any cost, just as Devon did.

"So here's to Devon and Maria," Tony concluded. "May you live happily ever after."

There were several other people who toasted the couple, spouting happy platitudes and wishes, but neither Devon nor Eric did so. The evening ended in a stalemate cloaked in fable.

The next day, the wedding and reception proceeded under the same pretensions, but Gavin noticed bruises on his mother's wrists below her long-sleeved dress. Uncle Marco strutted, eyeing Tommy and Mickie, who had suspicious bulges under their jackets.

22.

AFTER HIS PHONE CALL WITH KATIE THE NIGHT
before—Christmas Eve back in the family house in Wellesley,
Gavin had a hard time getting to sleep. This was the first night
they'd spent apart in more than a year—since they got their
apartment in Manhattan's Chelsea neighborhood. But it was
important for her to be with her mother at Christmas. Mrs.
Goodwin's health was rapidly declining; she now had a
hospice nurse twenty-four seven.

Gavin lay in his old teen bedroom, awake in the pre-dawn
hours. His eyes followed dancing sparkles from the streetlight
through the pines, disco-blinking against his wall. He worried
about his own mother. But not because of her health. He'd heard
them arguing the night before. Well, mostly he heard his father.
Tony's booming voice could rival a nuclear explosion, especially
when he was angry and drunk, which was obviously the case last
night. And then there were the occasional thumps coming from
their bedroom. Gavin hoped those sounds were nothing more
than objects being thrown about.

He gave up on sleep, rose from bed and pulled on his baggy
old sweats and holey slippers. He could make some coffee and
toast, then enjoy a little peace and quiet before Devon and his
entourage got up. Since the wedding that summer, Gavin had

begun to think of his brother as a trio—Devon plus Maria and Eric, his brother's shadow. There'd be no peace after they were all awake. Maybe he could work on the restaurant's menu and provisions order for the following week. He was glad the owners let him take two days off, but he still had to do his job. It was a competitive industry.

The marble tile of the kitchen floor, cold reaching through his slippers to his bare feet, jolted him into complete wakefulness. He went into the family room and turned on the lights circling the aromatic fir. He loved the Christmas holidays, but it didn't feel very festive in the house now. Tension hung in the air so dense it could have peeled the wallpaper.

Once Gavin settled down with his coffee and toast, he tried to dispel his concerns. His father had been like that for as long as he could remember. And on the occasions when his mother sported poorly camouflaged bruises, she never complained, instead waving her hand in dismissal, as if it were an expected rite of marriage. Yet he couldn't shake the sense of foreboding gripping him that morning, clawing at his throat.

Just then he heard Tony's Wagnerian bellow start up again, booming drama from his parents' bedroom, reverberating down the rear stairs to the kitchen.

Jesus, doesn't he ever stop? Wasn't last night enough? It's Christmas, for Chrissake!

Next, the sound of their bedroom door opening into the hall, followed by Tony yelling, "Don't you walk away from me, you smart-ass cunt!" His voice echoed throughout the house. "You think you're better than me, with your *P.h.D.*," Tony drew out Colleen's title with derision. "You're nothin' but a stupid slut."

Gavin stood, hesitating. Should he do something? Tony had made it much worse on his mother the last time he tried to intervene. But that day he'd had enough.

He rushed to the back hall and arrived just as a *SMACK* and a weak cry rippled from above. In the same surreal moment, his mother's body plummeted over the stairs in slow motion, initially airborne as if shot from a cannon then tumbling in flailing somersaults, her temple hitting the newel post before landing at his feet with a final sickening crack of skull on hardwood floor.

Gavin dropped down beside her, holding her head while blood began trickling from her ears and nose, her eyes staring without seeing. The earth stilled its rotation.

Gavin's vision spun in nightmarish flashes. He looked up to the top of the stairs. No one was there. He froze for a cold moment. His coffee and toast wanted to escape his stomach, to turn back time. He jumped up, headed for the kitchen phone to call for help, losing his breakfast along the way.

After calling 911, Gavin rushed back to his mother, desperately searching for a pulse, talking to her, urging her to rouse. Her body parts seemed misaligned, head divergent from her unmoving chest, shoulder askew. He tried pumping her chest to breathe, but it was futile. He wasn't breathing either, and he wasn't sure his heart was beating. He sat motionless beside her.

Tony stood in the kitchen with a drink, three-fingers neat, staring at the floor. Devon called out to Gavin, "Did you call an ambulance, Twinkie?" while he foraged in the fridge for something to eat. Maria and Eric watched morning cartoons on television in the family room, snickering. Gavin continued sitting on the floor beside his mother at the base of the stairs. He held her hand and talked softly to her, telling her she was loved. His chest lurched with suppressed sobs.

When the doorbell rang. Devon yelled, "Finally! They took long enough to get here!" He took a big bite of his morning glory muffin and flicked a shower of crumbs to the floor. "Anyone gonna get the door?" Gavin had already run to open the door and usher the attendants to his mother. An EMT crouched to check for pulse then quickly assessed the angle of her twisted neck and the pupils of her open eyes. He shook his head and looked up to Gavin, whose distraught face contorted in spasms.

Gavin groaned. "I didn't get here in time to stop it."

"Stop what?"

"My mother...," Gavin's outstretched arm swung an arc over the stairs and trembled toward Colleen. He couldn't speak.

The EMT—a twenty-something baby-faced young man—cocked his head at Gavin, seeming to wait for the rest of his sentence.

"I called the police," Gavin croaked, his voice barely audible.

"We can't do anything until they get here."

Then Tony broke in, still carrying his nearly empty glass. "What d'ya mean, you can't do anything? Take her to the hospital!"

The EMT stood up and turned to Tony. "I'm sorry sir, but she's gone. Is she your wife?"

The howling of police sirens wound down as they pulled up outside. A weathered officer strode in through the open front door. Spotting Tony, he said, "Hey, man, what's happening?"

"Jeez, Gus. I'm glad it's you. God, I don't know what happened, but there she is. My wife," Tony shook his head slowly. "Maybe she tripped on the rug up there in the hall or something." He dropped his gaze and put his hand—the one that wasn't holding his drink—over his face. He looked grim and despondent. More like a kid who's been caught doing something naughty than a man who just killed his wife.

Devon added, "Yeah, poor Mom was always sort of clumsy, getting bruises and cuts."

Upon hearing Devon's lie, Gavin's rage broke through his grief. "I was in the kitchen and heard it all! Dad was yelling at Mom upstairs, then I ran here just as Dad hit her. But I was too late to stop her from...just *sailing* down the stairs!" He flung his arm as he shouted, glowering at his father, then at his brother.

The officer turned to the EMT with an eyeroll. "Go ahead and take her to the hospital."

"Can they save her? Or is that where they do an autopsy?" Gavin moaned.

"They'll determine what's appropriate," the officer said. He turned to stand beside Tony and said low, "Sorry this happened, man. We'll take care of everything."

It began to dawn on Gavin what was happening now, knowing his father's history of bribing his way out of problems. He lunged toward the officer and Tony. "What do you mean, you'll take care of everything? My father hit my mother and threw her down the stairs!"

"Just calm down, young man," the officer said, pulling Gavin away. "You didn't see that happen, now, did you?"

Devon stood behind his father and aimed what seemed to be a warning look toward his brother.

Gavin insisted on riding in the ambulance with his mother. When they arrived at the hospital, he followed the gurney and rushed to tell his story to everyone who would listen. But Gus, the police officer, appeared just in time to dismiss Gavin's claims.

Gavin had never had to deal with anyone's death firsthand before that day. Certainly not such a cruel death. His mother was the only caring advocate he had in his family, helping him navigate around its landmines. Now he stood alone in the cold hallway of Newton-Wellesley Hospital, trembling under a flood of emotions. The image of his mother plummeting toward him, violently thrown at his feet, replayed its assault. He had been too late to stop it, and guilt crushed him for his failure. It felt to him like he had been attacked too, and now was in some sort of danger.

Gavin scanned the hallway. He'd been there years before. That summer seven years ago, when he would have done anything to save his brother. Giving blood, coming nearly every day to see him. The summer when everything turned bad, when his other half went necrotic.

He had to get out of there. He ran. Past nurses, doctors, and his O'Malley grandparents who'd just arrived. With no idea where he was going, but propelled by his medal-winning cross-country legs. No idea whether he was running to or away from something or someone. His stride became longer, faster, as if he were in a race for his life. Streets, cars, buildings, trees, people, all passed by for miles, in a blur.

Until he collided head-on into a passing jogger, throwing both of them to the ground.

"Gavin?" Dr. Pedersen croaked, his deflated breath a barely audible whisper.

Gavin rolled onto his side and attempted to rise. His sweatpants were torn out at the knee, red peeking through, matched by a spreading bloom at his elbow. "Dr. Pedersen," Gavin exhaled, flat and exhausted, like a man overboard surrendering to the approach of a rescue raft.

Dr. Pedersen rose and lifted Gavin to his feet.

Gavin's face—knotted in a kind of anguish far beyond the pain of his physical injury—instantly informed his old high school counselor that something other than skinning his knee was gravely wrong.

"There's a bench in the little park just ahead, son," Pedersen gestured, leading Gavin by his unscathed elbow and eyeing his attire, inappropriate for running. "Let's sit there for a minute so you can catch your breath."

Stubborn patches of snow lurked in the shade beneath bushes, emanating a chill that defied the hopeful sun of Christmas Day. Gavin's entire body rocked with violent shaking, suppressed rage battling with despair.

Dr. Pedersen put his arm around Gavin's shoulder. "What's going on, Gavin?"

Gavin coughed. "My Mom." Doubled over as if to vomit

again. "He killed her."

Dr. Pedersen slumped in shocked regret. And pity that Gavin's only lifeline in his family had become the ultimate victim of its dysfunction. He remained silent, stifling reaction. He waited.

"I was too late...couldn't stop it...couldn't save her..." Volcanic sobs erupted from him.

Pedersen's breath caught. "I'm so sorry, son." Although he was deeply saddened for Gavin's sake, he'd heard enough over the years that he wasn't too surprised to get that news. "Please don't blame yourself. You can't be responsible for saving everyone. Not even your mother."

Gavin's jaw set. "But she put up with his shit all these years." His voice rose, a primal roar. "She just took his crap—verbal, physical, and made excuses for him—rationalized it!" He pounded his fist on the bench in rage, then doubled over as if he'd been gut-punched.

Dr. Pedersen laid his hand on Gavin's convulsing back. "Abuse can destroy a person's self-confidence in their own agency, their belief in their ability or even right to defend themself. Your mother couldn't save herself." Rubbing Gavin's back as his shuddering gradually subsided, he withheld further questions or comments. It wasn't the right time.

Dr. Pedersen helped Gavin to his feet. "You need to go somewhere warm. And safe." He waved to a taxi that was just pulling away from discharging a passenger. "Where—"

Instantly Gavin whimpered "Katie", sounding like a child who lost his teddy bear.

Later, his O'Malley grandparents retrieved Gavin and took him to their house, where they grieved with him. When Gavin coughed out how his mother had landed at his feet, his grandmother cried, "That's a double tragedy, traumatizing you, dear boy." His grandparents stayed by his side all day, through the night, until the next morning.

Gavin got through the ensuing days in a numb fog.

———

Years later, much of what followed would be a blur for him. The fruitless appeals to the Chief of Police and Chief Medical Examiner. The autopsy concluding Colleen's injuries were accidental, with no indication of current or prior physical abuse. His father publicly mourning the "unfortunate fall" that took the life of his "dear wife". And his twin's dismissal. "You're being a maudlin sissy, Gav," Devon said. "Just stop crying and get on with your life. You can't change anything now."

Yet a few good memories would persist through the blur. Being surrounded during the funeral and burial by people who held him up. Saved him. His O'Malley grandparents rose above their own sadness to support him in the midst of the palpable grief tinged with outrage that smothered everyone there. Dr. Pedersen, Katie and her mother, Tray, many other friends gathered around him in heavy snow at the graveside, while Tony and Devon stood stiffly, displaying no visible emotion over the tragedy. Gavin was surprised to notice Frank Rizzo standing unobtrusively at the periphery of the mourners; why would he be there?

As everyone began dispersing after the service, Dr. Pedersen approached Gavin and placed a hand on him. "You mustn't feel responsible, son. And please remember that I'm always available for you anytime you'd like to talk. I'm as close as your phone or email."

"Thank you," Gavin murmured, unable to say much more at that point.

"I know how painful your mother's death is for you, Gavin," Pedersen spoke soft and low. "But I hope you'll think about whether her way of dealing with abuse was any different than how you deal with Devon's and your father's abuse of you. It's an important question for you to consider, in order to save yourself."

The muscles in Gavin's back went rigid. His breath held. Pedersen's question hit him like a brain freeze, and stayed with him in the months ahead. He suspected there may be some link between the answer to that and everything else that was toxic in their family. Including his suspicion that his father had paid someone off (Gus? The Medical Examiner?) to whitewash his mother's death. He vowed that justice—or karma—would prevail. Eventually.

23.

FOR MONTHS AFTER HIS MOTHER'S DEATH, GAVIN felt like a part of him had died too. But Katie supported him with her love and encouragement. His work in the restaurant helped, keeping him busy and engaged. And the owners made him Executive Chef. Tray, Pedersen and other friends stayed in touch with him frequently, checking in on his state of mind. Yet he never forgot Pedersen's parting question. And he purposely did not contact his father or his twin; neither did they contact him. But his visitor more than a year later would set in motion another tragedy, and reveal much more.

As usual in New York restaurants on a Tuesday night, it had been intensely busy earlier in the evening, but at that hour things were winding down. Gavin stepped back from the heat and took a gulp of water. He looked at the clock. One more hour for the kitchen, another two hours for cleanup. He paused to call Katie and give her a virtual hug before she went to bed. Life had been difficult for her after her mother died, as they also struggled to pay off her mother's medical bills.

Matt the busser came into the kitchen just as Gavin ended

his call. "Hey, Gav, you should see this guy at the bar," he said. "He's been sitting there most of the night. I think he might be half in the bag. Hope we can get him out of here before we close."

"And I hope Jason has cut him off," Gavin said. "We don't need the liability."

"Oh, and he asked for you," Matt recalled, almost an afterthought.

"Really?" Gavin was surprised but curious. "Well, things are slow right now, I'll go out and check. Can you handle the kitchen for a minute, Gabe?" he asked his sous chef.

Gavin rubbed his chin, willing the stubble to become a beard, and pushed through the swinging doors out of the kitchen, passing through the nearly empty dining room. One of the regulars saw him and called out, "Hey Chef! That brodetto was amazing!" Gavin smiled and gave a thumbs up before turning left into the bar. There was only one man sitting there. His beefy back was slumped over his half-finished drink. He clinked the ice in the amber liquid, swirling his glass on the polished wood. Gavin caught the bartender's eye, pointed to the man and gestured concern. Jason shrugged.

As Gavin drew closer, he thought there was something familiar about the man, judging from the back. He wiped his hands on his chef's apron and approached the guy. "Dad?!" he gasped.

Tony was the last person Gavin ever wanted to see again. He had finally gotten to the point of sleeping through the night without a nightmare of his mother plummeting to his feet, yet there in his restaurant the cause of all that was sitting in front of him. His father must want something. "Why are you even here?"

"I had business in the city, so I thought I'd look you up," Tony mumbled, and took a gulp of his drink.

Gavin studied his father. He hadn't seen him since his mother's funeral a year and a half before. It seemed so far in the past. He had an overwhelming urge to throw his father out of the restaurant on his ass. Not that he could lift him. The intervening time hadn't been kind to his father. Tony was overweight, looking drawn and beaten. Deep baggy circles under his eyes, cratered lines down jaundiced cheeks, ending in sagging jowls.

Gavin signaled Jason to bring him a beer. He took a sip, not taking his eyes off Tony. He didn't know what to say. After his mother died, he was haunted by his father's role in that 'accident' and his own failure to prevent it. And he still remembered Devon's cavalier attitude toward their mother's death, so he had no interest in seeing either his father or his brother again. Yet there Tony sat. And then he recalled what his mother had told him in the kitchen the day of high school graduation. That his father wasn't a bad man. "So, Dad...," he hesitated.

"I know you aren't thrilled to see me, Gavin," Tony said, and looked into his glass.

Gavin stammered, "Yeah, but...you *are* my father." As if that were sufficient to overcome all the hurt, the pain, the abuse through all the years.

Tony signaled the bartender for another drink. Gavin gave the negative signal to Jason.

"Y'know, son, you aren't the only one who feels bad about what happened to your mother."

Yet no admission of having anything to do with it, Gavin noted.

"She was a good woman," Tony mumbled, reaching over to clink his glass to Gavin's.

Gavin almost dropped his beer mid-air. He stared at his father.

"Your brother, on the other hand..."

So that's the real reason he's here. Gavin finally got it. He remained silent, wary.

"Devon's been running some of my stores," Tony frowned,

shaking his head. "Turns out he's a real fuck-up."

Gavin almost laughed. *Took you long enough to figure that out.*

"He's got us involved in stuff I never wanted anything to do with, thinking he's so damned smart. And my asshole brother Marco helped drag him into it. But the Rizzo family was always into it, and Frank's boy Tommy made capo in the Boston operations. You don't mess around with these guys, unless you want to get killed."

"Wait, Dad. 'Boston operations?' Are you talking about the mafia—the mob?"

"Bingo." Tony finished the last of his drink and slammed the glass down on the bar. "Mafia, mob, all the same."

"But didn't you piss off the Rizzos when Devon married Maria?"

"Yeah, well...Frankie Rizzo was always on my ass when we were kids. Real tough guy, more than all the machos in our neighborhood. So for your brother's wedding, I had to show Rizzo us DiMasis are tougher than the Rizzos." Tony paused. "Besides, I didn't want Devon anywhere near the Rizzos in the North End on that day."

He sighed and looked with weary eyes to Gavin. "Y'know, when I was growing up, guys had to be tough. I always figured your brother was the tough one, but 'tough' ain't all it's cracked up to be. Look who finally won the Rizzo faceoff."

"So what're you going to do?"

"Duck for cover. But your brother thinks he can beat 'em. He's crazy."

"Dad, Devon actually does have...uh...mental health issues."

"You think I don't know that?" Tony popped his head up and looked at Gavin with the eyes of a defeated man. He sighed. "Son, I came here to apologize to you. I know I didn't treat you very fair when you were a kid, and I favored your brother. I was wrong. So wrong."

Gavin felt like his world had just turned upside down. He

didn't know what he could say to his father now. An apology couldn't erase—or even assuage—all the damage to his self-worth over the years. He thought he'd finally put all that behind him. But now he didn't know what to think, with his father sitting beside him humbled and contrite.

"And y'know, son, I'm proud of you," Tony nodded slowly while speaking through ice cubes cracking as he chewed. "Really proud. Sorry it took me so long to appreciate what you do, how hard you work at what makes you happy."

Gavin was beginning to wonder if someone had swapped his father out with a body double. Never in his wildest dreams could he have imagined his father would apologize; that was completely out of character for the man he grew up with. While he maintained a tense vigilance, expecting the real Tony DiMasi to re-appear any minute, he realized his shoulders were still hunched tightly, as if preparing for the humiliating put-downs he'd grown up with. Muscle memories of old hurts triggered his retreat response.

"I appreciate your saying that, Dad," Gavin eked out the words. He guessed it was better late than never. But what did his father want? Understanding, forgiveness, or something else?

Tony took a deep inhale, as if gearing himself for a difficult task. "On another subject, did you ever wonder why your Nonno DiMasi didn't give his liquor business to Joey?"

Gavin was disappointed in Tony's abrupt change of subject. He wanted to get a better understanding of what had brought his father to what seemed like an epiphany, the realization that Devon wasn't the winner they'd always asserted, and that he, Gavin, had in fact achieved merit.

Maybe Tony's question would open the door to what had caused his change of heart. Gavin remembered his mother mentioning it the day of their high school commencement; Joey was the oldest son and 'rightful heir,' but Tony got the business. "I guess I always assumed Uncle Joey didn't want it.

Is there some other reason?"

"Well, Pop never wanted to have anything to do with the racketeering and other crap that was going on in the North End. Other parts of Boston, too."

"You mean the mob was operating in the North End when Grandpa was there?"

"Yeah, it's been goin' strong since the early nineteen-hundreds. Still is today, 2002—but it's the twenty-first-century version. Drugs. Big business." Tony paused and looked at Gavin, whose mouth was hanging open. He shook his head in a way that mocked the naïveté of Gavin's sheltered generation and went on. "Pop saw what happened to people who got caught up in all that stuff when he was back home in Italy—you know, the Cosa Nostra, the Black Hand, other criminal gangs. But then it was all around us in the North End, like it was the rats that came over on the boats with guys from Italy."

Gavin was gobsmacked as he listened to his father, who had a faraway look in his eyes as if he were replaying an old movie—one in which Tony was a bit player.

Tony stared straight ahead, without seeing, at the lineup of alcohol behind the bar, and went on. "When Pop opened his store on Prince Street, Phil Buccola and J.L. Lombardo were the mob bosses working out of the North End. Them and their capos extorted him, threatened to put him out of business if he didn't pay. Your Uncle Joey was born around that time."

"Really? Did Grandpa pay?" Gavin probed. "And what's 'capos?'"

"Of course he paid. There was no choice, if you wanted to stay in business or stay alive, and protect your family. But Pops never got over being pissed about how the Mob put the squeeze on him." Tony said. "Oh, and a capo is like a captain. Of goons in this case. Capos report to a boss higher up."

Just then the busser came into the bar. "Excuse me, Chef. We just took the order from our last customer seating of the night. Gabe says he can handle it. Would you and your guest like anything?"

"Thanks, Matt. I'll have some coffee. Dad, would you like anything before the kitchen closes? And maybe some coffee?"

"Yeah, I guess I should have some coffee," Tony grunted. "And an order of that Sfogliatelle Riccia I saw on the menu. Let's see if it's as good as my Nonna used to make."

"Our pastry chef made a batch this afternoon. I hope it can measure up." Gavin was intrigued with Tony's story, hoping it would help clarify why his father had always been so hard to love, or even like. "So go on with your story, Dad. This is all new to me—you never talked about it when we were kids."

"Yeah, well, I always wanted to protect you two," Tony said, pausing. "So let's see, where was I? Oh yeah, the mob in the North End. When I was growing up, the boss was Enrico Tameleo, and Frank Cucchiara was underboss. 'Cheeseman.'"

"Cheeseman?" Gavin snorted.

"Yeah, can you believe it? The mob liked to hang weird monikers on their guys. I think he had a cheese shop somewhere. And even today, there's a consigliere they call 'Big Cheese' DiNunzio, he has a cheese shop on Endicott Street, he must weigh more'n three hundred pounds," Tony shook his head and plopped another ice cube in his mouth. "So anyway, your Uncle Joey was all in with those guys—running stuff for them, doing collections. Pops was worried, afraid Joey would get into big trouble, told him he had to be smarter and tougher than those guys. It's like Pop wanted Joey to even the score after the mob screwing with his business. But then one time Joey fucked up. Braggin' to some guy who turns out to be undercover FBI. Cheeseman ordered a hit on him, so one of his capos had him shot, beat to shit and cut him up good and left him for dead. But my hard-headed big brother didn't croak. Ever notice Joey's not too bright? He used to be, before that."

"So that's why you got the business instead of Uncle Joey?"

"Well, Joey had to get out of town, for sure." Tony was on

a roll, dredging up memories of family and heritage, as if his DNA were vibrating the lyrics of his youth, recalling every name, every detail. "Pop sent Joey to live with his old Zia Francesca up in Marblehead. That was around the same time that Cheeseman offed himself, so the boss in Providence—Raymond Patriarca—kinda lost sight of what had happened and Joey sorta slipped through the cracks. But with his history and his...y'know, handicap, he wouldn't have been able to run the business anyway. So Pop had me take it over, but made me promise I'd only open stores outside the reach of the mob, and that I'd never get involved with them. No way, no how."

"Wow." Gavin was literally speechless as all this began to sink in, like a foreign language and culture. He was beginning to gain a new perspective on his father, who had survived a culture of violence and honored *his* father, keeping promises.

"That was around the same time your mom was pregnant with you two. God, she was the best thing ever happened to me."

Gavin drew back, incredulous at hearing his father say something that was totally contrary to what he'd experienced his whole life. His entire worldview turned upside down, as if he'd just learned that tornadoes were actually angels tickling the earth.

But Tony didn't notice or pause, and continued to prattle on in his usual way, now pumped with bygone memories. "So since Colleen's family's from Wellesley, I figured that was *totally* beyond reach of the mob, and decided to move there, to protect her and you boys. Good thing I did, because that was when the Angiulo brothers came on the scene and even though they didn't like violence or drugs, rival gangs brought it all to them in the North End. After Whitey Bulger from Southie started singing to the Feds, his Winter Hill stooges over in Somerville started trying to go after Angiulo's territory and things got worse. It was shoot 'em up time all around Boston—North End, Charlestown, Southie..."

Although still reeling from his father's unbelievable meta-morphosis from macho tough guy to considerate family guy, Gavin continued to be mesmerized by the story. He'd heard vague things about mob activity in Boston but had never paid much attention, like it was a Hollywood movie. Now his father's story brought it into family. Good thing he was only half Italian. But that wouldn't stop Devon.

"When was the last time you talked to Devon?" Tony asked.

Yep, there it is. The reason his father was there, camping out at the bar in his restaurant. "I haven't seen him since Mom's funeral," Gavin said through clenched teeth. He didn't want to recall that painful day. He waited for his father to divulge his real objectives.

"Well, he's in trouble. Playin' with fire, like I warned him not to. But you know his 'disorder' makes him a risk-taker. He's a sucker for stupid stuff. I guess that standoff with the Rizzo clan at his wedding had the opposite effect. Tipped things from flirting with the mob to all-out warfare. And when Pete Limone—'Chief Crazy Horse'—replaced old 'Sonny Boy' Rizzo, Tommy's uncle, as underboss to Patriarca, it all became deadly. One of Devon's guys got killed. The whole business has changed, they're moving drugs, getting tangled up with big companies, funny business with stock trading...and still the old stuff like liquor and prostitution. Your brother thinks he's gonna get out, but that don't happen once you're in."

Gavin's head spun with all the bizarre names and inter-necine battles. It was all a blur, but the bottom line was clear. His twin had gotten into dangerous business.

Tony slowly savored a bite of his dessert. "This is good, son. Glad to see you're finally doing Italian food. Different than what I grew up with, but it's good." He was silent for a while, taking another bite. "I'm afraid something really bad is gonna happen. Can you talk to Devon? You two may have had your problems, but he respects you. You're the sane reasonable twin; your opinion matters to him."

Gavin's beer threatened to come up as his stomach heaved. It felt like he was going to be sucked into a dark pit of rapacious vipers...just like when he was growing up with Devon.

24.

GAVIN DIDN'T WANT TO GO TO BOSTON. BUT even as he consented to his father's plea, he nevertheless steeled himself to repel any hint of abuse from his brother, or his father. Although—if Tony's story was sincere—Gavin was beginning to understand the culture in which his dad grew up, and the decisions that were intended to protect his family.

Still, Gavin was worried about his brother's safety. He was all too familiar with Devon's bravado, despite risks and dangers obvious to everyone but him. Or maybe it *was* obvious to him, and that just made him want to go up against it anyway, like some kind of adrenaline junkie.

"Hey, Gav," Devon called. "You left me a message. What's up?"

"I was calling to see if we could get together," Gavin said. "I want to discuss your proposition—y'know, about working with you in your business."

"Oh, great!" Devon crowed. "It's about time you came to your senses about that, little brother. Can you come up here? I'm pretty busy right now and can't break away to come to New York, but next Monday is my birthday!"

"Our birthday," Gavin corrected.

Gavin's restaurant wasn't open on Mondays, so they

arranged to meet then. He drove his Jeep Wrangler over four hours in heavy traffic to get there by noon.

When he finally made it to the North End, he navigated the narrow one-way Prince Street around delivery trucks and vans. As he was pulling into the reserved space in front of the store, Devon spotted him from the window and ran out to greet him. "Twinkie!" he cried. "Welcome to my world! Come on in so I can show you what I've done to the place. I bet you've missed me, little brother."

"Happy birthday, Dev," Gavin said. He wondered how Devon would respond when he had to burst his balloon that day.

"Thanks!" Devon crowed. "Twenty-four—and look how successful I am!" He opened the door to the store, ushering Gavin in and flipping the door sign to 'Closed.' "See what I've done with the lighting? No more harsh glaring industrial stuff, just focused spots onto each shelf, so people can read the labels. And the ceiling painted black helps with ambiance, too. You notice the hardwood floor? Classy, huh? And how about the rough-hewn narrow-plank wood walls? It's evocative of the inside of a wine or whiskey barrel, *and* it absorbs sound." He tipped up his chin, clearly proud of himself. If he were wearing suspenders, he might have tucked his thumbs under them in a cocky pose.

Gavin smiled. "Cool, Dev. I'm glad you're doing something you're excited about."

Devon laughed and clapped him on the back. "Remember, I'm the twin with good taste and class." Next he pointed Gavin to a glassed-in room on the right. "That's my temperature-controlled wine area. And here," he guided Gavin into another room with a long curved bar, "is the tasting room. I hold VIP events here at least once a month. And here," he opened a rustic wooden door to a dimly lit room with posh seating at the rear of the store, "is my cards and cigar room, where I do some serious business."

"What kind of business?" Gavin prompted.

"Let's go in and sit down, where we can talk in private." As they entered the room, Devon touched an inconspicuous point on the wall that opened a small cabinet door and pulled out a gun. "This is my security," he said, brandishing the small weapon. "You always have to be careful."

The hair on the back of Gavin's neck bristled.

Devon ushered his brother to a poker table surrounded by leather club chairs. As they sat, he leaned back, clasped his hands behind his neck like a man fully in charge of his domain. "I've learned so much about this business since Dad brought me in. When I first saw the store here on Prince Street, I thought I wanted to relocate it over to Hanover Street. That's the main drag in the North End, where most of the other commercial establishments are. Everyone goes there, even the tourists."

"Did Dad nix the idea?"

"No, actually, he thought it was a great idea. Sort of mainstream the business, take it out of the shadows. But his reaction told me it would be the worst thing I could do. The other part of my business needs to operate in the shadows."

Here it comes. "What kind of business?"

"Some stuff that's not exactly mainstream, but it's what really powerful men in New England do. And I make a ton of money."

"You're saying your business includes doing some things that're illegal, right?"

"It's only illegal if you get caught."

"And you don't think you'll get caught?"

"Damn straight. I'm too smart for these guys."

"And if you get caught, you're okay with prison? Like Angiulo, Russo, Quintana, Salemme...?" Gavin had done his homework.

Devon laughed, masking his surprise at Gavin's knowledge. "But *I* won't get caught."

"Just exactly what kind of things are you doing? Let's see...extortion?"

Devon nodded, with a smug smile. "You could call it that."

"Truck hijacking?"

"They do it to me—take my liquor shipments! I have to protect my business!"

"What's on those trucks you hijack, anything besides liquor?"

Devon squirmed.

"And...what else? Bribery? Bookmaking? Race fixing? Drug trafficking?"

Devon kept nodding like a bobblehead.

"And are you consuming the goods now? Like the drugs?"

"Okay, okay, that's enough, baby brother."

"Didn't one of your guys get killed? What was that about?"

"Hijacking a truck."

"Uh-huh. Was he the hijacker or the hijack-ee?"

"You don't understand how this works."

"Okay, help me understand. Other mob groups or their goons may not like what you're doing, or want to cut you out of your territory, or stop you from cutting into theirs, right?"

Devon slid further down into his chair, crossed his arms tight into himself and nodded almost imperceptibly.

"And they might resort to violence, right?"

"Maybe, but I can outsmart those rubes. You know I'm smarter than anyone else, Twinkie. Nothing's going to happen to me."

"Is that because you're such a lovable guy?"

"Exactly," Devon beamed a self-satisfied smile.

"So Crazy Horse Limone convinced you to expand your game, right?"

"Yes, and he'll protect me. And you too, when you go into business with me."

"And if he can't, or won't, what then?"

"Tell you what. Limone always holds court at the Gemini

Club in the afternoon. We were supposed to meet Dad for lunch at Café Pompei, the Angiulo family's old hangout," Devon said. "So let's have lunch with Dad then go over to see Limone at Gemini. He'll tell you. You do the work, they have your back."

"Devon, I just want you to be safe and not in jail. There are dozens of examples right here in the North End of really smart savvy guys who either went to prison or were killed. Or both."

"Aw, Twinkie—you care!" Devon squealed, putting his arm around Gavin's shoulder. "Well, I love you too, and want you to be almost as rich as I am. For starters, you can junk that old ragtop you drive for a new car!"

For all their differences, and despite his desperate need to get out from under his brother's asphyxiating efforts to control, manipulate and dominate him, Gavin did care. He sure didn't want Devon to get hurt. Or worse. He hoped he might have moved the needle a little that day by pointing out the obvious risks and danger. Maybe the lunch meeting with their father will finish the job—convince Devon to back away from his illegal activities. Especially the drugs, which hurt him more than anything.

When Devon led Gavin out of the store onto the street, he pointed a few doors up and said "That's where the Angiulo family lived. I saw old Frank a few years ago holding court on the sidewalk across the street from his house, to get the sun. Smart guy. Quiet. Like you."

"And he was in prison for fourteen years, right?"

"Well, yeah, someone ratted on him. But I got that covered."

As they walked the crowded sidewalk down the few blocks on Prince Street to Hanover, Gavin noticed that most people they passed seemed to know his brother. Although he observed a few men who, upon seeing Devon, seemed to duck and turn away, several other people greeted him by name. Some were even friendly, almost obsequious. There was also the reaction he and Devon had experienced all their lives—peoples' surprise or confusion in 'seeing double,' despite Gavin's struggling beard and their having aged. They were only twenty-four that day. But he suspected that their divergent lifestyles would ultimately affect not only their epigenomes but their appearance as well. Different expression lines and facial gestures from contrasting temperaments and attitudes would project the character of each as clearly as a neon sign.

They turned the corner and nearly ran smack into a morbidly obese man with aviator sunglasses that cut divots into the sides of his face. "Jeez, Red, where ya think you're going? And what? There's two of you now?"

"Sorry, Sammy. We didn't see you," Devon let out a guffaw.

But the big guy either didn't get the joke or didn't appreciate the humor. "You better watch it, asshole." As he waddled off, he turned back and said, "Spucky Spagnolo's lookin' for you."

Gavin thought he saw Devon briefly stiffen. "Everything okay?"

"Oh, sure. Some guy owes me money. Or I owe him, I forget." Devon chuckled and gave an elbow to Gavin's rib. "Look across the street. That's the peace garden outside St. Leonard's Church, where all Dad's family grew up. And down here on the right is Café Pompei. They usually open their wood-framed glass doors across the front for their version of an outdoor café on warm days like today. Best they can do with these narrow sidewalks."

But those glass doors weren't open that day. Devon opened the interior entry door to Café Pompei and walked in. A middle-aged guy in a stained t-shirt greeted him in a gravelly smoker's voice. "Hey Red, ya bring yer better half with ya today?"

"No, Dom, I just cloned myself," Devon deadpanned. "You decided to dress up today? Where's your regular white shirt?"

"I wasn't supposed to be here, but Alfred called in sick so

they brought me in," he explained, looking annoyed, and closed the door with a resounding click.

"My regular table upstairs in back?"

"Yer dad's already there, kid."

Devon led the way through the restaurant. Muted gray-blue walls with numerous large oil paintings—mostly Italian Renaissance with some abstracts, Italianate tile floors, period lighting, crown molding, contrasting red walls in alcoves. "This is a great place," Gavin said as he followed Devon up the stairs, sliding his hand along the curved wooden banister.

When they reached the top of the stairs, Gavin looked up to see a mural to rival Michelangelo painted in a large recessed oval in the ceiling. But the place seemed oddly deserted that day.

Devon led the way to the back of the restaurant and into an alcove with blood-red walls. Tony was already seated on the left side of the table with a hefty drink in his hand. "Well, it's about time, birthday boys. I was beginning to think I would have to drink alone."

"I've been trying to convince my baby brother to join me in my business," Devon said, and stood with his hands on his hips.

"And I've been trying to convince my ten-minutes-older brother that his business is illegal and potentially fatal," Gavin said, then slid into the right side of the half-circle leather banquette.

Devon slid in beside him and gave his brother a shit-eating grin.

"Well," Tony declared. He pounded his glass down on the white tablecloth. "I'm starving. Let's order some food and figure out how those two ends can meet. And Devon, don't think you're so damn smart. Listen to your brother."

Devon responded with a dramatic eye roll.

Dom from downstairs came soon to take their orders for drinks and food. "I sure am glad I called last night for a reservation, Dom. I see the place is *so* busy you have to be doorman, waiter, and please tell me you're not the cook," Devon drawled sarcasm. "If so, I'm sending my twin brother into the kitchen to save us all. He's the chef at Del Posto in Manhattan."

"We're always open for you, Red," Dom said. His tone oozed disdain. "And I don't think we'll need your brother's help today."

After Dom heard the orders (as a seasoned waiter, he didn't write them down), Tony excused himself to go to the men's room, a short distance to the left of the alcove.

Devon and Gavin dug into the breadsticks and resumed their earlier discussion. What happened next would ultimately determine the future of their twindom.

Devon finally looked up at the guy who'd arrived beside the table. "Ah, our drinks are finally here."

The man in a brown hat with its brim shading his face dropped the white tablecloth draped over his right arm, unveiling a black Glock in his hand. He took only a split second to point it, but Gavin would forever remember it all, frame-by-frame, in slow motion.

Tony emerged from the men's room just in time to lunge between that gun and his sons.

Gavin vaulted over the table and caught his father as he fell.

Devon ran.

The man turned toward Devon's back and shot again. Splatters of blood erupted from Devon as he ran. The guy tripped as he began the chase. But his target had already disappeared. And then so did he.

Gavin held his father, shouting for help.

Dom leaned against the opposite wall. Arms crossed, watching.

Gavin loosened his father's tie and collar. The red stain spread over his white shirt in a demented Rorschach pattern despite Gavin's fist pushing to staunch the flow. He looked into his father's eyes, under the drooping lids. "Dad, please don't die." He saw his father's lips moving.

Gavin put his ear close. Tony's whispers were nearly inaudible. Soft, mumbled, halting. Painful pauses between struggling words. "...always loved her....so beautiful....so damn smart...hate myself for hitting her....didn't mean to...make her fall..."

Gavin felt himself being sucked into a dark tunnel, but clawed his way back. He didn't want his father to die absent grace. "I forgive you, Dad," he whispered.

"...save yourself, son..." Tony gasped one last breath.

Gavin touched his father's vacant eyes and closed his lids. Angry red tentacles crawled across Tony's shirt, exposing a twisted tale, one locked inside him for generations. In that pattern Gavin saw the shape of his father's past and that of *his* fathers, the model of truculent dominance and captious misogyny that maimed human dignity, destroyed his mother, warped and defiled Devon's identity, distorted and crippled his own self-determination, polluting the lives of every DiMasi. Including his father, who lay before him a martyr to the expectations of his ancestors and to the legacy he imposed on his twins.

Gavin vowed to break the chain of macho toughness, reverse the cultural expectations that had perverted his childhood and his identity. He stood, hearing banging downstairs. Boston police officers couldn't get in. The door was locked. Dom went to open it. When the first officer saw Gavin, he growled, "Red, what'd you do this time?"

25.

GAVIN MET KATIE AT THE SECURITY EXIT AT LOGAN.
When he saw her, something bound up inside him released its
knots. He almost dropped to his knees, struck by a glow that
seemed to surround her like a beacon of goodness and sanity.
She was the only person who knew everything about him and
his messed-up family, yet still stuck with him.

He enveloped her in a smothering embrace and knew she
would understand the cataclysmic spasms erupting from his
chest.

"Oh, sweetheart," Katie murmured while she stroked his
back with her one hand that wasn't immobilized in Gavin's
crush. "I'm so sorry. We have a lot to talk about."

"Yes." Gavin sighed and released a cleansing breath he'd
been holding for hours. "Let's get out of here."

Gavin had called Katie after his father was killed. She
immediately gathered enough clothes from their apartment
for them both and caught a flight to Boston to be with him. As
he negotiated traffic out of the tunnel and drove to Wellesley,
she rested her hand on his thigh. "What have the police said?"

"They haven't said much of anything," Gavin said. The
grim set of his jaw twitched morse code in the headlights of
oncoming vehicles. "I talked with them for over an hour. They

seem more interested in locating Devon than finding Dad's killer. And they don't think there's anything suspicious about the restaurant locking up with us being the only customers in there. Like the whole thing was planned, and we were sitting ducks."

"Do you have any idea where Devon is?"

"I went over to his fancy waterfront condo, but he wasn't there." Gavin swerved erratically around a slow-moving truck. "The place stank and it was a trashy mess. Eric was there and Maria was 'taking a nap,'" he air-quoted with both hands off the steering wheel. "When she came out, she looked and acted like she was stoned, then freaked when she saw blood on me. When I told them what happened, neither of them seemed surprised or concerned. But when I asked if they knew where Devon might be, they shut down, like they were afraid of something."

"Wow. Sounds like they might know something but aren't telling."

"Yeah. And the police hadn't even been there yet! They were just pulling up as I was leaving."

"What about your dad's family?"

"Oh, poor old Grandpa DiMasi," Gavin sighed, shaking his head. "He's been going downhill since Grandma died; I'm not sure how he'll get through this. I called my uncles to meet me at the nursing home so he'd have support when I told him. Uncle Joey came, but Uncle Marco didn't. Maybe he didn't get my voicemail. Grandpa almost passed out when I told him. He collapsed into a chair and just sat there trembling. Then he got mad, really bitter, and growled something like, 'I told Tony that kid would be the death of him.'"

"Poor guy. Do you know yet what the funeral arrangements will be?"

"Grandpa DiMasi and Uncle Joey were no help on that. They were both totally gut-punched by the news," Gavin said. "But Grandpa and Grandma O'Malley are meeting us at their house. She's now Assistant Dean of Wellesley College, so they live in a faculty house across from the campus. They're going to help me figure it out. I guess the responsibility falls on me." He became silent, as if pausing for divine inspiration from the blur of brake lights ahead. "Y'know, it's so ironic. I had just gotten to the point of—well, *beginning* to understand my father, after all the years of feeling like he was an ass. I think maybe he was even trying to make amends, in his own macho way..." His voice cracked.

"I'm so sorry, Gav," Katie whispered, stroking his thigh.

When Gavin pulled into his grandparents' driveway, his heart calmed for the first time all day. As he helped Katie from the car, the O'Malleys came out of the house to greet them. They seemed to rush Gavin into the house, as if something were urgent.

Gavin didn't know how he would have managed without his O'Malley grandparents. During a long talk over tea, they all agreed that his father should be buried next to his mother in Wellesley's Woodlawn Cemetery. Gavin insisted on having the funeral mass in St. Leonard's in the North End. Even though it would be a slow seventeen-mile drive from there to the gravesite, he thought he owed it to his father, and to Grandpa DiMasi, who never wanted his family to get involved with the mob.

Gavin continued leaving phone messages for Devon and Marco. His worry escalated.

Grandpa and Grandma O'Malley promised to go with Gavin the next day to all the places where arrangements had to be made—the morgue, funeral home, church, cemetery. They would help Gavin post the death notice in the papers, make decisions on all the details, contact the family's estate attorney for reading of the will, and work through Gavin's overwhelming weight of regret. And his feelings of guilt. He hadn't saved his father.

"Thank you so much, Grandpa and Grandma," Gavin said as the discussion wrapped up. "What time should we join you in the morning?"

"Why don't you and Katie stay here with us tonight," Grandma O'Malley declared. There was no question mark at the end of her sentence. "There are clean sheets on the guest room bed."

"Thanks, Grandma, but I think I've already kept you up too late," Gavin said. "We'll go over to Mom and Dad's house and see you in the morning."

Grandpa O'Malley spoke up, "I don't think that's a good idea, son. You need to stay here. We have a good security system, and campus police are keeping an eye on the house." He looked intently at Gavin.

Gavin suddenly understood. "You think someone may come after me?" His voice went up a register.

"You did witness a murder, son, and they haven't caught the guy who did it."

And so it was settled. When Gavin entered the guest room, his mind flashed back to times he and Devon had stayed with their grandparents when they were little—the times after their parents had been fighting and his mother had visible bruises. It was a different house back then, but everything in the room was the same. The white-painted antique iron bed, handmade wedding-ring quilt, lace curtains, floral wallpaper, family pictures all around. He felt safe.

Long after Gavin and Katie turned out the lights, they lay in bed and continued to whisper, until she finally drifted off, leaving Gavin with his mind churning and his heart weeping.

It was almost two a.m. when he popped up, gasping. Which woke Katie. "What's wrong?"

"I saw it. All of it."

"It must be traumatic for you."

"But it was all a blur then, and now I saw it again, just as I was falling off to sleep."

"I'm sorry it's haunting you, Gav."

"But this is good! Now I remember everything, see

everything," Gavin's words rushed out in a torrent as he bounded out of bed and paced around the room. "Some guy named Sammy—huge overweight guy—told Devon that some-one named Spucky was looking for him...Italian-sounding last name...started with an 'S'...three syllables I think...it'll come to me. Devon looked nervous when he heard that. And I saw the guy with the gun. I'd sort of had a flash—just a fleeting zing of familiarity about him at the time. Now I'm pretty sure it was a druggie from our high school days—Jimbo Halloran, a couple years older than us. Maybe he works for the Spucky guy? And I distinctly remember the guy Dom in the restaurant, just standing and watching, all calm, after Dad was shot, like he was in on the set-up. I see it all now."

"So are you going to take all that to the police in the morning?"

"Well, yes, but they didn't seem too interested in finding the killer when I talked to them yesterday."

"Gavin, I hesitate to say this, but could it be they're covering up for someone, sort of looking the other way?"

Gavin stopped pacing. He began shivering despite the warmth of July, and realized he'd been stomping around the room in his boxers. He hopped back into bed, pulled the sheet over his bare chest and snuggled into Katie's warmth. "I have a better idea. Tray Harris is Deputy Chief of Police over in Somerville. I'll call him. He'll know what to do." He instantly began snoring.

26.

GRANDMA O'MALLEY MUST HAVE THOUGHT GOOD food—lots of it—could heal traumatic wounds. The fragrant aromas of bacon, apple cinnamon muffins and a savory frittata woke Gavin and Katie before eight o'clock.

Just as they were done picking at breakfast, Gavin's phone rang.

"Hey, Gav," Tray said. "I heard about what happened yesterday. You okay?"

Gavin stood and walked away from the kitchen table. "Not really. I was going to call you this morning. We need to talk."

"Damn straight we do. Where are you?"

"At my O'Malley grandparents' house in Wellesley."

"Give me the address and I'll be there in half an hour."

True to his word, Tray pulled up in his cruiser less than thirty minutes later, without lights or siren. "You remember my grandparents?" Gavin asked and welcomed his friend into the kitchen.

"It's been more than a year, but of course. Drs. O'Malley, good to see you again." Tray shook their hands. "And thanks for taking care of Gavin."

"Grandpa is going to go with me to make all the arrangements for the funeral," Gavin explained.

"Hold on," Tray said. "Is there somewhere you and I can talk?"

Gavin understood his friend's intent. "All right, we can go into the den." He looked to his grandfather, who nodded approval. "I'm going to get another cup of coffee. You want some?"

"No thanks. I've already had too much caffeine this morning."

As soon as they went into the den, Tray shut the door and got right to the point. "You need to get out of town, man."

"I have to make arrangements for my dad's funeral," Gavin objected. "And be there for the service and burial."

"You have a death wish? They know you saw who shot your father. They're after your brother, too."

"Shit." Gavin dropped into his grandfather's recliner chair.

"Yeah, we have the Irish mob in Somerville and Southie—remnants of the old Winter Hill gang." Tray leaned against the desk. "They have a long competition with the Italian mob in Boston and Providence. So we stay tuned to what's going on. The word is out there."

"That explains the reaction I got from the police in the North End." Gavin nodded.

"Like what? They didn't want to talk about your dad, only about where's Devon?"

"Bingo." Gavin hesitated. "I...I think I know who did it."

"Really?"

Gavin related what he'd seen, including names.

"That jibes with what I've heard...Spucky Spagnolo," Tray said. "Well, I think you should stay away from the North End. And definitely do *not* give those names to the police there."

Gavin stopped, as the weight of Tray's admonitions sank in. This was serious.

"Have you decided on a funeral home?" Tray pulled his friend back to the present.

Gavin blinked. "Not yet. We want to have the mass in St.

Leonard's and the burial here in Woodlawn."

"Where your mother was buried." Tray nodded slowly with a downcast look, as if recalling an old nightmare. "So...I can make arrangements with Waterman's on Commercial Street, and with St. Leonard's. I can use my badge to get the morgue to release your dad to Waterman's, if you make the call. Use your cell phone. You may have to sign a form. Do your grandparents have a fax machine here?"

"I think so, but if not, my grandmother can use one at the college."

"Use one at the college, so no one links the number to where you are," Tray began. "Then you and your grandparents can handle arrangements at Woodlawn. But you're going to need protection when you show up at the wake, the mass and the burial. I'll drive you in a squad car; that'll send a message. And I can get one of my buddies to be there, in plain clothes."

Gavin took in a deep breath. No words came out. Then, "What about my brother? I think he got hit with Jimbo's second shot, but he was able to keep on running."

"So far, I haven't heard that anyone knows where he is."

"He might be somewhere with my Uncle Marco, if anyone knows where he is."

"I'll put out some feelers. You gonna be okay, Gav?" Tray faced him and lay his hand on Gavin's shoulder. "I know you and your dad had some issues, but still..."

"That's the sad part," Gavin murmured. "Just a couple weeks ago, he came around and apologized, and told me a bunch of stuff that helped me understand him better. So it's like I was just getting to know him, and now he's gone."

"Remember what Pedersen always told you," Tray gripped Gavin's shoulder. "You are not responsible for saving everyone. Just save yourself."

"And Katie," Gavin nodded with grim determination.

After Tray left, Gavin filled his grandparents in on the plan. Then he took Katie into the den and closed the door. He hesitated, tense and nervous, like a rocket ready to launch. "What would you think about going on a honeymoon far away?"

Katie drew back in surprise. "Honeymoon?" she gasped. "That usually comes *after* the wedding."

"Well, that too," Gavin said, looking down with an embarrassed shrug.

"Gavin, that is the weirdest marriage proposal I've ever heard of," Katie said. "What prompted that?"

"We have to leave. They know I saw who killed my dad. I can't put you in danger too."

"But that's a lame reason for getting married."

"Katie, I have loved you, and wanted to be your husband, for so long—"

"And I love you too, Gav. You've always been so supportive of me, and my mother, too." Katie touched her hand to his cheek. "You're so good and kind. Unbelievably so."

"So is that a yes?"

"Can we sit down over here?" Katie motioned to the sofa.

Gavin's heart sank as he sat down. He was almost afraid to look at her.

Katie took his hand. "Gavin, you've given me the family I've never had. But you probably wouldn't be surprised that I might wonder whether there's something hidden in you that's a mirror of the dysfunctional stuff in your family. Your brother, your father, violence..."

Gavin nodded. "I've thought about that, too, Katie. It's something I've been afraid of for years. Maybe that's why it's always been so hard for me to fight back at them, afraid I might lose my temper."

"Well, you've had good reason to fight back. That's self-defense. But there's a line..."

"Do you think I'm capable of crossing that line? Being abusive?"

"I've never seen any of that in you. But..."

"I can't live without you Katie," Gavin pleaded. "I know that sounds melodramatic, but it's true. I don't know what I'd do without you. I promise you I will *never* hurt you. If you ever see any slight hint of that from me, you can and should walk out. After you kick me in the—"

"I don't want for us to be apart either, Gav," Katie said, almost in a whisper. "And I've never seen any reason, yet, to distrust you."

Gavin looked at her with fear and hope dueling all over him.

"Because I love you, and believe in you, I choose to trust you," Katie said slowly, locking eyes with him. "My experience with your family has taught me to recognize early indicators of abuse, so my trust comes equipped with that radar. Sort of like sleeping with one eye open."

Gavin nodded soberly. "If you prefer, marriage can wait till you feel more assured, Kat," He offered. "But I really have to get out of here, and I don't want to leave without you."

Katie squeezed his hand as a tiny smile parted her lips. "Well, you can't leave without me. Someone's got to take care of you. But just because we've been together since high school doesn't mean you can get away without proposing in the proper, romantic way." She crossed her arms and tipped up her chin.

Gavin quickly dropped to both knees before Katie and solemnly took her hand. "Will you, Kathryn Angela Goodwin, marry me?" he asked.

Katie giggled. "Much better."

"Is *that* a yes?"

"Yes, silly."

For a moment Gavin looked like a lost little boy. "I wish we could do the big wedding you deserve."

"I wish my mother was still alive..."

"I do too. Do you think she'd approve?"

"Of course. She loved you, and she always thought we'd get married eventually. It's just that I wish I would have her here to share it. And to lean on." Katie looked down. "Like, I don't have anyone to give me away, but you have your family. Your grandparents, uncle..."

"Family. Such as it is," Gavin mumbled. "But they already see you as part of the family, Kat. They're not as important as our safety is right now. Tray thinks that even if we just go back to New York, the mob has branches there too."

"So where would we go?"

"I'm thinking Hawaii. Not Honolulu, on O'ahu. One of the lesser islands, like maybe Kauai. I know a fellow CIA alum out there..."

27.

DEVON DIDN'T SHOW UP AT THE READING OF THE
will. Gavin learned that their father had just updated the will
the week before. He had left everything to his twins, to be
shared equally. Although he wanted no part of the liquor
business, his father had named him Executor with specific
instructions to take care of Devon. So nothing would change.

He recoiled at the thought of having to continue babysitting his twin. It was like he could never get away from the
dysfunction, which had finally become a life-or-death challenge.

The funeral home was a bland squat structure surrounded
by multi-story brick buildings on busy Commercial Street,
across from a skating rink on the waterfront edge of the North
End. Inside, subtle lighting, crown molding and large Persian-
style carpets attempted to lend an air of dignity to the otherwise depressing reality of death.

The room in which Tony in his casket was on view was
crowded that evening. Men in dark suits outnumbered women
by a wide margin. They milled about, among an overabun-
dance of floral arrangements, stiffly uncomfortable, hands in
pockets. Most seemed to be looking over their shoulder or
casting glances around the room, checking to see who was

there, who wasn't. Others had the flat practiced look of simply going through the motions.

Still no Devon. Where was he? Was he okay? Was he still alive?

Marco arrived, helping Joey hold up Grandpa DiMasi, who appeared shaken and ashen. Upon spotting his uncle, Gavin approached him. "Uncle Marco! I've been trying to reach you."

"Uh, yeah," Marco mumbled, not looking at him. "I've been out of town. Sorry about your dad."

"He was also your brother!" Gavin spat, disturbed by his uncle's detached attitude. "Have you seen Devon? Do you know where he is?"

"No." Marco abruptly turned to walk away.

Gavin caught his arm to stop him and spoke low into his ear. "Look, Uncle Marco. Just tell me whether my brother's still alive. Can you at least do that?"

"I don't know nothing, kid. And you should keep your mouth shut," he growled, and yanked his arm from Gavin. He walked over to where the Rizzo clan—including Maria and Eric—were huddled. They were all whispering, heads down and eyes darting.

Fury raged inside Gavin. He wanted to beat the shit out of his uncle, pummel the truth out of him, out of all the people standing around in this room pretending to mourn, pretending to know nothing. As if human life didn't matter. As if his father was a disposable commodity. And as if he could ever be whole without his other half.

As smoke signals of nascent violence emanated from Gavin, he was suddenly surrounded by the embraces of Tray, Katie, and his grandparents. Tray whispered in his ear, "Don't do it, Gav."

Gavin's muscles slowly released their tension as he fought to stifle bitter sobs. Anger, grief, frustration, helplessness all churned within him. He'd been robbed of his mother, his father, possibly his brother. He couldn't save any of them. And everyone was lying.

At least Katie and his grandparents were with him, and his best friend Tray was there, along with one of his fellow officers, both in funeral-appropriate attire.

Gavin looked around, seeing so many people he didn't know. Were any of them complicit in his father's death? Did any of them want to kill *him* now? He walked to his father's casket, kneeled and made the sign of the cross. His father looked peaceful, benign, nothing like the conflicted man he'd grown up with. Multiple opposing thoughts swirled in Gavin's head. He wondered whether he could ever sort it all out and finally achieve peace.

When he stood, a short thin man with a deeply lined tan approached him and extended his hand. "Hello, I guess you're Tony's son," he said. "I'm Harry Marino. Your dad and I worked together for many years. Great guy. I'm sorry for your loss."

"Thank you. I'm Gavin," he said, eyeing the man carefully. He reminded Gavin of a slimy lizard.

"It's terrible what happened. Do you know who did it?"

Gavin remembered what Tray told him. He mustn't give any indication that he knew anything, or even thought he knew. "I wish I did, sir," Gavin said. "It all happened so fast, it was just a blur. I was so focused on trying to help my father, I didn't really see anything else."

"I understand. It's such a tragedy. Well, good luck." And he was gone.

Visiting hours seemed to drag on. Gavin scrutinized every person there. He hoped Tray and his fellow officers might recognize whether any of them were known mobsters or suspects. Then he saw Frank Rizzo, Maria's father, breaking away from his family huddle and walking toward him with his hand out. "Gavin. I haven't seen you since your mother's burial," he began, clasping Gavin's hand in his and looking directly into his eyes. "And now this, another tragedy. Me and your father, we had our problems, but he didn't deserve to go this way. I'm sorry. You and your mother were always good people. I hope you can put this behind you and get on with your life. A good and happy life." He paused, still clasping Gavin's hand in both of his. "You like to travel?"

"Uh, sure. And thank you, sir," Gavin muttered, dumbfounded as Rizzo released his hand and walked away. Gavin opened his hand. A small silver charm lay nestled in his palm. He wondered why Rizzo gave it to him, then stuck it in his pocket.

When the hours of the wake were finally over and all the guests had gone, Gavin talked with the funeral director to confirm arrangements for services the next day. Tray gathered the guest book and cards attached to flowers. Although it was unlikely that any guilty party would provide their real name, it was necessary to follow all evidence.

"The limo will take you and your family back to Wellesley," Tray told Gavin as they exited the funeral home. "I'll ride with you; you'll be safe." He didn't mention the bullet-resistant tinted windows of the vehicle.

Tray rode in the enclosed front seat next to the limo driver, to monitor activity on his police radio, and to give the family privacy. But a heavy blanket of silence covered them all the way to Wellesley.

Once they arrived, Tray motioned Gavin to join him in the den. "Okay, so one of my friends from State Police will be outside your place tonight; he's coordinating with campus police," he said. "My buddy at the wake saw some guys he recognized, so I'll be looking into that."

———————

Gavin couldn't sleep that night. He couldn't stop worrying about Devon, hoping he was alive, hoping no one had come to finish the job. Long after Katie had drifted off to sleep, he gave up on sleep. He picked up his clothes from a side chair and tiptoed out of the room, gently closing the door behind him. Once he'd dressed in the den, he keyed in the house security code and stepped outside. He saw the unmarked car across the street, where the driver appeared asleep. Hoping the guy was a deep sleeper, he got into his Jeep and started the engine. Good thing he'd recently had it serviced and the muffler replaced; it wasn't as noisy as it had been. He pulled slowly out of the driveway with his headlights off.

At first he just drove around aimlessly. But then he found himself headed east on the Pike.

28.

GAVIN WOKE IN THE MORNING WITH AN OVER-bearing sense of dread. Every breath came as a struggle, as if a giant pillow were slowly suffocating him. Maybe Katie was right. He couldn't be sure what might be hidden dormant inside him.

Katie sensed Gavin's tension and stroked him softly. "We're all here for you, Sweetheart. We'll get through this together."

Gavin appreciated that, but his fear had escalated. Every little sound startled him. His neck muscles were stiff from tension. And from whipping his head around, looking behind him. Fear weighed him down to his knees. The overcast day and threatening clouds on the horizon seemed foreboding.

Tray's cruiser pulled into the driveway. He got out of his car to greet Gavin when he came out of the house, and pulled him aside. "Gav, I have some news."

"What?" That was all he could cough out.

"There was a fire around three o'clock this morning in the North End."

Gavin held his breath.

"Your brother's building..."

Gavin braced himself on the limo. "Was anyone hurt?" He

continued holding his breath.

"Two guys inside. They'd been shot."

"Who—?"

"Jimbo Halloran and Spucky Spagnolo."

"Where's Devon?"

"He wasn't there in the rubble. And we haven't found the responsible weapon yet."

"Does anyone know where he is?"

"No, man. But we're still looking. Probably for different reasons now."

Gavin's hand trembled as he got into the limo with Katie and his grandparents. He continued shivering as the car neared Boston, as if he'd stepped into a deep freezer to quell the fire within him.

St. Leonard's Church sat directly on the sidewalk of Prince Street in the North End. Its lush peace garden, with beautiful statuaries, was situated to its right on the corner of Hanover Street. Across Hanover, Prince Street was closed off due to the fire the night before. The smell of the conflagration still lingered in the air.

The exterior of St. Leonard's was unremarkable. In Romanesque Revival architecture, its squared asymmetry was represented in muscular unadorned brick, crowded by the surrounding newer brick buildings of the North End. There were two unequal square towers at each corner of the front, one with a pyramid on its top. There was no steeple, but over its apse at the back of the church perched a large white dome topped by a comparatively small plain cross.

But the interior of St. Leonard's was extravagantly ornate, thanks to the Italian immigrants who built it in the late 1800s. When Gavin walked into the church that morning, emotions took his breath away. He was bringing his father home.

Gavin remembered Frank Rizzo boasting about St. Leonard's before Devon's wedding. He hadn't been exaggerating. High above the altar, the concave mural of cherubim raising

Mary into heaven turned his joints to rubber. All the tension in him flowed out like a river, as if he were being baptized all over again, washed of all sin.

Devon didn't appear at the funeral service. Gavin's worry grew. Tray discouraged Gavin from speaking at his father's funeral. Too risky.

After the Catholic mass, during the long ride from St. Leonard's to Woodlawn Cemetery in Wellesley, Gavin closed his eyes and prayed, fingering the charm in his pocket. He couldn't remember the last time he'd prayed, much less when he might have meant it. But now he pleaded with God—if indeed there was a God—for his brother to be alive, to be safe. He begged for a sign.

Fierce winds churned roiling clouds across dark skies, but rain held off during the graveside ceremony. Mourners clustered uncomfortably around the plot. Joey had pushed Grandpa DiMasi to the graveside in a wheelchair, but Devon, Maria, Eric, the Rizzos, and even Marco were nowhere in sight. Tray joined Katie and the O'Malley grandparents, along with a few friends from high school and some of their former teachers, including Dr. Pedersen. After the military salute for Tony's service in Vietnam, soldiers folded the American flag into its iconic triangular form and presented it to Gavin. He was surprised by a feeling that he didn't deserve it, that it should go to Devon, then remembered what Dr. Pedersen had said—that abuse can rob a victim of self-confidence and belief in their own value. He caught himself; he thought he had overcome the inferior role he'd grown up with.

Gavin placed a white rose on his father's casket, then thanked each person as they left. He thought he caught a glimpse of Frank Rizzo's back, getting into a car ahead.

Gavin stayed behind while his father was lowered into the grave, then picked up a handful of dirt and dropped it onto the casket below as a final farewell. He turned to the adjacent grave and put his hand on his mother's headstone. He knelt in front of it and whispered, "He loved you, Mom. He really did. And he was sorry for the way he treated you. I forgave him. You understood him, so I hope you'll forgive him and welcome him home beside you."

He wiped tears from his cheeks, bit his quivering lips and stood.

Tray left the graveside and started up his police car to escort the limousine along the winding tree-lined path out of the cemetery. His car was well ahead when Gavin got into the limo to join Katie. He scanned out the window, hoping for a sign as the limo began a slow exit from the cemetery.

Suddenly Gavin caught a blur of someone with red hair darting behind a tree. "STOP!!" he yelled, opening the door and jumping out while the limo was still moving. He ran, zig-zagging around headstones and trees, finally catching up with Devon, tackling him onto the ground as Katie stared aghast out the window.

"Where the fuck did you go? You've made a mess of everything, you goddamned son of a bitch! And you expect me and everyone else to clean up after you!" He punched and pounded his brother with decades of pent-up fury, like a dormant volcano erupting. Finally both were breathless, but the hot lava of Gavin's anger lingered.

"Nice to see you, too, baby brother," Devon moaned through a bloody lip.

"Get up, asshole." There was a large bandage covering Devon's right ear and neck. Gavin recalled the spray of red from his brother as he ran from the shooter.

Devon just stayed on the ground, rolling like a puppy wanting its belly rubbed. "I have to lay low, Gav," he said. "They're after me."

"Who's after you?"

"Some guys from Providence. I can't tell you."

"What're you going to do?"

"I've got to go into hiding. And you should, too."

"Yeah, they know I saw who did it! This is all because of you—you think you're so damn smart. And Dad is dead, thanks to you, too!"

"Why should you care, Twinkie? Dad was always a jerk to you."

"He's our father. He had his own problems."

"And he gave those problems to me."

"Oh, poor you. The Chosen One."

"Well, I know what *you* did, Twinkie." Devon purred, attempting a conspiratorial half-smile. "Thanks—I didn't think you cared. But your secret is safe with me—I take back all those 'Goodie Gavin' jabs."

"You're a real fuck-up, aren't you? Just look what you've done to all of us!" Gavin knew that Katie had just seen his violent outburst, the effect Devon had on him.

"Ah, but I'm the best fuck up anywhere, all-time best." Devon laughed, wincing from his bruises and patting his bandage, which was blossoming red. He struggled to rise from the ground, holding his hand up to his brother.

Gavin didn't oblige. "Well, I value my life. I don't want you anywhere near me and Katie."

"Gav, I wish we could be like we always were," Devon mumbled, his mouth beginning to swell and blood streaming from his nose. "I love you. I always have," he whined in a thready whisper.

"Well, I *never* want to go back to that dysfunction, so just stay away from me," Gavin said. "But keep out of trouble." He turned to leave, then turned back. "And stay alive."

He strode back to the limousine just as Tray was running to him from his car, to see what was going on. Devon had already disappeared.

When Gavin got into the limo, Katie put her arm around him. "You finally fought back, Gav. It's okay."

But he knew it was far from over.

Gavin and Katie appeared at the Norfolk County Circuit Court in Canton the next morning to pick up their marriage license. They were then joined by Grandma and Grandpa O'Malley, Tray who was serving as Gavin's best man, and Dr. Pedersen. On most occasions a wedding would be cause for joy and happiness among participants, but what had triggered the timing of this ceremony cast a tense urgency over the group. Something akin to a shotgun wedding.

They all stood impatiently as the Justice of the Peace droned through the traditional marriage ceremony. When the officiant came to the part where he asked, "Who gives this woman in marriage to this man?", Grandpa stepped forward to claim responsibility, squeezing Katie's shoulder. She smiled her gratitude, blinking wetness from her eyes.

Katie wanted to speak her own vows. "Gavin O'Malley DiMasi, I've loved you since we were fifteen years old. You've always been attentive and caring, hearing my heart, feeling my joys and my pains, putting me first in your priorities. Your intelligence, passion, creativity and diligence have inspired me to be more and do more than I ever thought possible. Your constant unconditional love and belief in me—and in us—is what will keep me by your side all the days of my life. I'm so honored to be your wife, and I know we'll make a wonderful life together, with all its ups and downs. I love you now and forever."

Gavin stammered. He was surprised. He hadn't prepared, or even thought about, speaking his own vows. In that moment, the gravity of what was happening began to overwhelm him. Fleeing to Kauai was his desperate rush to escape danger. His father had just been killed. By a bullet meant for his brother. Gavin knew who did it, and they knew he knew. But he also held tightly to another secret.

Yet there he stood beside the woman he'd loved for almost a decade, whose good family had its own tragedies, who nevertheless loved him despite all the toxicity and tragedy drowning his life. He had been powerless to save his mother, his father, his twin brother, and even himself. And now he was bringing the woman he loved beyond all measure into the dangerous mess that was his life. How could he protect her? The hopelessness of that burden, that guilt, clawed at him, thrashing him from total collapse to running away.

He felt Katie squeeze his hands. He looked into her radiant face. His heart had been broken many times, but at that moment it was full of gratitude for the remarkable woman who loved him despite everything. He swallowed the lump in his throat and spoke. "Kathryn Angela Goodwin, I'm so lucky to have earned your love. You're the strongest person I know. You've been my loyal supporter through more bad situations than a life partner should ever have to deal with, yet you've stuck by me in spite of all that. I pledge to always try to earn your love, loyalty and trust. I'll be your most ardent supporter, through all the challenges that may come your way. Our way. Together we'll have a good life, rich in love and caring, constant through good times and bad. I'll love you always." Then with an urgent ferocity he added, "And I will protect you with my life."

Katie drew back with startled eyes upon hearing the vehemence in Gavin's final pledge.

The Justice of the Peace fidgeted impatiently. Weddings in his dreary office were usually a perfunctory ritual. He hurried through the balance of the ceremony, quickly getting to the conclusion: "I now pronounce you husband and wife."

With soft applause, the grandparents and Tray surrounded the newlyweds with hugs and blessings. Dr. Pedersen approached Gavin as the hug-circle broke up. "I'm proud of you, Gavin. It hasn't been easy."

"Right. Not easy. In fact, deadly."

"But you will finally triumph over family tragedy."

"With half the family gone, does the dysfunction go down by half?"

"The ghost of past dysfunction remains. But you're getting distance, and a fresh start. You will be victorious," Pedersen declared, in a firm command. "You always know how to reach me if you want to talk."

"But no chamomile tea."

Tray broke in. "Excuse me, Dr. Pedersen. It's time for me to drive the newlyweds to the airport." He quickly ushered Gavin and Katie out of the courthouse and into his police car. "Sorry I didn't paint 'Just Married' on the car, guys," he joked.

Gavin held Katie in the back seat. He hadn't thought much about the Grateful Dead since that concert with Tray in high school, but just then the lyrics of one of their songs whispered from his memory. *"Don't wanna be treated this a-way, Goin' where the climate suits my clothes..."*

When Tray pulled up to the departure curb at Logan, he got out to say goodbye to his friends. He pulled Gavin aside and spoke low. "Be careful and stay safe. I'll be in touch. Love you, man."

———————

As the airplane lifted, rising through clouds and leaving earth far below, Gavin cuddled into Katie's warmth beside him. His wife. He fingered the charm in his pocket and pulled it out to inspect it. In that moment he recognized that it depicted Saint Christopher, the patron saint of travelers. Parts of the prayer from childhood came back to him.

> *St. Christopher, protect me today in all my travels along the road's way. Give your warning sign if danger is near so that I may stop while the path is clear. Be at my window and*

*direct me through when the vision blurs. Carry
me safely to my destined place, like you carried
Christ in your close embrace.*

Now he understood. Frank Rizzo was urging him to travel.
To leave town, for his safety.

29.

IT WAS THE BEST NIGHT'S SLEEP GAVIN HAD HAD IN a very long time. No bad dreams or nagging worries, only the total surrender of complete exhaustion from a day of hiking in Waimea Canyon. He enjoyed the touch of cool cotton sheets against his skin as he lay beside his wife, whose soft snoring always made him love her even more. He relished those words...*my wife.*

After two weeks in Kauai, he still hadn't fully adjusted to the time difference. He'd awakened before four o'clock. It was ten a.m. back home; so he had managed to compensate by three or four hours.

Smells of saltwater drifted through the open windows of their resort suite. Shadows of surrounding palms moved in silence on the walls of their bedroom. It would be another two hours before the crowing and clucking of the local population of feral chickens would waken Katie.

Gavin carefully got out of bed, quietly pulled on his shorts and went out through the sliding door. His bare feet felt the cool dew on stiff Bermuda grass as he walked the short distance toward the beach. Although the sun hadn't yet risen, the area was sufficiently illuminated by the unimpeded starlight of the night sky, and the resort's safety lamps.

Waves lapped the shore in rhythmic order, with quiet seduction. There was no moon on this night. When he reached the sand, he scrunched his toes into the coarse damp grains. Sparkles of light danced the Milky Way on gentle Pacific ripples. He recalled waves earlier in the week had been a lot stronger—violent, even. Gavin stood and filled his lungs with salty air, suspended in calm.

Their time on the island had been the perfect escape from the drama back home. Between exploring, hiking, boating, ziplining, and walking the beaches, Gavin had frequented many restaurants, talked with chefs, studied local cuisine and agriculture. But as he considered the return flight in two days, his euphoria gave way to dread. Like stirring a béchamel past the point of perfection and seeing it curdle into gelatinous lumps.

He walked a short way up the beach and sat down on a large boulder. Every one of his senses were both stimulated and soothed. Rhythmic surf keeping time with his heartbeat. Soft breezes caressing his skin and playing with his hair. Fresh air heaving off Pacific waters, teasing his nostrils and renewing his lungs. Tastes of last night's tuna poke reminiscing on his tongue. Adrift in calm, every muscle melding into his surroundings, lost in time and space. As if in a trance, his thoughts floated, unfettered...to the beauty of the island, the kindness and authenticity of the people, the creative originality of the culture, the richness of indigenous history...

Dawn gradually crept in, brightening the sky in expanding colors, pulling up the sun from behind the horizon bit by bit. As its beams pierced Gavin's eyes, a charge of energy coursed through him, sparking his languor into purpose. He jumped up and ran back to their unit in the resort. Disregarding the need for quiet, he flung open the slider, which roused Katie from sleep. "Hey, Gav," her voice croaked. "You up already?"

Gavin ran to the bed and jumped on his wife, holding her in his arms and smothering her with kisses.

"Whoa!" Katie coughed, trying to open her eyes still matted with sleep. "What's up with you, Tiger?"

Gavin rolled over and lay beside her. "What would you think about moving here?"

"Moving here?" she squeaked, sleep still clinging to her voice. "To Kauai? Like, not just our honeymoon?"

"Yes!" Gavin cheered, his face nearly cracking with excitement. "The chef up in Princeville told me yesterday he's leaving, going to a restaurant on the Big Island. He's impressed with my background. He said he would recommend me to take over for him!"

"You could have any chef position you want back home, Gav."

"You overestimate me, Kat. But Devon's 'Mob Avengers' may still be after me, and I don't think they can find me here. I have to protect you, too."

"Is that the main reason you want to move here?" Katie looked into his eyes, suddenly serious, and stroked his arm.

Gavin looked down, nodding. "Sweetie, I *have* to get as far away from Devon as possible," he said. "It feels like he has suffocated me all our lives. I have to leave all that behind, be my own man, not just Devon's twin. I don't think I can really thrive if I don't completely break free of him." Gavin rolled over on the bed toward Katie, curled in a near-fetal position. He searched her face for a sign of understanding.

His words rushed out, as if convincing Katie was a matter of life or death—his as well as hers. "Our marriage could suffer from that tension, too, if we don't get away. I know you love it here! It'll be a low-stress place to raise a family, and you can put your degree and experience to work for plenty of businesses here on the island. Maybe you can open your own art gallery!"

Katie placed her finger on Gavin's lips. "I get it. But we need to consider the cost of living here, whether we can afford it, find a place to live, and be totally sure."

30.

THE SMELL. IT STRUCK GAVIN RIGHT OFF, EVEN
before Manu opened the door. Noxious, acrid. It triggered
something long stored in his memory closet. But he couldn't
quite put his finger on it.

Manu had been pitching Gavin for several weeks to check
out a few of his properties. "Hot chef like you should have his
own restaurant—the island needs you!"

Finally Gavin relented, more out of curiosity than serious
interest. This was the third property Manu had shown him,
the last in his current inventory. "The last guys here left the
island," Manu complained. "They owed me more than six
months, and totally skipped out on the rest of the lease."

"What kind of restaurant was here before?" Gavin asked.
He looked at Katie and raised his eyebrow, soliciting her
reaction.

"Chinese. They were from Taiwan," Manu said, guiding
Gavin and Katie through the abandoned space. "It's a mess,
but you can completely gut it and make it into your dream.
Almost two thousand square feet plus the covered patio. You
can screen it pretty easy if you want. And there's an option for
the smaller space next door. Both places are already zoned for
restaurant with alcohol license, and the location is perfect for

driving traffic to your door."

"Looks like they left in a real hurry," Katie said, looking around at the haphazard piles of restaurant supplies and structural materials. Her eyes landed on the overhead panels, grease-stained asbestos. "What's above that ceiling tile?"

Manu looked around and grabbed a stray board, pushing up one of the grimy drop-ceiling panels. "You can see it's wide open to the underside of the high slanted roof. So you could even have a vaulted ceiling effect if you wanted."

"What about permits?" Gavin asked. "I hear it's almost impossible for *haole* to get approvals."

"Ah, that's the advantage of leasing from me," Manu chuckled, slapping Gavin on the back. "I own the property so as *kanaka maoli* I can push the right people. And besides, man, you've already made a reputation on the island. Everybody loves the gourmet chef from Princeville Resort. You've been written up in all the island guides."

Gavin walked around, envisioning his new kitchen, and what he could do with the space. In the distance, Nounou Mountain (locally known as Sleeping Giant), verdant in the morning sun, seemed to project a glow—a blessing—onto the rear patio. He imagined tables crowded with people, an open kitchen with a woodfired grill, a bustling bar...

But he was getting ahead of himself. He wasn't sure if he was ready for owning his own restaurant at all, or if this location would be the best. Or what Katie thought.

Manu excused himself to take a call, walking out to the back patio.

"What are you thinking?" Katie whispered.

"Wondering what you thought," Gavin grinned sheepishly.

"I think it could be perfect."

"Do you think we're ready?"

"You've always wanted to create your own brand, your

own cuisine. Which you're limited in doing, by the resort owners in Princeville."

"I don't know...We've only been on the island for less than a year. I'm not even twenty-five yet. With almost zero credit history. No one's going to give us financing."

"That ex-CIA chef who came to visit—Andre something, the one who has chains on O'ahu and Maui. He really encouraged you, and he's very successful. Maybe he would co-sign."

"The whole process could be really high stress and risky," Gavin shook his head.

"I already have four clients, so that should help qualify us for loans," Katie said. "And risk? All of life is a gamble."

"Well, if you think the space looks promising, and you're prepared for a lot of pressure, we can do the due diligence, and then if everything checks out, decide if we want to go for it."

Manu came back in from the patio. "Well, what do you think, man? That was another guy who's really interested. He wants to put in a barbeque joint."

"Another one?" Gavin groaned. The island had an overload of lousy barbeques. "What did you say you're asking?" Gavin prodded. Questions and uncertainty swirled in his head. The process of liquidating his dad's assets was still ongoing, slow and complex; as Executor of his father's estate, he hoped he could get approval for an advance for the deposit. Then he had no idea whether Andre would co-sign the loan for the rest. And he didn't know where Devon was, to split the estate with him, so he'd have to hold half of everything in an escrow account...

"I think those idiots had at least three fires here their first year," Manu grumbled, gesturing to some charred boards and evading Gavin's question. "I know that'll never happen with you, Gav."

And then it came to him. The smell. Years ago, senior year of high school. Waking up at three in the morning, the acrid stench of burning fat intruding through his window. Turned out it was from a fire at the Chinese restaurant up on Route 9. He had jumped out of bed and run down the hall to his brother's room to see if the smell had wakened Devon. His twin was gone.

Later that night, shots of gunfire interrupted Gavin's dream, giving way to crackles of fire, smoke rising, billowing, flames growing higher, surrounding him, explosions, walls tumbling upon him...He woke groaning, panting as if he were being chased by malevolent demons.

31.

TWO MONTHS LATER ON GAVIN'S DAY OFF, HE WAS awakened at seven-thirty by Katie retching in the bathroom of their small house in Kapa'a. He silently hoped she hadn't caught a bug. There was so much to do as they ramped up all the requisite processes for completing their restaurant.

But soon he sniffed the smoky fragrance of Kona peaberry coffee brewing, rolled out of bed and shuffled into the kitchen. "Morning, beautiful," he whispered into Katie's loose curls, kissing her neck from behind.

"Did you sleep well?" she asked, pouring a big cup for him.

"Yeah. Never enough, though." He raised his arms high and stretched long, with the roar of a wild primate, then with a big sigh sat down at their thrift-shop table and began prattling on between bites of bagel. "Today we need to get the architect to finish the plan revisions, make sure they're compliant with commercial codes—I can't believe there's like more than fifty requirements on that checklist! Then get Manu to re-submit the plans and talk to each of the what?—*ten* different DPW departments!—so we can fast-track our permits. Then we meet with the carpenters and electricians to finalize their contracts. Then we're meeting with the bank, right? What are you telling your clients? Things are going to get really intense..."

Katie stood watching Gavin with a patient smile.

He looked up, realizing his wife hadn't spoken. "Are you all right, Kat? I heard you getting sick in the bathroom this morning. You haven't caught something, have you?"

Katie's smile widened. She turned around to pick up a short white plastic stick from the counter and put it on the table in front of Gavin. It had two parallel red lines in a small window across its middle. Gavin looked closely, unsure of what he was seeing. Finally the words beside the window sank in.

"PREGNANT?" he screamed, jumping up from his chair and throwing his arms around Katie, lifting her in the air and swinging her around. Then just as quickly he set her down gently in a chair, knelt beside her, took her hands in his and began to prattle on again—but more urgently. "Oh, I'm sorry. We have to be careful. Are you going to be okay? We need to go see a doctor! How do you feel? When are you due? Shouldn't you be in bed? We have to cancel the restaurant deal!"

At that point Katie began giggling uncontrollably. She placed her hand on Gavin's mouth. "Shush, silly," she stifled her laughter. "I don't have a deadly illness. We're just going to have a baby. It's not like pregnancy is a disability or handicap. And we certainly aren't going to back out of our restaurant."

"But there's so much to do!" Gavin moaned.

"Don't worry. I have a comprehensive checklist, timeline, contacts, what equipment and furnishings to order, what staff we need to hire, suppliers to engage, blah-blah...You still have to work in Princeville six days a week, and that's why I'm here. We've got this. The whole nine yards."

Gavin stared at her, once again awed by her grit. This beautiful delicate woman. Who could guess?

Katie tweaked his nose. "But you still haven't explained to me why it's nine yards instead of ten, like for a first down."

Gavin laughed and hugged her. "But how can you do all

that when you're pregnant?"

"It's not like I'm going to be building the place and hauling stuff, Gav. Besides, we should be open for business by the time I'm five or six months along. Chill."

———————

Katie and Gavin would soon realize the naïveté of assuming a reasonable schedule.

As in many places, Kauai's public officials—such as the Inspectors and Permit Officers in county departments—often went off to the state capital (another island in this case) for weeks at a time, some of them demonstrating incompetence when they finally returned. The interdependencies among departments could stymie forward progress even further, resulting in many steps of Katie's complex flowchart exploding with additional required steps. Despite Manu's native status and Andre's influence at the state level, the project lurched along in a maddeningly glacial pace.

But by November, thanks to their dogged determination and hard work—and Katie's effectiveness as project manager—they were planning to open 'Ono Kūloko (Local Taste) the week of Thanksgiving. With Katie's eye for design, the place was stunning on a modest budget. Recycled wood lent a rustic air, and paired with corrugated steel, faux granite counters and tabletops, and clusters of Edison light fixtures hanging from the vaulted ceiling, the result was both warm and sleek contemporary.

They would begin with a "soft opening", with no PR fanfare and a limited number of invited guests, followed by a slow rollout. That would allow time for any unanticipated issues to arise and be corrected before too many customers strained the process. Fortunately, Thanksgiving was the last Thursday in November that year, giving them more time to prepare. Gavin had prepared menus around locally-sourced ingredients, perfected his sauces, trained kitchen staff, installed special cooling systems for the microbrew kegs, and a hundred other requisite things to ensure readiness.

Gavin rubbed Katie's belly. "How're you feeling, Kat?" he asked, a week away from their opening day.

"Happy we aren't having twins," Katie grunted, hitching up her eight-months-pregnant abdomen with both hands.

"Are you gonna be okay?" Gavin asked, peering into her face. "Promise me you won't do too much. You have me, and now a staff to help out. You don't have to keep on doing everything."

"I promise," Katie sighed, lifting her butt onto one of the sleek bar stools that had just been delivered.

"Are you nervous?"

"I think we're as prepared as anyone can possibly be for the opening."

"I mean about the baby," Gavin stroked her belly again.

"We have another month, Gav," Katie did an eye roll and shook her head. "No need to get worked up about it. Let's just get through opening our restaurant. One thing at a time."

Gavin stood in front of her and pulled her into his chest. "You're more important to me than anything in the world, sweetheart. You, and our baby. Way more important than the restaurant."

"We're going to be okay, Gav. Just rolling it out slowly before we get too many surprises."

But they hadn't accounted for island gossip. Their soft opening with invited guests was supposed to kick off at five o'clock on the Monday before Thanksgiving. Shortly after four that afternoon, cars began arriving in their parking lot. Soon the lot was full and cars were circling, looking for parking places across the highway. People began banging on the front door of the restaurant and a line formed out on the sidewalk.

Katie had required the wait staff to come in early so she could review training and procedures with them, and get everything set up. Gavin had assembled his kitchen crew early and had already started the woodfired grill to build up its heat. So by four-thirty, Katie decided to begin letting people in, treating everyone to their choice of a drink from among the twenty-three microbrews on tap, wine or champagne.

The night became one protracted scramble. Their maiden voyage opening was anything but slow, and it certainly didn't "roll". It stampeded, like an out-of-control herd of wild horses. By eight o'clock, Katie finally complied with Gavin's insistence that she sit, and at ten o'clock she agreed to go home to bed. By eleven o'clock the crowd had drained the entire inventory Gavin had provisioned for the week. By closing time, they had served almost four hundred customers. After cleaning up the place, Gavin didn't get home until two in the morning.

It was still dark when he got up at five-thirty the next morning. The sun wouldn't rise for another hour and a half. He couldn't count on the local farmers, suppliers and abattoir to deliver what he needed before the restaurant had to prepare for its first lunch that day, so he began driving to each location to get enough for midday; he would order provisions to be delivered for that night and week when he arrived at each. As he drove, he listened to the local radio host announcing the weather for the day, ads for car dealers and tour guides, then, "The hottest thing on the island last night was in Kapa'a—the opening of a new urban chic restaurant, 'Ono Kūloko. Our reporter Jenny Stevens was there, and tells us it was packed with people enjoying an exciting menu of locally-sourced food and beverages created by Gavin DiMasi, former gourmet chef at Princeville Resort. Jenny tells me that everyone who is anyone in Kapa'a was there—and some VIPs from O'ahu, too. So there you have it. Looks like DiMasi's new venture is the next 'In Place' to be!"

So much for soft openings and slow rollouts.

Soon, every wedding planner and hotel concierge on the island began recommending their clients to 'Ono Kūloko.

Reporters from all media requested interviews, which were published and distributed widely, including international tour guides. Large floral tributes arrived at the restaurant daily—including congratulatory bouquets from the O'Malley grandparents, Tray and Dr. Pedersen.

Gavin rarely got much more than three or four hours sleep each night. Katie managed to get five or six hours. Aside from that first opening Monday, the restaurant's normal schedule would be Tuesday through Sunday, with Mondays serving as the time for deep clean, payroll, ordering, bill-paying, and bookkeeping. Not for sleeping.

32.

ALTHOUGH GAVIN AND KATIE MANAGED TO SLEEP till eight that first Monday after Thanksgiving, the days of getting a good night's sleep were soon over. On the next Monday a week later, Katie felt a tremor before dawn. And then an earthquake.

Katie had wanted to have a home birth with *palekeiki*—a midwife trained in local culture practices—but Gavin was so worried and overprotective that he insisted on a hospital birth. All during Katie's labor that day, Gavin was by her side, doing everything they'd practiced in their Lamaze classes. Between each round of contractions, he fussed over his wife, offering ice chips, rubbing her back, holding her hand, mopping her forehead, asking how she felt. And pacing.

"Gavin dear," Katie murmured. "Will you please just relax? Everything's okay...oh, here comes another one...*(pant-pant-pant...)*"

Margaret Colleen DiMasi arrived at 2:05 that afternoon, almost two weeks early, weighing six pounds ten ounces and equipped with a healthy set of lungs. Gavin was the first to hold little Maggie, who carried the names of both Katie's mother and Gavin's. He was overcome with a dizzying eupho-ria that nearly swept him off his feet. Giggling and crying at the same time, fearful he could do something wrong or hurt the baby, he handed her to Katie.

"She's so beautiful, Kat. Oh my god, she's so perfect."

"It looks like she has orangey-red fuzz on her head, Gav."

"And she has your nose, Mama."

"I can't wait to take her home. How soon will they release me?"

"Tomorrow," the doctor interjected as he walked into the room. "Providing everything is okay. Right now the new dad needs to leave and let the new mother rest."

"I'll be back later, Kat," Gavin said, kissing her as he reluctantly left. He was almost more exhausted than the new mother was. But when he walked outside the Mahelona Medical Center into the sunshine, he wanted to jump, shout, and turn cartwheels. His heart was so deliriously full he couldn't contain himself. A joy he'd never felt before washed over him like a powerful tsunami, taking his breath away.

He began running. Up the hill in the direction of their house, but with no intention of going home. He just ran, as if there were some magical destination that might reflect his happiness, confer validation that he was worthy of such a wondrous blessing. That precious healthy baby, his amazing wife. There was something sacred, even holy about the miracle that just occurred. What had he done to deserve this?

As he ran, he approached the sharply angled outlines of a contemporary building he'd passed daily but never really paid attention to. He hadn't been in a church since his father's death, but now he slowed, drawn to the open door of Saint Catherine's Catholic Church.

The interior of the little church was simple, although warmer and more embracing than the exterior. No stained-glass windows, but light streamed in through plain windows under a vaulted industrial-beam ceiling, illuminating colorful murals interpreting Bible scenes in Hawaiian terms and telling stories of the parish history and its people. Austere contemporary wood benches lined up in front of the altar. A breathless silence hung in the space.

Gavin walked gingerly down the aisle, as if fearful of disturbing the quiet. He lowered himself onto the edge of the front bench and looked at the altar. It wasn't perched on an elevated sanctuary as in most churches he'd been in. Behind it was a mural of the cross surrounded by indigenous peoples. It all seemed accessible, connected to real day-to-day life. It felt personal, so present. Unlike the grand, distant, ethereal Saint John's he grew up in, or Saint Leonard's where his father grew up. This was a life he could embrace in reverence and humility, be a part of, not stand back in awe. It was the culture in which he would raise his daughter.

The last time he'd prayed, he asked for a sign that his brother was still alive. Now he prayed to God for the strength and wisdom to keep his daughter and wife safe.

33.

ALTHOUGH THREE-WEEK-OLD MAGGIE OBLIGED her parents by still being asleep in her bassinet at seven-thirty that Christmas morning, there would be no rest.

First the doorbell and then pounding on the front door dragged Gavin out of bed, and triggered Maggie's morning aria. Gavin prepared to chew someone out for disturbing his family on Christmas morning. Instead, when he opened the door, the bottom fell out of his world.

Below a coal black buzz cut, the ghostly white face of his double taunted. A dark trepidation overcame Gavin, like in a horror movie where the evil clown keeps coming back, after you thought you'd vanquished it forever.

"Twinkie!" shrieked Devon. He barged past his brother with his arms full of wrapped gifts. A gaunt graying Eric trailed behind him with more gifts.

"Merry Christmas!" Devon crowed as he stalked around Gavin's living room and into the kitchen. "Your place is really little, Gav. I guess your restaurant business isn't very successful. And I don't smell coffee for my breakfast, Julia. And no bacon either. I thought you're supposed to be a famous chef now!"

Warring thoughts competed in Gavin's brain, fear surpassing dread. He thought he'd shed his brother forever, the poison that shackled his identity, his personhood. Now his impulse was torn between assault and running. The presence of his twin in his house—his sacred ground—felt life-threating.

Gavin tried to control himself, level his voice. "The last time I saw you, I told you to stay away from me and Katie, that I never wanted to see you again," he eked out one word at a time.

"But I brought gifts, Gav! For you, your lovely wife, your baby girl!"

Gavin could feel the effects of his two a.m. closing-up beer somersaulting in his stomach. Devon seemed to know all about his current life, which clanged alarm bells in his head. If Devon knew all that and managed to find him, so could the mob. And where Devon was, could they be far behind? The monster had returned for Gavin. And his family. He might run, but he couldn't hide.

Katie peeked down the hall to see what was going on, clutching Maggie to her breast. Gavin caught her eye and tele-graphed a subtle negatory. She ducked back into their bed-room.

"Devon, I want you and your boyfriend gone," he spat. "Now."

"Aw, Twinkie," Devon whined. "I came to make peace, and to help you! You're going to need my experience to make your restaurant successful. I know more about business than any-one!"

Gavin advanced toward his brother, one determined stride after the other. "I don't need anything from you, asshole. You're a danger to my family and a toxic parasite to me," he growled. "I'll give you sixty seconds to walk out the door, or I call my police officer friend."

"Oh, is that Puna Mahi'ai? That fat turd? He's *my* friend—I hung out with him last night."

"You're never going to stop taking over my life, are you?

Isn't it enough you've fucked up your own life, you have to take me down with you?" Gavin raised himself up, as if he were growing a foot taller than his brother, expanding like the Incredible Hulk, complete with seething green Hulk fury. "Get. The fuck. Out. Of here!" his voice boomed from deep within him. The earth trembled. "And take this damned shit with you." He kicked a box, sending it sailing out the open door with the precision of a field goal. "I don't want any of it, and I sure don't want you."

In an instant, Gavin transformed into a human bulldozer, spreading his arms wide and scooping his brother and Eric in one fell swoop toward the door, throwing and kicking gifts behind them. Boxes of all sizes took flight, just like the chess pieces Gavin had always yearned to send airborne.

He finally launched Devon off the top of his stairs in a contorted somersault, sailing and tumbling like his mother did. Landing on Gavin's front lawn, the former wrestler had lost whatever skills he once had and lay helpless in the grass.

Gavin slammed and locked the door behind him. The mantra Dr. Pedersen and Tray had drummed into him began its beat again. *You aren't responsible for saving everyone. Just save yourself.* He couldn't save his sociopathic brother. But Katie and their baby were now the only family that mattered. Where his true self resided.

He scrambled for his phone and called Puna's cell.

"Hey, buddy," Gavin tried to calm his voice. "You on duty today?"

"Not till this afternoon, Gav. It's gonna be tough though. I've been up since five, thanks to my kids so excited to open their Christmas presents. My third cup of coffee isn't much help."

"Sorry to bother you on Christmas, Man. Would it be okay if I came over for a few minutes? Something's happened, kind of important."

"If it's important to you, of course. I'll have Nalani put on a fresh pot of coffee."

"I'm bringing Katie and the baby with me. Can't leave them alone now."

Gavin hung up before he could notice Puna's puzzled silence.

"Do you really think Devon would come back and make a scene?" Katie asked as Gavin abruptly rushed her and Maggie out the door. "I sure don't want Maggie exposed to DiMasi madness."

"I don't know. I'm just really worried about him showing up out of the blue. Like, how did he find me?"

"Sweetie, articles about our restaurant and you the famous chef were published not just here, but in travel magazines distributed on the mainland too."

"Crap. Maybe no one in the Boston Mob reads travel magazines."

When they arrived at Puna's house, his friend greeted him with a cup of coffee. With whiskey in it and topped by a dollop of whipped cream. "I know your middle name is Irish, and I'm guessing you might need this..."

"You're a genius."

Puna motioned Gavin out to his back patio in the shadow of Sleeping Giant. Puna's land was a *kuleana* (responsibility) plot that had been in his family for generations, having been awarded to his *maka'āinana* (commoner) ancestors in 1850 during the *Mahele* (divide), as compensation for their having worked the land. Katie stayed behind to chat with Nalani and share Maggie with their three kids. The oldest, fourteen-year-old Anela, hovered over Maggie, undoubtedly hoping to become the baby's sitter.

"So what's up?" Puna began, before he'd fully settled into his broad koa wood chair.

That was one reason Gavin liked Puna. No bullshit, straight to the point.

"Did you see a guy from the mainland last night with a

black buzz cut, pale skin?" Gavin asked.

Puna paused to think. "Yeah. Said his name was Dave something. Real friendly guy. Something about his face reminded me of you, actually. He looked like he used shoe polish on his hair," he smirked.

"I never told you I have a brother. That was Devon, my identical twin."

Puna drew back with a confused look.

"He dyed his hair because he's running from the mob. Boston Mob."

"Holy shit. What'd he do to piss them off?"

"Stupid stuff. Because he's so fucking smart. So they put out a hit on him, guy came with a gun, my dad stepped in and got the bullet instead. I was there and saw who did it, so they're probably looking for both of us now."

"Holy shit. Your father?"

"Died. Yes."

"That's why you moved here."

"Yeah. To avoid the mob *and* my brother."

"I'm sure you're glad the mob hasn't got to him. But why do you want to avoid him?"

"Well, I'm glad he's still alive, but not that he showed up here. If he managed to find me, that means the mob can too, and if they're following him, they might find me too."

Puna gazed out to the mountain and nodded slowly, processing all that.

"On top of that, my brother is mentally ill. Sociopathic. There are times he's even psychopathic. I don't want him around me or my family."

Puna drew back, incredulous. "Really? He seemed like a nice guy."

"He's been diagnosed with Malignant Narcissistic Personality Disorder."

"That's a mouthful."

"People with that disorder are very charming, but it's a foil for being deceitful and manipulative. They need to dominate, be seen as the best in everything even if they're actually not. Devon's been messing with me since we were kids, convincing me I'm a loser, he's a winner, and I'm nothing without him."

"Well, that sure isn't true."

"It's like he's obsessed with owning me. Controlling me."

"This is all heavy shit, Gav. As your friend, I'm really sorry. I'm not sure if there's anything I can do as a police officer though, unless you can get a restraining order. That's gonna be hard if you can't prove he's physically threatening you."

"Yeah, I know. But if I call you the next time he comes creeping around me and my family, maybe he could be arrested for trespassing. Or if he's still using..."

"What, drugs?"

"Yeah, big time. Trafficking too."

"Did he ever get caught?"

"Yes, but he didn't serve time or anything. Just rehab."

"But that has to be on his record, and a rehab deal usually requires staying clean after."

"So you're saying that if he's caught with it now, he could be put away. But dredging up that old charge could trigger a tip to the mob on where he is now..."

"Which would also tip them to where you are."

"Catch-22."

A resigned silence settled between the two friends.

"One thing I don't get is the 'identical' twin thing," Puna said. "How can one of you have a mental illness and the other be straight arrow?"

"Yes, it's weird. Personalities can be different; they aren't tied to genetics or DNA, like some mental illnesses are. But my mom—she was a shrink—said something about 'epigenetic alteration' from his drug use and injuries in car accidents. Those things can sometimes cause changes to how specific genes are expressed, which can affect ways of thinking and behavior..." Gavin shrugged hopelessly. "I've always just joked it's because we're mirror twins—you know, reverse images, opposite personalities."

Puna shook his head. "Weird shit, man." He patted Gavin's shoulder. "Oh, by the way, Anela's track coach said he'd love it if you could help train the cross-country team once a week. Your restaurant's closed on Mondays, right?"

Gavin suppressed an eye roll, thinking of his typical Mondays.

34.

NO ONE ON THE ISLAND SAW DEVON AFTER THAT. Gavin hoped he was gone for good. But still alive.

The first letter arrived at the Princeville Resort right after the holidays. The concierge there called Gavin.

"Hey Gavin, Moe here. Did you get in trouble with the Department of Health?"

"What do you mean?"

"We got a letter from someone saying they got food poisoning from eating at your restaurant, advising us not to send our guests there."

"That's the first I heard about it," Gavin said. "We haven't had anyone from Food Safety come here since we opened."

"Well, someone said they got sick there. Maybe they didn't report it to the health department."

"But why wouldn't they report it—to us or the health department? Did it come from someone on the island?"

"It's postmarked from California, but the name isn't one of the guests we've had recently."

"I'll call Inspector Lee. By the way, what's the postmark date on the envelope?"

"Let's see...December 29."

Red flags popped up. Gavin felt like he'd fallen into a

bottomless hole. Just when he thought he'd left both abuse and danger behind on the mainland. "Can you save that letter and the envelope it came in?" he asked through clenched teeth. "I'll come by to get it, to give to Lee. I'm sure he'll want it."

"Uh, I think I should give it to him, Gav. Not that I don't trust you or anything."

"Sure, I understand. But I'd like copies. Maybe the date or name might ring a bell, so we can track down what could've made someone sick."

Inspector Richard Lee came to *'Ono Kūloko* before eleven o'clock the following Tuesday morning, unannounced. He slapped a bright yellow official-looking notice on the door: "Closed Until Further Notice by Order of Kauai Department of Health". He explained to Gavin that the inspection process could take as long as two hours, after which the closure could be either lifted or continued, depending on outcomes.

Gavin was glad Inspector Lee came before the restaurant had opened for lunch, but the kitchen staff were already prepping food for the midday crowd. And he knew word would get out about that ominous sticker on his door, announcing some sort of problem at *'Ono Kūloko*. That would really hurt business. His gut sprouted more red flags.

An hour later, Inspector Lee came to Gavin with a checklist, asking when was the last time the exhaust hood over the woodfired grill had been cleaned, when the last spray for insects and other pests was done, what cleaners were used in daily cleaning, and so forth. He had already noted temperature settings and current readings of freezer and refrigerators, and of the water heater and dishwasher. Katie and Gavin kept meticulous logs on all that information, updated daily. After Lee recorded all required information, he gave Gavin a copy of his report—an "A+" rating, along with copies of the letter and envelope Princeville Resort had received.

The name on the envelope caught Gavin's attention right away. 'Ulysses D. Masters'...Umberto DiMasi? "Has anyone checked to see if this person exists at this address?"

"Not to my knowledge, Gavin," Lee said, then looked down like an embarrassed child. "I know you run a tight ship here, but I have to do my job, follow up on any and all complaints."

"Even from nonexistent addresses and bogus names?" Gavin asked,

"It's out of my hands. I just follow orders."

"I understand. But it casts suspicion on my restaurant and drives customers away. Today I lost my entire lunchtime business, and I don't know how much that big yellow notice will affect business going forward. You know we've always been better than code, obsessively clean and safe."

Inspector Lee nodded and pursed his lips. "We couldn't find a thing wrong today, or even marginal. Of course we might be doing surprise inspections at any time in the future, but if so I'll try to time it to avoid disrupting your business," the Inspector said as he removed the notice from the front door and left. Gavin scrutinized the typewritten letter for any clues to its origin. There was something in the wording that felt wrong, something in the phrasing, but he couldn't quite put his finger on it. He then faxed the inspection report to Moe in Princeville.

Gavin's friend Puna stopped by the restaurant the next afternoon. "I heard you got shut down by the health department."

"You're not the only one," Gavin grumbled.

"So what did you do?"

"Nothing, apparently." He pulled out his copy of the letter and envelope. "This was sent from California the first Monday after I kicked Devon out on Christmas morning."

"You think he sent it?"

"No one has complained to us, or to the health department, about getting sick. They just sent this horseshit directly to Princeville. Moe says the name doesn't match any guests they've had recently, and there apparently isn't anyone by that name at the return address. But the name sort of mirrors Devon Umberto DiMasi. Could be just a coincidence I guess."

"Maybe just someone with a weak stomach. Or some guy who thought he should get a bigger piece of steak. Weird that it came snail mail. Everyone communicates by email these days—it *is* 2004. That would be easier to trace of course. If it happens again the same way—no evidence, unsubstantiated name and address, we should start keeping a file. I'll let Richard Lee and his boss know."

Business was down more than ten percent the rest of that week, but gradually began inching up. Katie amped up postings on their Facebook page, with mouth-watering photos of their food and drinks. Gavin crafted new cocktails, featured a different menu item daily and announced special Happy Hour deals. Fearful that the public attention might invite another bogus complaint, they nevertheless began posting a Valentine's Day special the first week of February, so couples could make plans.

Five days later Gavin got a call from Janice at the Wyndham in Princeville. "Hey, Chef! Haven't seen you in a while," she began. "Did you get in trouble with the health department?"

"Let me guess," Gavin sighed. "You got a letter. Was it postmarked from California?"

"Yes!" Janice said, surprised. "Do you know this Danielle Manson person who got sick in your restaurant?"

Gavin thought that the similarities to Devon's name in this and the prior letter were way too obvious, like his brother was taunting him. Wanted him to know he had the power to make or break him. "No," Gavin growled, "there is no such person, and no one has reported getting sick in our restaurant—neither to us nor to the health department," He went on to explain. "Inspector Lee will want that letter and the envelope it came in, and both I and Officer Mahiʻai will need copies. That's the second letter in a little more than a month. Someone is trying to tank my business."

"Oh, wow, Gavin, that's awful! I couldn't believe that you, of all people, would have anything other than a pristine operation. Do you know who's doing this?"

"We have our suspicions, but we can't prove anything yet. That's why Puna wants to collect the evidence. Do you need help getting the stuff to Richard Lee and Puna?"

"No, I have to be in Lihue later today on business. I'll drop off the original to the health department and a copy for Puna. And a copy for you on my way back to Princeville. If you treat me to one of your IPAs," Janice teased.

"Along with any meal of your choice, my friend."

Gavin left messages with both Inspector Lee and Puna that Janice would be bringing the latest letter to their offices.

Lee was considerate enough to show up the following Tuesday morning at nine-thirty, eliminating the need to put a 'Closed' sign on the restaurant, since they didn't open until eleven-thirty. "This one's nearly identical to the last one, Gavin. Just a different name and address. We did a search and there's no such address, and no one by that name in Santa Monica. You've clearly pissed someone off."

"Yeah, we think we know who it is, but without finger-prints we can't prove anything."

"So sorry, Chef," Lee mumbled, fidgeting with his clip-board. "I'll just do what I have to do and we can sign the forms so I can be on my way. There's another place up the beach I have to go to, that won't be so lucky."

After Lee was done, Gavin faxed the A+ report to Janice. Then his cell phone buzzed.

"Bet you can't guess who this is," the sonorous bass teased.

"Holy shit—Tray, you son of a gun!" Gavin yelled, laugh-ing, relieved, almost weeping, as if he'd just been saved from the firing squad. He didn't realize he missed and needed his friend so badly until that moment, as he felt weak with relief. "It's been so long—too long! How the hell are you? Where are you? When are you gonna come see us?" he prattled on, as he usually did when he was excited.

Tray waited for his friend to wind down. "You done now, man?" he teased. "I'm calling to tell you that I'll be in Kauai later this week—the thirteenth through the fifteenth."

"Oh, my god!!" Gavin hooted. "That's over Valentine's weekend, and the restaurant will be crowded, so I'm not sure how much time I can spend with you." Gavin tried to dismiss his worry that if gossip leaked out about the health department coming again, there might not be a crowd. "When are you getting here?"

"Friday night late..."

"Oh, that's perfect! Come straight to the restaurant. The crowd will be thinning out and I can break off and let the staff earn their keep while you and I catch up. Sit at the counter in front of our open kitchen and I'll feed you, along with some great microbrews. So what brings you to Hawaii?"

"A surprise. We'll talk Friday!"

When Gavin told Katie that Tray was coming, she was so excited to see him but disappointed she couldn't get a sitter on short notice and come to the restaurant Friday night. Gavin said he'd try to get a sitter so she could come the following night, but he had already planned to surprise her with a sitter for the night of Valentine's Day.

Around nine-thirty Friday night Tray walked in, with a stunningly beautiful young woman on his arm. He had acquired a more mature look in the past couple of years, his gleaming fresh-scrubbed face now sporting neat chin whiskers and mustache, topped by the early stages of a receding hairline. He gave the hostess his name; Gavin had alerted her to expect his friend and where to seat him. When Gavin turned and saw Tray, he quickly wiped his hands on his apron and rushed forward to greet his friend. If anyone were observing, they would think the two hadn't seen each other for a decade, instead of only two years.

Tray spoke first. "Gavin, this is Hannah Fong. She just defended her PhD dissertation at BU. She and her family live on O'ahu, near Waikiki."

"So happy to meet you, Hannah!" Gavin said, reaching out to take her hand. "So Hannah's your surprise, Tray?" He signaled a server to bring menus and flights of microbrews for his guests.

"Part of it," Tray smiled.

"There's more?"

"Hannah, would you like to tell him?"

Hannah cracked a knowing smile and held up her left hand, where a sparkling diamond graced her ring finger. "We're getting married in September."

"Oh my God! Congratulations!" Gavin shouted, drawing them both into a giant hug.

"And you're the Best Man," said Tray.

"Wow," Gavin said, uncharacteristically speechless. "I'm honored. It's so great you're getting married. Wait till Katie hears—she'll be thrilled for you! And Hannah, if you ever want to get the real inside dirt on this guy, you know where to find me."

Hannah giggled and cast a teasing glance at Tray.

"But there's more," Tray added.

"More surprises?"

"I'm leaving the police force."

"Leaving? But your whole family eats, sleeps and dreams blue!"

"I'm going to Quantico."

Gavin looked puzzled.

"FBI training. Twenty weeks. Five months."

"Holy shit!" Gavin gasped. "What do your dad and brothers think of that?"

Tray looked down and scrunched his mouth. "Both my parents are thrilled. So's Abe. But Kyrone, not so much. Like I was afraid, he got pulled into the life, and FBI took him and a couple other cops down. He's waiting trial now, in a treatment facility."

"Oh shit. I'm so sorry," Gavin said. "If you're in FBI, could you intervene for him?"

Tray shook his head vigorously. "Not a chance, man. I'm just lucky they still accepted me, with that going down in my family."

"Damn. Then after training, will you be stationed in all kinds of different places?"

"It's possible. Maybe not immediately, but over time. There's an office on O'ahu—in Honolulu—so I'll request that. I hear headquarters honors assignment requests in more than half of cases. And Hannah already has a research position lined up at the University there."

Anakoni—Koni, Gavin's sous chef—placed an order of Gavin's signature style tuna poke and a mile-high mound of chickpea-battered onion rings on the counter for Tray and Hannah. "Mmm...beautiful—and smells so good!" Hannah said. "Before I dig in, can you point me to the ladies room? Oh and Tray, can you order me a glass of white wine to have with that poke?"

As Hannah left, Tray asked, "So have you heard anything from your brother?"

"Oh yesss...," Gavin sighed. "He and his boy Eric showed up on our doorstep early Christmas morning with armloads of gifts and shit. He'd buzzcut his hair and dyed it black. And whined that he missed me, all that crap. I kicked his ass out, told him to never come near me and my family again."

"The mob is still alive and well, y'know," Tray said. "Carmen DiNunzio—'Big Cheese' just took over from 'Sonny Boy' Rizzo as underboss, and Pete Limone—'Chief Crazy Horse'—became Consigliere last year. He's still pissed that his two boys got killed. These guys don't forgive and forget."

"That's not the only problem I have."

"Sure. Your brother could bring those guys to your door."

"There's something else that's got my suspicions up." Gavin held up a finger with a promise to be back in a minute and slipped into the back office. When he returned, he placed his copies of the letters to resorts on the counter for Tray. "We've never gotten any complaints of anyone getting sick here, nor has the health department, but these letters were sent from California to local resorts out of the blue, telling them not to send their guests to the restaurant. The first one was sent the Monday after Christmas, after I kicked Devon out. The latest one came after I posted special deals on Facebook for Valentine's Day."

Tray scanned the letters. "Have you ever had any complaints before?"

"None. The first time the Food Safety Inspector did a surprise visit after Princeville gave him this letter, shut down the place during lunch and couldn't find anything wrong. The second time, they figured it was probably a hoax and just did the short-form process. It's getting to be routine. But it eats at me, keeps me on edge and awake at night."

"The timing could just be coincidental with Devon's visit."

"Could be. But no one's ever complained about getting sick here, or anything else about the restaurant. The names and addresses are bogus, they mirror Devon's name, and there's also something about those letters. maybe the wording, that's nagging at me. Can't put my finger on it."

"Well, keep the letters and envelopes. A pattern may emerge."

"Yeah," Gavin exhaled long, as if he were trying to expel toxins, and stuck the letters into his pocket. "So what are you giving Hannah for Valentine's Day? We're giving a red rose tomorrow night to every woman who comes in. And Katie will be here, too—we got a sitter for Maggie. Daughter of a police friend of mine."

"You have this thing for law enforcement, huh?" Tray laughed, then saw Hannah returning from the ladies' room.

"You think I should give her something more than this little trip to Kauai?" he grinned and extended his arm to ease Hannah onto the counter stool. "Hey, Babe, you'll be able to meet Katie tomorrow night. She'll be here for Valentine's dinner."

"You two should come over to the house for breakfast too," Gavin urged. "So you can meet our little Maggie," he added with a proud beaming smile. "I'll already be here at the restaurant, but I know Katie is excited to see Tray again, and she'll love to meet Hannah!"

Gavin felt so...whole again, like in the warmest sense of *home*, with his best friend there next to him. The friend who'd pulled his ass out of deep dark holes. He needed Tray now more than ever.

35.

GAVIN HAD BEGUN TO DISCERN A PATTERN. EVERY few months, within a week or so of 'Ono Kūloko posting a big event on Facebook or being featured in a news article or magazine, another letter would arrive at another resort or hotel—The Cliffs, Waipouli Beach, etc.,—or to travel services such as wedding planners or tour guides. Each letter registered a similar complaint in nearly identical terms. But businesses in Kauai comprised a relatively small and tight-knit community, so it soon became known that some sort of con was afoot, and response to these letters became routine.

Puna set up the procedure and the Chamber of Commerce communicated it throughout Kauai to all businesses. The letter recipient was instructed to watch for letters of the type shown in the attached image, not open it, and give the envelope and letter to Puna, who would collect fingerprints from the letter then give it to Lee, who would arrange an "inspection" and give a copy to Gavin. But in each case, there remained something that eluded Gavin, some cryptic code in the letters taunting him.

On that July Monday he drove to the Kunoa abattoir, which was the only one on the island he would allow to supply his meat due to their Temple Grandin-defined humane treatment of the animals. As he navigated the narrow road, he thought of what he knew his staff were planning for his upcoming birthday. He—and Devon—would be twenty-six years old. He wondered where his brother was. Whether he was safe.

Gavin's angst churned in his head, intensified by the surreal green blur of passing overgrowth in the former sugar plantation. Then something tweaked his peripheral vision. White and tan specs twinkling morse code from the thicket. He pulled over and got out of his truck to investigate, breathing in loamy smells of rich earth damp from recent rains. Faint mewling squeaks beckoned from the brush, drawing him into a dank lair. Two tiny puppies maybe less than a month old quivered in hunger. Or fear. One writhed forward on its belly in urgent heaves, dragging an unnaturally bent leg behind. Its tiny head thrust toward him with piercing eyes demanding attention. Gavin reached to pick it up, then stiffened as he saw the other pup cautiously peek from under a fern. Caked blood from a missing eye and ear bore witness to the terrifying evil of violent abuse. Suppressing the retching convulsion in his stomach, Gavin pulled off his shirt, wrapped both pups into it and carried them to his truck, vowing to save them from whatever heinous beast had done this to them.

Gavin sped to the nearest animal clinic while patting the twin pups on the seat beside him. He'd never met the vet there, and hoped she was a miracle worker. But the vet said both pups had been cruelly abused and should be put down. Gavin refused. He rescued them. He would take care of them, nurse them back to health, give them a chance at life.

After cleaning, suturing and patching the eye and ear on one pup, she set its broken leg and that of the other pup, but issued a warning. "Both pups have been severely traumatized. Although their x-rays don't show major internal damage, we'd need scans to be sure. But with their young age and condition, they might not survive major surgical intervention. And even if their physical damage heals, they won't be good pets. Their behavior—their character—will be off in some ways."

Gavin looked down at those sweet pups—twins. Like he and Devon were. Whoever did this was a monster. Bitter anger stung his eyes. Victims shouldn't have to pay with their lives. He was overwhelmed with a fierce determination to protect and defend them, the same commitment he had for Katie and Maggie. He was certain that with love and patience, these two pups would thrive, and their unique identity and character would emerge.

When Gavin brought the pups home, Maggie was instantly enthralled. Something her size, moving and making noises! Just over seven months old, she had recently graduated from belly-scooting to four-limbed crawling. But now to welcome her new friends she reverted to belly-scooting, just as they were doing. Within days, Patches, the one-eyed one-eared pup, seemed to have shrugged off both his physical and emotional abuse with unbridled glee and broad puppy smile, trailing Maggie wherever she went. But Beggar, who first batted his big eyes at Gavin, became more sluggish and weaker every day, lying around and whimpering sadly.

"Gav, I'm taking Beggar to the vet," Katie said on Monday, after the pups' first week.

"I'll go too, but we're taking him to a different vet. That one just wanted to give up and put our guys to sleep."

"'Our guys'?" Katie grinned.

"Well, sure. We rescued them, gave them names. They're part of the family now," Gavin said, lifting Maggie into her car seat. "Right, Mags?"

"I love you, Tiger," Katie whispered.

All five DiMasi family members went off to the new naturopathic animal clinic up near Honua Lani Gardens. The vet there, Dr. Thomas, had a thick brush of white Afro and an accent that Gavin thought might be Caribbean. When the doctor saw the commitment Gavin and Katie had to raise the puppies despite their injuries, he seemed to intensify his focus and attention.

After Dr. Thomas examined Patches and Beggar, he ordered bloodwork, CT scans and parasite treatment for both pups. While his assistant began with Patches, he held Beggar in his arms and talked with Gavin and Katie. "I wish I knew who tortured these poor animals," he stroked Beggar. "Despite Patches' external injuries, he seems to be doing well. The tests should confirm that."

"That's great, but what about Beggar?"

Dr. Thomas shook his head. "I heard fluid in his lungs, and his heartbeat is thready and irregular. I'm not optimistic."

"But he was more lively and aggressive than Patches when I found them!" Gavin was surprised and confused.

"Sometimes animals will exhibit outgoing or aggressive behavior when they're in greatest need, most desperate. On the other hand, Patches' injuries were visible, so he wanted to hide them from you; you were a stranger at that point. Animals can be reticent to expose their vulnerability—their weakness—to strangers."

It struck Gavin that puppy twins were similar in those ways to human twins. And this kind man was clearly an animal whisperer. Or psychiatrist.

"So we need to see what Beggar's scan shows, right?" Katie asked.

"Yes, that will determine what we can do," Dr. Thomas nodded. "Most internal injuries can only be repaired by surgery, if at all." The old vet scratched under the pup's jaw, then handed Beggar to his assistant who'd come in with Patches' tomography films, releasing an excited squirming Patches, who immediately executed a three-legged hobble to Maggie. The vet scrutinized the images. "Patches doesn't appear to have any serious internal issues, from what we can see in the scan. We'll have Beggar's results in a few minutes if you'd like to wait. Can we get you some water?"

Gavin and Katie exchanged worried glances, silently processing the doctor's Catch-22 prognosis for Beggar.

When the assistant returned with Beggar and his films, Dr. Thomas looked at them, shaking his head with sadness. "I'm afraid that the damage to his lungs and liver is extensive, which is the cause of fluid accumulation. Surgery would be both uncertain and risky."

"So what can we do, Doctor?"

"We can give him medications to help reduce fluids in his lungs and to support his liver," Dr. Thomas began. "But that may have limited effect, given the extent of damage."

"So you're saying the best thing we can do is try the meds and hope for the best?" Gavin whined in a mournful plea.

"This puppy knows he's loved," Dr. Thomas said. "Regardless of outcome, he isn't suffering. I see him watching your baby. He's sad, resigned."

As Beggar quietly took his final breaths a week later, he was surrounded by Patches, Maggie, Gavin and Katie. Despite Dr. Thomas's reassurances, guilt lurked at the edges of Gavin's grief. He had failed to save one puppy. Beggar.

He hoped he could save Devon. From himself.

36.

"WE'LL BE JUST FINE, GAV," KATIE SAID. "YOU DE-
serve a day off. You've been training Koni for ten months now,
so just trust him. I'll be there in case anything needs an
'executive decision.'"

Gavin and Tray were spending the day before Tray's
wedding, hiking in forest and cliff trails. It was a best-friend
retreat, in lieu of a bachelor's party. "But what about Maggie?"
Gavin asked. "This is the first time she's spent a whole day
without one of us."

"Anela will be watching her at Puna and Nalani's place.
And of course Nalani will oversee Anela," Katie smiled. "Maggie loves it there, and she'll have a whole family taking care of
her and Patches. You're so cute when you do your worrywart
thing," Katie teased.

"But she's just started trying to stand alone. What if she
tries to walk, and falls?"

"And what if you might have fun and relax!"

"I'm so glad Tray got assigned to the Honolulu office,"
Gavin smiled and began loading his backpack. "By the way,
the artwork you put up yesterday looks great. A lot of people
commented on it."

The art gallery Katie acquired had its grand re-opening

under its new name—*Makakū* (creativity)—over Labor Day weekend. One of her marketing tactics was to hang pieces from the gallery in *'Ono Kūloko*. The addition of color to the cool grays, wood and steel of the restaurant lent a dynamic vibe to the space. "I hope it helps business. I've just signed three new artists."

"And you've sold how many pieces in your first three weeks?"

Katie beamed. "Twenty-two!"

"Pretty soon I can retire and be your 'kept man,'" Gavin laughed.

"Nice try, Tiger."

"C'mon, Tray," Gavin teased. "What d'ya think this is gonna be, a walk in the park? Here's a backpack for you, loaded with water. You're going to need it."

"All right, all right," Tray grumbled, pulling off his running shoes and putting on the hiking boots Gavin brought him.

"We need to get up to the lookout early, before the trade winds bring in the clouds obscuring the view. Is Hannah here?"

"No, she's spending the day with her mother and bridesmaids. They're all getting their hair and nails done, last-minute adjustments on their dresses, all that stuff."

As Gavin drove up Waimea Canyon Drive, he explained the geological history of the island—formed five million years ago by a volcanic eruption that's now mount Wai'ale'ale, that people from Polynesia began coming to the island in the 1200s in dugout canoes bringing plants they'd need to survive on volcanic soil, and that Waimea Canyon is one of the wettest places on earth, getting 466 inches of rain a year. He pointed out magnificent vistas along the way...twin Waipo'o and Wai'alae Falls, Red Dirt Falls, multicolored striped canyon cliffs rivalling the Grand Canyon, majestic mountain ranges in all directions.

"You ever think about being a tour guide, Gav?"

"I just love this place," Gavin laughed. "Did your family come out here for your wedding?"

"Oh sure, they wouldn't miss it. Even Kyrone. He's on probation now, had to get special dispensation to come."

"Has he made peace with you being in the FBI?"

"Yeah, sort of. We kind of avoid the subject for now."

"So what's it like in the Honolulu office, G-man?"

"I just got there a month ago. So far it's good. The location is key for stuff going on between U.S. and PAC RIM."

"So you might end up traveling to the Far East, eh?"

Gavin pulled his truck into the Kalalau Lookout in Kōke'e State Park a little before nine o'clock. "The road ends farther on at the Pu'u o Kila Lookout, but this lookout gives a wider view to not just the North—the Kalalau Valley—but also the west, the Honopu Valley and a great view of the ocean, in the direction we'll be hiking."

The two friends walked to the fence at the outer edge of the lookout. "Holy shit," Tray whistled. "This is amazing."

"You ain't seen nothing yet," Gavin laughed. The two-mile-wide Kalalau Valley beyond the lookout dropped to brilliant blue waters of the Pacific sparkling four thousand feet below. "This point alone gets more than seventy inches of rain a year."

"More than Seattle?"

"Yep. So down there is the NaPali coastline—sheer high cliffs all along most of the northern and western shores of the island. You should take Hannah on one of the sailboat cruises around the NaPali coastline. Stunning! Dozens of movies have been filmed there. There are wave- and wind-carved sea caves and inlets all along the way. We could hike there on the Kalalau Trail, but it's eleven miles long each way and pretty grueling."

"Yeah, I think I'll pass on that one," Tray smirked.

"Now turn this direction. Down there is the Honopu Valley, leading to the western coast of NaPali. We'll be taking a three-mile trail—Awa'awa'puhi—south of Honopu. It joins up with the Nu'alolo Cliff trail and ends at the Lolo Vista—killer views of both the Awa'awa'puhi and Nualolo Aina Valleys, lots of beautiful falls dumping all that rainwater, and the signature folding spires of NaPali cliffs dropping down to the surf..."

"Now that you've described it so well, I don't need to go—save my energy for tomorrow!"

"Wait—weren't you the big quarterback superstar? And didn't your FBI training get you in even better shape?"

"Not at this elevation, man."

"Our hike will only take about three hours there and back—a little over six miles total. And I brought lunch and we both have plenty of water. This'll be good training for marriage," Gavin laughed.

They drove back down the road to Mile Marker 17 and parked where the trail began, at over four thousand feet. As they set out, it was a relatively peaceful stroll heading west through high forest, with Gavin identifying native dryland plants along the way. After the first mile the forest began to give way to barren landscapes as NaPali gradually came into view, and the sweeping Awa'awa'puhi Valley opened up to broader ocean vistas. When the trail merged with the Nualolo Cliff Trail, mountain goats clinging to steep slopes confirmed they were in precipitous terrain.

At one point they encountered somewhat slippery rocks on the trail. "Take it easy here, Tray. Good thing you have those hiking boots," Gavin said.

"Not very fashionable, though."

"But really macho."

"Right..."

With several stops and pauses for water and to take in the views, eventually the flat grassy ridgetop of Lolo Vista, edged by red rock, appeared ahead. Tray dropped to the grass with a relieved sigh. "I guess that wasn't so bad. Most of the way flat or downhill."

"Yeah, but unless you want this hike to be five miles longer, we're going back the same way."

"Uphill," Tray groaned.

Gavin pulled out sandwiches and fruit for their lunch. "Look down there!" he pointed to the churning Pacific 2500 feet below, where pods of spinner porpoises were leaping out of the water and showing off for cheering passengers in a catamaran sailboat.

Tray got up and walked forward for a better look.

"Tray, get back, that scree is loose, you'll—"

At the same time Gavin jumped up to run toward his friend, the red scree slid out from under Tray, sending him feet-first toward the edge of the cliff. Gavin vaulted himself airborne in a belly-flop onto the red rocks, sliding forward just in time to grab Tray's arm, digging his toes into the ground to brake their trajectory.

Tray tucked his heels into the side of the cliff under his butt, to wriggle back onto the flat ledge, with Gavin pulling on his arms. Once they were both back on solid terrain, they looked at each other and began snort-laughing in relief.

"I think you just saved my life, Gav," Tray said.

"Payback for you saving mine, in more ways than one."

"So...guess I could eat that sandwich now."

"Let's hope one of those goats didn't get into our food."

As they devoured the food Gavin brought, the breathtaking views of the NaPali coastline left them speechless. Finally Tray spoke. "I can't believe I'm getting married tomorrow. I mean, of course I can believe it, and Hannah is awesome, but it's going to be a whole different life. I'm the first guy in the family getting married. I just hope I can do it right."

"Yeah, marriage is a big responsibility. Sometimes feels so humbling, like am I up to it? It's the most important thing in my life right now," Gavin nodded slowly, gazing off into the distance. "I heard someone say once that real love is placing someone else's life above your own, and that's how I feel about Katie and Maggie. My god, Maggie. My heart just swells every time I look at her, think about her."

"Oh, I'm afraid to even start thinking about kids. I have to be sure I get the marriage thing right first." He rolled up one of his sleeves and flashed a tattoo of two hearts linked, with 'Hannah' and the wedding date. "I had this done yesterday at Little Tsunami in Kapa'a to remind me."

"Wow, now that's commitment!" Gavin laughed and admired the artwork. "So it's up to us guys to be sure our families are protected, safe and happy. That's huge. Hannah's lucky you're in law enforcement."

"But you take on the job of protecting and fixing everyone, Gav. It's nice that you feel a responsibility for all of humankind, but if they won't accept responsibility for themselves too, they can pull you down with them. Remember what Pedersen told you. Save yourself first, or you're useless to anyone else."

Gavin went silent. He knew that, somewhere in his head. So why was he consistently compelled to help Devon, stand by him, save him, even after the times he'd made a show of kicking his twin to the ground?

"Besides," Tray laughed. "We both have tough, smart, capable women in our lives who can totally kick butt, and probably protect us if we need it."

While they finished eating, Tray turned on a playlist he'd stored on his cell phone. Gavin recognized some of their shared favorites from years past, but didn't recognize one strident tune that seemed to elicit reverent attention from Tray. When it was over, Gavin asked "What was that song?"

"*Lift Every Voice and Sing*," Tray said. "It's sort of the black national anthem."

"Wow—really? What are the words, and how did that come to be, like, a thing?"

"It started as a poem in 1900 celebrating Abraham Lincoln's birthday, then it was set to music as a hymn. It's about liberty and hope, a '*song full of the faith that the dark past has taught.*' It's a prayer of thanksgiving for faithfulness and freedom. Sort of like a song of determination to rise above slavery and oppression."

"That's so awesome. I need a song. My own anthem of freedom from—"

"Yep, you do," Tray nodded. "You aren't still on that Grateful Dead kick, are you?"

"Uh, no. that seems so lame now."

"So why is it so hard to break free of your brother, Gav?"

"Oh, god. Aside from the obvious twin hook?" Gavin smirked. "Despite years of trying to get away from it, rise above it, I've had more years—formative years—being told I'm a loser and that what I think, feel and do are stupid or delusional. And that Devon is the only twin who knows what's real, so I'm lost if anything happens to him. It's sort of embedded deep in my definition of who I am, so I doubt myself."

"Even though everything you've ever done is totally opposite of 'loser.' That's just so much bullshit. You must know that."

"Yeah, I know it in my head, but it's hard to keep from being pulled back in, because he's my twin. And he's a master manipulator. And he's the only family I have left."

"And you think you failed in your savior role with your mom and dad, so you can't fail with Devon."

"I guess. Something like that."

"Well, you have your own family now. And 'family' is more than blood. Think of all the people who know how decent and awesome you are. Like me, all your friends on this island, your grandparents, and Pedersen, who'll never give up on you."

Gavin stared out at the horizon, then smiled when he thought of Frank Rizzo, the most unlikely advocate.

"The master manipulator is just trying to salvage his self-worth by hacking yours. On top of the damage your dad did to you."

"Right," Gavin turned to Tray with raised eyebrows. "I'm beginning to realize that Dad was sort of a product of his childhood and culture, where guys had to be tough. It was their role. So he expected the same thing from us. Of course I wasn't like that, so he projected toughness onto Devon and always said I was the wimp. Until he needed me to save my twin, and that was what I had to do. My job, my role in life."

"There's a difference between tough and strong, Gav. You're totally strong, and we wouldn't be friends if you were your dad's version of tough." Tray pulled a banana from Gavin's backpack. "So can you just resign from that babysitting job?"

"Easier said than done. But I'm trying."

"At least you've stopped trying to fix him."

"There's no fixing possible. I just don't want him to die."

Silence seemed to be the only response to that.

"Hey, I guess we'd better head back, if we're going to show up in time for the rehearsal dinner."

"Yeah, I sure don't want Hannah to blame me for making you late for that!"

37.

THERE HAD BEEN NO LETTERS IN MORE THAN A month. Gavin and Katie were beginning to hope it was all over, that the harassment had run its course. But a week after Katie put up a social media post announcing the restaurant's Halloween festivities, Inspector Lee showed up on Tuesday morning with two assistants and slapped the big yellow sign on the front door.

Gavin's heart sank, then his anger peaked. "I was hoping this was over, Inspector," Gavin said, struggling to keep his annoyance out of his voice. It wasn't Richard Lee's fault. "I thought we all understood that some anonymous jackass was just out to ruin our business."

"Yeah well, this time it's different."

"Different how?"

"I can't talk about it."

"You can't talk about it? Why? Can't I be told what the problem is, what we're being accused of?"

"There were multiple letters. They all went to government officials."

"What?!" Gavin yelled, charging out from behind the bar, where he'd been hooking up a new keg.

"I can't say anything else. But you're probably going to be

shut down for at least a week, if not more."

Halloween was huge in Kauai. Huge. People go all-out with outrageous costumes; entire neighborhoods shut down with neighbors vying for best candy offerings, decorations, displays, lights, music, sound effects, scary gimmicks, house of horrors, parades. These were serious traditions. Then after the kids all get their treats, the grownups flood restaurants and bars for their adult treats.

'Ono Kūloko would lose a ton of business during this holiday, not to mention the days it was closed before and after. The whole island would know they were shut down. It would take months to recover their reputation and their business.

Gavin called Puna. No answer. He left a message.

He called Manu, the *kanaka maoli* owner of the property he was leasing.

"Hey, Gavin!" Manu answered. "How's everything going? You ready for your first Halloween?"

"We were, but we got shut down."

"What'd you do, man?"

"Nothing. Some unknown asshole from the mainland is trying to ruin us. Sending letters to resorts with lies about getting sick, filth in our restaurant, that kind of crap. And now their latest trick is sending to government officials. Do you know a lawyer?"

"Holy shit! I can give you the woman I use, but if you don't know who the guy is, you can't sue. Maybe you need a P.I.?"

"Police are already involved—Sergeant Mahi'ai—but now that it's gotten to government people, maybe it'll be elevated to the Chief. I want legal help so I can sue the county for shutting me down with zero evidence based on anonymous letters from someone with a bogus name and address."

"Then you'll need Amy's senior partner, Joe Sugimura. He's gone up against county officials in the past. I'll text you his info."

Gavin's cell phone buzzed; Puna was calling back. "I heard

about it from Inspector Lee," Puna said. "So did the county Mayor, three Council members, the District Health Officer, Prosecuting Attorney, and Chief of Police. I just got a copy of the Chief's letter."

"Jesus H Christ."

"You have Lee and his boys there now?"

"Yeah, and they put the big yellow sign of doom on the door. Lee says I'll be shut down for at least a week, maybe more. Apparently the big guys are spooked."

"Soon as they're done, come down to HQ and take a look at this letter. Maybe something might ring a bell."

It was after two o'clock when Gavin pulled into County Police HQ in Lihue. After he signed in at security, Puna took him into an unadorned fluorescent-lighted meeting room and gave him a cup of coffee before placing a letter on the table in front of him. "Exact copies of this letter were sent to seven people in county government, all on the same date, from San Jose California, with the name and address in the signature as return address on each envelope. Because the other letters had only gone to businesses in Kauai, we hadn't warned government officials not to open the envelopes. So we won't be able to get prints from these."

Gavin read the letter in front of him:

"My family and I ate at the 'Ono Kūloko restaurant in Kapa'a, Kauai on October 19, 2004. We noticed that everything was very dirty. The table hadn't been cleaned for some time, and the floors had more than the minor debris one might expect from the prior seating. The cutlery wasn't thoroughly clean, with hardened food particles between fork tines and on knives. When our food was served, the meat tasted rancid, and we actually found live bugs on the salad. When we went to the bathrooms, they were not only so disgustingly dirty we couldn't use them, but my *daughter saw a mouse scurry behind the overflowing wastebasket of the ladies' room.*

"I have previously been an official in the health department of the small town where I used to live, and I can assure you I know more about restaurant cleanliness than anyone else; I am an expert in that regard. I must say that I've never been to a restaurant as filthy and unsafe as 'Ono Kūloko."

The letter was sent, without a signature, by someone named Daniel Martin. "We've tried to find someone with that name at that address, but we struck out," Puna said.

"Too bad he didn't actually sign it. I might have something with Devon's writing, that we could compare, for proof. But now I finally realize what's been bothering me—"

"Gav, because this has gone to elected officials, it's raised the stakes. So we have two other people coming here to meet about it at two-thirty."

"Who?"

Puna turned as a clerk came to the door to usher in a middle-aged woman. "Come on in, Abby, and have a seat. Can I get you anything?"

"No, thanks. And this must be Gavin DiMasi. I'm Abby Palakiko, Postmaster for Kauai. I recognize you, from eating at your restaurant, but we've never had the chance to talk."

Just then a surprisingly young senior police officer walked in. "Hello, Gavin. I'm Kauai Police Chief Adam Kahananui. I've eaten in your restaurant too. I don't think there's anyone on the island who hasn't," he smiled.

"So I guess you're here to discuss this letter that went to several government people?" Gavin said.

Chief Kahananui sat at the head of the table and took the role of spokesman. "We've all eaten in your restaurant and have never seen anything close to what is described in this letter, Gavin. Same with the health inspectors and everyone else. The letter makes some libelous assertions. Of course we all know the only rodents we have on the island go after birds' eggs out in the brush," the Chief scoffed. "We'll need to look into the other claims. Whoever wrote the letter can't be located at the address he claims. So unless further investigation discovers something credible in what he says, at this point we suspect it's fraudulent. Yet because it's libelous and was sent through USPS to elected officials across state lines, it's a federal crime. That's why Abby and I are here."

Puna spoke next. "So the Chief has decided that we'll contact all government officials and staffers, and again remind every hotel, travel company, wedding planner, caterer, all your partners on the island, and instruct them to not open any future envelopes looking like these, and instead forward to the station with the case number we've opened. This is so we can open the envelopes with gloves on and check for fingerprints on the letters," he explained.

"What about the Hawaii and Kauai publications that review restaurants?" Gavin asked. "People coming to the island use those as bibles. We've been the featured restaurant in several of them. And I may have more businesses to add to your list."

"You can give me anyone else you think we should contact," Abby Palakiko said. "These communications will originate from my office and will be signed by me and Chief Kahananui."

"I appreciate that," Gavin said. "I think I know who's doing this. And from this letter I finally recognized something that makes me certain who's doing it, but there's no proof."

"What's that, Gavin?" Puna asked.

"I realized that something in this letter is in every letter I've seen so far—something that my brother always says. 'I know more about'—whatever the topic is—'than anyone, and I'm the expert.' Check the other letters, you'll see some form of that in all of them. And that's my brother's constant refrain."

"Why would your brother do this?" Abby asked.

Gavin took a deep breath. "He has a mental illness—Malignant Narcissistic Personality Disorder. One symptom is claiming superior abilities over everyone on any topic. Another symptom is trying to manipulate and control people, especially specific victims. In this case, me, his twin. Because I refuse to allow that, and because I've achieved some level of success, he's compelled to destroy me."

"How long has he been like this?" the Chief asked.

"Almost our whole lives, but it reached a sociopathic level by the time we were sixteen. And now it's gotten much worse."

"Oh my god," Abby said. "Your whole life. I am so sorry."

Puna spoke up now. "Gavin, you should tell them about the other thing, that you told me."

"Uhm, yeah," Gavin hesitated. "My brother developed a substance abuse problem. Which isn't unusual for someone with his disorder. And because he took over our father's liquor business based in the Italian North End of Boston, he got involved with the Boston Mob. Trafficking drugs is part of their business model. He got caught and did rehab instead of time."

The Chief slowly shook his head, grim. "And I always pegged you as straight and vanilla with apple pie. Sorry, man."

"We should inform all government officials—and their assistants or mail rooms—to be on the lookout for envelopes like this, not open them and give them to us," Puna said.

"I think we should get our court psychiatrist involved in this case too," the Chief interjected, "to see if there's a way to trip him up, get him to reveal himself."

"The mob is still after my brother," Gavin mumbled. "They're after me too. I saw who tried to kill him and missed, killing our dad."

A stunned silence cast paralysis over the room.

Lacking verifiable evidence and having only one suspicious person complaining, the Mayor—with the urging of Chief Kahananui—directed the Department of Health to lift the closure of 'Ono Kūloko. So Gavin was able to open the next day, Wednesday before the Halloween weekend. News had gotten around, though, so business was off from what it should have been.

But after Halloween, business rebounded to nearly full swing. Just as bad news travels, so does good news, and gossip about the bizarre hoax affecting one of the most popular restaurants on the island had spread fast.

On Friday after the Veteran's Day holiday, the restaurant was extremely busy, so Gavin didn't notice the text until more than an hour after Puna sent it:

"Better come. This one's bad."

Besides being a good friend, Puna was the officer responsible for maintaining evidence and case files on the barrage of letters attacking 'Ono Kūloko, and he helped Gavin and Katie file complaints. There were two separate case numbers, one for letters sent to private businesses, and one for those sent to public officials.

When Gavin saw Puna's text, he couldn't imagine anything worse than all the other letters someone sent to people across the island. None of those damning messages had ever been sent to him, or to the restaurant. The letters were always posted from somewhere in California, and the return names and addresses were always bogus. Although he had every reason to know who was sending them, the police couldn't really do much without hard evidence.

After responding to Puna's text that he was on his way, Gavin hesitated whether to tell Katie just yet. She usually stressed out each time they learned of a new letter. He looked out to the dining area, where nearly every table was occupied, even during midafternoon. He turned to Anakoni, his sous chef. "Hey Koni, I have to run out for a while—should be back in a couple hours. You're in charge, okay?"

"Well, yeah," Koni said. "But we're really packed."

"I'm sure you can handle it. Pete's here; he can help."

As Gavin headed for the back door, Katie came into the kitchen looking for one of the servers. "Where are you going?" she asked.

"We're down low on tomatoes and onions—don't know how that happened," Gavin said, not looking at his wife.

"Well that's bad timing," Katie grumbled. "Can't you send someone else?"

"Not really," Gavin mumbled and gave her a quick hug. "I'll be back as soon as I can."

And he was gone, peeling out of the parking lot and praying that traffic didn't slow him down on the way. The one main road around the island could get seriously clogged this time of day.

When Gavin finally made it to the station in Lihue, Puna wasn't at his desk. Another officer pointed to a room back in the corner. The door was closed, so the officer ushered him down the hall and knocked on the door before opening it slightly. "DiMasi's here; you want him to come in?"

"Yes, of course," Puna said.

Before Gavin entered the room, he saw through the window that there were other people sitting around the table with Puna. Then he saw that one of them was Tray, which was simultaneously a relief and concerning. Was he here in his FBI capacity? Why?

"Gavin, c'mon in and sit down," Puna said, and introduced everyone around the table. "You've met Kauai's Police Chief Adam Kahananui and our Postmaster Abby Palakiko. We also have State Chief of Police Stan Davis, Postmaster General Brandon Elefante and FBI Agent Trayvon Harris. Can we get you anything to drink, Gavin?"

Gavin's heart skipped a beat or two. He nodded to Tray, telegraphing a quizzical look. If these heavy-hitters were here to talk about another letter complaining about his restaurant, it must be really bad. "Uh, water would be fine."

"You might need something stronger, my friend," Puna said low.

Oh shit, what now? Gavin dropped into a chair.

Puna handed him a familiar-looking white envelope and letter. Gavin's hands trembled a little as he read the letter, jumping immediately to the highlighted lines:

> *"Our daughter worked this summer at the 'Ono Kūloko restaurant on Kauai, owned by Gavin DiMasi. She left there abruptly after two weeks and came back home. She just disclosed to us that she had been sexually harassed and assaulted by the owner. I'm a psychiatrist and I know more about sexual assault than anyone; I'm a renowned expert in the field. You must arrest this monster and shut him down."*

Gavin's mouth fell open in disbelief, then erupted into unhinged rage. He jumped up from his chair, sending it backward and crashing to the floor with a loud bang. He pounded the table furiously, causing several idle pens to clatter. "Sexual assault now? You've GOT to be shitting me! That's fucking CRAZY!" He looked around the table and realized he'd lost control. He wasn't helping his credibility. He lifted his chair and sat down, gritting his teeth. He closed his eyes and took several deep breaths, trying to calm himself, then with great effort spoke in a measured tone, "Sorry, guys. I'll take that double bourbon now, Puna. This is nuts. We know very well who's sending these lies. My mentally ill twin Devon. His trademark line is right there. 'I know more about' blah, blah. 'I'm an expert' blah, blah. And besides, all the females working for us this summer are still with us."

Chief Kahananui spoke up now. "Gavin, this letter was sent both to the Kauai police as well as to state law enforcement in Honolulu. The crime of sexual assault is a serious one, so we have to conduct a thorough investigation."

Chief Davis broke in, "Officer Mahi'ai tells us that this seems to be an escalation of a series of letters complaining about getting sick in your restaurant, despite consistently high marks from the health department and Safety. They were all sent from different locations in California by people with different names, none of which have checked out as legitimate. And in a quick search, whoever sent this latest letter doesn't seem to exist at the address they claim. either. But we've barely begun the investigation, and now we've brought in the FBI," turning with a nod to Tray. "As you know, sending libelous letters to government officials is mail fraud, a federal crime. And because this one is claiming sexual abuse, we've had to involve FBI."

Gavin didn't know whether to cheer or cry. He hoped that having his friend on the case wouldn't be considered a conflict of interest, and that Tray could finally end the harassment torturing him.

"Do you have anything that might have your brother's fingerprints?" Davis asked.

"I don't think so. We're obviously estranged."

"We'll need your fingerprints, and saliva for DNA testing," Davis said. "So we can differentiate your prints from any others on the letters."

"Gavin, what kind of twin are you?" Tray interjected for the benefit of the others. He knew the answer and its implication for fingerprints.

"We're identical mirror twins. Monozygotic, monochorionic, and monoamniotic."

Tray nodded and turned to the others at the table. "So there may likely be similarities in whorls and loops of fingerprints if those on the letters are Gavin's twin's. Never exact of course, but much greater statistically than by chance. Our experts can determine probability the prints are from Devon."

After being fingerprinted and giving his saliva to another officer, Gavin began the drive back to the restaurant. He had been gone more than two hours. His staff, and his wife, would not be pleased. But for the first time he felt hopeful that with Tray's help, he might finally break the chains between him and his twin.

38.

WEEKS PASSED WITH NO NEW LETTERS AND NOTHING definitive from police or FBI, although Tray frequently kept in touch by email. Gavin couldn't stop looking over his shoulder, expecting it to resume any day. Especially after the leading Kauai magazine published a cover story and four-page article on Chef Gavin and the new oyster bar he'd just opened next to 'Ono Kūloko.

Gavin and Katie were extremely busy that holiday season, planning Christmas and New year's festivities for both restaurants and Katie's art gallery. And of course planning Maggie's first birthday and second Christmas.

Then the Monday before Christmas, Tray called.

Gavin's heart skipped a beat, hoping his friend would have news of a breakthrough. "Have you found anything?"

"We haven't been able to get much more than partial prints from the letters we have," Tray said. "A couple similarities to your prints, nothing definitive. But I called to see if your brother has reached out to you?"

"No..." Gavin held his breath. "Why do you ask?"

"He's on the island."

"Here in Kauai?" Gavin's mouth went dry.

"We were scouring through public data last week, looking

for anything on Devon. He bought a place in Princeville six weeks ago, hired contractors to do some work on it, and just flew in two days ago. Him and some guy, Eric Malone."

"Oh, shit. If you could find that out, I'm sure the mob could too."

"If they're still looking for him. If they still care. We haven't heard any recent chatter mentioning Devon."

"Well if that's the case, it's good. But now if he's here, he'll probably start hassling me all over again."

"Yeah, that's why I wanted you to know. Prepare you. If it gets bad, I'm sure Puna can help you get a restraining order."

"Like that would stop him."

"Sorry, Gav."

"Well thanks for the warning, I guess. Hope he doesn't show up on our doorstep Christmas morning like last year."

"Don't let him in, man," Tray said. "Unless you think you can get his prints on something."

"Hmph. Now that's an idea..." Gavin paused.

"Don't do anything risky, Gav," Tray cautioned.

"Right..."

Tray broke Gavin's grim silence. "On a happier note, how's Katie and Maggie?"

"Oh, Maggie's walking now—running, actually—and Katie's art gallery is doing well, even turning a small profit," Gavin perked up. "How's Hannah, and marriage?"

"Marriage is great—should've done it long ago. And Hannah joined a biotech research team at Hawai'i Pacific. She'll start teaching one class next semester." Tray paused while someone on his end talked to him. "Hey Gav, I gotta sign off. Let's talk on Christmas and catch up a little more. I'll send you the address of Devon's place in Princeville—let me know if you need anything else."

Gavin thought about what his friend said. Maybe he *could* get Devon's fingerprints. Not just partial prints. But he'd still need the same prints to be lifted off one of those illegal letters.

Or some other crime scene.

That night, his restaurant's "Contact Us" link received a cryptic note from an unidentified person, saying only:

"For Expert advice, contact DUDM@xyzmail.net"

It didn't require a forensic expert to determine that note was from Devon Umberto DiMasi, Expert at Everything. A conflicting three-way tug of war launched within Gavin. The long-standing twin allegiance versus Devon's history of manipulation and abuse, versus his own desire to collect Devon's fingerprints. He hesitated, his cursor poised over 'reply.' He wanted to carefully manage trapping his brother, getting his prints. So should he wait till the next day to reply? To show he wouldn't be manipulated or controlled, wasn't eager to get back into his brother's orbit.

It took enormous restraint to shut down the computer and go to bed. But he didn't sleep.

Early the next morning, as Gavin was leaving for the restaurant, his phone pinged with a message from Tray to his personal email. Devon's new house was at the end of a dead-end road—Kaohe—in the Kilauea area of Princeville. He called Katie from his truck.

"Morning, Katie-Kat," he said.

"You left the house early this morning, Tiger," Katie said. "And you were doing a lot of that tossing and turning trick all night. What's going on?"

"Devon's on the island."

"Oh, NOooo..."

"Tray told me about it yesterday and sent me his address this morning. So lock up the house all day—whether you're home or out. In fact, if you can take Maggie and Patches and go visit Nalani, that would be even better."

"We can't do that indefinitely, Gav."

"Yeah, I know. I don't know how we're going to deal with this long term. But he sent a message through the restaurant's 'Contact' page, giving his email. I'm going to make him wait for a response, but not so long that he gets desperate and comes knocking on our door—the house or the restaurant. I want to meet him in some neutral place and trick him into getting his fingerprints."

"That'll require some finesse. And risk getting you caught up in his manipulation again."

"Yes, but until we can shut down his game, we need to keep you and Maggie safe."

———

Koni and other restaurant staff gave Gavin a hard time because he seemed so spacey and distracted all day. His mind was in a whirl, toying with different ideas on how to get Devon's fingerprints without contamination by other prints or sacrificing full-finger images. He also kept looking at the restaurant entry, worrying that his brother might become desperate for attention and decide to descend on 'Ono Kūloko. He finally had a plan for getting Devon's prints.

Late that night, Gavin replied to Devon's message, playing along with his game, while showing him that he knew where he lived:

DUDM,

Welcome to the island. I understand you have moved into your newly renovated home in Princeville. I'd love to bring you a "Welcome Basket" of culinary delights from our restaurant. Please let me know when is a convenient time for you.

Best regards, GODM

Almost immediately—as if he had been sitting poised next to his keyboard—Devon responded:

Tomorrow, Wimp. 11 a.m.

That day would be Christmas Eve, when the restaurant would be packed and frenzied before closing early. Devon was most likely aware of the disruption and inconvenience of that timing for the restaurant. But Gavin had solicited "a convenient time for you," so...

———————

Gavin's breakfast threatened to erupt with every bump in the road. He had informed Katie, Tray and Puna of his plan, in case something went wrong. Now as he drove north on the Kuhio Highway, he checked the basket beside him and worried whether he could succeed in his mission without getting pulled into his brother's dysfunction. His madness.

He turned off the highway and drove the lush winding Kalihiwai Road, then onto Kaohe Road all the way to the end. There perched on the crest of the cliff overlooking Kalihiwai Bay was a large gray stucco mansion with a three-story tower rising from one end. Devon had never appreciated subtlety.

Gavin pulled his truck in front of the house and stared. Easily large enough for a family of twelve, the house reminded him of a fortress. Straight boxy exterior walls, square windows placed high, as if preventing outsiders from seeing inside. He was surprised there wasn't a moat and drawbridge. There was something forbidding about it, like a wolf guarding its den. Threatening, as if entrance could result in absorption, a visitor merging or fusing with the monster inside, succumbing to Devon's voracious endocytosis.

He picked up his basket, which held a bottle of wine, two wine glasses and corkscrew, along with baguettes, goat cheese, fresh figs, knives and cloth napkins. With the exclusion of the handle, everything in the basket had been wiped clean of any possible prints and placed with gloved hands. As Gavin climbed the wide stairs to the front door, he felt eyes watching him. The door had a heavy brass knocker in the form of a clenched fist. When he lifted the knocker and let it fall onto its strike plate, the resounding thud seemed to vibrate throughout the house.

Gavin waited for his brother, or someone, to respond. He lifted the knocker and let it fall again. He was about to give up and leave when the door opened. Devon's black buzz cut had given way to a shoulder-length unkempt frizzy red.

"Twinkie!" Devon squealed, throwing his arm around Gavin's neck in a headlock and ushering his brother into his house. Their footsteps and voices echoed in the sparsely furnished house. "What have you brought me?" Devon asked, grabbing the basket from Gavin.

"Some of our best wine, along with two crystal wine glasses and some fruit and cheese," Gavin said. "I thought we could toast your new residence."

"First I want to show you around my place!" Devon said. "As you know, I'm an expert in design."

"Great," Gavin murmured. He hoped Devon's 'show and tell' wouldn't derail his plan. "I don't have a lot of time though, and I want to be sure to toast your happiness before I have to go. You have a huge house! By the way, where's Maria?"

"Oh, she OD'd a couple years ago," Devon shrugged. "Do you see this antique pool table? It was once owned by Earthquake McCready!"

Whoever that is. "I'm sorry about Maria; that must have been so hard. Is Eric with you?"

"He's off getting some groceries now. Or whatever."

Gavin tried to hurry Devon's room-by-room tour, narrated with ostentatious boasting. All the rooms were cold, hollow, white with black or gray. But when they reached the last room on the top floor—Devon's "office"—Gavin was surprised to see more furnishings there than in any of the other rooms. It almost seemed occupied by humans, unlike the spare showroom character of the rest of the house.

In the center of the floor lay a magnificent leopard's pelt. Its four limbs splayed out unnaturally, its once-proud head frozen in mid-roar, teeth bared, glassy eyes aglow, its dappled spots like the art of gods. Taken from a magnificent nearly extinct animal, testament to its killer's—and by conveyance, its owner's—dominance. Gavin couldn't bring himself to walk on such a "rug", so he gingerly stepped around it to the opposite wall, where he stopped short at the sight of a small painting on one wall. More than a little disturbing, it was dark in color and subject matter, crowded content, sinister form, containing demons, half-human animals and machines. It seemed foreboding, as if depicting the end of the world. "Who painted that?" Gavin asked.

"You obviously know nothing about great art," Devon sneered. "That's by the famous fifteenth-century artist Hieronymus Bosch."

"Oh." It almost made his skin crawl.

"Pull out the left side, Twinkie. Like you're opening a door."

Gavin cast a skeptical look at his brother.

"Go on. Do it."

Tentatively, Gavin slipped his fingers under the left edge of the frame and lifted cautiously. As Devon promised, the frame was hinged on the right and opened out, like a door. On the white wall behind the painting, a sketch of a zombie-like skeletal head mocked, with a round black object affixed to the center of its voided nasal cavity.

"Push that button in the middle of his face, Gav."

When Gavin cautiously pressed, a sound whirred and a section of wall beside the Bosch slid open, revealing a well-lighted circular room. Gavin looked in, and up, where a four-windowed cupola climaxed high above. This was the top of the tower he saw from outside.

"I had this tower added to the house when I renovated it.

For my safe room, if they ever come after me. You might want to keep that in mind, Twinkie..."

Gavin understood what his brother was implying with that taunt. He wouldn't take the bait. Not now.

"That's cool, Dev. Thanks for showing me around. I really hope you're happy here. Why don't we drink a toast to your safety and happiness before I have to leave?"

Back on the first floor, Gavin took the colorful cloth napkins from the basket, ceremoniously placing one on each side of the small steel table in Devon's kitchen. "Would you like to open the wine, or shall I?"

"You go ahead, Julia."

"Okay. Pull out those crystal wine glasses while I open the wine. Oh, and you can set out the cheese and baguettes if you'd like to have some now."

Gavin wrapped a napkin around the wine bottle to open it, then poured some into each glass. Devon lifted his glass by the bowl, as Gavin knew he would, and raised it in a toast. "To me, my fabulous house, and my little brother welcoming me back!"

Gavin raised his glass by its stem in an air toast to his twin, "Cheers! Let me know what you think of that wine?"

Devon placed his lips on the rim and took a drink. "It's okay. I've had better."

"Swirl it, give it a little air, then taste again."

"Oh sure, Julia. That's the expert protocol." He gripped the bowl to swirl and drank more. "Yeah, that's a little better. You think we should finish this bottle?"

"I can have a little more, but then you should finish it. I have to drive back to the restaurant. We're really busy today."

"Oh, Goodie Gavin. Sure, I'll finish it."

When Gavin finally extricated himself from Devon's house and pulled his truck away, he was tempted to peel out and speed down the highway, as if evil forces were pursuing him. But he drove carefully, with his heart still racing, sweaty palms and white knuckles gripping the steering wheel. He wondered how long it would take his brother to realize that only one wine glass was on the table. Or maybe he wouldn't notice; he had a glass for himself, the only thing that mattered. Gavin looked over to be sure Devon's glass—wrapped in the plastic bag he'd brought to avoid wiping or smudging any prints— was securely cradled in one of Katie's kitchen towels.

On the drive back to Kapa'a, Gavin left a message for Tray. "I think I got Devon's prints."

39.

PUNA WAS ON DUTY CHRISTMAS AFTERNOON, just as he was the year before. So Gavin arranged to deliver his precious cargo to him at the station in Lihue, handling it carefully, gingerly, like it was a ticking time bomb.

"So, how'd you manage it?" Puna asked. While Gavin recounted his clandestine caper, Puna extracted two glasses from his desk drawer and poured a thick creamy liquid into each glass. "Nalani made this eggnog and wanted me to give you a Christmas cheer." He pulled out a little airplane-sized bottle of rum and emptied it into Gavin's glass. "Congrats, man."

Gavin clinked his friend's virgin glass and sat stiffly on a chair next to Puna's desk. There were three other desks in the cluttered room in Kauai police headquarters, all unoccupied that day, except for Puna. "How soon can you get it down to the FBI?"

"After we log, tag and secure it, I'll contact them to see whether they want to fly up and get it, or if they want us to come down to deliver it," Puna downed his eggnog and licked his lips. "This is Saturday, so probably can't happen till Monday earliest." Puna looked at Gavin's furrowed brow and put his beefy hand on his shoulder. "I know you're really anxious for things to move along, Gav. We'll all do the best we can."

Gavin hugged his friend. "Merry Christmas, man. And thanks. Katie has gifts for Nalani and your kids, so we'll be stopping by your place later today. Maybe there'll be some more of that delicious eggnog left!"

On his drive back home, Gavin called Tray, who promised to fly up first thing Monday to get the evidence and take it back to FBI's forensic lab. Gavin's muscles began to release, as he realized his good fortune in having such loyal supportive friends.

Gavin had been so hopeful that Devon's fingerprints could be matched to some prints on the envelopes and letters, but so far that wasn't the case. The best he could hope for was that his brother would keep his distance, although Devon called Gavin's cell phone nearly every day. After the first call, Gavin recognized the number so didn't pick up and had Katie do the same. But Devon left long messages each time, whining and pleading for 'Twinkie' to come see him, feigning sadness, remorse, illness, or end-of-world disasters to get his attention.

Gavin told Puna about the phone calls. "I'm surprised he isn't showing up at your house or at the restaurant," Puna said. "You didn't see him in your New Year's Eve crowd on Friday, did you?"

"No," Gavin shook his head slowly. "I'm surprised we haven't seen him too. Actually, it makes me suspicious, worried that he has something up his sleeve, planning something."

"Well, if he comes around your place, I'll help you with a restraining order."

"Which could be too little, too late."

"Sorry, man. Best we can do."

But then the phone calls stopped. Which worried Gavin

even more.

On a crowded Friday night two weeks later, Gavin had to go over to the bar to help install a new keg of the restaurant's most popular brew. He was focused and single-minded in his task, so didn't notice who exactly was sitting at the bar. Until he heard a somewhat familiar male voice with a North End accent. He stiffened.

"I see you're still wearing the Saint Christopher I gave you."

Gavin tried to avoid showing his fear. Without looking up, he said "Never take it off," then slowly stood and faced Frank Rizzo as if it wasn't at all surprising to see him there, in Kauai, at Gavin's restaurant.

"Thought I'd take a little vacation," Rizzo smiled. "And visit the number one restaurant in Kauai."

"Good to see you, sir. My condolences on the passing of your daughter," Gavin said.

Rizzo nodded with a grimace.

Gavin forced the squeak of nervousness from his voice. "What are you drinking?"

Rizzo raised his empty glass. "Just waiting for that keg to be connected for my refill."

Gavin turned to his bartender. "Nate, pour this gentleman that new IPA, on the house. You'll like this one, Mr. Rizzo."

"That's good of you, young man," Rizzo said. "I'll enjoy that even more if you have a few minutes to sit with me."

Gavin knew he really needed to get back to the open kitchen, but figured Koni could handle things. Turning down an 'invitation' like that from Frank Rizzo might not be good for his health. Besides, he had questions. Whether or not he'd get straight answers was another matter.

"And one for me too, Nate." Gavin settled onto the end bar stool beside Rizzo. He didn't know how to proceed, so after clinking his glass to Rizzo's, he opened with the standard insipid question. "So what brings you to Kauai?"

"I wanted to see you, Chef. And enjoy your award-winning cuisine."

"Have you eaten?"

"Yeah, I had to try your famous tuna poke—did I say that right? Then I had your ribeye. Everything was even better than the reviews."

Gavin was exhausted from holding his breath. He decided to come straight to the point. "Why are you really here, sir?"

Rizzo smiled. "I *did* decide to take a vacation. Really. The choice of Kauai was because of you."

"Should I be worried?"

"No. That's one reason I'm here. I'm now the top capo in all New England, and I've issued a 'do not touch' order to protect you. You're good people, you just got tangled up because of your brother."

"What about Devon? Should he be worried?"

"Well, to be honest—I can be straight with you, right?" Rizzo looked at Gavin.

Gavin nodded, fearing the worst, but he had to know.

"That's the other reason I'm here."

Gavin's breath caught.

"We know your brother's here on the island. But we can see he's not in the business. Too...um...confused to be a threat. Making amends now would be like flogging a wounded animal. No lesson learned, no 'sweet revenge.'"

Gavin had no words. He didn't know what to say. Frank Rizzo had just implied that Devon was too crazy to bother wasting a bullet on.

"So put it all behind you, young man," Rizzo said. "Your father didn't have to die. The guys responsible for that fuck-up got what they deserved," Rizzo stared meaningfully into Gavin's eyes. "You've built a successful life here, so now you and your little family enjoy it."

Rizzo downed his beer, patted Gavin on his back and stood to leave. "But keep on wearing Saint Christopher."

40.

GAVIN UNLOCKED THE BACK DOOR TO THE RESTAU-
rant before six a.m. as morning light began to glow in the east.
He was late that Tuesday, the day after '*Ono Kūloko's* special
Valentine's Day celebration. He was exhausted. Everything
seemed to have gone wrong before he could even get out of
the house that morning. Engine trouble, Maggie's tantrum,
plumbing problem. And still no match to Devon's prints.

He hoped the rest of the day would be better. He had a lot
of preparations for the restaurant's Saint Patrick's Day celebration in a few weeks; he wanted it to be even better than the
previous year's. It seemed to be the cycle—from one celebration to the next, to maintain their ranking on the island. With
all the press coverage he'd been getting since Christmas—being
named 'Number One' on the island—the restaurant was consistently at capacity.

Anakoni's car wasn't in the lot. That was odd. Koni was so
predictable, usually arriving before Gavin did at five-thirty.

Gavin heaved his pack onto the stainless-steel counter just
inside the door and flipped on the lights. The kitchen gleamed
in perfect order, just as he and his staff had left it after
Monday's deep clean. He went to the walk-in cooler to double-
check inventory. Of course he'd done that last night, but he

was anal. Everyone teased that he had OCD. But he hadn't achieved success by being careless or relying on assumptions. Things can change. He didn't like surprises.

He pushed down on the lever handle to unlock the heavy door to the cooler, which was wired to automatically turn on the lights inside. He was greeted by pitch black darkness, and temperatures that didn't feel as cold as usual.

"Oh, shit!" Gavin shouted, pounding his fist on the metal door. His entire inventory—including the big shipment he'd received midafternoon the day before—could be at risk. Good thing the restaurant didn't open for breakfast; maybe he had time to recover before the lunch crowd. He ran back to the electrical panel and opened it. The breaker controlling the cooler was off; he wondered what tripped it. He switched it on but it immediately tripped off again. Maybe there was a short somewhere. He grabbed a flashlight on his way back to the cooler to investigate.

Then he stumbled. He looked down and saw cables splayed out on the floor, their cut ends naked and exposed. He froze in place, eyes wide, scanning. He slowly turned his head around, first to one side then to the other, gripping the flashlight like a weapon. He reached over to the magnetic strip over the prep table and grabbed a large knife, then tiptoed cautiously out of the kitchen. He turned on the entire bank of 'urban chic' Edison lights in the dining area, where chairs were inverted atop tables like dead bugs. He peered all around, behind the bar, in the restrooms and closets. Nothing. No one.

Gavin picked up the restaurant phone to call police. The line was dead. He reached into his pack for his cell phone, but he must have left it in his truck. He ran out back and opened his truck door, reaching for his phone in its usual place. It wasn't there. He searched the entire vehicle; no luck. He could drive to the nearest gas station, where he knew he could use the phone to call police. When he turned his key in the truck's ignition, he heard the empty click-click-click of a dead starter.

Now he was panicked, his breath held motionless in his tightened throat. He didn't know whether to run or if he'd be safer inside. Surely Koni would be coming soon, and other staff would arrive by nine. He ran into the restaurant, locked the door and headed into the kitchen. As he walked past the cooler, he briefly flicked his flashlight toward the opening and rushed on.

Two steps later, he realized he'd just seen empty shelves. He turned back and stood in the open doorway, his flashlight penetrating the darkness. Residual smells of absent produce, fish and meat taunted his nostrils. Without knowing why, he entered the cooler. Behind the door, lying on the floor in a small pool of blood, Koni groaned.

The cooler door slammed shut behind him and Gavin heard the lever turn on the other side.

In darkness, with no sounds and motionless air, time stood still. It may have been sixty seconds or sixty minutes, during which Gavin checked Koni's pulse and injuries, tied them with cloth strips torn from his shirt, then his flashlight batteries died. Banging on the thick heavy door of the cooler or trying to open it would be fruitless. His mind explored every obvious, creative, innovative and ridiculous alternative imaginable— and tried a few, such as crossing wires in the ceiling light to make signals (the lines were dead), but came up empty.

With two people consuming limited oxygen, he wasn't sure how long either of them could last. Koni wasn't any help as he drifted in and out of consciousness. Gavin fingered the Saint Christopher charm hanging from his neck. Did Devon do this? Was he so desperate for attention, for control? Or was he out for revenge? Did Devon notice that his brother took the wine glass he'd used, and suspected it was for capturing his fingerprints? Unfortunately, none of the letters had prints that had more than twelve points that matched Devon's prints on the glass.

What was the sound he heard now, something so loud it managed to penetrate the thickness of the cooler? Was that an alarm? A smoke alarm? His mind reeled with visions of another fire...no, it couldn't be. Or was it? The mob getting even? But Rizzo said he'd ordered them off. He felt the cooler door. It was beginning to feel warm, hot in places, despite its insulation and thickness. At least he and Koni wouldn't burn to death. But asphyxiation could be worse.

Minutes passed like hours while he waited, expecting to lose consciousness. Then he heard, below the alarms, a scratching on the cooler door. The lever turned, the door opened, and Patches rushed in from the flames, with a fireman right behind. Gavin scooped up Patches, told the fireman about Koni, and lurched toward the door.

Out in the parking lot, fire trucks battled the blaze and an ambulance carried Koni away. Gavin noticed Puna talking with the Fire Chief.

Katie stood at the edge of the commotion, then rushed to embrace him.

"How—why?" Gavin sputtered.

"I'm so glad you're safe!" Katie cried, hugging him tighter. "I realized you'd left your phone behind when it buzzed with a message. It said 'It's payback time,' from a number I didn't recognize. I called Puna and came right away. By the time I got here, all the emergency vehicles were here."

Patches jumped excitedly on his old friend. "Hey Patches," Gavin reached down to hug his pal. "For a one-eyed one-eared mutt, you're pretty damn smart. Thanks for finding me in that cooler." Then he was suddenly frantic, "Where's Maggie?"

"In the car asleep, Dear."

"What time is it?"

Katie looked at her watch. "Quarter of seven."

Is that all? But it felt like hours...

———————

A week later, Tray called. "Gavin." He began, his voice sounding like an official statement with full stop at the end. "Good news." Again, the terse statement.

Gavin caught his breath.

"Your brother's fingerprints from his wine glass were matched to evidence from the fire. We issued an arrest warrant and Kauai police are arresting him now. You should not be there."

Puna related details to Gavin afterward. When police arrived at Devon's Princeville house to charge him with arson, assault and attempted murder, Devon began ranting incoherently. As they led him away in handcuffs, he kept yelling, "It's all your fault, Twinkie! I'm the best, but you had to ruin everything!"

41.

GAVIN

I PUT DOWN MY DRILL AND TAKE A BREAK FROM THE work. I nod to Gene the electrical contractor and weave my way past all the works-in-progress and go to the open door of the patio. One of our typical mid-afternoon downpours masks the view of Sleeping Giant.

It's been months, but we're getting there. It still amazes me when I think about how many people came out to help us after the fire. After FBI completed their investigation, Tray stuck around to help pull my head out of quicksand. Like, knowing my brother tried to kill me was a little depressing... even though I try to remind myself that came from his illness and he really didn't want me dead, just under his control.

But then Puna organized help from the police force—sort of a modern version of barn-raising. It's as if the whole island kind of took it personally. Customers, competitors, politicians, even the insurance company—who ever thought *insurance companies* could actually care? And our suppliers! Amazing. We'll be back operational soon. Koni's concussion doesn't seem to have slowed him down. He—and all the staff—have really stood by us. They're even planning a birthday party for me, targeting that day for a grand re-opening.

So maybe Tray was right. Even though it's hard for me to

accept. I guess I'm not a loser. All those people wouldn't have wasted their time helping a loser.

But I'm not "Goodie Gavin" either.

I have to get more air. I go out onto the patio. Fine mists of rain manage to get through the screens. It smells fresh and new, washing away dust in the parking lot to revive fragrances of pikake and plumeria. Feels great, like it's waking me up. Which I really need. Haven't been sleeping well.

Oh, jeez. That cat out there is hassling a nene. Not smart. Those little geese can get nasty to protect their nest. Mothers are like that. Like Katie. And Mom. Mom wasn't capable of 'nasty,' but she became stubbornly insistent trying to defend me from Dad's and Devon's shit, and keeping Dad from excusing Devon's behavior. Nice try, Mom, but the problem was bigger than you. Bigger than all of us. It took me way too long to finally realize that.

The plumber comes out to the patio. "Hey Gavin, I'm going out to get more pipe and some different fittings. You need anything?"

"No, I don't think so. Careful out there. Drivers can get stupid in this rain."

So yeah, I'm having a hard time sleeping. Nightmares when I do. Katie's been great. Patient, understanding, supportive. Calming me when I wake up yelling, disturbing her sleep. Even Maggie and Patches seem to be extra sweet and loving now.

When I was locked in that cooler in the dark, the alarms going off, the door feeling hot, afraid I wouldn't live to be twenty-seven, wouldn't see Katie and Maggie again, I thought maybe Rizzo was lying and the mob wanted payback for killing their two guys. Setting that fire.

I still can't believe I did that, still have bad dreams and nightmares about that night, three years later. I relive the whole scene all the time, doing the 'what-ifs' in my head. What if I hadn't gone there that night? Would Devon have gone, gotten killed, or killed them? What if Devon hadn't shown me where he hid his gun? Those guys were waiting for Devon, and then they started shooting at me. Did I just get lucky, or is there a killer in me?

Rizzo said those guys got what they deserved for messing up, like it's an occupational hazard or something. Katie said basically the same thing when I told her. But still...

What if my brother had never messed with the mob in the first place?

What if I didn't think it was my job to take care of my brother, no matter what he does?

Of course it *was* my job. I remember Dad the night of our sixteenth birthday party. "What the fuck, boy, why weren't you watching him?" and "C'mon, boy, you're gonna save your brother's life." When Devon was in the hospital, I had to give blood, go see Devon every day. When he came home, I had to babysit him, make sure he did his therapy routines. I had to go to the same college with him and stay in the same fucking room with him, watch out for him. Damn near destroyed me. When he was in drug rehab, I had to drive up from New York to give him 'encouragement'—which didn't help. When he got crosswise with the mob, Dad begged me to go up and 'talk some sense' into him.

It took me a long time to understand that the problem was bigger than that, bigger than all of us. Dad's attitudes and behavior were shaped by Grampa and probably his father before him, and the culture where they grew up. Guys had to be tough, get ahead by knocking other people down, cutting corners. And if they weren't the best, they had to fake it. Dad raised us the same way. Which resulted in Devon not only aping those same attitudes but also getting into risky behavior and developing mental illness.

We were all pre-programmed. Mom didn't have a chance against the force of that. And Dad finally realized the futility of that 'program' in the end.

I've finally begun to pull myself out of it, re-program myself, take the controls away from all that, away from Devon. But what about him, the golden boy? He was never really "golden", was he? Devon was as much victim as I was, just in a different way. Dad pushed him into a no-win situation. Devon was supposed to be the winner, but Dad didn't show him *how,* only *what.* Dad's tough macho Italian mob roots sure didn't provide a good role model for how to excel at much of anything. Yet if Devon didn't fulfill Dad's expectations, he risked losing Dad's love. Devon was trapped in a role with no script, no stage direction. A paper dragon.

And now he's trapped in his hollow existence. Does he realize how Dad, Grandpa, and probably generations of men before that, determined who he would become? Maybe if I can help him understand that, I can finally save him.

The rain has stopped, almost as quickly as it began, parting the clouds. The sun sizzles the wet blacktop in the parking lot and steam rises. I have to get back to work on this place. I press the playlist on my phone. Bon Jovi belts out 'It's My Life'...Yeah. *"It's now or never...I just want to live while I'm alive..."*

42.

THERE WAS NO RESPONSE WHEN GAVIN KNOCKED on Devon's door. His brother had been out on bail awaiting trial for more than three months, with an ankle monitor, all the while calling Gavin, begging and whining.

Gavin found the door unlocked, and cautiously entered. Devon's palatial house was completely dark inside. All the drapes and blinds—and even windows—were closed against the piercing brilliance of a hot July afternoon. The air in the house was humid and stale, lacking oxygen. No air conditioner or lights. He called out to Devon and wandered around looking for him. He finally found his brother sitting huddled in the corner of his bedroom, wrapped in a soiled blanket. Odors of dried-up food on the dishes littering the room assaulted Gavin's nostrils. And another foul smell he didn't want to acknowledge. Flies buzzed around the garbage. He'd never seen his twin in such a state.

Gavin stood in the doorway. "What's going on, Devon?" he prodded. "You wanted to see me, said it was urgent."

"Good to know I can still get you to do what I tell you to do, little brother," Devon sneered. Or at least it sounded like one of his derisive insults, even muffled behind that disgusting blanket.

"I'll give you two minutes to tell me what you want," Gavin said. "Then I'm gone."

Devon poked his head out of his blanket. Gavin's breath caught in his throat. His brother's hair was greasy and matted, turning his red into a slick dark brown. He clearly hadn't showered or shaved in a very long time. His eyes darted around the room and his lips contorted, as if he feared monsters might be lurking in every corner.

"Eric left me," he muttered in a whisper.

"Well, what do you expect, Dev?" Gavin said. "You've been abusing him for years."

"I'm the best thing that ever happened to him, you idiot," Devon threw off his blanket and stood clumsily, flailing wizened arms and exposing his naked emaciated body. "He can't do that to me—I won't let him get away with it!" he screamed.

Gavin took a step back. "What are you going to do, Dev? Suddenly become a nice guy to get him back?"

"You'll see. He'll be sorry," Devon snarled. "And so will everyone else."

"Well, Dev," Gavin began, hesitating. "I'm sorry. For a lot of things. Sorry that Dad pushed you into being something you're not. Sorry you felt like you had to be the person Dad always expected you to be, or else. Sorry you never had the opportunity to choose who you really wanted to be, and discover what it takes to be that person—"

"What the fuck're you talking about, Wimp! I did it! I am who I want to be—the best! I made so much money, I'm so successful, everyone is jealous! Eric couldn't handle it!"

Looking at Devon's physical state, and his deranged rant, Gavin was suddenly fearful. That he might lose his brother to psychosis. "Devon, I'm worried about you. You need help. Beyond anything I can do."

"Get the fuck out of here, Twinkie," Devon coughed, his voice raspy, screaming. "You're worthless to me. Dad always knew it. He sacrificed his life for ME, not you!"

Pedersen always told Gavin he couldn't save everyone. But this was his brother. His twin. He'd always thought of Devon as his other half, and only recently recognized the self-defeating nature of that term, which implied neither was whole without the other. But in fact, each of them was a separate person, in charge of his actions and his life.

Gavin turned to leave and looked back at Devon, who was slumped on his floor, leaning against the wall, urine beginning to pool around him. On his way out the door, he thought he heard a thumping, but couldn't tell where the sound was coming from.

He called Social Services from his cell phone on the drive back to Kapa'a.

43.

DEVON

TWINKIE THINKS I NEED *HELP?!* THE ONLY HELP I need is to get this damn monitor off my ankle.

Well, I guess it is true, in another way. I need Gavin's help, but that's what he's supposed to do anyway. Protect me, take care of me. It's always been that way. I'm the smartest twin, I have big ideas, I'm a visionary. So I'm a risk-taker and sometimes things go off the rails. Dad always expected Gavin to look out for me, protect the Golden Goose...or was that the goose that lays the golden eggs?

Oh yeah, that's it. I'm the Golden Boy. Like Dad always said.

What does that mean? That I was anointed—for what? To be or do what? Always be the best, right? Always be the winner. What was the competition? What did I win?

I won this fashionable ankle bracelet.

Oh, if my friends could see me now...what was that dumb song?

Where are my friends? Who are my friends? Eric's a loser. Forget about him. Whatever happened to Cecil? He loved me. And Jimbo? Oh yeah, he's dead. Gavin killed him. Right. Gavin has to protect me. Because I'm the best. I'm his better half. He can't live without me.

I think I need to have my eyes checked. Things are looking a little fuzzy. And what's that over there, moving around? I didn't think there are mice on Kauai, but something's over there going after my leftovers from last night...not last night...when was it I had pizza delivered? That was hilarious. The guy was so shocked when I came to the door with no clothes on, that he ran away without getting paid! Looked like he'd seen a zombie or something. Funny. I wasn't going to pay him anyway.

I had that nightmare again. Except I wasn't asleep. The one where all these people are laughing at me and saying I'm nothing, a nobody, a fraud. Except they weren't turning away and leaving. They were chasing me, coming after me, like they were going to lynch me or something. Rattled the shit out of me. Felt like I was going to die.

What's it like to die? They say your whole life passes in front of you when you're dying, like a flash of everything you've done, people you've known. Some people I wouldn't want to remember in my final minutes. Spucky, Limone...

What was I saying? Friends...Gavin's the only friend I have now. What's a friend supposed to be, anyway? Gavin *has* to always be there for me. Because we're stuck together, two halves of a whole. And because Dad always told him to. Without me, he's only half a person. Does your twin count in the 'friend' category? I always thought so. Friends are supposed to do stuff for you, like Gavin does, right? And do they think I'm *their* friend? Do I have to do stuff for *them?* Besides grace them with my presence and let them do things for me? I guess I never really got the friend thing...

There's a lot of stuff I never really got, now that I think about it. Like, what does it take to be "The Best"? Dad always said I was the best, but I never got what I was supposed to *do* to be the best. Winning at everything was what I was supposed to do, I suppose, and when I didn't actually "win"—like valedictorian—I could just *say* I won, or say someone cheated, or the thing wasn't important and I wasn't even trying to win, or make logical explanations. And everyone bought it and I was still a winner, right? Because if I wasn't, Dad wouldn't still like me. Love me.

He was always such a tough guy. My role model. I guess that's the way guys were in the North End. Like the Rizzo clan, Dad's competition. It was always so important to Dad to win that battle, but he didn't. Because they were part of the mob, and so I played that game too, so I could win for both of us. Then Dad protected me, and he lost. The game. His life.

Too bad. Dad wasn't a winner.

Oh, shit. Actually piss. Just lost it, here in my comfy corner. I can go over to the other corner. Crawl. Eric can clean it up. Oops, I forgot. He's gone. Loser.

Now what was I saying? Oh yeah. Dad. Always insisted I was the best, the winner. But he wasn't a winner, so why did he expect me to be one? He got his first store from Grandpa DiMasi, then with Mom's family money got more stores, but I know firsthand he wasn't doing very well. No big profits. That's why I decided to branch out. Because Dad raised me as "The Best," "The Winner." But that was like programming a robot without installing a power supply.

Maybe that's why all those people are coming after me, telling me I'm a fraud. They know. They want to kill me! But maybe they just want to kill the "winner" in me, because that's the fraud part. But then what's left?

Here I am, my whole life's passing in front of me, but I don't think I'm dying. Yet. I'm checking out my body now, and it isn't looking too good. Maybe if I took a shower...

Besides, I can't die. Gavin would be left, as only half a man. He'd no longer have a purpose—to take care of me, like Dad programmed him to be. I'm his power supply.

Codependency's got a bad rap.

44.

GAVIN GOT THE CALL IN THE MIDDLE OF HIS STAFF
and more than a hundred customers singing 'Happy Birthday'
to him during the restaurant's grand re-opening.

He violated every speed limit on the way. When he finally
arrived, there was nowhere to park his car. Several squad cars,
a fire truck and two ambulances crowded the street in random
angles, evidence they'd each come separately in extreme haste.
Personnel from those vehicles, along with dozens of other
people—likely curious neighbors—milled about, talking among
themselves under gray skies. A few of the gawkers had
brought out folding chairs to sit comfortably and observe
whatever event had summoned such a convergence of first
responders.

He barely missed a small dog running in front of him as
he screeched into an illegal spot and frantically sprang from
his car, heart pounding from his chest.

Puna ran from a cluster of policemen to intercept him,
planting his broad girth in his friend's pathway and both his
beefy hands onto Gavin's shoulders. "Gav, stop," Puna halted
him. "You can't go in there."

"I came as fast as I could! What's going on?" Gavin
screamed in panic. "Are all those cops and ambulances here

for Devon?" He couldn't catch his breath. "I just saw him a couple weeks ago—" he coughed in a helpless whisper.

"Look, Gav," Puna stammered, his eyes averted, whether in embarrassment, sorrow, or both. "We got a call from KIUC. They came to turn off your brother's electric and they smelled something."

Just then Gavin saw, over Puna's shoulder, two men navigating a gurney out of Devon's mansion. A white sheet covered the top and a stiffly bent grayish arm dangled off the right side. He broke free of Puna's grasp and rushed through yellow police tape to pull the sheet up in a frenzy. It was Eric. Deteriorated flesh. How long had he...? A memory flashed to Gavin, the thumping he'd heard the last time he left Devon's house. But where was his brother now? He whirled around and began running toward the house.

But Chief Kahananui, wearing plastic gloves and white face mask, stopped him before he mounted the steps. "I'm sorry, Gavin, this is a crime scene. You can't go in there now."

"Crime scene? Where's my brother!" Gavin shouted, lunging toward the Chief.

"We've searched the house, man. He's not there," the Chief said, taking Gavin's arm to steer him back.

But Gavin pulled away and vaulted up the front steps three at a time. He covered his nose, assaulted by acrid odors billowing from the open doorway. He heard the Chief's whistle behind him, calling out to an officer to intercept him. Evading the officer by cutting through the kitchen pantry to the back stairs, he flew up the two flights to Devon's top floor study.

He took a deep breath, then strode with wary steps across Devon's leopardskin rug. Its spots rose and swirled around him. Dizzy, nearly swooning, he lifted the apocalyptic Hieronymus Bosch painting. His hands trembled as he pressed the button behind it, then agonized as the wall to Devon's "safe place" slowly opened.

Gavin lurched into the circular tower. He gasped and fell to his knees. Consciousness left him.

≈ ≈ ≈ ≈ ≈ ≈ ≈ ≈ ≈ ≈ ≈ ≈

Sun breaks through the day's dark clouds. Light streams from the clerestory above, creating sparkling showers of dust motes, illuminating Gavin's twin in a glorified aura. His open lips curl in a crooked sneer. Opaque green eyes glare, the leopard trapped. His naked body spins and sways in a gust of air from two floors below, a pendulum out of time. Blood-red words mark the wall behind him.

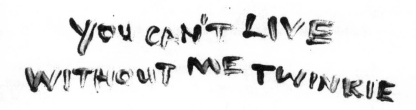

EPILOGUE

THE LAST TWO MONTHS HAVE BEEN ROUGH ON Katie. She's had to do it all. Manage the restaurant, her art gallery, Maggie and Patches. And Gavin. Good thing they have dependable staff and friends. Including a mercy mission from Dr. Pedersen.

Tray came up from Honolulu last week to spend time with Gavin. The two of them went off on an expanded three-day version of the hike they did last year, along the NaPali coast. Their own version of 'burning man.' Katie expects them to return later today.

It's Monday and she is in the restaurant office balancing the books, doing payroll and ordering supplies. Maggie plays with a toy truck on the floor beside her. Staff are busy deep-cleaning the kitchen and dining room. The back door opens; Katie looks up to see Gavin walking in. With a peaceful beatific smile, he sets down his phone and hits his playlist, with a grin toward her. During his hike with Tray, he had become a Nina Simone fan. Now his anthem rings out..."*It's a new dawn, It's a new day, It's a new life, For me...And I'm feeling good...*"

He walks to Katie, kisses her gently, and picks up Maggie.

"Welcome back, Tiger. How was your hike with Tray?"

"Awesome. I'm back for real now." He pulls up his sleeve. "I got a tattoo at the same place Tray got his. Devon will no longer control me, but he'll always be with me."

BOOK CLUB
DISCUSSION QUESTIONS

1. This is a novel about a family. Multiple generations of a family. What experiences, expectations and beliefs—in each generation—do you think drives the behavior of each character? In Tony's father, Tony, Colleen's parents, Colleen, and each of the twins?

2. From the first chapter, and sporadically throughout the novel, we see evidence of gaslighting behaviors — from whom, toward whom? How are those behaviors different from benign interpersonal behavior such as teasing or joking? What purpose do those behaviors serve for the gaslighter, and how does it affect the recipient[s] of that behavior?

3. Why do you think Tony has decided to label, and treat, Gavin as the lesser of the twins, and Devon as the "winner"? What was it about each of the twins that influenced Tony's choice? What was it in Tony, and his background, that drove him to pick winners vs losers, even in his own children?

4. Although clearly intelligent and accomplished, Colleen is slow to assert herself, both for her own welfare as well

as for her sons. Why do you think that is? What are the prior and current conditions in her life that influence that reluctance?

5. The relationship between Colleen and Tony is complex. Both are victims, in different ways, of different forces. Explore the dynamics of class conflict and cultural expectations, as well as marital love and fealty. Do you find Colleen a sympathetic character? What about Tony?

6. Dr. Pedersen is a loyal supporter of Gavin, during high school and the decade beyond. Speculate on their relationship, and what may have been the factors in Pedersen's life and/or profession that influence his tenacious devotion and dedication to Gavin's plight?

7. Gavin has been victimized by domestic and narcissistic abuse throughout his formative years. We want him to assert himself, fight back, leave the abuse, but he keeps being sucked back in, "like a moth to the flame." How indelible are the scars from such abuse, experienced early and persistently in life? How difficult is it to break away from the abuser, especially when it's from your identical twin brother, who is himself a victim?

8. Katie has had her own family challenges. What do you think draws her to Gavin, and more importantly, what keeps her there? She may be reluctant to stay with someone whose family is so toxic. She wonders whether that dysfunction will manifest in Gavin and in their relationship. How does she handle those concerns? Is that a gamble?

9. Tray is a loyal best friend to Gavin, although their family, racial and socioeconomic status are quite different. What do you think draws them together, and keeps them so loyal to each other?

10. The mind and motivations of a sociopathic narcissist are difficult to fathom. Why do you think Devon abuses, taunts, and tries to ruin or even kill Gavin? Control? Jealousy? Fear of rejection, of losing the only person who is obligated to love him?

11. The theme of salvation is persistent throughout the novel, regarding each of the main characters, and some of the minor characters. Can you identify the cases where a character either does (or should) save someone, or is/should be saved by another character?

12. Each DiMasi family member has secrets. What are they?

13. Is Devon's final outcome a curse or blessing for Gavin?

ABOUT ATMOSPHERE PRESS

Atmosphere Press is an independent, full-service publisher for excellent books in all genres and for all audiences. Learn more about what we do at atmospherepress.com.

We encourage you to check out some of Atmosphere's latest releases, which are available at Amazon.com and via order from your local bookstore:

Dancing with David, a novel by Siegfried Johnson

The Friendship Quilts, a novel by June Calender

My Significant Nobody, a novel by Stevie D. Parker

Nine Days, a novel by Judy Lannon

Shining New Testament: The Cloning of Jay Christ, a novel by Cliff Williamson

Shadows of Robyst, a novel by K. E. Maroudas

Home Within a Landscape, a novel by Alexey L. Kovalev

Motherhood, a novel by Siamak Vakili

Death, The Pharmacist, a novel by D. Ike Horst

Mystery of the Lost Years, a novel by Bobby J. Bixler

Bone Deep Bonds, a novel by B. G. Arnold

Terriers in the Jungle, a novel by Georja Umano

Into the Emerald Dream, a novel by Autumn Allen

His Name Was Ellis, a novel by Joseph Libonati

The Cup, a novel by D. P. Hardwick

The Empathy Academy, a novel by Dustin Grinnell

Tholocco's Wake, a novel by W. W. VanOverbeke

Dying to Live, a novel by Barbara Macpherson Reyelts

Looking for Lawson, a novel by Mark Kirby

Yosef's Path: Lessons from my Father, a novel by Jane Leclere Doyle

ABOUT THE AUTHOR

Leslie Kain received her BA in Psychology from Wellesley College and an MBA from Boston University, so the setting of *Secrets In The Mirror* is familiar to her. She draws from her careers in psychology and government intelligence to create stories of inner conflict and resolution. Leslie has had short stories published in several literary journals; *Secrets In The Mirror* is her first published novel. She thanks the team at Atmosphere Press, her husband, critique partners, WFWA friends, and cat Sheba for all their encouragement and help.